13
DATES

D0967508

ALSO BY MATT DUNN

Best Man
The Ex-Boyfriend's Handbook
From Here to Paternity
Ex-Girlfriends United
The Good Bride Guide
The Accidental Proposal
A Day at the Office
What Might Have Been
Home
A Christmas Day at the Office

13 DATES

MATT DUNN

LAKE UNION
PUBLISHING

This is a work of fiction. Names, characters, organizations, places, events, and incidents are either products of the author's imagination or are used fictitiously. Any resemblance to actual persons, living or dead, or actual events is purely coincidental.

Text copyright © 2017 by Matt Dunn
All rights reserved.

No part of this book may be reproduced, or stored in a retrieval system, or transmitted in any form or by any means, electronic, mechanical, photocopying, recording, or otherwise, without express written permission of the publisher.

Published by Lake Union Publishing, Seattle

www.apub.com

Amazon, the Amazon logo, and Lake Union Publishing are trademarks of Amazon.com, Inc., or its affiliates.

ISBN-13: 9781612185798
ISBN-10: 1612185797

Cover design by Lisa Horton

Printed in the United States of America

For Tina. Forever.

1.

I fall in love with Angel the moment I see her.

Though when I think about this later, I realise it's *before* I see her – more accurately, when I *hear* her, in Starbucks (and even more accurately, at 12.46 p.m. on Saturday, 6 May, 2017). She's standing in front of me in the queue, and unlike the people before her, who all seem to have ordered their coffee just the way they want it in terms of type, strength, size, temperature, and almost what the cow that provided the milk's been eating, like their lives depend on getting it right, when it comes to her turn, Angel just stares up at the menu board as if she's only just spotted it.

'Next,' says the barista impatiently. He looks like he's been put together in the Starbucks factory – slightly too-bushy beard, shiny, pomaded, slicked-into-a-huge-quiff hair, shirtsleeves rolled up just enough to expose the tattoos on his forearms – and his brusque enquiry makes Angel jump.

'Are you sure? Only I can't see any racks of clothes, and it says "Starbucks" on your apron . . .' She fixes him with what I imagine (because I haven't seen her face yet) is a smile, even though it isn't returned very sincerely, and there and then I'm struck by just how attractive, how *sexy*, how . . . mesmerising, a GSOH can be. 'What's good here?'

'The coffee.'

'Well, in that case, I'll have one of those.'

The barista sighs. '*Which* one of those?'

Angel peers up at the board again (not the done thing in Starbucks, apparently, given the tutting coming from the queue behind me), folds her arms, then simply says, 'Flat white?' like she's guessing the final answer on *Who Wants to Be a Millionaire* and actually has *no idea* what a flat white is. Though in her defence, she possibly hasn't, because this is Richmond (West London, not Yorkshire), a town that gentrified when Shoreditch was still in short trousers (metaphorically, as opposed to ones that show a bit of mankle), and nowadays is more hip replacement than hipster.

In truth, I don't really notice her until she speaks, not because she doesn't look good from behind – she's tall, slim, with a ton of bright-red hair piled messily on top of her head, and wearing a pair of workout pants and a figure-hugging neon T-shirt; and I'm that simplest of Pavlovian life forms, the single human male, after all, so of course she's *registered*. But even though I'm sure it's possible to fall in love with someone from behind, the 'love' thing doesn't happen to me until I hear her voice, and mainly because her tone is just so . . . upbeat, I guess. Playful, even when doing something as mundane as ordering a coffee. The kind of voice that if she was a judge kicking your act off *Britain's Got Talent* or a doctor giving you some bad news, you probably wouldn't feel too upset about it.

'How do you want it?' says the barista impatiently, perhaps a bit irked at having to spend what must be no more than a second or two longer than usual taking her order.

'I'm guessing you'd suggest 'to go'?'

He gives her a look. 'Extra hot?'

'You're not so bad yourself,' says Angel, diffusing his bad mood in an instant, and making me wish desperately that *I* was someone who someone like Angel would say something like that to. Which is possibly why, when the barista does what I'm suddenly desperate to do, and asks her what her name is, and she says 'Angel', I can't help myself, so I say 'Angel' too, just to get the feel of it.

Trouble is, I've said it just as the noise from the coffee machine behind the counter stops, so she turns around, and it's even worse, because she's *gorgeous*, in a 'describe your ideal woman' kind of way (even though she's probably not at all what I'd have described *before* I first saw her), and I suddenly lose all sense of, well, *everything*.

She smiles at me, her expression a mixture of interest and amusement, her mouth turned up at the sides but her forehead slightly wrinkled, as if she thinks she's heard something but she's not sure what, and *that's* the moment that seals the deal. But because I've just fallen in love – something that's happened to me, let me think, *never* in all my thirty-five years – all I can do is stare back at her, and after a second or two she evidently starts to find this a little disconcerting, so she gives an almost-imperceptible shrug as if she's imagined the whole thing, then turns back towards the counter.

Sensing this is a window of opportunity that might never open again, I mentally kick myself up the backside and take a deep breath. 'Angel?'

'Do we know each other?' she says, glancing over her shoulder at me.

Ever the smooth operator, my mumbled 'Um, no' puts us in danger of being over almost before we've even begun, though I just about keep the window cracked open with my hastily tacked-on 'That's really your name?'

She nods. 'Angel by name, Angel by nature . . . Actually, scratch that second part.' She flashes me a smile. 'Why shouldn't it be?'

'No, no, it absolutely *should* be,' I say, then worry that sounds cheesier than it was meant to. 'In the sense that you can, of course, choose to call yourself exactly what you wish, and not that you *are* an angel. Though I'm sure you're very—'

'It's short for "Angela",' says Angel, counting out her two pounds sixty and handing it over to the barista.

'Right.' My heart's pounding, and for some reason I can't seem to formulate my thoughts to concentrate on anything but Angel's absolute loveliness, because it takes me an uncomfortably long time to come up with: 'Not really *short*, then.'

'Short*er*.'

'True.' I think for a moment, aware that I have to be nimble on my feet. But like the uncoordinated old weatherman who's always the first to be booted off *Strictly*, the best follow-up I can manage is: 'Well, I think it's a beautiful name. "Angel", I mean. Not that there's anything wrong with "Angela" . . .'

'Thank you. I'll be sure to pass that on to my parents,' she says, stepping around to the side of the counter. 'Seeing as they're the ones who chose it.'

'Right. Um, thanks. So . . .'

There's more tutting from behind me, which I assume is a criticism of my chat-up technique, until I realise Angel's sidestep has put me at the front of the queue – for ordering a coffee, at least. Hurriedly, I move into the space Angel's just vacated, and seeing as I've never been in here before, I order the first thing that comes into my head.

'I'll have what she's having.'

'Name?' says the barista.

'Angel,' I say, assuming he wants to know who 'she' is.

'*Your* name.'

'Noah,' I say, loudly enough for Angel to hear, even though I suspect the window of opportunity has already slammed shut – on my fingers. And while I'm grateful that Angel now knows *my* name, I'm a little mystified as to why they should be asking. 'Um, why?'

'For the coffee,' says the barista, as if explaining something to an unruly toddler, then nods towards where a different man with an identical hair-and-beard-and-tattoos combination (which I'm beginning to suspect is part of the uniform) is fussing over a machine that wouldn't look out of place in NASA Mission Control. And while I'm confused about why the coffee needs to know my name, perhaps this is some new ethical approach, like carbon offsetting: I know what I'm drinking, so it's only fair that what I'm drinking knows me. 'So . . .'

'So?' I say, at the precise moment I realise he's indicating the display on the till.

I manage to find the exact change, but instead of seeming pleased when I smugly hand it over, the barista gives me a look, and it's only then I notice the tips cup on the counter in front of me. Embarrassed, I root around in my pocket for an extra twenty pence, but I've only got a fifty-pence piece, and I'm pretty sure dropping it in and removing change from the cup is possibly worse than not leaving a tip in the first place, so I decide to tough it out.

I'm now faced with the dilemma that I don't have a clue what to do: whether I'm supposed to go and sit down and someone will bring my coffee to me, or go and stand where Angel is waiting (which I don't dare do, because then I might have to talk to her). But Angel seems to sense my discomfort, because she does that nodding thing while widening her eyes, which I take as an invitation to step out of the queue and join her.

'Thanks.'

'Your first time?'

I'm not sure whether she means being here in Starbucks or ordering a flat white, but thinking about it, the answer's the same to both of those questions.

'Is it that obvious?'

Angel makes a face that's part sympathy, part pity.

'I don't normally like these places, but I'm on my way to a' – I stop talking for a moment, worried that admitting to Angel that I'm on my way to a blind date might not be the best approach – 'meeting, and I needed the toilet' – I hesitate again, because Angel's making the 'too much information' face, then decide I'm already in too far – 'and some, you know, *meetings*, are already stressful enough without the extra pressure of a full bladder, and I don't like to have to go to the toilet in the first half hour of meeting – I mean, *a* meeting – partly because then I think the person I'm, well . . .'

'Meeting?' suggests Angel, so I nod enthusiastically, mainly because I'm relieved she's still paying attention.

'. . . will think I'm doing that because I'm nervous, and even though I *am* nervous, I don't want them to know that, or use the time that I'm in the toilet as an opportunity to form a negative opinion about me, or even leave . . .' I take a quick breath, sensing now would be a good time for a sprint finish to the end of my story. 'Anyway, I was only in the queue because I felt guilty about coming in to Starbucks and using their toilet without actually buying anything, so I decided I should get a coffee.'

Angel waits until she's sure I've finished, then she narrows her eyes. 'Even though that's a bit counterproductive?'

'How so?'

'Firstly, you're replacing the liquid you've just gotten rid of.'

I shrug at her, insofar as you can shrug *at* someone. 'Circle of life, and all that.'

Angel makes the 'that was deep' face. 'And secondly, caffeine's a diuretic. So you're actually going to end up needing the toilet more.'

'Ah.'

'Though you probably shouldn't feel guilty about using a Starbucks toilet.'

'Why not?'

'Given their alleged non-payment of corporation tax.'

She says that rather loudly, but the staff behind the counter don't seem to notice. Or care.

'Right,' I say, giving her a conspiratorial wink, even though I don't actually know what she's talking about – and which, when I catch sight of my reflection in the mirror behind the counter, possibly looks a bit creepy. And creepy's the last thing I want Angel to think I am, mainly because – and the revelation almost makes me go weak at the knees – something's telling me *she's the one.* And when you've never met 'the one', when you've had enough trouble simply trying to meet 'the next one', when you've always assumed the process would be like going on a long drive and eventually realising you'd arrived at your destination, rather than a head-on collision before you've even got out of first gear, and suddenly you find yourself standing right in front of the person you know you could fall in love with, if you haven't already . . .

I start to panic, worried that at any moment Angel's coffee's going to be ready, while mine will still be in production, and unless I can come up with some wonderfully charming line, she's going to be out of my life faster than you can say 'White Chocolate Mocha Light Frappuccino' (whatever *that* is). But thankfully, in an economy-of-scale kind of way, and no doubt attempting to maximise the profits that – according to Angel – Starbucks allegedly doesn't declare, the barista has made our coffees simultaneously.

'Two flat whites,' he tells us, placing our drinks side by side on the counter as if they, at least, are a couple.

'Oh, we're not together,' says Angel, and although my 'unfortunately' gets a smile, I'm so convinced I've blown it that it's all I can do to grab the nearest one and make a run for it. But I've only managed to get a yard or so when Angel taps me on the shoulder.

'You've got my coffee.'

'What?'

'My coffee.' I follow Angel's gaze towards my cup, which I only now notice has 'Angel' written in black pen on the side.

I know it's futile, but I go through the motions of checking hers, then act surprised to find my name – or at least, 'NOEL' – scrawled on it.

'They're the same, though?'

'Are you asking me, or telling me?'

'Well, both, I suppose.' I hold my coffee next to hers for a moment so she can compare the two. 'They're both flat whites.'

'But that one's mine. Or at least, it was meant to be.'

As was us meeting, I want to say, though in its place, the best I can come up with is: 'Don't you just want to drink mine instead?'

'It wouldn't feel right.'

'Even though they're *exactly* the same?'

Angel peers at her cup suspiciously. 'But this one's got your name on it.'

'That's not actually my name.'

'Why would you give them a false name?'

'I didn't.'

'Well, then . . .' Angel is giving me a look which seems to suggest she's enjoying toying with me. Or that I'm a little bit crazy. And right now, I can't argue with her on the second point.

'No, they made a mistake.'

'As did you,' says Angel.

I don't quite know how to take that, so I concede defeat and hand her my (or rather, her) coffee, and Angel lets out a satisfied sigh.

'I've seen complex hostage swaps that were easier,' she says, which makes me burst out laughing.

'Okay. Well . . .' And then, because I can't think of anything else to say, I say 'Cheers', and 'clink' my cup against hers (a little too enthusiastically, perhaps, because the 'clinking' action spills a little bit of my coffee through the hole in the lid, which nearly lands on Angel's feet), then look around for somewhere to sit. There's a table in the corner with a couple of chairs, or a single uncomfortable-looking stool by the wooden ledge thing in the window, so I do the decent thing and aim for the window seat, but just as I'm about to sit down, a large guy in a leather jacket muscles past me and nabs the stool from under my nose.

I'm thinking about remonstrating with him, even though he's twice my size, when I'm aware of someone standing behind me, and when I turn around, it's Angel.

'There's a table there,' she says, nodding towards the corner of the café.

'You take it.'

'No, that's fine.'

'I insist.'

'Please.'

'No, honestly, I'll stand . . .' I'm aware this is getting ridiculous, and chances are, two more men in leather jackets are going to come along and nab it, but as Marlon – my number two at work, and the person the inventor of Tinder probably had in mind when they were designing their app – always says, where women are concerned, 'if you snooze, you lose' (and if that's the case, then compared to him, I'm currently the Rip Van Winkle of dating).

'Suit yourself,' says Angel. 'But there are two chairs.'

It takes me a second or two too long to cotton on to her meaning – something I know she can tell, given her 'Duh!' response to my awkward 'Are you suggesting we sit . . . together?' Then, as she starts towards the table, I sigh loudly, as if I'm doing her a huge favour, and quickly follow her. 'Okay,' I say, 'I won't bother you.'

As Angel's eye-rolling tells me that ship has already sailed, I hang back to let her choose the chair she prefers, then move the other one to a sort of no-man's-land position, not too far away from the table that I have to stretch to reach my coffee, just close enough that the couple at the next table won't feel I'm trying to eavesdrop on them, and sit down.

'This is a bit awkward, isn't it?'

Angel lowers her voice. 'Drinking our coffees here, when we got them 'to go'?' she says, casting a furtive glance over at the counter.

'No, I meant . . .'

Angel rolls her eyes again. 'I know what you meant. Shouldn't be, though, seeing as we're already on first-name terms.'

'But we're not. Like I said, they got it wrong. It's actually "Noah".'

As I take the opportunity to edge my chair closer to the table in a series of childish jump/bumps, rather than do the simple thing and just stand up and move it, Angel raises both eyebrows. 'Interesting name.'

'It rained for forty days and nights before I was born.' It's been my standard 'amusing' answer for years, but it's only now, sitting in front of someone I'm obviously desperate to impress, that I see just how lame it is. 'Sorry. Bad joke. So . . .'

'So what?'

'So you're a virgin, too? Starbucks, I mean . . .' I add, reddening quickly.

'No, just this Starbucks. My first flat white, though.'

'And will there be a second?'

'Too soon to tell.' Angel tilts her almost-full mug towards me to show me how much she's drunk. 'Early signs are encouraging, though. It's kind of like a coffee milkshake, but . . .'

'Hot.'

'Exactly. Hot. Besides, life should be all about new experiences, so . . .'

As Angel takes another sip, I'm conscious that I'm staring, as if waiting for more of her fascinating opinion about what she's drinking, so I avert my eyes, then notice the word (well, *words*) 'parkrun' emblazoned across the front of her T-shirt, and then I'm conscious that I'm staring at her chest, so I point at it (which, on reflection, is probably worse), and in the absence of anything else to say, all I can do is blurt out: 'Parkrun'?

'That's right,' says Angel, though in a tone that suggests she's merely complimenting me on having the reading ability of a five-year-old. 'Do you run?'

'No. I mean, I *can* run, obviously. I just don't. I've got a car, and . . . Well, the only thing I run now is a gallery, if you see what I—'

'A gallery?' Angel raises both eyebrows. 'As in "art"?'

I nod. The quotation marks Angel's put around the word are quite appropriate given some of the stuff we exhibit. 'Are there any other types?'

She thinks for a moment. 'Shooting.'

'Right. Well, no, this is definitely art. Though we do occasionally have some photography exhibitions, which I guess you could say is—'

'Whereabouts?'

'Here, in Richmond. On Church Road.'

'I've walked past it.'

'But you've never been in?'

'Are you asking me or telling me?' says Angel.

There's an amused expression on her face, as if she's expecting me to follow up with: 'Telling – I'd have remembered.' But I'm not that smooth, so 'Asking' is what I say.

'And how did you wind up doing that?'

'Well, funny story . . .'

Angel looks at me expectantly, and I suddenly feel under so much pressure to make a good impression, to have her rolling on the floor with my 'funny story', that I hesitate. In my experience, a lot of people say 'it's a funny story', then they go on to tell a story that's not funny at all. And sitting here in front of Angel, I desperately don't want to be one of those people.

'Well?'

'Actually, I'm not sure.'

'Sure of what?'

'That it's a funny story.'

She takes another mouthful of coffee. 'Not even "funny" as in "weird"?'

'It's neither, now I think about it.'

11

'Right,' says Angel, though she's looking as if she's beginning to regret restarting the conversation – and to be honest, I'm having second thoughts myself.

'Running a gallery's a bit like running a shop,' I blurt out, when she doesn't ask anything more. 'Although we don't pay for the stock. We have an opening night, invite loads of people – most of whom only turn up for the free drinks – after which the artist gets to have their work displayed on the walls for a month or two, then people come in and look at it and, occasionally, someone buys something. Then we split the money with the artist and . . .' I take a too-big gulp of coffee, then take the serviette Angel's offering me to wipe the foam from the tip of my nose. 'That's it, really. It's hardly rocket science.'

'And do you enjoy it?'

I think for a moment. 'I do, actually. I mean, we're a business and everything, so mostly we have to show what sells, of course, and quite frankly, some of that stuff's a bit . . . Anyway, every now and again I get a chance to exhibit a young artist who wouldn't normally be able to get any gallery space . . . and that's what I like the most.'

'That's good,' says Angel. 'It's rare you meet someone who actually enjoys their job. So well done you.'

'Thanks,' I say, a little taken aback at the compliment. 'What about you?'

'What about me?'

'What do you do? Where do you live? That kind of thing.'

'Are we really going to do this?' says Angel, an amused expression on her face.

'Do what?'

'Exchange personal information like we're playing tennis.'

'What's wrong with that?'

'People should be spontaneous. Work things out as they go along. Find out about each other from what they do, rather than what they say – "action is character", and all that. Otherwise you might as well just present them with a questionnaire.'

'A questionnaire?'

'You know, "do you want children?", "if you had a dog, what type of dog would it be?", "how much do you earn?", "is it better to be good-looking or clever?" . . .' She mimes a yawn, so I laugh, although I hope she can't tell that I'm not finding this funny at all, because I used to think that kind of thing was a *brilliant* idea – a great way to cut through all the rubbish so you could make an informed decision about a potential partner from the get-go. And yet now, as Angel spouts on about how relationships don't quite work like that, and that getting together with someone isn't based on logic or compatibility or the answers to a questionnaire that's probably been written by someone who's single anyway, and how life is a rollercoaster, and when you meet someone, well, you're jumping into the seat next to them and hoping you can hold on, that the ups and the downs and the bends don't throw you out, and if you *do* manage to stay put, eventually you might start to enjoy the ride, I'm feeling a bit terrified. Because where she's concerned, I'm starting to see the attraction.

'Anyway,' she says eventually. 'I don't want to get all *Jerry Maguire* on you, but compatibility *is* all about two halves making a whole. Yin and yang. Opposites attract, and all that. Life – *relationships* – should be unpredictable. Full of surprises. That's what makes them interesting. Fun. Exciting. Put two people together based on some tick-in-the-box approach, and that's just boring.'

'Really.'

'I don't make the rules up. But it's true.'

'Says who?'

'Says *science*,' says Angel, in a way that suggests she's amazed not everyone knows this.

'Huh?'

'I read it in a magazine.'

'Just because some Bridget Jones clone writing in *Cosmo* thinks—'

'*New Scientist*, actually,' says Angel, smirking at me.

'Ah.'

'Yes, *ah*,' says Angel, downing a huge gulp of coffee.

I try not to stare as she licks the moustache of foam from her top lip. 'But surely, for the average person—'

'Let me stop you there. How many people do you know who fit the definition of "average"? I certainly don't.'

'I couldn't possibly comment. Seeing as you didn't answer any of my original questions.'

'Nice move!' says Angel, then she sighs good-naturedly. 'Okay . . . I'm twenty-nine years old. I'm not a natural redhead. I recently got a tattoo—'

'Whereabouts?'

'In a tattoo parlour in Brighton,' she says, without missing a beat. 'My favourite colour's black, and yes, I know, technically black's not a colour, but an absence of colour. I work for a charity . . .' Angel stops talking as I hold up both hands in a 'slow down' kind of way.

'Work for a charity?' I have to stop myself from shaking my head in disbelief. Angel's not like anyone I've ever met before – she's interesting, intriguing, incredible, and lots of other words beginning with 'i' (including, I'm beginning to suspect, 'ideal'), and it's all I can do not to glance around Starbucks to check we're not being filmed for some new reality dating show where they surprise you with your perfect woman. 'That's very . . . worthy.'

Angel does a little bow, as if accepting an award. 'Now, what else . . .' She thinks for a moment. 'I play the ukulele. I collect Converse trainers.' She straightens one leg out, so I can see the bright-red canvas basketball boots she's wearing. 'And that's about it. So tell me – are we compatible, do you think?'

'Er . . .'

She's looking at me in a 'game, set and match' kind of way, and I'm so conclusively beaten that I don't have the faintest idea of where to go from here – but then, fortunately, she lets out a short, tinkling laugh.

'All this factual stuff . . .' Angel waves a hand in the air, as if what she's describing is whirling around us. 'It doesn't define us. It's a part of us, but who we are – rather than what we are – is a lot more interesting. Don't you think?'

There's a pause, one that lasts so long that I manage to finish the rest of my coffee, then Angel sighs. 'Or maybe you don't,' she says. 'Which would be a shame. What time's your meeting?'

'What meeting?'

'The one you were on your way to when you stopped in here for a—'

'Shit!'

'Bit too much information there, Noah, TBH.'

'Sorry. No, I mean . . .' I show Angel my watch, then realise that unless she knows what time my date was, then the gesture's pretty pointless. 'It was ten minutes ago.'

'Nothing important, I hope?'

'It's . . .' I feel myself start to colour again. 'Well, it's sort of, um, a date.'

'A *date*?' Perhaps I imagine it, but Angel's face falls a little. 'Don't tell me – Tinder?'

When I don't say anything, Angel frowns. 'No need to be embarrassed. Lots of people meet their future ex that way.'

'You said "don't tell me". Though no, it isn't Tinder. It's a proper date.'

Angel widens her eyes. 'A *proper* date.'

'That's right,' I say, as she takes another mouthful of coffee. 'Well, a blind date. Which is still—' I don't get a chance to complete the sentence, as Angel bursts out laughing, spraying coffee over the table.

'Sorry.'

'What's so funny?'

'A blind date.' She shakes her head as she dabs at the table with a serviette. 'I'm actually impressed. Though you don't strike me as the type.'

'This is . . . was . . . or rather, *will be* my first.'

'Well, let's hope it'll be your last.'

'You mean because she and I will end up getting married, having kids and living happily ever after, or because it'll be so bad that I never go on another?'

'You believe whichever one suits you.'

'Well, I'd have gone for the first one if you hadn't just poured scorn – not to mention hot milk – on my romantic ideals.'

Angel snorts with laughter again, though fortunately this one's caffeine-free. 'Hey – don't listen to a word I'm saying. I think it's great you're being so spontaneous, and doing something you've never done before. Besides, relationships and me don't really go together.'

'Because?'

'Just because,' she says cryptically.

'Well, if you don't date, how can you be so sure that—'

'I never said I didn't date . . .' Angel hesitates, though not long enough for me to come up with an appropriate interruption, then she smiles. 'Though I will give you one piece of advice, if you want you and this girl to have any chance of a second one.'

'Which is?'

She leans across the table and nudges me. 'Show up for your first.'

'Right,' I say, though I already know my date with Wei is going to be a comparative let-down. I could listen to Angel reading the phone directory, to be honest – her voice is so animated, her face seems to change expression every few seconds – and as I stare miserably into my empty mug, Angel obviously misinterprets my disappointment, because she looks a little guilty.

'I'm sorry,' she says. 'I didn't mean to burst your bubble.'

'Oh no, don't worry,' I say, as defiantly as I can. 'My bubble's still . . .' I search for the right word.

'Inflated?'

'Unburst.'

Angel peers at me as if she's considering a challenge in Scrabble, then she finishes the last of her coffee and stands up. 'Well, it was nice talking to you, Noah, but people to see, places to go, things to do . . .'

'Right. Of course,' I say, leaping out of my chair so quickly I almost knock it over, and follow her to the door. 'Me too.'

'I was talking about you.'

'Oh. Okay. Well, like I said, I've got a date, so I ought to . . . I mean, I shouldn't really—'

Angel silences me with a smile. 'I understand.'

'Okay. So . . . Bye.'

'Bye, Noah. And good luck!'

And while I know I should say something, *anything*, just to try to prolong the conversation, or get her phone number, or do whatever else normal people would do in this situation, the best I can manage (and I'll kick myself later), is the world's most inappropriate thumbs-up. And a double one, at that.

Angel smiles, then – just before she disappears through the door, and quite possibly out of my life – she pauses, and looks back over her shoulder at me. And when I don't say or do anything (although it's possible I imagine it), she gives a wistful shrug.

'I hope it goes well,' she says.

So I nod and say, 'Thanks,' though I'm already hoping it doesn't.

2.

On reflection, meeting the love of your life on the way to a blind date with someone else probably isn't the best preparation, and to be honest, given how my head's spinning having just met Angel, I'd rather not go. But when you're thirty-five years old, with a sense that everything you want in terms of getting married, settling down, having kids is slipping away from you, and when the five-or-so relationships you've had that you thought were 'serious' actually turned out to be laughable, and your chat-up skills are as poor as the ones Angel's just experienced, and is probably currently cringing at, going on a blind date that the guy you work with set up because he's tired of your miserable moaning is pretty much your last available option.

Still, according to Marlon, Wei is a funny, smart, pretty Chinese girl (although when I asked him why – if that was the case – *he* wasn't going out with her, he got a little shifty), so I'm keeping an open mind. I can only hope that she is too, given that she's also going to be a pretty *angry* Chinese girl since, thanks to my Angel diversion, I'm half an hour late for our date.

Not that she looks that angry. Although that could simply be because she seems to have already met someone else, judging by the slicked-back-haired/shirt-not-tucked-in/skinny-jean-wearing man sitting on the stool next to (the girl I assume must be) her at the bar.

At least, I *think* it's her – she's the only Chinese girl in here – though of course, it might be someone else entirely. Wei might have gotten tired of waiting and left already. In which case, the only thing I might be interrupting is someone else's date.

For a moment, I don't know what to do: go and introduce myself and risk getting punched in the face, or give up on the date entirely, though given my abject failure with Angel earlier, giving up really isn't an option. Then I have a brainwave.

I stroll up to the bar and position myself next to where she's sitting, sideways on, her back to me, wave the barman over and order myself an Estrella. As he cracks the cap off the bottle, I clear my throat.

'I'm supposed to be meeting someone here,' I say, loudly enough for them to hear me, too. 'Her name's Wei. Has anyone . . . ?'

As I let my voice trail off, I'm aware of the girl next to me swivelling around on her seat. I turn to smile briefly at her, and she frowns back at me.

'*I'm* Wei,' she says. 'Who are you?'

'I'm Noah.' I nod my thanks at the barman, who sticks out his lower lip in an 'I didn't do anything' way, then glance nervously at the man Wei's been entertaining. 'We've got a—'

'. . . date. Yes, I know. But *this* is Noah,' she says, jabbing a thumb back over her shoulder.

'Your name's Noah too?'

'Er, yeah?' says the man, sounding a little unsure of himself.

'Really?'

'Yeah.'

For a moment, the three of us act like we're doing the mannequin challenge. I've never met another Noah. Never even heard of one, apart from the Ark guy. And what are the chances that two of us have come into the same bar, at the same time that Wei is expecting to meet . . .

In a flash, it occurs to me what must have happened: He's walked in, seen a single, attractive girl sitting at the bar, strolled confidently over and said hello. She's said, 'Are you Noah?' And sensing an opening, thinking maybe she's been stood up, he's said, 'Yes.'

The trouble is, what happens now? Wei's obviously been having a good time with him. I'm late. Even though he's quite clearly trying to hijack my date, and that must be against some code or other, I sense I'm still starting so far on the back foot, the slightest nudge would send me toppling over. And the most glaring factor of all: I can't stop thinking about Angel.

'Well, what are the chances?' I say, trying to ignore the fact that Wei's looking like she's hoping they're pretty high.

'Have you got any ID?'

This comes not from Wei, but from fake Noah. He's obviously clutching at straws, thinking that if I can't *prove* I'm Wei's original date, he's still got a chance. Though judging by the way Wei's peering at me suspiciously, he's got that anyway.

'Yes,' I say. 'Have you?'

'Not on me, no,' says fake Noah quickly.

'Okay, well, who was it who set us up?'

'I'm not going to say, am I?' says fake Noah.

'Why not?'

'Because then you'll say the same person, and that doesn't get us anywhere, does it?'

As I scowl at him, Wei clears her throat. 'How about if you both say it on three?'

'On three as in "one-two, say it"?' I ask. 'Or "one-two-three, say it"? Which would technically be "on four".'

'I'll count to three,' says Wei. 'Then you say it.'

'So on four?' says fake Noah.

'Yes, on four,' says Wei exasperatedly.

I glower at fake Noah as she counts; then, when it's time to speak, I start to say 'Marlon', but pause halfway. Marlon's not a common name, and quite frankly, if fake Noah can guess it, then he's the better man.

But the 'Mar . . .' he's copied from me is as far as he gets, and I smile smugly at him as his elongation of the syllable starts to get ridiculous.

'. . . tin?' he suggests eventually.

'. . . lon,' I say triumphantly. Though the way Wei's face immediately falls, it feels like a hollow victory.

'Fair enough.' He flashes a sheepish smile at me as he jumps down from his stool. 'But you can't blame me for trying.'

I'm just about to take my rightful place on the winner's podium/ bar stool at Wei's side, when fake Noah stops in his tracks. 'But before I go, Wei, just ask yourself this,' he says. 'Who would you rather go home with? Someone who left you waiting on your own in a pub for the best part of half an hour, or someone who saw you sitting at the bar, thought you were so gorgeous he knew he had to come over and talk to you or he'd never forgive himself, was even prepared to pretend to be *him*' – he points at me dismissively – 'just to get to know you better.'

He's good, I have to admit. After a speech like that, if he *does* go, and I try to salvage what's left of my date with Wei, then not only am I in the doghouse for being so late, but I'll also always be playing catch-up to whatever-his-real-name-is here, and I'm not sure I can recover from either of those two things. But do I even really want to, given how Angel knocked me off my feet earlier?

To her credit, Wei's looking like she feels a little awkward that she's been sitting here flirting with someone else, even though she didn't *know* she'd been sitting here flirting with someone else (and even though that's exactly what I've been doing in Starbucks). And while it occurs to me to point out that if he's been lying about being me, he's probably been lying about lots of other things too, that could come across a bit like sour grapes. Besides, all of a sudden, it's *me* who feels a fraud, because this *is* how it should be: People's eyes meeting across a crowded room (or even a half-empty bar). Them getting to know each other. Talking. Flirting. Finding a spark. Not being artificially put together in a 'she's single, you're single' kind of way. Because maybe, actually, it's not all about having things in common. Sometimes it's more about having nothing in common. Possibly like Angel and I, well, have or don't have. I can't quite work it out.

Perhaps Wei and fake Noah were meant to meet. Maybe me bumping into Angel and arriving here late was part of some grand, cosmic master plan to get Wei and fake Noah together, just as me needing the toilet then feeling so guilty I bought a coffee might be me-and-Angel's funny story to tell *our* grandkids.

So instead, I pick up my drink, silently cheers the two of them, and stroll out of the bar with a mumbled 'good luck!'

And the funny thing is, I mean it.

The gallery I run is at the bottom of Church Road, in an old newsagent's, nestled between an Indian restaurant (The Spice is Right) and a shop that never seems to be open (with no name, but with a display of garish plastic raincoats in the window, and that someone once told me is a front for a mail-order rubber and fetish-wear business).

In truth, the gallery doesn't take much running, partly because we don't get many customers – those people who do come in either just want to pass a few minutes while they're waiting for a table next door, or need a breather on their way up the hill to Richmond Park. In any case, like I told Angel, running a gallery's easy: once a month we take all the old stuff down, replace it with new stuff, invite a few people round (usually the artist's friends and family) for a couple of glasses of cava to celebrate the opening of a new 'show' (it used to be champagne, but when you sell as few pieces as we do, cava makes economic sense), then sit and wait for people to come in and maybe buy something.

Fortunately, just often enough, someone *does* buy something, especially if we've been lucky and the local paper has given us a review, though that doesn't happen very often – we're hardly the Tate Modern, and even if we were, the *Richmond Informer* doesn't do 'modern'. Then, Marlon and I will take it in turns to experience the adrenaline rush of fixing a small red sticky dot to the painting's caption card – though we rarely run out of dots, if you know what I'm saying, and to be honest, neither of us can ever remember whose turn it is next.

When I get back this afternoon, Marlon's waiting for me by the door. Dressed in his trademark black-suit-and-shirt combination (which I always kid him makes him look more like gallery security than someone with a degree in Fine Art from Cambridge), he's a younger, better-looking Denzel Washington (if Denzel Washington was six-foot-four inches tall and nearly as wide). And while at first I think his hopping from one foot to the other with excitement is because he's sold a painting (or even two), it's actually for less-commercial reasons.

'So?'

'So what?'

Marlon glares at me, then he grabs me by the shoulders and steers me into the chair behind the desk. 'How did it go?' he asks, angling the desk lamp so it's shining directly into my face.

'How did what go?'

'Wei?'

I push the lamp away as Marlon perches on the edge of the desk. 'Well, *No Wei* might be more appropriate.'

'Please tell me you mean that in a Brangelina/Kimye/Bennifer way.'

'What on earth are you talking about?'

'I used to date a girl who worked on the celebrity-gossip desk for the *Daily Mail*. Noah and Wei – *Nowei*.' He laces his fingers together, as if to demonstrate the merging of the names. 'Rather than "no way" . . .'

I shake my head slowly, and Marlon's face falls. 'What did you do?'

'Why do you automatically assume it was *me*?'

'All right. What did *she* do?'

'She didn't do anything either.'

'Huh?'

'For me, I mean. At least, I know she's never going to be the love of my life.'

'You can't really tell that after just one date.'

'Yes, you can,' I say, though I don't dare admit we didn't even have one. Or admit that the reason for *that* was the girl I fell in love with on the way there.

'You can't. It takes thirteen dates to fall in love.'

'Says who?'

'I read it in a magazine.'

'Don't tell me – *New Scientist*?'

'*Cosmo*.' He laughs. 'Which doesn't make it any less true.'

'Why thirteen?'

Marlon starts counting off on his fingers. 'First date, the attraction is there, otherwise *you* wouldn't be, obviously, and usually so is a lot of alcohol, which kind of writes it off in terms of anything you can draw a meaningful or significant conclusion from. Second to fourth, things become a bit more "real" – you begin to find out whether you actually *like* them as well as fancy them, and trust me, for a relationship to work, you've got to have both those things. By the fifth, sixth and seventh, you've probably slept together, written off the first bad sex to performance anxiety, and started to form an opinion as to whether it's the kind of sex you'll be happy doing long-term. Getting personal, as well as getting to know them as a person. Eighth, ninth and tenth . . . Maybe you haven't bothered to shave, maybe *she* hasn't, perhaps you get annoyed at the way they speak to a waiter, or start to suspect they only buy a copy of the *Big Issue* when you're with them. Then, the next couple of dates is when you have to work out whether the little idiosyncrasies they have – the way they eat, for example, or choose from a menu – which you found so quirky when you first met them, are things you can live with, or if they're eventually going to make you want to stab them in the leg with a fork. Once you've got past all of that? Well, then and only then is when the "love" part really starts. And all of that apparently takes . . . ?'

He holds up both fists, splays his fingers, then bends seven of them back down.

'Thirteen dates. I get it. Thank you, Yoda. Although I'm not so sure,' I say, because while I can see some sense in what Marlon's saying, what's just happened to me with Angel is the complete opposite. 'I mean, *fall* in love . . . "Fall" suggests something quick. You don't fall off a cliff and drift gently down to the ground, do you? You hit the ground, and with a bang.'

'Hang on, Billy-no-dates. You're arguing with a magazine – no, a *bible* – written by women, for women . . .' He grins. 'Why do you think I never go out with anyone more than a handful of times?'

'Yes, well,' I say, smarting a little from his 'Billy-no-dates' quip. 'It's wonderful that you're so concerned not to leave a trail of broken hearts behind you, but—'

Marlon silences me with a look. 'We're not talking about me here, are we, Noah? So tell me – what happened?'

'Well, funny story.'

Marlon rolls his eyes, then heads into the back to put the kettle on. Given how busy the gallery normally gets, we both know I'll have plenty of time to tell him.

The house I live in is a large, stucco-fronted semi in a part of Richmond called The Vineyard. Whether there was ever an actual vineyard there, I'm not sure – nowadays, the Duke's Head pub and an Oddbins are the only things we have that contain wine (unless you count the drunk guy who seems to live on the bench outside the church hall). The rest of the area is full of eye-wateringly expensive houses, and in truth, I'm lucky to be here – the room I rent from my elderly landlady, Mary, is well below the market rate.

Not that she needs the money – I suspect it's more for the company. Her husband, Stan, died ten years ago, and they didn't have any kids; as she often reminds me, I'm 'the grandson she never had' – and even though I often tease her about charging her 'grandson' rent, it's an arrangement that suits us both fine.

When I get home that evening, Mary's standing in the kitchen, alternately frowning at the glass door of the microwave and jabbing at the buttons as if she's trying to find BBC One. She hasn't heard me come in, and I don't want to give her a heart attack, so I rap my knuckles on the kitchen worktop, just loudly enough to make her look round.

'Oh, hello, Noah. Good day?'

'And a good day to you, Lady Mary.' I bow theatrically at her – she's a huge fan of *Downton Abbey* – and she waves regally back. 'It was . . . interesting.'

'How so?'

'I met someone.'

'That must have made a change. Normally you don't get that many customers.'

'Ha ha. No, I mean a *girl*.'

'You didn't think Marlon would set you up on a blind date with a *man*, did you?'

'It, um, wasn't actually on the blind date.' I take her elbow and lower her into a chair. 'It was beforehand. In Starbucks.'

'Oh yes?'

Mary's looking up at me expectantly, so I perch obediently on the edge of the kitchen table. 'Not much to tell, really. Her name's Angel. She was in front of me in the queue and . . . Anyway, there was a bit of a misunderstanding, and we got chatting, and it turns out that she's funny, and smart, and kind, and gorgeous, and a real individual, and . . .' Mary puts a hand to her mouth, trying to hide a smile, so I stop mid-flow. 'What?'

'You said there wasn't that much to tell.' She reaches creakingly over and pats me on the knee. 'And what does this Angel do?'

'She works for a charity.'

'Which one?'

'Um . . .'

'Is she local?'

'Er . . .'

'I hope you didn't talk about *you* the whole time?'

'Well, no. We talked about . . . well, *everything.*'

'It sounds like the two of you had a lovely time. Did you ask her for her Twitter address, or whatever it is you do nowadays?'

'Um, no.'

'Why ever not? Playing hard to get, was she?'

'More like impossible to get. She said she doesn't really "do" relationships.'

'Did you ask her if she wanted to "do" one with you?'

'I . . . No.'

'Why not?'

'Well, because I was on my way to a date. And how would that have looked?'

'I'd have been flattered.'

'And your last date was?'

Mary thinks for a moment. 'Nineteen sixty-six.'

'Exactly.' I flash her a grin. 'Things have changed since then.'

'And not for the better, from what I've heard. All this swapping left, right and centre . . .'

'*Swiping.*'

'Either way,' says Mary, though I'm pretty sure she's not referring to direction of a swipe. 'You youngsters seem to have forgotten what romance is.'

'We haven't forgotten. Things just work differently nowadays.'

'Or don't work,' says Mary. 'Given how high the divorce rate is.'

'Yes, well,' I say, which I realise is pretty much saying nothing at all. 'All I've ever wanted is to meet a nice girl, settle down, have kids. And then when I *do* meet a nice girl, I can't do anything about it, because I'm on my way to meet another girl.'

'You sound like you're pretty smitten. And it sounds to me like she felt the same.'

I hesitate for a moment. On the one hand, there was definitely a spark between us. But on the other, as Marlon often points out, I'm thirty-five years old and still single, with a trail of failed relationships and (probably) missed opportunities behind me, and therefore my reading of these situations perhaps isn't as reliable as I'd like.

'Maybe. Although apparently it takes thirteen dates to fall in love with someone, so . . .'

'*Thirteen* dates?'

'According to Marlon.'

'He'd know, I suppose. Though that seems like a strange number.'

'I suppose it takes that long to realise if you like them or not, to find out what you have in common, that sort of thing,' I say, deciding to give her an abridged version of Marlon's earlier explanation, and Mary nods thoughtfully.

'That might be true, you know. When my Stan first started courting me, I didn't want to know. But gradually he wore me down . . .' She looks up at me suddenly. 'That's what you should do!'

'Wear her down?'

'By taking her on thirteen dates,' she says, as if it's as easy as that. 'See if you can't get her to fall in love with you. And it'll help you.'

'To?'

'Make sure you're thinking with the right part of your anatomy.'

'You mean my head,' I say, trying my best not to blush. 'Rather than my, ahem, trousers?'

'I meant your heart. But that too.'

'Maybe. But thirteen dates are going to be tricky to get to, Mary. Especially if she won't even, to use your earlier phrase, "do" *one*.'

'I don't know. What exactly constitutes a first date nowadays?'

I shrug. 'You sit down and talk. Perhaps over a coffee.'

'Well, it seems to me that you and this Angel have already done that.' Mary smiles mischievously, then she pats me on the knee again. 'Which means it's one down, twelve to go.'

3.

Of course, *actually* asking Angel out is dependent on being able to speak to her again, and despite spending the best part of the next week hanging out at Starbucks, there's no sign of her. And seeing as I don't know where she works, or where she lives, or even her surname (which, despite Marlon's best efforts, makes tracking her down on Facebook impossible), that kind of means that that's, well, *that*.

By the Friday, I'm kicking myself for not asking for her number – especially since *she* was the one who invited *me* to share her table – in fact, I'm so miserable, I'm starting to wish we'd never met. And I suspect Marlon's feeling the same way, given how fed up he's becoming with me walking round the gallery looking like the world's come to an end.

'I don't know why I'm so obsessed,' I say, as we prepare the invitations for the forthcoming show. 'It's not as if she's even my type.'

'Do you *have* a type?'

I nod as I run through a list of my exes in my head (although, worryingly, running through the complete list doesn't actually take that long) – all of them 'sensible choices', as my mum and dad would say, on the odd occasions I'd take one home to meet them. 'Insofar as they're usually the complete opposite of Angel.'

'So, the type you could see yourself marrying. Having kids with.'

'Seeing as that's what I want, yes,' I say, though I'm conscious that 'want' is underplaying it a little.

'Refresh my memory. How many of these women did you actually end up marrying and having kids with?'

'What? None of them!'

'Well, they weren't really your type, then, were they?' Marlon sighs. 'Angel didn't say anything about where she lived?'

'Nope.'

'Or more about what she did, apart from the charity thing?'

'For the hundredth time, no.'

'Any other clues?'

'Such as?'

Marlon narrows his eyes. 'How she was dressed. It's amazing what you can work out from the details.'

'Well, she didn't have a McDonald's uniform on, if that's what you're getting at.'

'Okay, what *was* she wearing?'

I narrow my eyes and try to picture her, worried the vision that was Angel might soon begin to fade. 'Trainers. Grey leggings. A T-shirt with "parkrun" written on the fro—'

'Boom!' says Marlon, slamming the back of his fingers into the palm of his other hand.

'I beg your pardon?'

'She *parkruns.*'

'She what?'

'Parkrun. It's a running thing.'

'Don't tell me – in the park?'

Marlon applauds sarcastically. 'Every Saturday morning.'

I stare back at him, though it takes an embarrassingly long time before the penny drops. 'But . . . tomorrow's Saturday.'

Marlon nods enthusiastically, and reaches for his phone. 'Here we go,' he says, after a quick Google. '"Parkrun. We organise free weekly timed runs all over the world. Held in pleasant parkland on weekend mornings, our runs are open to all – from juniors and first-timers to

Olympians and octogenarians . . ." And super-hot women called Angel.'
He looks up at me. 'I made that last bit up.'

'Really.'

He nods. 'So all you need to do is turn up at' – he jabs at the
screen – 'nine o'clock tomorrow morning, go for a little jog around
the park, *et voilà!*'

'Right. Great. Erm, how "little", exactly?'

'Hold on . . .' He peers at his phone. 'Five kilometres.'

'Five kilometres?'

'It's not that far. You know how to run?'

'I know how to do lots of things. Doesn't mean I can, though.'

'I'm sure you'll manage. The thrill of the chase, and all that. And
remember what you'll be chasing.'

'That still doesn't mean she'll go out with me, does it. Particularly
if I'm a jelly-legged, panting wreck.'

'Sounds to me like you're describing your first meeting.' Marlon
grins. 'Anyway, according to the website, it's just for fun.'

'Fun. Like school cross-country races were?'

'It's not a race – "just you against the clock", it says. And more
importantly, apparently they all go for coffee afterwards. So all you need
to do is turn up, do the run, go for that coffee, then sidle up to her in
a "fancy seeing you here" kind of way, and . . .'

He does the *boom* thing again, and I smile nervously, though I'm
not sure what I'm more worried about – having to run that far, or the
prospect of seeing Angel again. Because what if I'm wrong, and I've
imagined the 'spark' between us?

Then again, what if I'm right?

And although my current level of exercise on a Saturday morning
tops out at rolling over in bed to hit 'Snooze' on my alarm, I already
know that if I want a second date with Angel, I don't have a lot of choice.

A quick trip to the TK Maxx in Kew Retail Park has provided me with a pair of running shoes, and while I'm not sure how effective trainers named after (and not much more expensive than, thanks to the shop's heavy discount policy) my favourite chocolate bar will be, the Adidas Boost I'm wearing are apparently designed to 'change everything you think you knew about what fast, cushioned and comfortable feels like'. And even though I'm not sure I had the faintest idea about how that felt in the first place, more importantly they're also bright orange. Which means the ambulance crew should be able to find me without too much trouble in the event of a cardiac arrest.

I've decided to come in disguise – or at least, a hoodie, baseball cap and sunglasses – just in case I look so bad that I don't want Angel to recognise me (or I decide to quit halfway), but even the extra layers aren't doing much against the chilly morning. It's two minutes to nine, and in the fifteen freezing minutes I've been here, I haven't been able to spot her amongst the forty-or-so variously shaped-and-sized people, dressed in an assortment of running gear, stood shivering in this corner of Richmond Park. While some of them are enthusiastically stamping their feet or performing a few on-the-spot sprints to keep warm, I don't dare – I've a feeling I'm going to need all my energy for the actual run.

I peer through the dense cloud of mist that appears every time I breathe out, and scan through the assembled runners again. It's looking like I've had a wasted journey, and a hot cup of coffee and something decidedly unhealthy from the nearest café are looking a lot more attractive than a meaningless slog around the park, but before I can sneak off, a man wearing a bright yellow gilet with 'STEWARD' written on the back calls us all to attention.

'Morning!' he says, his tone incredibly cheery, although that's probably because he's not going to be running this morning. 'I'm Stewart. Yes, yes, I know, Stewart the steward . . .' He pauses as a smattering of laughter – though it could simply be a chattering of teeth – comes from the assembled runners. 'Now, are there any first-timers here?'

Before I know what I'm doing, I put my hand up, then hurriedly lower it again as I wait for the rather surprising round of applause to die down. 'Sorry,' I say hesitantly. 'Did you mean first time here, or first time running? Because it's not. My first time running. Ever, I mean.'

Stewart rolls his eyes in a 'this one's trouble' way, and I can't help but notice that a few of the other runners have edged away from me – in the way that experienced skiers keep their distance from newbies on the slopes – as if there's a danger I might knock them over. 'Well, welcome to parkrun,' he says, then he turns his attention back to the group. 'I know it's a bit chilly, so I won't keep you long, but we do have a presentation to make – for a hundred parkruns. Where's Eleanor?'

There's another round of applause – quite a bit louder than the one I just received, though I suppose that's understandable – then an old lady at the front puts her hand up.

'Well done!' says Stewart, handing her a T-shirt with '100' written on it, which by the looks of her could actually be her age, and as she slips it on, I start to feel a little better. If Eleanor can manage a hundred of these things, then how hard can they be?

'Right. Just to remind you,' continues Stewart, 'the course follows the road, then turns left towards Sheen Gate, left again by the car park, then follow the path to just past Cambrian Gate . . .' Though, to be honest, I've zoned out at this point. I'm already sure I'm going to be nowhere near the front, given the number of much-more-athletic-than-me people in obscenely fitting tights performing some vigorous last-minute stretches around me, so I'm hardly going to need to know the exact route, and while there's a possibility that everyone else will sprint off so quickly that I've got no one to follow, Stewart's 'there'll be stewards at every corner' reassures me on that front. Until I suddenly think: *What if one of those stewards is Angel?*

As I debate whether to attempt a few last-minute stretches myself, Stewart blows a whistle, and I'm almost knocked over by the stampede towards the start line. 'Are we all ready?' he asks.

'As I'll ever be,' I say, under my breath.

He blows the whistle a second time, and there's a mass beeping as almost all the front row press 'Start' on their stopwatches, though as they all sprint off down the path (and I reluctantly jog off in pursuit), it takes me about a hundred metres to realise two things: firstly, that parkrun's not 'just for fun', for most of the runners at least, as the majority of the leaders seem to have set off at a pace that would exhaust Mo Farah (one in particular is so quick that he might even *be* Mo Farah, and even though we're only supposed to complete the one lap, I'm already worried about him lapping me); and secondly, if Angel *is* stewarding somewhere out on the course, then chances are she'll have gone for a coffee and disappeared off home before I even reach her.

Already gasping for breath, I force myself to put one foot in front of the other, cursing the fact that my new trainers are rubbing but determined to make it to the first turn, hoping Angel might be there – though, by now, as much because that means I'll have a reason to stop.

By some miracle, I make it, though there's no sign of her, and from what I can make out, she's not at the next turn either. The half a dozen oldies – Eleanor included – that I set off in front of are gradually catching me up, and as a mother pushing a double buggy the size of a small off-roader steams past me, I'm desperate to quit.

I kneel down, pretending my shoelace has come undone, planning (once everyone's gone past) to sneak away, but as Eleanor draws level, to my horror, she waits for me.

And as she helps me up with an encouraging 'Come on, lad,' then shuffles off in front of me, it's all I can do not to trip her up.

By the time I eventually limp into work, it's nearly midday. There was no sign of Angel anywhere on the course (I forced myself to walk-jog the whole way round, just to make sure), and the pain I'm currently feeling from my blisters, stiff calves, aching thighs and (for some reason) sore nipples isn't made any easier by Marlon's throwaway observation that 'she must do a different one', and my subsequent finding out that almost *every* local park has a parkrun. Which means I'm going to have to go and put myself through this torture *every* Saturday morning if I want to find her.

To make things worse, while I'd rather spend the rest of the day in a seated position behind the desk (or at home in bed), there's a crisis at the gallery I have to deal with. Once a year, we show 'hot local artist' (his words, though he's American, and not even in the slightest bit cool) Hank Martin's latest collection, but for some reason, Hank (or Hanksy, as he's started to sign his paintings, in a desperate attempt to secure some street cred) hasn't confirmed he'll be ready in time. With his opening planned for next Saturday night, last month's paintings already taken down and the invitations already sent out, Hanksy, like Angel, is looking like a no-show.

'Still no news,' says Marlon when I walk back in after an emergency trip to Boots – incorporating a quick detour past Starbucks, *just in case* – for ibuprofen. 'And he's not answering his phone.'

'Well, maybe he's got wet paint on his hands. Did you leave a message?'

'I did. Threatening to break his fingers if we don't see something soon.'

'Marlon, that's very, um, *kind* of you, but breaking his fingers is hardly going to speed up his painting.'

'Haven't you seen *My Left Foot*? Which, to be honest, is what some of Hanksy's stuff looks like it's been painted with.' Marlon glances up at the empty walls. 'This is a gallery, Noah. We're supposed to have paintings on display. That's how it works. Otherwise there's nothing for people to see. Or, more importantly, buy.'

'You know what Hank's like. He probably just wants to put the finishing touches to them all before he delivers them.'

'He should have finished them weeks ago.'

I put on my best approximation of Hank's Californian drawl. '*You never actually finish a painting. You just decide to stop working on it.* Though he'd better decide to stop working on them all by Saturday otherwise he – and *we* – will be in serious trouble.' I nod at a pile of rectangular packages on the floor. 'What are they?'

'The frames.'

'Great. How many invites have we sent out?'

Marlon taps a couple of times on his iPad. 'A hundred, give or take.'

I sigh, then fold my arms and nod at the frames. 'Tell you what. Let's wait and see if the works arrive on Monday, and if not, we'll just hang the empty frames. That'll give us an idea of what goes where. Then when the paintings arrive, all we have to do is—'

'Put them in the frames.' Marlon gives me a little salute. 'Way ahead of you. Coffee?'

'I'll get them,' I say. And even though I know it's probably futile, I check my reflection in the window, head out through the door and limp painfully back to Starbucks.

4.

When I get up on Monday morning, Mary's nowhere to be seen. This is strange, because even at her age, a trip to the local Sainsbury's – the only reason she'd probably have for going out at this time of day – can be completed in less than ten minutes. And when I get back from my own trip to Sainsbury's (just to check she hasn't had an accident on the way there or back, and to pick up a triple chocolate muffin for breakfast), a shout of 'Help!' from the back garden sends me running – still a little painfully – through the house.

'Mary?'

'Over here, Noah.' Mary looks up from where she's sitting, in the corner of the patio, at the bottom of the steps that lead down to the garden. 'Thank goodness! I thought you might have left for work.'

'Hold on,' I say, leaping down the steps and nearly falling myself.

Mary gazes wistfully up at the iron railing. 'If I'd held on, I wouldn't be lying here now.'

'What happened?'

'I fell. Again.'

I squat down beside her. 'Have you hurt yourself?'

'I'm not sure. I can't seem to get up, although that's nothing new. And my wrist . . .' She's cradling her left hand in her right, and seems a little pale, so I hurriedly slip my phone out of my pocket.

'I'll call an ambulance.'

'No, I'll be fine. If you could perhaps just give me a . . .' Mary winces as I try to help her up, then slumps against the garden wall. 'Actually, on second thoughts, you'd better leave me where I am.'

'I don't think that's such a good idea. It's not the warmest of days.'

'I didn't mean . . .'

As I dial 999, Mary smiles at my attempt to lighten the situation, and once I'm sure the ambulance is on its way, and I've texted Marlon to tell him I'll be late, I sit back down next to her. 'Did you want anything? A cup of tea?'

Mary shakes her head. 'No. Just chat to me. Take my mind off my predicament.'

'What about?'

'How you're getting on with that Angel girl, for example.'

'I've almost given up on her, to be honest,' I say miserably.

'Why?'

'There's been no sign of her in Starbucks, she wasn't at the park on Saturday morning, I don't have the first idea where she lives or works, and aside from walking up and down George Street all day in the hope she walks past, or putting a missing persons ad in the *Informer* . . .' I sigh. 'I guess it just wasn't meant to be.'

'Oh, Noah. Don't be such a . . .' Mary frowns. 'What's that word that begins with a "p"?'

'Pessimist?'

'No – "pussy". What if this girl *is* the love of your life? And you've given up on her after a week?'

'But I don't know what else to—'

'Just keep looking.' Mary smiles. 'You found her once, you'll find her again. Richmond's a small place. You're bound to bump into each other.'

'Maybe.'

Mary rolls her eyes at me, and I smile back at her. 'Did you want me to come to the hospital with you?'

'As long as I'm not keeping you from anything,' she says. 'Like a hot date?'

I glower at her good-naturedly. We both know the answer to that.

The ambulance men are the kind of big, strapping, capable guys who make me look (and feel) pretty pathetic – though that's possibly due to me being unable to contain my excitement when they tell me if I want to go with Mary to the hospital, I'll have to sit up front. And even though I'm slightly disappointed that they don't switch on the siren, or even the flashing lights – and actually drive a lot slower than *I* normally would – given the last few days, the ambulance ride stands a good chance of being the highlight of my week.

As Mary's taken in for her X-ray, I settle down in the waiting room with a cup of molten-hot-but-tasteless coffee from the vending machine in the corner, and flick through the copy of *Classic Car* I've found in the pile of dog-eared magazines on a table in the corner, amazed how, given that there's only a certain number of classic cars, they manage to keep thinking of new stuff to write about them.

But even though the articles don't seem to have moved on, I'm wondering whether *I* need to. I've been obsessing about Angel for the best part of a week, even though (and despite what Marlon says) she's clearly not my type. And by the looks of things, I'm never going to see her again anyway, so what's the point? I'm only wasting my time.

Then again, it's not as if I'm beating eligible women off with a stick, is it? And Angel and I had a connection, I'm sure of it – so Marlon might be right, and I might be wrong about what my 'type' actually is. And if he's right about that, and right about this 'thirteen dates' stuff, then I owe it to myself (and my chances of future emotional/domestic/paternal happiness) to try to track her down, and then . . . Well, do my best to take it one day, or rather one *date*, at a time.

I sigh, loudly enough to wake up the old man sitting opposite me who's been snoring loudly since I sat down, and stare hopelessly up at the flickering light on the ceiling, replaying my encounter with Angel over and over in my mind, looking for some sign, some clue, some way to find her. But every time, all I can think about is the look she gave me when she left. How hopeful her expression was. And how hopeless I was at responding.

An hour later, I'm contemplating 'treating' myself to a second cup of coffee – or maybe even risking the tea (though to be honest, given how tasteless the coffee is, it'll probably be hard to tell the difference), and wondering whether *Take a Break* is really an appropriately named magazine for an accident and emergency waiting room, when Mary reappears, escorted by a young male nurse.

'How is it?'

She raises her arm to proudly show me the bright purple cast encasing her wrist. 'Double fracture.'

'Show off. Nice colour.'

'I'm going to dye my hair to match.'

The nurse smiles. 'Now remember, Mary,' he says, 'we'll see you back here in a month to have the cast removed. Here's your prescription for painkillers.' He hands her a piece of paper. 'And don't overdo things. Have you got someone to look after you?'

'No, I don't—'

'Yes, she does,' I say quickly. 'Shall we go home?'

'Well, seeing as a game of tennis is probably out of the question.' Mary pats the nurse on the arm. 'Thank you, dear. Do we get another ride in the ambulance?'

The nurse shakes his head. 'I'm afraid not. There's a taxi rank out the front, though.'

'A taxi it is, then,' says Mary, then she loops her good arm through mine. 'Come on, Noah. My treat.'

'Ooh!' I say mock-excitedly, though as we make our way towards the exit, my heart actually does skip a beat: Angel's coming out of one of the consulting rooms at the far end of the corridor. She's just as I remember her – not surprising, really, given that her face is burned indelibly into my brain – and dressed in a combination of tartan mini-skirt, smart shirt and a (different) pair of Converse All-Stars that, worn together, makes for an interesting work outfit.

As she slots a pair of headphones into her ears and jabs at the screen of her phone, I open my mouth to shout her name, then realise she probably won't hear me if I do. But Mary's still clamped onto my arm, and at the rate we're walking, Angel will be gone before we get outside.

'What's the rush?' says Mary, as I attempt to hurry her along a little.

'That's her!'

'Who?'

'The girl I told you about.'

'What girl?'

'From last week?'

'The blind date?'

'The other one. Angel.'

'Oh,' says Mary, clearly confused, followed by a much more loaded 'Oh!' With difficulty, she locates her glasses on the string around her neck and puts them on. 'She's pretty.'

'Isn't she?' I say proudly, then I stop dead in my tracks. In Starbucks, dressed casually, she seemed approachable, but here, now . . . I'd be embarrassed to even be caught looking.

As Angel slips her phone into her pocket and starts walking away from us, I mentally facepalm. What was I thinking – that someone like her would ever be interested in someone like me? As I pretend to be fascinated by a poster on the wall that, embarrassingly, is talking about sexually transmitted diseases, Mary gives my arm a tug.

'What's the matter? Go and talk to her!'

'She's . . . Now I see her again . . . I just think she might be . . .'

'What?'

'Out of my league.'

'Why would you ever think that?'

'Trust me. I know.'

Mary looks at me as if I'm being ridiculous. Which I probably am. 'Just go and say hello.'

'I can't.'

'Why not?'

'Because I'm . . .' *Paralysed by fear*, while being the right answer, probably isn't the one that'll show me in the best light. 'Well, I'm helping you, aren't I?'

Mary gives me a look that suggests it's the other way round. 'Go on. And hurry up,' she urges, as Angel strides purposefully towards the exit. 'She's getting away!'

'Hold on. Is this some kind of set-up?'

'Oh, Noah, you've caught me out. I waited until I heard you get up this morning, then I threw myself head-first down the garden steps, simply because I knew this Angel girl would be at the hospital.' Mary smiles, and shakes her head. 'Sometimes, in life, we all need a little luck, Noah. And a little push.'

'Yes, well . . .' I stare miserably at the door Angel's just disappeared through. 'She's gone now. It's too late.'

'No, it isn't,' says Mary, clamping my arm beneath hers and almost dragging me along the corridor and out towards the taxi rank, just in time to see Angel climbing into the lead cab.

As the taxi pulls away, Mary hurries us over to where the driver of the next cab is waiting, leaning out of his window and about to light a cigarette, which she snatches from his lips, then hands politely back to him.

'Hey! I was about to—'

'Drive us somewhere,' says Mary sweetly. 'Isn't that right?'

The driver sighs, and starts to climb out of the cab to get the door for her, but Mary's already ahead of him. 'Come on, Noah,' she says, jumping in, then shimmying along the back seat and beckoning for me to follow her.

'Where to, love?' says the driver.

'Follow that cab!' says Mary, pointing at Angel's taxi as it heads off down the road, and the driver laughs.

'What?'

'The taxi that was parked in front of you. If it's not too much trouble, I'd very much like you to follow it.'

'But . . .'

'And it's "pardon", not "what".'

'Listen, lady—'

'Today would be nice,' says Mary, quite a bit less sweetly, and the driver scowls at her in his rear-view mirror.

'I don't know what you think this is, but—'

Mary waves her arm threateningly in the air – though she could just be showing off her new plaster cast. 'Just drive, will you?'

Evidently knowing better than to argue with Mary's tone, the driver hurriedly turns the ignition key. I just about manage to get Mary's seat-belt fastened before there's a screech of tyres, then we're off.

After the relative calmness of the ambulance trip, the taxi ride more than makes up for it. We career off down the road, but don't make it through the lights in time, which means we have to slam our brakes on while Angel's cab sails off into the distance. Then it's a frantic chase around the one-way system through the town centre, until we spot them heading past the station. Thanks to an undertaking manoeuvre involving a bus that almost sends *us* to the undertakers, we eventually slot in two cars behind them at the roundabout, then tail them along the dual carriageway until, finally, Angel's taxi pulls up outside a large building with 'THE POPPY FACTORY' written in huge letters on the front.

'Ta-da!' announces Mary, as Angel jumps out of her cab, then hurries up the steps and into the building.

As we slow down to look for a parking space, I take a deep breath and undo my seatbelt, sure Mary's going to insist I go in after her, *and* sit in the cab and watch me until I come out with her number, a bit like when my mother wouldn't let me leave the dinner table before I'd finished everything on my plate. But instead of directing the driver to stop somewhere and let me out, Mary just taps him on the shoulder. 'Well done,' she says. 'You can take us home now.'

As she gives him the address, I frown, and wonder whether she's having another one of what she's begun referring to more frequently as her 'senior moments'.

'Is that it?'

'*You're welcome*, you mean?'

'I don't . . .'

'Oh, Noah. I was hardly going to put you on the spot,' says Mary, patting me on the knee.

'But . . .'

'You said you didn't have any way of getting in touch with her. Well, now you do.'

'Huh?'

'It's called a telephone,' says Mary, pointing to the sign on the front of the building. 'You go home, calm down, then find the number in the telephone directory. Then all you have to do is ring her. Unless you *would* like us to let you out here?'

I narrow my eyes at her, then refasten my seatbelt. Even though the journey home's a lot more sedate, somehow I feel I might be in for a bumpy ride.

5.

The Poppy Factory turns out to be a charity that produces, perhaps not surprisingly, poppies. Not real ones, but the commemorative poppies that the Royal British Legion sells or that go into wreaths and the like, and are made by 'veterans with health conditions or impairments', according to their website.

Finding Angel's number – or rather, finding Angel's office's number, turns out to be the easy part. Mainly because when I eventually pluck up the courage to call – which takes a few goes – the automated phone system completely catches me out.

'Thank you for calling The Poppy Factory,' it says. 'For the extension of the person you're calling, please press "hash", followed by their extension number. For the company directory, please key in the first letter of the surname of the person you're calling.'

There's a pause, after which I almost expect to hear the voice saying *come on, then!*, and then I end the call and stare at the handset, unable to believe that I've been beaten at the first hurdle. What are my options: call back, hit 'hash' followed by a number at random, and say, 'I'm sorry, I was after Angel' to whoever – if anyone – answers, or even just call twenty-six times and work my way through the whole internal directory? Besides, maybe she's 'Angela' at work, rather than 'Angel', which might make that twice as hard, or something. Plus there's the small matter of how exactly I'm going to ask her out, and then how I'm going to counter what's sure to be her 'no' in reply.

'Zero,' says Marlon, when he gets in later that morning, and I nervously explain my dilemma to him.

'I've been called worse.'

'No – hit "zero". Whenever you call somewhere and you don't want to go through the automatic system, just press the "zero" key. It takes you straight to the operator.'

'How do you know that?'

Marlon shrugs. 'I used to date a girl who worked for BT. She knew how to press all the right buttons.'

I widen my eyes at him, then before I can lose my nerve, pick up the phone, make for the privacy of the gallery's toilet and redial Angel's office number. Though the woman who answers with a curt 'switchboard?' when I follow Marlon's instructions is the type who makes doctors' receptionists seem welcoming.

'Oh. Hi. Yes. Hello. Can I, um, speak to Angel please?'

'Angel who?' is her stern reply, which stumps me, although I suppose I should have anticipated this, and I'm frantically trying to picture Angel's coffee cup in Starbucks to see whether there was a surname written on the side too, when the receptionist, evidently tired of my three-second pause, follows the question up with an even sterner 'Hello?'

'How many Angels do you have?' I say, trying for a jokey manner, gambling on the fact that I've been on this earth for thirty-five years and Angel's the first Angel I've met, so the chances of there being two in the same office must be extremely small. As, I'm starting to fear, are my chances of being put through, until the receptionist – evidently deciding her day is too short to behave like a Dobermann on the phone with someone who obviously sort-of knows who he's calling for – lets out a loud sigh.

'Extension three-three-six,' she says coldly, in a 'don't waste my time next time' kind of way.

'Thank y—'

'Who shall I say is calling?'

'Noah.'

'Just "Noah"?'

'Well, there's no one else on the line, if that's what you—'

'And where shall I say you're calling from?'

I'm smart enough to know she doesn't really want me to say 'the toilet', but don't have the nerve to say 'it's a personal call', worried that they might not be allowed. I'd give the name of the gallery, but in my panic, I seem to have forgotten it.

Fortunately, just as I'm conscious the pause is getting uncomfortable, I have a brainwave.

'Starbucks,' I say.

'Hello?' says Angel, so quickly that it takes me by surprise, and in a tone that suggests even after that Gestapo-like grilling, the receptionist hasn't bothered to tell her who's calling, a fact reinforced by the way she responds to my cheery 'Hello!' with a tentative 'Who is this?'

'It's Noah.'

'Noah?'

Her tone is difficult to read, not to mention the fact that it's hard to work out whether it's actually her from her first five words. But there can't be two Angels in her office, and while it's possible she might have forgotten who I am, it could be that the slight uplift at the end of her voice might simply be an indication of pleasant surprise to be hearing from me. I tell myself it's the latter, and soldier on.

'Yes. You know, from Starbucks? Last Saturday?' I add, though probably needlessly. How many Noahs might she meet in Starbucks that I need to define it by the exact day?

'Oh, *that* Noah,' says Angel, and I immediately feel stupid – or rather, that there might be more of us than I thought. And not just fake ones. 'How did you get my number?'

'I, um, saw you the other day, followed you to your office, then googled it.'

I've blurted that out without thinking about it, and I stare at the handset in horror – if ever there was a reason to put the phone down, I've just given her one. But instead, Angel starts laughing, which I have to take as a good sign, rather than a sign she's going to have me arrested for stalking.

'You followed me to my office?'

'Well, yes. I wouldn't have, under normal circumstances, but Mary – that's the old lady I live with – she made me do it, and . . .'

Angel laughs again. 'Well, that explains it. How are you?'

'I'm good. You?'

'Yeah. Great. Thanks.' She says these three words non-committedly, as if she's wondering why on earth I'm calling. Then again, she probably is.

'Are you busy?'

I catch sight of myself in the mirror above the sink, and realise that I'm cringing. I know exactly what I'm doing: stalling for time, by throwing out question after question, meaning she's got to come up with something to say, rather than me coming out with the *actual* reason I'm phoning. But I wouldn't be phoning if I could help it – after all, who calls nowadays for anything, let alone to ask someone out? According to Marlon, it should definitely be via text, or by email, or WhatsApp, or even swiping left or right (or whatever way Tinder works). Not by *actually speaking* to the person you want to spend hours with, actually speaking to. And certainly not by using a phone for *phoning*.

'Well, I'm at work, so I suppose I ought to say yes, in case my boss is listening.' Angel lets out that short, tinkling laugh again, and I'm reminded it's one of the things I really like about her. One of the many things. Even though I hardly know her at all.

'Oh. Right. Should I let you get on?'

There's the sound of someone gagging from the other side of the toilet door, so I throw it open to see Marlon, standing as if he's had his ear pressed against it. He straightens up and mimes hanging himself, and to be honest, if he *actually* had some rope, I'd probably ask him if I could borrow it.

'I'm not *really* that busy, Noah.' Angel's dropped her voice to a whisper.

'Poppies all made, are they?'

'I don't actually make them. I'm a designer. We have a team of people who do that.'

'So, you're not a veteran, then?'

'Do I *look* like a veteran?'

'I'm . . . not sure,' I say, never having met a veteran in my life.

'Trust me, I'm not.' Angel laughs again. 'So, did you ring for a chat, or . . . ?'

Then it hits me. She's a modern, independent, attractive, smart (if a little kooky), clued-up woman. She knows *exactly* why I'm phoning her. Unless she left something behind in Starbucks and I'm calling to return it (and we both know that's not the case), there can be *no possible reason* for me to be on the phone now unless I'm intending on asking her out, and she took my call, which (if the receptionist *did* tell her it was me) probably means she's not completely averse to the idea of seeing me again. Plus she hasn't asked me how my blind date went – though given that I'm calling her now, I'm sure she can probably guess. And while you'd think all of that would fill me with confidence, all of a sudden the pressure starts to get to me. This isn't me: putting myself on the line (literally) for someone I know nothing about. Thinking we might have a future simply because our eyes met across a crowded Starbucks and we had a fun conversation.

She likes roller-coaster rides. Unpredictability. Surprises. I'm a long-game player – I have to plan to be spontaneous. Like my biblical name-sake, I like to know what's coming.

'Um . . .'

'Because like I said, I'm at work, so I can't really . . .'

It's then that I completely bottle it. But in my defence, asking someone out is hard. Especially when – and I've just at this precise moment realised this is the case – you're convinced they're going to turn you down.

'Right. Sure. Well, okay. So, I'll see you around?'

'You'll *see me around*?' she repeats (though I might be imagining the question mark at the end of the sentence), and all at once, I'm convinced she's about half a second from putting the phone down (and to be honest, I'm surprised she's kept talking this long).

I know I have to think on my feet, because I *won't* see her around – even after a week, that's become pretty clear. We don't go to the same places, or at least, not at the same times, so unless I embark on some pretty serious stalking (or Mary falls over and breaks her other wrist and Angel just happens to be at the hospital again), that's never going to happen.

Then, suddenly, from somewhere, I spot a chink of light at the end of the tunnel. *This* is spontaneous. Maybe I *can* be that guy. I'm taking a risk by calling her, after all, so perhaps I already am. And she's bound to respond to that. To *me*. Isn't she?

I step out of the toilet, take a breath, then take another. 'Yes, well, that's actually why I'm calling. Because I haven't. Seen you around. So I was wondering if you fancied . . .' *Me?* Can't say that. 'Whether you might like to go . . .' *Out with me?* Nope, because Angel's 'relationships and me don't really go together' the other day is still ringing in my ears. *Think.* 'For . . .' *Ever?* No. What's the most non-committal thing I can think of? 'A coffee.'

'A *coffee*?'

I grit my teeth at how disappointed Angel sounds. 'No. Of course. Silly of me. Why would you want to, when we've already had . . .' My voice trails off, and I pace anxiously around the gallery, desperate for inspiration, Marlon a step or two behind me. Trouble is, given that we've taken down the old show, and are still waiting for Hanksy to deliver his stuff, all I've got to look at is a big fat nothing – which just about sums up my life right now. So instead of coming straight back at her with something else (and surely *anything* else would be better than my pathetic 'coffee' suggestion), all I can do is miserably assume the worst. 'Listen, Noah,' says Angel, after a few moments that feel like about half an hour. 'I've got a meeting, so . . .'

Suddenly, I realise the light at the end of the tunnel isn't perhaps as bright as I thought it was. It isn't even an oncoming train. And even if it *was* a train, it's going in the opposite direction. And I've missed it.

'Don't go!'

'To the meeting?'

Anyone smoother would say 'no, bunk off, come out with me and we'll go and do something fun instead', but as I'm beginning to realise, I'm about as smooth as the coarsest-grade sandpaper. And because I don't say anything, because I *can't* say anything, Angel says, 'I'm sorry,' even though *I'm* the sorry one, and then she puts the phone down. And to be honest, I can't blame her.

As I slump dejectedly into my chair, Marlon perches on the end of my desk. 'A *coffee*.'

'No, thanks. I—'

'I wasn't offering. I was criticising. You chump,' he says, and I can't argue with his assessment.

'My mind just went blank. And I should have remembered.'

'Remembered what?'

'Angel. She's all about new experiences. Never doing the same thing twice. So what do I go and do? Ask her to do exactly the same thing we did last week.'

'Call her back. Quick.'

'I can't.'

'She'll be flattered.'

'There's a fine line between flattery and harassment.' I fold my arms. 'If she's not interested, she's not interested.'

'How can you possibly think she's not interested?'

'Hello? No second date?'

'She took your call. She stayed talking to you long past the point that even *I* would . . .'

'What do you mean by that?'

'In spite of all your quite frankly ridiculous attempts to prolong the conversation' – Marlon shakes his head in a mixture of disbelief and pity – 'she's probably thinking *you're* not interested, if the best you could come up with after all that was a *coffee*. She probably thought you lost interest after speaking to her again.' He picks up the phone, and holds it out towards me. 'Think of somewhere else to take her.'

'Out for dinner, or someth—'

I stop talking, because Marlon is miming the biggest yawn imaginable. 'Dinner?' he says, when he catches me glaring at him.

'That's right.'

'You can't come up with anything more original?'

'What's wrong with asking her out for dinner? Everyone has to eat.'

'Aha!'

'What does *that* mean?'

'Noah, you've got no idea how this dating lark works, do you? How many *dinners* we have to force down in the quest to find someone. It's the most awkward thing imaginable, sitting there, staring at each other, trying to think of things to say in between mouthfuls or until the next course arrives, hoping you haven't got something stuck in your teeth, wondering whether there's garlic in that sauce you're trying not to drip down your shirt . . .'

'Actually, I've got *every* idea how this dating lark works. It works . . . well, like that. A series of dates—'

'Dinners?'

'Okay, maybe dinner-dates, while you work out whether you get on well enough to, you know, take things to the next level.'

'You mean the "horizontal" one?'

'Maybe.'

'And that's worked for you so far, has it? Like you having a "type" has?' He sighs. 'Be original. Ask her somewhere she's never been before. To do something *you've* never done before. Make it a new experience for the both of you. You'll find out a lot more about each other than you will just sitting across from her in some restaurant.'

I glare at him again, though this time I'm annoyed because I can see he's right. 'How can I possibly pick something she's never done before?'

Marlon thinks for a moment. 'You could invite her to the opening.'

'What?'

'I bet she's never seen a Hanksy before.'

I stare miserably at the empty walls. 'She's not likely to see one now, even if she turns up.'

Marlon fires up his laptop, and navigates to the invite screen. 'Go on,' he says. 'It'll give you something to talk about. And what have you got to lose?'

'Nothing, I suppose,' I say. Though the actual answer is: *everything*.

It takes an hour or so to hang the frames (which, much to Marlon's amusement, because I have my phone on speaker, includes me fielding the usual five-minute weekly check-in call from my mum and dad, where my mum sets a new record in reminding me not to leave it 'too late' to give her the grandkids she's desperate for. Though I decline from asking her 'too late' for who).

Now all we have to do is cross our fingers that the actual artworks arrive sometime between now and Saturday, and seeing as there's no point in both of us hanging around here being bored, I give Marlon the rest of the day off, and so I'm sitting here preparing caption tags for the twenty or so paintings we hope are coming when a figure walks past the front window, stops dead in his tracks, then mounts the steps to the gallery.

The door's locked, though we have a buzzer system (it's not really for security purposes – our stuff is rarely the kind of thing you'd want to buy, let alone steal – but it gives the place an air of exclusivity, and makes sure we're awake whenever a potential customer walks in), and as whoever it is presses (and holds) the button, I'm about to go over and tell them we're closed, but then I recognise the flouncy shirt, velvet jacket and cravat. It's Patrick Welsh, pompous art critic for the *Informer*, his column, 'Wallcoverings', is so far up its own backside you'd need a torch and a very long arm to read it.

I'm a little surprised. Patrick usually only turns up to openings – presumably solely for the free drink or six he always manages to consume, seeing as he never even mentions us in any of his columns. Though given how he normally savages every show he goes to, I suppose I should be grateful.

I watch him through the glass – more than a little puzzled, as he seems to be finding something fascinating about the selection of empty frames hung up around the gallery – then buzz the door open. But before I can intercept him, he marches on in.

'I'm sorry, Patrick, we're clo—'

'Is this the new Hanksy show?'

I nod. 'Well, it will be. We don't open until—'

'You don't mind if I get a sneak preview?'

'Well, it's more of a "Blanksy" at the moment, so . . .'

Patrick pulls a small-leather-notebook-and-pen set out from his pocket, uncaps the pen with a flourish and starts to jot something down. '*Blanksy*, you say. That's good.' He nods at the nearest frame. 'Controversial, as ever.'

'Well, he likes to leave us hanging . . .'

'Quite.' Patrick takes a step closer to the wall, places the glasses strung around his neck precariously on the bridge of his nose, and examines the empty space where a painting should be. 'I mean, I suppose it's kind of a commentary on today's art scene, isn't it?'

'It's . . . What?'

'That art really is in the eye of the beholder. By not showing anything, he's inviting us to create our own art, in a way. To stare at the emptiness *through* the frame, focusing on the blankness, the very wall itself. Telling us that whatever one's gaze is aimed at, it's all really open to interpretation. Wouldn't you say?'

I have to swallow a laugh. Patrick actually thinks *this* is the show. And while I know I should point out that we're still waiting for the actual paintings, I've watched him drink way too many glasses of our cava not to want a little payback.

'That's an interesting point of view.' I fold my arms and join him in quiet contemplation of the empty frame in front of us. 'I think this is my favourite,' I say. 'There's just something about the . . .'

'Emptiness?'

'Exactly.'

'What's it called?'

'Hold on.' I head back to my desk, pick up the first caption I see, and when I fix it next to the frame, Patrick nods sagely.

'*Boy with a Vase*. Interesting title.'

'Isn't it?'

'I mean, it's almost as if he's daring us to picture that boy. What is he doing? What colour is the vase? Why is he holding it? Indeed, where is he taking it? Has he stolen it, perhaps to sell, so he can buy food?'

'Or drugs?' I suggest.

'Perhaps he made it. Or he's going to smash it out of mischief, or maybe he's simply carrying it back to his mother, who's told him to fill it with water so she can adorn it with a bright array of freshly cut flowers?'

'Or . . .' I pause, mainly because Patrick's looking at me, his pen poised as if he's intending to quote me. 'Well, the possibilities are endless.'

'Infinite.'

'In fact, it's as if the artist's making *us* do the work.' *Instead of pulling his finger out and delivering what he promised*, I think.

Patrick frowns contemplatively. 'That's good. I might just steal that for my review, if you don't mind?'

'You're actually going to *review* this?'

'Of course!' says Patrick. 'If you don't mind?'

And it's mean of me, I know, but if I've learned something from my brief dealings with Angel, sometimes you have to grab these opportunities with both hands – mainly because they may never come around again. So instead of setting him straight, and knowing full well that he'll write this up and then probably become a laughing stock, I simply shrug.

'Be my guest,' I say.

6.

Marlon's right. Inviting Angel to the gallery opening is a brilliant idea. Firstly – *hopefully* – it'll be 'new' for her; secondly, sending her an invite means I don't have to embarrass myself on the phone to her again; and thirdly, I'm finding it impossible to come up with anything else for the two of us to do. Even though something might be new for me, I don't get out much, whereas Angel looks like the kind of girl who's probably hardly ever home. And while the opening might be a disaster (seeing as we still don't have any actual artwork, not to mention the fact that there's going to be a bogus review in Saturday's *Informer*), at least I can be sure that Angel will never have been to anything like it.

Marlon offered to go round and 'speak' to Hanksy directly, but I'm a little worried about what that might entail. So, instead, I've just had an awkward phone call (my second of the day) with Hanksy to check what's going on: our conversation culminated in him telling me 'you can't put a timescale on art', which, while being the kind of naff thing he usually comes out with, isn't exactly the kind of argument I can use with the people I've invited to come and see – and hopefully buy – it. A fact I repeated to him in no uncertain terms, although my suspicion is it fell on deaf ears.

Calling Angel's a lot easier, partly because I know her extension number now (so I can avoid the Rottweiler of a receptionist), but mainly because it's gone seven, and I'm pretty sure she'll have left for the day. Even so, my hands are shaking a little as I dial, but a careful press of 'three', 'three', and 'six' puts me through, and after a moment, there's a click.

'You've reached the voicemail for Angel Fallon. I'm sorry I can't take your call right now, but please leave a message, and . . .'

. . . and for a moment, I'm almost tempted to do exactly that. It's good to hear her voice again – the tone of her message, when she doesn't have a clue who's calling, suggests such hope, such a positive attitude, as if she's expecting to be delighted by the conversation, with whoever it is. But in the end, I put the phone straight down, not because I'm too scared she'll realise it's me (although I am), but because for the first time in a long, long time, I've gotten exactly what I wanted.

I sit at my desk for a moment or two while I wait for my heart rate to drop below the danger zone, then I write 'No coffee, I promise!' on the invite, fill in 'Fallon' after 'Angel' above The Poppy Factory's address on the front of the envelope, stick the invite inside and a stamp in the top right-hand corner – then (once I'm absolutely sure it's firmly stuck) head out towards the postbox.

When I get back home, and after a fruitless hour or so trying to work out some witty repartee (or rather, make sure I'm not just a mumbling wreck) in case Angel actually turns up on Saturday night, Mary knocks on my door. She's looking a little distressed, and at once I think she's had another accident.

'Is everything okay?' I ask anxiously.

She stares at me, a little puzzled. 'You know, I've completely forgotten what I came up here for.'

'How's the wrist? Not hurting, I hope?'

Mary shakes her head. 'Nothing that a couple of aspirin and a large gin won't see off.'

I take her by the arm, and help her back downstairs. 'You shouldn't be coming up here. All these stairs aren't good for you. Just shout if you need me.'

'Rubbish.' She pats her thighs. 'What is it they say? "Use it, or lose it"?'

I smile grimly. If that's true, then there are certain parts of my body I should be worried about dropping off.

'What if you have another fall?'

'Noah, it's touching how worried you are about me, but you shouldn't wrap me in cotton wool. Or anyone, for that matter. Because it's only going to make you worry they're more fragile than they already are. And everyone falls, Noah. At some point. You just have to hope someone's home to pick you up.' She stops halfway along the hallway. 'Oh, yes – *that* was the reason I came up.'

'What was?'

'I've decided I should look at a few homes.'

'Homes?'

I follow her into the front room, and Mary hands me a bunch of leaflets from the dining table. 'Retirement homes. Or rather, care homes. I wondered if you'd have a read through a few of these for me?'

'Of course. But what's brought this on?'

Mary sweeps a hand around in the air in front of her to indicate the whole house. 'Everything. This place is a lot to look after. My fall. And I keep forgetting things. The other day, when I'd finished my shopping, I spent half an hour trying to remember where I'd parked my car.'

'You don't have a car.'

'I realise that now. So I thought, before I do something really silly, or hurt myself badly, I ought to at least see what my options are.'

'Well, one of your options is to let me look after you a bit more. I can do your shopping. Cook you dinner. Although by "cook", I mean get us both a takeaway.'

'Now now, Noah, that's very sweet of you. But you've got your own life to lead. And you certainly shouldn't have to worry about me.'

'But you love this house.'

'Sometimes, sadly, that's not the deciding factor.'

I flick quickly through a few of the leaflets she's handed me. At first glance, most of them look like houses even the Addams Family would run a mile from. 'Tell you what,' I say, fixing a smile on my face. 'Once you get that cast off, why don't you and I go and check them out in person?'

'Noah, I couldn't possibly ask you to—'

'It'd be my pleasure,' I say, realising it'd also be a chance for her to see just how bad they are, and that she'd be better off staying here. Especially with me to help her manage. 'Let's make a day of it.'

Mary thinks for a moment, then her face lights up. 'We could stop off for lunch. My treat.'

'It's a date!' I say. And I don't mind. After all, if Angel doesn't turn up to the opening, it's likely to be the only date I've got to look forward to.

7.

It's half past eight on Saturday morning – two weeks since I met Angel – and the ungodly hour finds me lacing up my running shoes again. Angel hasn't RSVP'd to my invitation, which would suggest she's not coming this evening, and if that turns out to be the case, another parkrun is my best bet of seeing her. Without being arrested for stalking, that is.

Besides, bumping into her 'accidentally' will give me a chance to play it, well, if not 'cool', exactly, given how sweaty and red-faced running five 'K' (as I'm learning I should refer to it) makes me, at least I can act all nonchalant, as if I don't mind if she turns up tonight or not. Though there's probably more chance of me pulling a muscle than pulling *that* off.

I've dismissed Bushy Park, Kingston, Gunnersbury and Wimbledon Common as being too far away, which means the Old Deer Park parkrun is my best bet for finding Angel this morning, though when I get there, it's more a case of *Oh Dear* Park, as she's nowhere to be seen amongst the assembled runners. What's even worse is that this parkrun turns out to be three laps, rather than one, of Old Deer Park. And while I'm assured it's the same 5K distance (and just that the park is smaller than Richmond Park), for someone who hated cross country at school, there's something psychologically off-putting about having to go round three times.

I have managed a couple of mid-week runs (though the word 'jog' would be more appropriate; as would the other word – well, *words* – 'fast' and 'walk' and 'long sit-down') in preparation, but I'm still relieved to see the competition seems a little less *athletic* than the Richmond Park one last Saturday. Sure, there are a couple of long-and-lean-limbed, raring-to-go, Olympic-hopeful types, built (as my dad likes to say) like a 'racing snake', but on the whole, the field seems a good ten-or-so years older, with enough Eleanor-types in attendance to justify a renaming to Old *Dear* Park. Right at the front, there's a huge middle-aged man – not just tall, but massively wide as well, somewhere between fit and fat, like an ex-Olympic rower who's in transition to a career in competitive eating. He's clutching a lead, and on the other end is a slightly manic-looking dog, which barks excitedly every time any of the other runners approach, despite his owner's repeated cries of 'Be quiet, Rocket!'

Yet again, there's no sign of Angel amongst the marshals or the runners – according to the website, you get a parkrun T-shirt for doing either – and I'd be in danger of starting to believe I might have imagined it if I hadn't mentioned it to reassure her I hadn't simply been staring at her chest. Still, perseverance is what's called for – I already know I'll try every local parkrun if I have to, even if it kills me. Which – looking out at the ominously muddy circuit – it might.

Nervously, I fiddle with my sunglasses, make sure my hood's up and – not for the first time – wonder what on earth I'm doing here. Three laps of a park on a grey Saturday morning in the kind of outfit you see people wearing on CCTV captures on *Crimewatch* is probably the least likely thing ever to impress a potential new girlfriend. Ever.

Reluctantly, I take my place on the start line and wait for the whistle, then set off at a steady pace, falling into step behind a grey-haired man in the kind of running shorts that used to be fashionable in the seventies, hence they're now only worn by the over-seventies, and which show a lot more leg than you'd ideally like to see on an older person. For the first two-thirds of the first lap, things seem to be going okay, and my running feels almost easy, though it's only when I reach the start of the final third I realise why: the long uphill stretch to the turn, which means the bit I've just run was, in fact, downhill.

In vain, I try to hang on (metaphorically) to the old man in front of me, but as he starts to disappear off into the distance (which is a blessing, given those shorts), it's all I can do not to come to an abrupt stop. My breath's coming in huge gasps, my legs feel heavy – although by some miracle, I make it to the top of the hill – and I'd pull out now if I could, if not for the bunch of cheering, clapping supporters egging me on at the turn.

Determinedly, I head off on lap two, thankful at least for the down-hill part, trying not to think about how I've got to do it all again – twice. At least there's been no sign of Angel at any of the turns – even though I'm in my disguise again, there's no way I'd want her to see me like this, then for her to turn up this evening and perhaps put two and two together.

By the time I've made it halfway round, the front runners have already lapped me, and it occurs to me that I could pretend I'm one of them. Finish after this lap, and try to kid the organisers that I've done three laps rather than two. But if I'm ever going to find Angel and ensure that our parkrun meeting isn't a total disaster, that starts by being able to at least complete a course that every (other) man, woman and dog seems to have no trouble with.

Getting to where it *actually* starts, though, is even harder than last time – the hill seems to have increased in steepness to such a degree that, even if I do make it round a third lap, I'm going to need some mountaineering gear to get to the finish line. What isn't helping is the incessant barking that I can hear from behind me, and what's worse is, it's getting closer.

Exhausted, I glance back over my shoulder to see Rocket and his owner haring up the hill towards me. Maybe *that's* the secret. Perhaps I can borrow a dog for next week, because from what I can see, having one actually seems to be an advantage: Rocket's straining so hard at the lead he seems to be pulling his owner round. It's no wonder you don't see dogs at the Olympics. They're probably on the banned list, along with blood doping and steroids.

Being lapped by the leaders I can just about take, but being lapped by a man and his *dog* . . .

Although my thighs are hurting, my heart feels like it's about to burst through my chest and the blisters that are surely developing on my feet courtesy of my weighed-down-with-a-ton-of-mud trainers will probably have me hobbling for the next week or so, there's nothing for it but to grit my teeth and concentrate on putting one foot in front of the other, while trying to ignore the four legs gaining at my heels, not to mention the sarcastic Road Runner-esque '*meep meep*' Rocket's owner shouts as he approaches.

Trouble is, my idea of running fast uphill with another lap to go, and Rocket and his owner's sprint for the finish, don't sit that well together, and – obviously not prepared for a runner in front of them to almost be going backwards – Rocket has chased up to the left of me, with, unfortunately, his owner on my right. Which means Rocket's lead catches my trailing leg and sends my left foot the wrong side of my right one, and the three of us tumble down to the ground in a heap.

As I lie there, covered in mud, my legs tangled in the lead and with the wind knocked out of me, Rocket's tail going like this is the best game *ever*, his owner picks himself up and glares down at me.

'What do you think you're playing at?'

I look up at him as I struggle to catch my breath, presuming he doesn't want a complete rundown of my plan to get Angel to fall in love with me.

'What am I playing at?' I pant. 'You need to watch where you're going. Or, at least, your dog does.'

Rocket, to his credit, looks a little embarrassed, but while the man's gone red too, it's with anger.

'I was on for a PB!'

'A what?'

'A personal best. Which you've gone and messed up.'

'*I've* messed up?'

'By bloody well walking the course.'

'What?'

'Hello?' The man taps the logo on his T-shirt. 'Park*run* . . .'

'If you can't control your dog . . .' I feel the anger bubble up inside me, though the last thing I want to do is get into a fight. And particularly because, given the size of the man, the run isn't the only thing I might lose. 'Are dogs even allowed?'

'It's a *park*.'

'To run!'

'At least he can.'

'Maybe you should take him for his walk some other time.'

'Maybe you shouldn't run so slowly that you get lapped. Or shouldn't run at all . . .'

I size him up again, and decide to rein in my anger a bit. The guy is huge, and would be towering over me even if I wasn't lying on the grass at his feet. Besides, I think I've twisted my knee a little, which means running away probably isn't an option either.

As Rocket begins to lick my face, the man pulls him roughly away, and with a final glare, he and Rocket sprint off into the distance. I reluctantly haul myself to my feet, and gingerly set off towards the finish.

And it's then I decide something: Angel or no Angel, I'll be coming back here next week. I might not be able to win Angel over. But there's someone else I'll take great satisfaction in beating.

There are a hundred reasons why Angel might not turn up tonight. She might be busy. She might not like art. She might be washing her hair (though is that ever a real excuse?). She might not have got the invite. She might have got the invite and decided that, on balance, she's just not interested in me (and if that's the reason she doesn't come, and I've been wasting my time, I suppose there's nothing much more I can do). These are the thoughts that circulate around my head on a continuous loop from pretty much the exact moment I get to work. That is, until I remember I've got bigger problems.

Patrick's review comes out in the morning's *Informer*. On balance, I suppose it's a good one – words like 'controversial' and phrases like 'pushing the boundaries' are guaranteed to get bums on seats at an opening almost as much as offering free alcohol is.

Not that I see it – though by the time I've listened to the voicemails from Marlon and Hanksy, I feel I know it off by heart, which I should already – but Patrick's quoted me word for word. And in an unusually magnanimous gesture (that I could have done without), he's attributed the quotes to me.

I'm trying to convince myself that there's an upside to this. That I won't live to regret it (though Hanksy's promised that me living might not be on the cards if he's made to look ridiculous as a result). That, assuming the review has kick-started Hanksy to deliver his paintings in time for tonight and loads of people actually turn up, given the publicity, we're bound to sell at least some of them. But when I spot a Hanksy-shaped figure crossing the road outside the gallery and storming angrily towards the door, I realise the chances of selling anything are pretty remote.

'You're empty-handed.'

I've meant that in relation to his artwork, though I'm glad to see Hanksy hasn't brought any weapons either.

'What?'

'I don't see any paintings.'

'Nor did Patrick Welsh.' Hanksy glares at me as he slams the door shut behind him with such force that it bounces open again. 'What did you think you were playing at?'

'What was *I* playing at? What are *you* playing at? We're supposed to be opening this evening, we've got dozens of people coming, and I've got nothing to show them. Literally.' I look accusingly at Hanksy, who's wandering around the gallery peering at his 'work'. 'Besides, it wasn't my fault he came in and jumped to the wrong conclusion.'

'And you didn't think to perhaps point out the error of his ways? I'm going to be a laughing stock. No one will ever take me seriously again. Or you, for that matter.'

'Or Patrick Welsh,' I suggest. 'Which is surely a good—'

'Excuse me . . .'

Neither of us has noticed the man who's evidently just walked into the gallery, and who's just cleared his throat nervously behind us.

'Can I help you?'

'I was wondering . . . *Boy with a Vase* . . .'

'What about it?' spits Hanksy.

'Is it for sale?'

'Pardon?'

'Is it for sale?' says the man, turning his attention back to the empty frame on the wall behind us. 'Only there doesn't seem to be a price list, and there's no red dot . . .'

'Well, funny story . . .' I say, and I'm about to launch into what's actually happened, but Hanksy shushes me.

'It is,' he says, holding out a hand for the man to shake. 'I'm the artist.' He turns and contemplates the frame, his arms folded. 'We've had a lot of interest.'

'I'll bet,' says the man. 'I read the review this morning. He was spot on.'

I stare at him, almost unable to believe I might be *sticking* a spot on if he actually buys it.

'So . . .' He reaches for his wallet. 'How much is . . . ?'

'It's . . .' Hanksy and I exchange glances. The frame's worth at best a fiver, but I've got to make some profit. 'Six . . .'

'. . . tee . . .' says Hanksy.

'. . . n.'

'Hundred,' says Hanksy, as if he's just played the winning card in a game of Top Trumps.

'Sixteen hundred?' The man frowns, and for a moment, I think Hanksy's blown it.

'That's the special "preview" price,' says Hanksy. 'The opening's this evening. And after that . . .'

'Well . . .'

'I'll even sign it for you.'

There's a pause, then: 'Done,' says the man, handing me his credit card.

You have been, I think.

As Hanksy gives him a tour round the rest of the 'exhibition', I process the payment, then ceremonially affix the small red sticky dot to the caption card. And while I don't believe in signs, or omens, or fate – for a moment, selling *Boy with a Vase* makes me think that miracles can actually happen.

In the end, I realise I needn't have spent the rest of the day a bundle of nerves, because (unlike everyone else we've invited, who virtually batter the door down in their rush to see Hanksy's brilliantly reviewed 'work') Angel arrives ten minutes after the show opens, marching confidently through the door as if she owns the place. She's dressed in a pair of what Marlon later points out are 'boyfriend' jeans (though my heart drops when I mis-hear him and think he's said they're 'her boyfriend's jeans') – with an AC/DC T-shirt she's cut the sleeves off, yet another pair of Converse and her hair down this time, and she looks just as beautiful – no, *more* beautiful – than I remember.

Which is why, the moment she walks in, my first instinct is to hide (well, not hide, exactly, but make myself not visible), which in a space the size of the gallery is a little difficult. And while the whole point of this rigmarole I've gone through to get her here (not to mention the parkruns) is so I can ask her out, spend some time together, work out over the course of thirteen dates whether we're compatible or if the bolt of lightning that struck me when I first saw her was just a flash in the pan, I can't hide all night. Though putting myself the other side of Marlon in a dark-side-of-the-moon way until I can think of a clever opening line will do for now.

'Is that her?'

'Who?'

Marlon rolls his eyes, then does a quick sidestep to reveal a glimpse of Angel, a strange smile on her face, peering in amusement at *Boy with a Vase*.

'Angel.'

'Keep your voice down!'

'What? Why?'

'She'll see me!'

Marlon sighs exasperatedly. 'Sorry, Noah. I didn't realise the whole point of you inviting her this evening was so you could play hide-and-seek. Go and talk to her!'

'What about?' I say, thinking that actually, now she's here, hide-and-seek is a much better option.

'The show might be an idea.'

'Okay, okay.'

Marlon hands me a couple of glasses of cava, which I drink, one after the other, until I realise he's probably meant for me to take one of them over for Angel.

'Sorry,' I say. 'Just a bit nervous.'

Marlon gives me the 'no shit' look, then hands me another two. 'Have you worked out what you're going to say?'

'I hadn't really thought that far ahead.'

'Well, I'm going to go and mingle,' says Marlon. 'And I suggest you do too.'

'Fine. Right. Yes.'

'Good luck.'

'You too,' I say, automatically, then – feeling rather like a lone wildebeest out in the Serengeti now that my Marlon-shaped cover has disappeared – I take a half step in the direction Angel's moving – rather swiftly round the show, I have to say – quickly chug one of the glasses down, swap the empty glass for another, then complete what feels like the longest journey in the world. Of course, while that's partly because my knee's killing me after my tangle with Rocket's lead earlier, it's still not long enough for me to come up with anything better than a faltering 'Hi'.

Angel swivels around, then smiles broadly, and says simply, 'Hey, you,' and my heart starts hammering so fast I'm sure she can probably see my jacket vibrate.

'You got the invite, then?'

'I did.' Angel looks left and right, then lowers her voice. 'Though don't tell the owner, but I'm one of those people who only turns up for the free drink!'

'I don't think he'd mind. At all,' I say, lowering my voice to match.

I'm not sure whether I should go in for a kiss on the cheek, but when Angel extends a hand towards me I guess that answers *that* question. Awkwardly, I transfer one of the two glasses of cava into the other hand, although the shape of them means that holding two in the same hand is actually rather difficult and I end up spilling half of one of them on the gallery floor.

'Rather formal, aren't you?' she says as I shake her hand, then she pulls me close and kisses me briefly on the cheek, and it's all I can do not to reach up and touch the spot where her lips have been. 'I thought you were going to hand one of those to me,' she says, nodding towards the glasses.

'What? Oh. Right. I am. I mean, I was, obviously.'

Angel regards me for a moment or two, and I wonder if she knows the kiss has thrown me. 'Well, go on then.'

'Sorry? Oh. Sure.'

It's intoxicating being this close to her. Either that, or the three glasses of cava I've downed in as many minutes are stronger than I thought. In any case, I'm conscious I've already run out of conversation. What can I say that's guaranteed to put the conversational ball firmly in her court? *I've got it!*

'Cheers!'

'Cheers,' replies Angel, clinking her glass against mine and hitting a double-fisted conversational backhand right back at me.

'So, um . . .' My voice trails off. While this has all the elements of a second date – a drink and a walk round an art exhibition – unless I up my game, it's going to be a very quick one. If that's the case, a third, let alone another eleven, is way beyond even my wildest dreams, and while I'm beginning to suspect I won't need thirteen dates to work out how I feel about Angel, I'm not sure even thirteen – especially if they're like this – will be enough for her to fall for me.

Angel's turning away, and though it's only to examine the painting (well, frame) in front of us, I'm already worried I'm losing her. 'What do you think?'

'Of . . . ?'

I nod at the frame in front of her, where the caption reads 'Woman, nude', and Angel leans in towards the frame, as if examining the (imaginary) brushstrokes. 'Not really my thing.'

'Nude women?' I've meant it . . . well, not even as a joke, really, but more like a conversation-maintainer, but perhaps understandably, Angel shoots me a look.

'I know it's your gallery, and I'm sure there's a certain type of person who loves this pretentious crap. But if you like this kind of thing, you're only a short distance away from thinking a pickled shark in a tank is art.' She sweeps a hand around the gallery. 'I mean, look at these people. They're pretending to be impressed by this . . .' She peers at the caption tag, but before she can say anything, Hanksy has pushed in between the two of us and is standing uncomfortably close to Angel. He's looking a little drunk, and also straight at her chest, so I put my arm around his shoulders in a 'matey' kind of way and steer him back a step.

'Angel, this is Hank. Hank, this is—'

'Call me Hanksy.'

'Hanksy.' Angel raises both eyebrows. 'You mean, like Banksy?'

'No way!' slurs Hanksy. 'I'm nothin' like Banksy.'

'No,' I say, followed by a whispered 'Because Banksy doesn't want anyone to know who he is' in Angel's ear.

'Angel, eh?' Hanksy leans in to kiss her, and she makes that face Sigourney Weaver does when the alien's getting too close, then he swivels round and stares at *Woman, nude* as if seeing it for the first time. Which he probably is. 'And what do you think of the show?'

'It's . . .' As Angel considers her response, I start to cringe. I've only known her for five minutes, and already I'm sure she's not one to mince her words. 'Interesting.'

Hanksy beams at her. 'Isn't it?' he says.

She nods at the next-door piece, which is simply called *Untitled*. 'And what does this represent, do you think?'

'About a thousand pounds, if Noah gets his arse in gear and sells it,' says Hanksy, before breaking into a peal of overenthusiastic laughter.

Angel frowns. 'Then again, you can't really call it a show, can you, because it's more of a no-show? Quite frankly, I'm sure there's better stuff produced by the average five-year-old and stuck up on fridge doors around the country. I tell you, the people who produce this kind of stuff should be ashamed of themselves. Trying to convince people with more money than sense that this is "art" and they should pay for it . . .' She takes a mouthful of cava. 'I'm sorry, Hank. I'm going on a bit. What's your connection to all this?'

'I, well . . .' Hanksy's looking a little conflicted. On the one hand, it's clear he fancies Angel, and having the ego that he does, can't possibly comprehend that the feeling might not be mutual. On the other, announcing that he's the 'star' of the 'show' after she's slated it might not be the smartest thing.

Angel smiles sweetly. 'Are you a reviewer? Well, I hope you're going to give this crap the slating it deserves.'

'No, I . . . I'm the artist.'

Angel makes a rather melodramatic 'oh god!' face, putting her hand over her open mouth for good measure. 'Oh. Well, just ignore me. I obviously don't know anything about art. I mean, I know what I like, obviously . . .'

Me too, I think, then realise I've said it out loud, *and* while I'm staring at her. I fix a smile on my face and lower my voice. 'Don't worry. This isn't actually typical of Hanksy's work. It's just that . . . Well, this actually *is* a funny story.'

I check there are no potential customers in earshot, and I'm just about to launch into it, when Marlon, saint that he is, walks over to rescue us. 'Hanksy,' he says. 'There's someone over there who wants to meet you.'

'I'm still meeting Angel,' protests Hanksy.

'Someone who's interested in buying a couple of pieces,' adds Marlon, and Hanksy's eyes light up.

'I'll see you later, Angel,' he says, blowing her a kiss before following Marlon to the other end of the gallery.

As Angel makes the 'not if I see you first' face, then glances at her watch, I start to panic. She's funny, and bright, and interesting, and honest (though I might possibly have some apologising to do to Hanksy tomorrow), and every minute I spend with her, I fall more and more in love with her, *and* become more and more unable to ask her out. And while normally I could expect to give her a guided tour of the exhibition, quite frankly that's a little difficult when there's nothing except for a series of empty frames to talk about. So I lead her over to the desk to show her our past catalogues, and talk her through the young artists we've promoted this year – ones with actual paintings – and Angel tells me about this guy called Nick at her work who could really do with a helping hand, and shows me some photos of his portfolio on her phone, and it's good, and when I promise her I'll find him some space on the wall, she tells me she could kiss me. Although she doesn't.

'Well,' she says eventually. 'People to see, places to go, things to do. So . . .'

'Don't go. Yet, I mean.'

Angel smiles. 'I really ought to,' she says, though I'm a little stumped as to what that means.

'Okay. But before you do . . .' I go to finish the last of my cava, then realise I already have, and try to disguise my attempted-drink-from-an-empty-glass by pretending to check a crack on the rim. 'Can I ask you something?'

'Sure. As long as it's not "will you go out with me?"'

'Ah.' There's a resounding thud – though perhaps I imagine it – as my heart hits the gallery's wooden floor. 'Right. Well, in that case . . . Why did you come tonight?'

Angel shrugs. 'I've never been to a gallery opening before.'

'You're all about new experiences, then?'

Angel nods. 'They're what make the world go round. That and the sun's gravitational force, obviously.'

I raise both eyebrows. 'Only new experiences?'

'It's kind of a philosophy of mine, along with "life's too short to wait in line". You've got to give everything a hundred and ten percent – and yes, I know that's not actually mathematically possible. Look at dogs.'

'How does looking at dogs fit in with . . . ?'

'No – I mean, as in their attitude. For example, they're supposed to have this amazing sense of smell, yet they still prefer to stick their noses right up another dog's backside. And that's me.'

'Not literally, I hope?'

'I mean in terms of living life full-on. Throwing yourself into things. Don't say "no" if "yes" might be interesting.'

'Well then, say yes to going out with me, because that might be interesting.'

'Noah, it's not that.'

'We could do fun things. Like, I don't know . . . Name something you've never done before?'

Angel narrows her eyes, as if she's trying to make out something on the opposite wall. 'Rock climbing.'

'Well, that . . . sounds like fun.'

'Noah, you seem like a lovely guy, but you're obviously . . . I mean, people who go on blind dates . . . It's because they're *desperate* to meet "the one". That's just not me. We're – *I'm* – so obviously different.'

'Whatever happened to opposites attract?'

'Attraction's not the problem.' Angel smiles regretfully, and opens her mouth as if about to explain further, before something flickers in her eyes. 'It's what we want that's so different.'

'Maybe it isn't,' I say, looking imploringly into her eyes. 'Especially if what we want is each other.'

It's a good line, even though I've absolutely no idea where it came from, and for a split second I think it's made all the difference, but after a pregnant pause that lasts so long it's in danger of having to be induced, Angel looks away. 'How about we just say that I'll think about it?' she says, about as non-committedly as anyone can, then she hands me her glass, leans in and briefly kisses me on the cheek again. 'Thanks, Noah,' she says, in a way that sounds like the kindest dumping ever.

'At least let me walk you to the door?'

'Do you think you can manage?'

'How do you mean?'

'You're limping.'

'Oh *that*? That's nothing. I just . . .' Angel's making her way towards the exit, and I realise full disclosure is the only thing that might gain me a bit of time. Though hopefully not of the 'jail' variety. 'Well, I was at parkrun, and . . .'

Angel pauses, mid-step. 'I'm confused. When we first met, you said you didn't run.'

'I don't. Not really. But I was desperate to find you again, and I remembered you were wearing that parkrun T-shirt, so last week I went to the Richmond one to try to find you. Then this morning it was Old Deer Park. Process of elimination, you see . . .' I stop talking. Angel's expression has changed, and although it's almost imperceptible, there's a definite . . . well, *softening* is the word I'd use.

'Noah, that's really . . . I mean, I'm flattered that you . . . Nobody's ever . . . Well, most men think swiping right is all the effort they have to put in. Whereas you . . .'

'Ran five K. Twice!' I remind her. She's walking towards the door again, though not quite as quickly as before, so I exaggerate my limp a little, grimacing with every step. 'Come on,' I say. 'Come rock climbing. With me.'

I know it's probably not the most romantic of suggestions, and possibly not the best activity for a date – and also that I'm seriously going for the sympathy vote – but for some reason, it seems to work, because Angel looks at me for a moment, then smiles again.

'Okay,' she says, before heading out of the door.

And just like that, we're on for date number three.

8.

Rock climbing?'

Marlon starts to laugh as he dumps an armful of cava bottles into the recycling bin, and I feel a little offended. 'Why not?'

'I know you said you'd fallen for her, but I hope you're not planning to take that literally?'

'Ha ha. Very funny.'

'And when is this momentous event taking place?'

'I'm going to shoot for Tuesday night.'

Marlon scratches his head. 'Interesting night for a date.'

'I'm trying to strike a balance between "desperate to see her again" and "playing it cool".'

'I see "desperate" won.' Marlon laughs again. 'And where is this momentous event taking place?'

'Here in Richmond. Well, Sheen, to be precise,' I say, pointing to the advert in the *Informer*. 'Sheen Indoor Climbing Centre.'

'*Sick*,' says Marlon, though it takes me a moment to realise he's referring to the centre's acronym, rather than using some slang word of approval. 'Do you like rock climbing?'

I shrug. 'I have no idea. "New experiences", she said. And there's no reason why that shouldn't apply to both of us.'

'So you've never been?'

'Well, no. I don't really like mountains. Or any high places. On account of my . . .'

'Your what?'

'Well, *vertigo*.'

Marlon stops, mid-recycle, and frowns at me. 'And you don't think that might be a problem?'

'Actually, no. Sheen *Indoor* Climbing Centre. You can't get vertigo indoors, surely? And besides, how high can it be?'

'High enough' is the answer to that question. Even standing on the ground, looking up in barely disguised horror at the artificial cliff face in front of me, my head is starting to swim. I already know I've bitten off more than I can chew, despite the hundreds of multicoloured 'holds' (I've been reading up so as to appear a bit more knowledgeable) that should mean even a beginner like me is able to scramble, Spiderman-like, to the top.

We're wearing safety harnesses too, which have done nothing to reassure me that I won't fall off, and which the twenty-something Australian (or New Zealandian, or somewhere down there) rock-god, steel-limbed instructor (Dirk, or Bear, or possibly even Rock) has spent ages ensuring fits perfectly on Angel – though his cursory hard tug on the part that goes between *my* legs makes me realise that if I *do* fall, the apparent halting of my headlong plummet by a canvas strap looped around my testicles means any extra activities that might have been on the cards this evening will definitely be off the table.

I swallow hard, and turn my attention back to the instructor, who's running through a number of safety points, though it's difficult to con-centrate on what he's saying given the vision of Angel in front of me, clad in a loose-fitting (in a way that you can see her bra through the armholes) 'Oasis' – the group, not the shop – T-shirt and a black pair of what I understand from the odd spam email I occasionally 'accidentally' click on are known as 'yoga pants'.

I've paid for a private session – just me, Angel and the instructor – to make it a bit more personal, though I'm beginning to regret this, given exactly how personal he's getting with her. Still, we're on a *date*. Our first proper one (even though I'm counting it as number three). And while Angel insisted we meet here rather than letting me pick her up, she assured me that she's 'never late'. Which, given that I got here half an hour early just in case, is a good thing.

I zone back in, just in time to hear the instructor say '. . . let go,' a phrase I'm imagining had the word 'don't' in front of it, but though I'm not sure, I don't dare ask him to repeat himself. Hopefully whatever he said won't be too important later on.

Dirk/Bear/Rock gives Angel's harness one final tweak, then he takes a step backwards. 'Right. Any questions?'

I glance across at the neighbouring wall, where a couple of toddlers seem to have made it up to the top in less time than it takes me to climb my stairs at home, then peer up at our 'beginners' section. Perhaps it's my imagination, but it seems to have got higher in the five minutes we've been standing here.

'Is it . . .' I nod towards Angel, inferring I'm asking out of concern for her welfare – but really, it's me I'm worried about. '. . . dangerous?'

'No more so than crossing the road.'

I think back to my near miss with a cycle courier when I stepped off the pavement earlier, and give him a semi-enthusiastic thumbs-up.

'Besides,' he says, his eyes fixed on Angel. 'I'll be belaying you the whole time.'

'I beg your pardon?'

'Belaying you. With the rope. So you can't fall off.' He indicates the pulley system hanging from the rock face behind him. 'Neither of you have done any climbing before, have you?'

Angel shakes her head, so I put my hand up gingerly. 'I had to go up into the loft yesterday. Does that count?'

'Not unless you went the long way, up the outside of the house. Oh, and you'll be needing these,' he says, handing us each a helmet.

'What's this for?'

'In case you fall.'

'I thought you said we wouldn't?'

'Like I said . . .' Rock/Dirk/Bear is looking at me as if he thinks I'm trouble. 'It's just in case.'

'And this is going to help, is it?' I say, rapping my knuckles on the thin plastic.

Rock/Dirk/Bear folds his arms – arms that are more like knotted ropes. 'It's for health and safety,' he says, which I take to mean *no, but you have to wear it anyway*.

'Right. Let's rock!'

As I smile politely at his joke, Angel takes her helmet and puts it on, tucking her hair behind her ears as she does so, and I have to stop myself from staring – even wearing a battered old plastic lid like this she still looks sexy. Hoping I'll look like some hunky workman rather than Bob the Builder in mine, I slip it on and fasten the strap underneath my jaw, ensuring it's tight enough to keep my teeth from chattering in fear. The only trouble is, my helmet's a little too big, which means when I look down, it slips forwards to cover my eyes. Which might not be a bad thing, given my fear of heights.

'So, is there a technique?'

'There is.' Doing a good impression of a mountain goat, Rock/Dirk/Bear leaps up onto the wall, grabbing a couple of handholds between vice-like fingers and arranging his legs in the kind of position a nine-year-old Russian gymnast might find difficult. 'Keep your body as close to the wall as possible,' he says, thrusting his hips forwards in a pervy way, 'and then . . . climb.'

He ascends the rock face with the grace of a ballet dancer, his hands and feet a blur, and touches the top like he's playing Tag with it, before descending at an equal pace. 'Right,' he says, leaping off the wall, pirouetting in the air and landing like an agile panther right in front of us. 'Who wants to go first?'

Now I have a dilemma: 'ladies first' would suggest that Angel should lead off, but the danger of that is she might think I'm chicken; but *me* going first, leading the way in a '*me man, me climb wall*' kind of way, runs the risk of Angel seeing just how pathetic I am. I might, of course, take to this like – well, a duck to water isn't perhaps the best of analogies – and get to the top with no trouble at all, then have the satisfaction of beaming down at her encouragingly; though given that looking down isn't an option (both from the point of view of my vertigo and my loose helmet), maybe I should just go first and concentrate on not making a fool of myself. But I don't get the chance, as Angel's already approaching the wall and dipping her fingers into the little bag of chalk we've been told will help us grip.

Dirk (I finally spot his name badge) clips the end of a piece of rope onto her harness, takes up the slack and nods towards the lowest handholds. 'Remember,' he says, 'the aim is always to keep three points of contact.'

'Email, mobile number and—' I can't even complete my joke before Dirk shoots me a look.

'On the *wall*,' he says, as if he has no sense of humour whatsoever. I hate him even more, and make a mental note not to take Angel on any more dates where there's a potential for fit instructors.

But as Angel starts to climb, I have to say, I'm impressed. Maybe it's because she's fearless, maybe it's because I'm enjoying the view as her yoga-panted backside reaches my eye level, but in actual fact, it's probably because I can't think of many other women who'd come somewhere like this on a date and throw themselves into it so wholeheartedly.

Though this impression lasts around another minute, as Angel gets about ten feet off the ground, then comes to an abrupt halt.

'Noah . . .'

'What's the matter?'

'I'm stuck.'

Dirk tugs gently on the rope. 'Just reach for the next hold, and move up to that.'

Angel glares down at him. 'I'm guessing your definition of the word "stuck" is different to mine?'

'Try coming back down to your last—'

'Hello!' says Angel. '*Stuck* – remember?'

I peer anxiously up at her, then nudge Dirk. 'Can't you go and get her?'

Dirk nods at the rope he's holding. 'I'm too busy making sure she doesn't fall off.'

'Shall I take over? Then you can climb up and . . .'

'Have you ever belayed anyone before?'

'To be honest, I'm not sure.'

'It's actually very technical.'

I frown. From what I can see, belaying seems to mainly involve holding on to a rope, which doesn't seem that technical to me. But maybe he's right – or maybe, like Dirk, you need forearms bigger than my thighs to be able to do it, and he's just trying to spare me the embarrassment (and spare Angel from falling to the ground). Which means there's nothing else for it.

I smile confidently up at Angel, dip my hands in the chalk bag (coating them in about half of its contents for good measure – after all, I might be gripping for two) and approach the wall. 'Hold on!'

'As opposed to?' says Angel, anxiously.

Gradually I start to ascend, and at the beginning, it's actually not too difficult – almost like climbing my loft ladder, in fact. The special rubber climbing shoes they've loaned us almost feel like they've got glue on the soles, and the chalk on my fingers helps me grip, too – although the rivers of sweat running from my palms are in danger of washing it off. I've made three or four moves, and surprisingly, it doesn't feel that high (though when I look round, and realise I've only reached Dirk's head height, I can see why), and while I'm not tied in to the safety rope, the floor's padded, and I'm not planning to fall off. Besides, with Angel stranded above me, I've got no choice but to go for it.

Steadily, I make my way up the wall, careful to remember the 'three points of contact' rule, and before long, I'm right beneath Angel. And while the view is something I'd enjoy under other circumstances, I've realised my first mistake. There's nothing for it but to make like a crab and traverse sideways, then continue upwards until we're level. Finally, carefully, I edge across, reach an arm around her back, and making sure I've got *four* points of contact solidly anchored, smile encouragingly at her.

'Hi.'

Angel looks nervously round at me. Her knuckles are white, and at once, I feel guilty about suggesting this for our first date. 'Not the best choice of word, Noah.'

'Don't worry. I've got you.'

'Who's got *you?*'

'Now, you're on a rope, so you can't fall. All you need to do is move a bit to your right, and you'll be able to start climbing again.'

'Start *climbing?*'

'It's better than the alternative,' I say, flicking my eyes downwards for a nanosecond, trying to ignore the fact that the padded floor looks a long way away. And not *that* padded.

'I can't seem to . . .' Angel is stretching her leg out, but her foot is inches away from the hold she's reaching for.

'Can you shift your body across a bit?'

'I'll try.'

Angel manages to move away from me a little, but she's still agonisingly short of the hold, so I carefully let go with my right hand, reach out and give her a push, though I've forgotten my hands are all chalky, and all I succeed in doing is leaving a perfect white imprint of my hand on her black-clad backside.

'Good,' I say, as she finally hooks her toes onto the hold. 'Now all you need to do is move your right hand up, grab the hold directly above you, and you should be able to make it to the top.'

'Wouldn't it be easier to go down?'

'You're halfway up already. And it'd be a shame to come so far and not at least try to summit.'

'Summit?' Angel gives me a look that suggests I'm maybe overstating things, then she hauls her body up, finds a convenient set of holds and begins to climb up the wall again. After a few more moves, she's at the top, grinning triumphantly down at me.

'I did it!'

'You did!'

'Thanks to you.'

'I'm not sure what I did,' I say, though I'm quite happy to take the credit.

'Okay, Angel,' calls Dirk from the floor. 'Well done. Now just lean back, let go, and I'll take your weight on the rope and belay you down.'

Angel frowns at him. 'You can do that?'

'Yup,' says Dirk.

'Well, why didn't you suggest that when I was stuck?'

''Cause you'd have never gone up again and climbed to the top, like you did. And Noah here wouldn't have had the chance to play the hero, either.'

I grin up at her, enjoying the 'hero' tag, and as Dirk starts to lower Angel down, I begin my descent. Trouble is, reaching for my first hold, I quickly realise that going up is a lot easier than coming down – unless you're descending on a rope – and unbelievably, now *I'm* stuck.

'Um, Dirk . . . ?'

But Dirk is too busy lowering Angel down pretty much right on top of him, and as I do a double take at this, my helmet slips down over my eyes, which means when I gingerly release my left hand to adjust it, I've forgotten it's the hand that's actually anchoring me in position, so letting go has the effect of spinning me round on the wall.

Frantically, I flail around and manage to grab on to a nearby hold, though I'm now facing outwards in a crucifix position, like Tom Cruise in the opening sequence from *Mission: Impossible II*. Which – even as a first-timer – I can tell isn't going to be the easiest position to climb down from.

'Dirk!'

'What?' says Dirk, a little exasperatedly, more interested in fussing with Angel's harness than paying attention to me.

'Help?'

'What are you playing at?'

'I'm not "playing" at anything.'

'Hold on,' he shouts. 'I'm coming up. Don't panic!'

There's a psychological phenomenon I've read about, and it's this: if someone says to you, 'Don't picture an elephant riding a bicycle,' then the first thing you do is picture exactly that. So the moment he tells me not to panic, I start to hyperventilate, and even in the tiny window of vision my loose helmet gives me, I can see I'm still a good ten feet or so above the ground, and that's more than enough to set my head spinning. What's worse is, thanks to Dirk's bellowed 'Don't panic!', almost everyone else in the whole climbing centre has stopped what they're doing to look at me. Including Angel.

There's only one way to salvage the situation, I realise. Ten feet is nothing, especially given the padded floor at the bottom of the wall, so I should be able to jump it quite safely. Not that I have the choice – as hard as it was to hang on the other way round, trying to hang on with my back to the wall (literally) is almost impossible.

'Don't worry,' I say, my voice sounding a lot more confident than I actually feel. 'I can jump down from here.'

'You're sure?' says Dirk.

'Yes,' I say, in a tone that could equally be taken as *no*.

I take a deep breath, and – grateful that my helmet prevents me from seeing what I'm doing – let go and drop ('jump' would suggest some active propulsion on my part) to the mat. Trouble is, Angel has stepped backwards to try to get out of the way, and she's still got the safety rope on, which winds round her ankles, so she falls over backwards, and when I hit the ground, I stumble forwards (in what would be a pretty impressive version of the beginning of a parachutist's roll if I'd done it on purpose) and land right on top of her.

As I gingerly reach up, push my helmet back and find myself staring into her eyes, Angel smiles.

'Well, *this* is awkward,' she says.

Yet the funny thing is, lying on top of her in what's effectively the missionary position, it doesn't feel awkward at all.

'You were a real gentleman.'

We're standing at the climbing centre's bar, where Angel's bought us both a pint, and I'm trying not to peer at the hand-shaped chalk imprint on her left buttock.

'You might change your mind if you could see what I can see.'

Angel follows my line of vision, then reaches down to brush it off. 'Even so, that was good of you to come to my rescue.'

'That was good of you to, ahem, catch me.'

'Any time,' she says, giving me the briefest of smiles, then she gestures with her pint glass over towards the wall, where Dirk has been pulled six feet into the air by a fat middle-aged man who's just fallen off, leaving the two of them hanging there like a pair of mismatched

Christmas tree decorations. 'Well, after this, I think I can safely say that climbing Everest would be the last thing on my bucket list.'

'It's the last thing on a lot of people's bucket lists. The last thing they *do*, anyway . . .'

'Well, *there's* a cheery thought.'

'Hey – this was your idea. "Something different," you said. "New experiences." And I'd never done this before either, so . . .'

Angel laughs.

'What's so funny?'

'It's just . . . other men I've gone out with – they've always wanted to appear so cool. Taking me to places they knew, or doing things they'd already done. No one's ever . . .'

'Been prepared to make a fool of themselves?'

Angel laughs again. 'Well, yes. My last boyfriend . . .' she says, and I don't pay attention to the rest of the story, which in retrospect is probably a mistake, because it might be useful information for later, i.e. it might help me avoid having that description applied to me at some time in the future . . . Anyway, the reason I don't pay attention is because I'm too busy mentally punching the air, because – and yes, I'm well aware this probably wouldn't stand up in court – in referring to her 'last' boyfriend, Angel is not only confirming that she's single, but also hinting that I'm – while perhaps not her 'current' boyfriend – am probably in the 'boyfriend' group, in the same way that a gorilla and a chimpanzee are both monkeys, even though they're very different (later I find they're actually both apes, not monkeys, but that doesn't dampen my enthusiasm at all). Anyway, the point of her story, I realise, as I sip my beer, is that by being *un*cool, I've apparently scored some serious brownie points. And fortunately, uncool is my natural state, so I can't lose!

'. . . but this was fun.'

'Which part? The bit where you got stuck on the wall? Or where I jumped on you from a height?'

Angel fake-scowls at me. 'All of it.' She glances at her watch, then finishes her lager and sets her glass down on the bar. 'But it's a school night, so . . .'

'So . . . ?' I say, wishing lager came in litre glasses so she'd have to stay longer.

'But Friday isn't. Well, technically it is, but Saturday isn't a school day, if you see what I mean, so . . .'

'So?'

'So . . .' Angel reaches across, picks my phone up from the bar and punches her mobile number into it. 'Call me,' she says.

Trying to play it cool, I just nod, but perhaps a little over-enthusiastically, because I've forgotten I'm still wearing my climbing helmet, and it slips down over my eyes again. But as Angel reaches across to help me loosen the strap, our hands touch, and the spark is so strong, I'm sure my eyes light up.

'What do you fancy doing?'

'You,' says Angel, and my heart leaps, but she follows it up quickly with '. . . decide,' so I tell myself to calm down.

'I'll find something you've never done before.'

Angel looks intrigued. 'Got any ideas?'

'Leave it with me,' I say, because quite frankly, not yet I don't.

I quickly finish the rest of my beer, then walk her out to the car park, where Angel peers at me for a moment, as if on the verge of some momentous decision, and then, to my stunned surprise, she kisses me – softly, tenderly, but all-too-briefly – on the lips, before jumping quickly into her car.

And as she pulls out of the car park, her 'call me' mime, holding an imaginary phone up to the side of her face, is one of the sweetest sights I've ever seen.

9.

The rest of the week passes without incident. While Mary's fractured wrist doesn't seem to be causing her too much pain, Marlon high-fives me with such force when I tell him how the climbing date went that he almost breaks mine too. I force myself to go for a run every day, and despite an incident with an over-territorial deer in Richmond Park (which at least means I've introduced a bit of speed work), I actually start to look forward to lacing up my trainers. We sell a few more of the Hanksys – or, as Marlon has christened them, 'the artwork formally known as *prints*'. And by the time Friday comes, though my hands are trembling when I call Angel's mobile, it's with excitement, rather than nerves.

'A drink?'

I'm glad we're speaking on the phone, so Angel can't see that I'm grinning like an idiot, though she's not sounding so impressed, and it's all I can do to stop myself from playing my joker already. 'That's right.'

'Noah . . .'

'It's not an ordinary drink.'

There's a pause, and then: 'Tell me more.'

'We're going for a drink . . . on a *horse!*'

There's a longer pause, during which I wonder whether I should have pointed out it's not the same horse and, in fact, the stables will give us one each, especially when Angel eventually breaks the silence with: 'I don't understand.'

'We get to the pub on a horse. Then have a drink. Then come back . . .'

'. . . on a horse?'

'You're way ahead of me.'

'So we're going horse riding?'

'Well, yeah. To a pub. And, you know, back again.'

There's a funny noise, which I realise is Angel squealing in delight. 'I *love* horse riding!'

'Ah. So you've been before?'

'Well, yes, but, not for a long time. Since . . . Well, that doesn't matter. That sounds lovely.'

'When was the last time you went? On a horse. Not, you know, for a drink.'

'When I was a little girl.'

I frown. That would suggest Angel doesn't love it quite as much as she's making out, but I'm not prepared to jeopardise the second set of brownie points I seem to have scored. Even so, the excitement in Angel's voice in unmistakable, so I de-frown and mentally pat myself on the back. (Googling 'exciting dates in West London' had only led me to a rather dodgy website where the 'exciting dates' were all women with their faces pixelated out, and I'd only come across the pub ride courtesy of a desperate search on TripAdvisor.) I punch the air with my free hand, pleased for the second time that Angel can't see me down the phone.

'So do we have a winner? Or rather, a *whinny*-er?'

I can almost hear Angel cringe at my bad joke – and in front of me, I can *see* Marlon doing exactly that. 'We might.'

'Great. Well, I've booked us a couple of, you know . . .'

'Horses?'

'You *have* been before. At, um, seven p.m. So . . .'

'Where?'

'Richmond Park. There's a stables. Some stables. I don't know if it's plural or singular . . .' I stop talking, conscious that if I keep coming out with stupid observations like this, it'll be me who's the singular one.

'Great.'

'Shall I pick you up?'

Angel hesitates for a moment, though whether it's because she doesn't want me to know where she lives – or even worse, doesn't want to go through that awkward drop-off-afterwards-or-come-up-for-coffee scenario – I'm not sure.

'That would be lovely,' she says, after a second or two that seems like a lifetime to me. 'I'll text you the address.'

'Great,' I say, then rush over to the window, ensuring I've got the maximum number of bars on my phone, concerned somehow her message won't get through, but I needn't have worried: my phone bleeps almost as soon as I end the call. And even though I want to wish away the next seven hours so I can see her again as quickly as possible, I can't, because there's something else I need to do first.

So I pick up my keys, leave Marlon holding the fort and make my way excitedly to my car.

Richmond Park is huge. Which means that even with the car's roof down for maximum visibility, it takes me a while to find the stables. And in the end, it's not the sign saying 'RIDING STABLES' just past Robin Hood Gate that catches my eye, but the pungent, eye-watering whiff of manure that seeps in through my nostrils.

Fortunately, given the park's twenty-miles-per-hour speed limit (which I've been struggling to keep to, even in my forty-year-old car) I manage to make the rather abrupt left turn into the entrance without too much protest from my tyres. As I park in front of what looks like a series of garden sheds joined together with the top half of their doors sawn off, a woman dressed in a pair of jodhpurs that look like they belong to someone several sizes smaller – and leading a scarily big horse – comes over to meet me.

'Hi,' she says. 'I'm a lady.'

I'm not quite sure what to say to that – especially since the fit of her jodhpurs isn't leaving her gender in any doubt – until I spot her name badge, and realise she's said (rather poshly), 'I'm *Melody*.'

'Hi.'

'Can I help you?'

'I hope so,' I say, clambering out of the car. 'I've got a couple of, you know . . .' *Places? Seats? Saddles?* I flick my eyes towards the horse, which is defecating to a quite impressive distance, and I'm glad its rear end isn't pointing towards my open-topped car. 'Booked for the pub ride this evening.'

'You're a little early.'

'I know.' I reach up to pat the horse's nose, like I've seen jockeys do after they've won the Grand National, but have second thoughts when the animal bares a set of vicious-looking teeth. 'But I wondered if I could take one out on a test ride beforehand.'

'A test ride?'

'This evening's a date, you see. And I've never ridden a horse. And my girlf— I mean, the girl I'm bringing – she has, and I don't want to look stupid, so I thought I could just . . .' I glance at the horse again, who – amazingly – is still pooing: there's already a pile of manure behind him that could fertilise the whole of Kew Gardens, and I'm beginning to think I should put my car's roof up, just in case.

'You've asked a girl to go riding on a date, and you've never ridden a horse?'

'Yes. And, um, no.'

'Going for the sympathy vote, eh?'

'That's a no, too. And therefore why I'm here . . .'

The woman sighs, then looks at her watch. 'Right. Well, there's a beginner's group going out in five minutes. You can join them if you like.'

'Brilliant. It won't be on . . .' I swallow hard, and glance at the horse she's holding. He's really very big, and if I was worried about my vertigo on the climbing wall . . . '*Him*, will it?'

'Relax. I'm sure we can find you one a bit more suitable.'

'Right,' I say, wondering if they do horses with stabilisers, like kids have when they're learning to ride a bike, or whether it'll be one of those Shetland pony-type mini horses instead. 'Oh, and just remember, when you see me later, I haven't been here today.'

'Fine,' says the woman. Though she's already wearing an expression suggesting she wishes that was the case.

I'm directed to the tack room, where a girl who looks about twelve hands me a helmet (which I check won't cover my eyes this time) and a pair of riding boots (which I'm assured will 'save my shoes', though I don't want to ask her from what). I quickly put them on, then hurry back outside, where a group of half a dozen primary-school-age kids are waiting excitedly on a mean-looking selection (herd? Flock? I really must read up) of horses. Melody, now in full riding gear, is standing impatiently next to them and holding a horse that, while not quite as terrifyingly tall as the one I saw when I arrived, is still fairly intimidating.

'He's hardly *My Little Pony*, is he?'

'Don't worry,' says Melody reassuringly. 'He's only fifteen hands. That's as in "high",' she adds, evidently noting my blank expression. 'Not fingers and thumbs.'

Which is all I'll be, I think. 'What's his name?'

'Centurion,' says the woman.

'Like in *Gladiator*?'

'No. Like the tank.'

I walk up to Centurion and give him a thorough once-over, although aside from checking he's actually got four legs, I'm not sure what else I should be looking for. He's solidly built, which I'm sure is good for stability rather than speed, and looks fairly placid, certainly compared to some of the other skittish mounts that are pacing and stamping their way round the stable yard. Not knowing exactly what to say to a horse, I settle for a friendly 'Hello, Centurion' – though that seems to do the trick, as he (and I'm sure it's a he, given the fire-hose-sized appendage hanging beneath him that's just started to give my riding boots a rinsing) looks at me briefly, snorts loudly, then turns his head away.

And it's here I encounter my first stumbling block: I've now got to get on in front of everyone, although it's probably better to embarrass myself in front of a group of kids now, rather than Angel later . . . Or perhaps not, I realise when the children all erupt into giggles at my first Fosbury Flop-ish attempt, as Centurion decides to take half a step away from me just as I'm mid-jump, leaving me on my backside on the floor.

As I pick myself up and dust myself off, relieved I haven't landed in the growing yellowish lake that's pooled beneath Centurion, Melody smiles sympathetically at me.

'Sorry,' I say. 'Like I mentioned, I've never done this before.'

Melody looks at me pityingly, as if to say she'd already have guessed that even if I *hadn't* told her. 'It's easy,' she says. 'Both hands on the saddle, then just put your foot in the stirrup and climb on.'

Holding onto the saddle's the easy part. Getting my foot high enough to put it into the stirrup not so much, and it's even something that master-of-the-splits Jean-Claude Van Damme might struggle with, especially in the tightish jeans I happen to be wearing. And then, when I do eventually manage to get my foot in there, Centurion decides to move a step forwards, sending me plummeting to the floor again, only this time with my foot still caught in the stirrup.

As the children almost wet themselves, I'm starting to regret this. All I need now is for Centurion to get spooked by their laughter, start running out of the gate and across the park, and I'll be dragged along the ground behind him, like you always see happening to the baddie in westerns. But before any of that can occur, Melody untangles my foot, grabs me under the shoulders and (rather impressively) hoists me back onto my feet.

'Hold on,' she says, walking across to the stables, fetching the kind of mini stepladder you see in short people's kitchens and setting it down in front of me. Unable to make eye contact, I mumble a quick 'thanks', climb up the couple of steps, grip the saddle firmly and vault on. The saddle's not the most comfortable, and the leather's a bit slippery – plus, Centurion's rather wide, which means the position my legs are in is probably more suited to giving birth than a gentle cross-country excursion. But I'm sure I'll get the hang of it. Or rather, I have to.

Melody marches over to her horse, which has been waiting obediently during my shenanigans, and climbs effortlessly on. 'Right, everyone,' she says, calling us all to attention. 'Just remember what I told you. Your horses should all follow each other, but just in case, a sideways pull with your left hand, and . . .' She gives her left rein the slightest of tugs and her horse obediently swivels to the left. 'Left you'll go. Do the same with the other hand . . .' She demonstrates, and her horse turns to the right. 'And that's pretty much all there is to it. Any questions?'

The kids are all chattering amongst themselves, seemingly oblivious to the challenge ahead, in that fearless way small children have when you see them on ski slopes and the like. I, on the other hand, raise an arm.

'Yes?' says Melody.

'What happens if he gets out of control? I might be thrown off.'

Melody nods at Centurion, who's looking as bored as it's possible for a horse to look. 'Oh, don't worry,' she says. 'He knows what he's doing.'

'Great,' I say, glad one of us does.

As the group heads out through the stables gate, Centurion takes one look at me as if to check I'm still on board, then ambles out behind them, and just like that, I'm *horse riding*. First impressions are that it's not that difficult: apart from coping with the mild front-to-back rocking, there's not much skill involved, the horses seem to know where they're going, the bridle path is pretty flat, and in any case, Centurion seems pretty sure-footed – so as long as I remember to duck for branches (a lesson I learn the hard way when I get a mouthful of oak leaves), I seem to be getting on okay. I'm at the back of the line too, so it's not as if anyone can see me as I awkwardly try to copy Melody's technique (which, at this speed, basically seems to be to just sit there).

As the ride progresses, I start to feel a little more confident – after all, 'sitting' is a skill I've mastered over my thirty-five years on this planet. So what if I'm doing it on something moving, and somewhat further than usual from the ground – the basics are still the same, even out here, at one with nature. And while my 'man parts' are a little too much at one with the saddle for my liking once we start trotting, and my backside is starting to get a little tender after the half an hour or so we've been riding, that's probably my own fault for not knowing how to keep my feet in the right position in the stirrups.

Importantly, though, I've hopefully learned enough to not embarrass myself in front of Angel later. I'll still look awkward enough that it should pass as my first time (and I already suspect that I'm not a natural horseman, so no amount of lessons is going to help me with that), but I'll be good enough that I can enjoy the trip to the pub and back this evening without the danger of ending up as a prize-winning clip on *You've Been Framed*. Now, instead of being thrown off, all I have to worry about is coming up with a couple of hours of witty, scintillating conversation, so Angel won't give me the heave-ho.

'Okay, everyone,' shouts Melody, after we've looped our way sedately round the pond in the middle of the park. 'Time to head back.'

As the other horses trot off obediently, Centurion seems to be flagging a little, perhaps because I'm not ten years old, so he's carrying twice the weight of the rest of them. After a few minutes, Melody breaks off from the front of the group and rides back to where I'm not quite keeping up the rear.

'How are you getting on?'

'Good,' I say, trying not to wince every time my backside hits the saddle, 'I think.'

'Excellent. In that case, did you fancy a little canter?'

I nod, even though I don't have the faintest idea what a 'canter' is.

'Great.' Melody beams at me, revealing a set of teeth that rival Centurion's. 'Come on, then!'

She steers her horse to a halt by the side of the bridle path, and with a level of skill that I manage to impress myself with, I manage to get Centurion up alongside Melody's horse and 'park' next to her.

'And a *canter* would be?'

'Somewhere between a trot and a gallop,' she says, making a strange clicking sound with her mouth, then she digs her heels into her horse's sides and the two of them set off in pursuit of the rest of the group.

I look down at Centurion, who's found a tuft of grass to munch on. 'Come on then.'

Centurion continues munching.

'Canter!'

Centurion munches some more.

'Please?'

I give the reins a half-hearted tug, and do my best impression of Melody's clicking noise, though it sounds more like I'm tutting in disgust at him. But instead of the requested canter, Centurion looks up at me as if to say *Really?*, shakes his mane and starts ambling reluctantly forwards, even slower than before.

Up ahead, Melody's rapidly disappearing from view, mainly because she's having to chase down the rest of the group, who seem to be racing each other back, and for a moment, I start to panic. Unless I take the main road, I don't know the way to the stables from here, and it's a big park, and if I've got to get Centurion back, drive home, get changed (so I don't smell of horses – a dead giveaway – though I've a feeling I'm also going to be spending a while in the shower), and get back here with Angel for seven o'clock, then I'd better get a move on.

I look down at Centurion, hoping he knows the way, taking some comfort that he certainly doesn't seem to be phased by us being out here on our own. Maybe you can get horses with the same sense of direction as homing pigeons – though there's only one way to find out. And while the prospect of being on a fast-moving horse frightens me a little, there's a speed limit in the park, which I'm sure he knows. And twenty miles an hour . . . well, that's only about three times as fast as I can run. How scary can it be?

I take a deep breath, make the clicking noise a little louder this time, then dig my heels gently into Centurion's sides. When nothing happens, I do it again, a little harder, and I'm just contemplating a full-throated 'yee-hah!' when I notice a bald man sitting on a bench in front of us. There's a pit bull at his feet, and as we draw level, the dog starts to growl. Then, as it lets out a full-throated bark, Centurion suddenly wakes up, surging forwards as if I've done a drag-start to get away from the lights.

As Centurion sprints headlong along the bridle path, it's all I can do to hang on, though to be honest, falling off would be a relief – the violent motion is repeatedly slamming my nether regions painfully against the hard leather saddle.

I've seen enough westerns to know you're supposed to do some sort of swinging action at this point, cleverly matching the motion of the horse with the movement of your buttocks. Unfortunately, my boots don't seem to be getting a lot of purchase on the stirrups – perhaps due to the inch or so of manure I've got caked on the soles that, when I attempt to raise myself up, and to my horror, suddenly makes my feet slip out of them. Which means that I've got no choice but to try to absorb the bumps with my testicles.

My earlier optimism about Centurion respecting the park's speed limit is proving futile, and as we go careering along the bumpy path, I realise I've got a choice to make: jump off, or try to get him under control. Getting my feet back in the stirrups is an impossibility given the way they're swinging around, and the reins provide little support.

I try hanging on to the stubby bit at the front of the saddle like a rodeo rider might, but I can't get a proper grip, and besides, I've been grasping the reins for dear life for the past half an hour, so my grip strength isn't quite what it might be.

After a minute or two, and with my chances of ever having children rapidly diminishing, I decide there's nothing for it, so desperately I lean forwards, and with a loud 'Sorry!' grab Centurion by the mane, though to my horror, that only seems to make him want to go faster.

I debate shouting 'Whoa!' at the top of my voice, though to be honest, given the bashing my bits and pieces are taking, I don't have much of a voice left, so I look around for a soft spot to jump to, but the bridle path looks painfully hard – and besides, jumping would involve getting some kind of foothold, and if I could do that, I wouldn't need to jump in the first place. As it is, just letting go and slipping off is my only hope, but then I run the risk of being trampled, or even worse, dragged at speed. With no other option, I grip as hard as I can with my legs round Centurion's middle, and extend my arms around his neck.

Finally, thankfully, my hope that he knows where he's going is rewarded when I spy the stables through a gap in the trees, and it's with considerable relief when Centurion does the same and slows down to a trot, eventually ambling in through the gate as if nothing's happened. Gingerly, I haul myself back upright and take hold of the reins again, and by some miracle manage to relocate my feet in the stirrups. The group of children are already there, their mothers happily snapping away on their camera phones, and as Centurion makes his way over to the water trough, Melody strides towards us.

'How did you get on?'

I nod towards the mini stepladder leaning against the side of the trough, assuming she's asking because I'm going to have to use the same method to get off again, then realisation hits. 'Oh, you mean on the ride?' My voice is an octave or so higher than before, and I think about going into detail, but then again, I've got to be back here in a few hours, and the last thing I want is to be banned. 'Great,' I say, hoping Melody thinks my eyes are watering with excitement.

'That's good.' Melody looks at the heavily perspiring Centurion, who seems to be gulping down most of the water in the trough, and pats him heartily on the shoulder (if horses *have* shoulders). 'It looks like you've given him quite the workout.'

I can't think how to answer that, so instead, I just slap my thigh in the way I've seen cowboys do, but when Melody looks at me strangely, I just mumble something about a wasp.

'We'll see you later, then,' she says.

I glance at Centurion, wondering whether the 'we' she's just used refers to him too. 'You will. And remember,' I add, 'you haven't seen me.'

As Melody gives me a look that suggests she wishes that was the case, I clamber inelegantly off. 'Oh, and any tips for later? Just so I don't look quite so . . .'

'Awkward?' She looks me up and down. 'Just try not to fall off.'

And all of a sudden, I'm back at the climbing wall again.

10.

Angel's sitting on the kerb outside her flat when I get there. It's in an old house just off the main road, in perhaps not the nicest part of town (though it's still Richmond, so 'not the nicest' part of town just means the Porsches, BMWs and Mercedes – or Mercedeses, or Mercedi, or whatever the plural is – parked in the street are a couple of years old as opposed to brand new). Besides, I can hardly draw any conclusions from that: the only reason I live on the 'nice' bit is because Mary gives me such a good deal on the room I rent.

In truth, I'm disappointed that I don't get the chance to go inside, or at least peek in over her shoulder through the door to see how she lives: whether she's messy, or has a week's worth of dirty dishes left in her sink, or a shrine to Satan daubed in virgin blood on her bedroom wall – anything to show me she's not perfect. Though, given how the fact that she's an impulsive, argumentative, outspoken thrill-seeker with a devil-may-care attitude and a weird shoe addiction (in summary, the polar opposite of anyone I've ever dated before) hasn't done that, I'm a little worried as to what exactly I'd need to see to make me change my mind.

I've showered – twice – and changed my clothes after my afternoon ride, and I'm now dressed in a pair of looser jeans (along with a pair of briefs under my boxer shorts for a bit of extra padding), plus I've popped a couple of ibuprofen to try to numb the tenderness in my nether regions. I'm still in a bit of pain but, all in all – and even though it's perhaps a little sneaky of me – I'm glad I've at least familiarised myself with this evening's mode of transport.

It's warm enough that I've still got the roof down, and when I beep the horn as I arrive, Angel's face lights up. She already looks the part, dressed in her 'boyfriend' jeans (which I take as a positive sign), a flannel shirt and what I'm beginning to suspect are the only type of shoes she ever wears – a pair of Converse, purple this time.

I've already planned to maintain my 'gallant' image, so I stop and jump out, aiming to run around the car and open the door for her but, because she gets in herself – and I'm too busy concentrating on walking as if I'm not in agony with every step – by the time I get round to her side of the car, she's already fastening her seatbelt, which makes me look a little foolish.

'Nice car,' she says, peering around the interior as I pretend that adjusting the passenger-door wing mirror is the reason for my little jaunt.

'Thanks.' I head back round to my side and climb into the driver's seat. 'It's an MGB Roadster. Nineteen seventy-two. Original wire wheels. Overdrive. Two careful owners. Then me . . .' I stop talking; Angel's making a face. 'What?'

'I said "nice car". Not "read me its CV".'

'Sorry.'

She sticks her tongue out, and I grin at her, then pull out into the traffic, head over the level crossing and accelerate up Queen's Road, planning to take Angel on a romantic top-down drive through the park on the way to the stables, though for some reason she makes me stop at the bottom of the hill to put the roof up. While I assume it's because she doesn't want her hair messed up, when we get to the park, she asks me to take it down again.

'Twenty miles an hour, okay?'

'Huh?'

'For your hair?'

Angel's frowning at me, so I decide to concentrate on driving instead, stealing the occasional glance at her under the pretence of pointing something out on her side of the car, which is perhaps a little dangerous, not because I worry we're going to crash, or run over one of the wild deer that roam around the park, but simply because each time I do, with her hair streaming in the wind, her face illuminated by the evening sun, I fall even more hopelessly in love.

At the stables, there's a group of riders, all round about our age, which I'm relieved to see after the overly judgemental kids who were here earlier – perhaps not a surprise, given that we're going to a pub. My stomach lurches a little when I spot Centurion, though he's now being ridden by an older lady who looks like she knows her way around a horse. Which does seem to be 'around the front', given how he's relieving himself again, in a way that makes Niagara Falls look like a leaky tap.

Melody is there, ticking everyone off on a clipboard, so I introduce myself with a perhaps overly loud 'Noah', and Angel nudges me.

'The perfect name for a horse rider,' she whispers. 'Because it rhymes with *whoa*.'

'Hey!' I tell her, as Melody directs us towards the tack room. 'I do the bad jokes.'

We collect our boots and helmets, and by the time we're ready, Angel's almost hopping from one foot to another in anticipation. When we're led to our horses, she expertly climbs up into the saddle, looking like she's going to burst with excitement. I'm determined not to embarrass myself this time, and by some miracle, I manage to haul myself on first time, causing Angel to raise both eyebrows.

'You've done this before!'

'Not before today, no,' I say. Which is true, if you think about it.

'So,' says Melody. 'We're going to ride through the park, and stop off at The New Inn for a drink or two, then head back just before sunset. Now, has anyone here not ridden a horse before?'

As everyone looks at everyone else, I suddenly remember I've forgotten I'm supposed to put my hand up, so I do.

'Noah, right?' says Melody, playing along, and I nod.

'Well, just . . .'

Even though I know she's doing it for my benefit in terms of Angel, rather than to make sure I'm okay, Melody runs through the same instructions as this afternoon, and then, after a quick safety briefing, we're off. I've ensured my stirrups are the right length, mainly because my backside is so tender from earlier, and it's amazing how the pain focuses my technique.

'Hey,' says Angel, bringing her horse up alongside mine proficiently. 'You're a natural.'

'Look who's talking.'

Angel laughs, digs her heels in and trots off in front of me. 'It's just like riding a bike,' she calls back over her shoulder. 'Well, except for the having-to-pedal part. And a lot more fun!'

And the funny thing is, it *is* fun, and not just because I'm mesmerised by the sight of Angel's bottom bouncing up and down just in front of me, or the fact that we're off for a drink (and on our fourth date!), *or* the fact that my plan seems to be working.

To my surprise, I find myself starting to relax and enjoy the scenery – as well as her company. I can see why Angel responded so enthusiastically: it's a lovely evening, and the park is so lushly green and countryside-like that if it weren't for the planes flying regularly overhead on their way to Heathrow, you'd forget you were in London; the horses are quiet (apart from the regular percussive farts that seem to be coming from the one behind me, something that sends the woman riding him into fits of giggles every time it happens); and it's a cliché, I know, but there's something about being out here like this, man and beast, surrounded by all this nature, on this eco-friendliest form of transport, in beautiful weather . . . While riding and I might not have been love at first sight, I can see how I might eventually come to feel that way about it.

Though the way my backside is hurting, whether I'll manage thirteen goes, I'm not so sure.

The 'drink' part of the date is fun, though it turns out to be more of a group thing than the romantic two-of-us evening I'd been hoping for. Plus, I almost embarrass myself when we get to the pub, tie the horses up outside and I ask Melody whether we should be padlocking them to something, like you would with your bike.

Angel's first at the bar, thanks to some clever use of her elbows/ fluttering of her eyelashes as required (though when I shrink in embarrassment at her pushing-in skills, she simply reminds me life's too short to wait in line, and I tell her I thought she'd meant that metaphorically), and then we nearly have our first argument when she insists on buying the drinks seeing as I've organised the ride, and I tell her I'll just have a half, and she thinks I'm only saying that because I don't want her to spend much money, but I insist it's because I'm driving, and she laughs, and tells me it's actually called 'riding', and, besides, you can't be drunk in charge of a horse, but I remind Angel I've got to drive her – and then me – home. Although I won't get what her 'maybe' response to the second leg of that journey means until much later.

When we eventually get back to the stables, she's looking a little flushed, though I put that down to the excitement of the canter on the way back as opposed to the two glasses of white wine she's had. We say goodbye to the rest of the group then head back to the car, and because it's looking as though it might rain, I pause before I get in.

'Roof up or down?'

'Are we driving home the same way?'

'Do you mean in terms of route and not technique?'

Angel rolls her eyes, then she thinks for a moment. 'Down,' she says.

I start the car and reverse carefully out of the stables, trying my best to avoid the various piles of manure, then head back through the park. And on this gorgeous evening, driving with Angel by my side, the wind in our hair, through this most beautiful of London settings, for the first time I've reason to be thankful for the normally frustrating speed limit, as it means I can spend longer in her company. She's got her eyes shut, and looks so lovely, so beautiful, so *alive*, in fact, that by the time we get back to her flat, I'm having to fight off a wave of insecurity and the feeling that she's 'slumming it' with me. What's worse is, there's a parking space right outside, which it's silly not to pull into, so I do. And then I face the dilemma about leaving the motor running, though it's a dilemma Angel puts an end to very quickly.

'Do you want to come up?'

More than anything in the world, I think.

'Unless you've got somewhere you need to be,' she adds, perhaps taking my lack of an answer for reluctance.

And though I feel the only place I *actually* need to be is with her, there's so much pressure that I can hardly speak. So I just nod and climb out of the car, then Angel gets out, and as I join her on the pavement, she stands up on tiptoe and whispers, 'Your motor's running' into my ear, and I'm about to tell her *too right it is* when I realise she means I've forgotten to switch the engine off.

With a guilty grin, I sprint round to my side of the car, turn the key in the ignition, then – without bothering to put the roof up or even lock the doors – follow her like a puppy dog up her steps.

Angel's place is tiny, even for a studio flat. Crammed into the eaves of the building, in what probably used to be a very small attic, it's the kind of place that makes the minuscule show flats they lay out in IKEA look positively spacious. There's a compact kitchenette in front of the window, a tiny dining table with two chairs, and a small, two-seater sofa against the wall, with the bed separated from the 'living' part by the coffee table rather than any kind of wall or curtain, which is at the same time both great *and* terrifying in terms of ease of access.

It's incredibly full of stuff, too, with more paintings on the walls than we have at the gallery (though right now, that's not too difficult), including a few colourful abstracts that look like Angel's painted them herself. There's a selection of books on her shelves ranging from *Bridget Jones* to *War and Peace*, an impressive line-up of Converse shoeboxes under the bed (which Angel catches me looking at, then makes the 'what can you do?' face), a clothes rail with what looks like a random selection from a charity shop in the corner, and a ukulele hanging on the back of the door. It couldn't belong to anyone but Angel. And I love it for that very reason.

'It's not much,' says Angel, smiling at my cursory inspection. 'But it's home.'

'It's lovely,' I say, still a little breathless from the four flights of stairs.

'Thanks. So . . . did you want a coffee?'

I look at my watch – it's automatic, but immediately I wish I could take the action back. 'Um, no, thank you. It's late, and . . . The caffeine, I mean.'

Angel looks at me strangely, then walks over and tugs open one of the kitchen cabinets. 'Okay, well, I've got some wine – though it might be off – brandy, Malibu, some tequila . . .'

I shake my head. 'Better not. Like I said earlier, I'm driving.'

'And like *I* said earlier – *maybe*.'

I stare at her for a moment, trying to process what she's just said, still not allowing myself to entertain the thought that she might have invited me up here to stay, which may very well mean for *sex*. Apart from a peck on the cheek at the gallery, and the briefest of lip-meetings outside the climbing centre, we haven't so much as held hands yet. And while I'm aware that makes me sound like a prude . . .

'In that case,' I say, aware that pause has probably lasted a lot longer than either of us would have liked, 'a brandy would be lovely.'

Angel looks around for a couple of glasses, but she can't find any clean ones, so she grabs two randomly out of the sink, has to wash them up, then dry them, and by the time she's handed me a rather generous measure of brandy, it's all I can do not to gulp it down in one to stop my hands from shaking. It's been a long time since I last had sex, and a long *long* time since I had sex as meaningful as this might be.

'Cheers,' she says, clinking her glass against mine.

'Cheers.'

'So . . .' She's standing very close to me, making eye contact as she sips her drink, so I take a mouthful of mine. The liquid burns the back of my throat, but I don't care – I'd welcome *anything* to divert my attention from, ahem, *other* parts of my body.

'So?'

Angel reaches a hand up for my glass, so I take another quick gulp, a bit like a toddler might when a parent's trying to remove a drink they're halfway through, then I let her take it from me. She puts the glasses down on the coffee table, grabs me by the hand and leads me to the foot of the bed – a walk of all of two paces – then she stands a foot or so away from me, unbuttons her shirt slowly, shrugs it off her shoulders and drops it on the floor between us.

'Your turn,' she says, her voice a little husky.

Given the vision of Angel standing there in her bra, close enough to reach out and touch, it takes a second or two for my brain to process what I'm supposed to do now. Quickly, and not quite as sexily as Angel, given that I haven't undone enough buttons to get my head through the neck hole first go, I pull my polo shirt off over my head and drop it on top of hers.

Angel keeps direct eye contact (which is good, because it means I don't have to surreptitiously hold my stomach in) as she kicks her shoes off, undoes her jeans and wriggles out of them. Then, cleverly using one foot, she hooks them up and drops them onto the rapidly growing pile of clothes in between us.

I reach down, pull my trainers and socks off in one go (mentally patting myself on the back for this, as it means I won't be stood there in underpants and socks later), then undo my belt, unbutton my jeans, shake them down to the floor and step out of them. I'm not quite as coordinated as Angel, so I have to bend down to pick them up to add them to the pile, and while this puts my head level with where I'm guessing Angel's tattoo might be, I'm too much of a gentleman (or too terrified) to look for it.

When I stand up again, Angel's grinning at me. Her eyes flick down to my boxer shorts, and I'm wondering how far this game has to go: her next move is her bra, obviously, though she's wearing one more item of clothing than me, so I'm going to be naked first. I could of course intervene. Step forward, pick her up and carry her the (admittedly) short distance to the bed. But to be quite honest, despite the fact I'm shortly going to be standing embarrassingly buck naked in front of her, this is one of the most enjoyable games I've played in a long while.

With the slightest of smirks on her face, Angel reaches round, unhooks her bra, then slips it off, keeping one arm across her breasts as she drops it onto the pile. I realise I've got no other option but to go for it, so – keeping my eyes firmly fixed on hers – I grab the waistband of my boxers, lower them to my ankles, and step confidently out of them. But when I stand back up again, Angel's looking puzzled.

I freeze, wondering what on earth it could be about my genitals that's causing so much consternation. Are they that weird-looking? Too small? Or – and I realise it'd only be as a result of any swellings caused by today's two horse rides – too big? But before I dare to check, Angel finds her voice again.

'Why are you wearing double underpants?'

I frown at her, peer down at my groin and go pale. I'd completely forgotten I'd put an extra pair on as padding, and now Angel's going to think . . . I can't even imagine what she's going to think.

'For the horse riding,' I say, as if that explains everything.

'Did you think it was going to be that scary?'

'No, it was for . . .' I exhale loudly, and decide that at this point, honesty is probably the best policy, so I'd better admit to my sneaky afternoon ride. 'I'm a bit tender.'

Angel raises both eyebrows. 'Dare I ask why? And where?'

'Well, funny story . . .' But I've been caught out, and while I'd like to come up with a clever answer, I can't think of anything apart from coming clean. 'I went riding earlier today too. I'd never been before, so I thought I'd better get a feel for it. Just so I wouldn't embarrass you. Or look stupid.'

'Like you do right now?'

'Um, yeah. Sometimes spontaneity takes a bit of planning.'

'For some people.' Angel rolls her eyes, then she laughs. 'So those were for cushioning?'

'Yup.'

'And did they work?' says Angel, taking half a step towards me.

'I'll tell you in the morning,' I say.

11.

I miss the following morning's parkrun, though that's mainly because I'm in so much agony after yesterday's exertions – *all of them* – that it's all I can do to get out of bed. And while I should be leaping up and punching the air while clicking my heels together – metaphorically, at least, given how knackered and sore I am – Angel's off-handedness towards me when I say goodbye to her is in such stark contrast to her hands-on approach last night, I can't help but feel a little deflated.

When I eventually limp into the gallery and lower myself gingerly into my chair, Marlon's smirking at me.

'What?'

'What do you mean, *what*?' he says, mock-indignantly.

'Your face is a picture.'

'It's the only thing in here that is, at the moment.' He straightens one of the Hanksy frames on the wall, then hands me a cushion from the bench in the middle of the room, and I gratefully slide it underneath my backside. 'I take it that's from the horse riding?'

'Mostly,' I say.

'Crikey, Noah. I know they say love is a battlefield, but you make it look like the one at the start of *Saving Private Ryan*.'

'I'd find that funny, if laughing didn't hurt. Everywhere.'

Marlon widens his eyes. 'And that's after only four dates? Impressive. For you.'

'Thanks. I think. But . . .'

'There's a "but"? Already?'

'It's just . . . Angel seemed a bit . . . distant this morning. Didn't really say much when I left.'

'Distant? Or too exhausted to speak? Because by the looks of you, that's a possibility.'

'Ha ha. Seriously, though. Does that happen a lot? You know, the morning after . . .'

Marlon puffs air out of his cheeks. 'I don't often hang around to find out, to be honest. But maybe she just wants to take it slow. After all, like you said, she doesn't do relationships, but she does date. And perhaps what happened last night was a little bit soon for her. Was it at her . . .'

'Flat? Yes. We'd just—'

'*Instigation*, I was going to say.'

I think back, trying – and failing – not to blush at the memory, then nod. 'Yup. Both times.'

Marlon makes the 'too much information' face. 'Hmm. Tricky one. I suppose it depends on what Angel thinks the difference is.'

'Right.' I pause, and then: 'Between?'

'Dating and a relationship.'

'Right.' I pause a bit longer this time, and then: 'So, generally, when *does* dating become a relationship?'

Marlon looks at me pityingly. 'Sometime between now and thirteen, hopefully! Although that's kind of down to you.'

'Down to *me*?'

'Two words,' he says, as he heads into the back to put the kettle on. 'Fire extinguisher.' And though it takes me almost as long to get his reference as it takes Marlon to make the coffee, when I do, it fills me with more than a little hope.

There's a fire extinguisher set into a recess in the wall in the corner of the gallery. It's bright red – like most fire extinguishers – about two feet tall, and next to it there's a little health and safety sign that says, simply, 'FIRE EXTINGUISHER'. I say this not in case you visit us one day and a fire happens to break out, but to point out that it's a normal, regular, ordinary, run-of-the-mill, standard-issue everyday fire extinguisher – the kind you see in any hospital, school, library, shop, restaurant or other public building. Which is why Marlon and I are mystified whenever – and it happens more than you'd think – someone stops in front of it, stares at it contemplatively for a minute or so, then flicks through the price list to see how much it costs.

And even though we insist it's not for sale, that doesn't stop people trying to bargain with us, as if we're simply playing hardball to drive the price up (though explaining it's our *actual* fire extinguisher generally puts an end to that conversation. And sends them scurrying, red-faced, for the door).

I say *this* not to poke fun at our visitors (I'd use the word 'customers', but the percentage of people who come in who actually buy anything would mean I'd fall foul of the Trade Descriptions Act) – we're grateful for every one of them (except the ones with bad body odour, or the ones who're just sheltering from the rain and feel they should pretend to be interested in whatever's on the walls, or the ones who sneer at the work and mutter, 'I could do better myself', loudly enough to ensure we hear them) – but just to illustrate that if you create the right environment, then you can get people to see the world differently. To put it another way, if you've been wandering round under the impression that empty picture frames are in fact 'art', then it's not too far of a leap of imagination to believe a fire extinguisher might be. So if I act like Angel and I are in a relationship, do all the things that people in relationships do, treat her to all intents and purposes like she's my girlfriend . . . well, it's just possible that she'll start thinking that way, too.

'So,' says Marlon, handing me a steaming mug of coffee. 'What's next?'

'I thought I'd take her away for the weekend. Next weekend. Get there in time for lunch on the Saturday, followed by a romantic dinner that evening, then find a decent pub for a Sunday roast, before heading back.'

Marlon looks impressed. 'Smart move.'

'A weekend away?'

'Trying to cram in as many dates as you can in as short a time as possible.'

I ignore the implication. Even though he's right. 'So I'm going to take next Saturday off. If that's okay?'

Marlon shrugs. 'You're the boss.'

Though where Angel's concerned, given her mood this morning, I'm really not sure I am.

12.

'Margate.'

There's something about the way Angel says the town's name – not quite a question, not even a statement of fact, but a sort of repetition that sounds like complete disbelief that I'd choose somewhere she obviously regards as the armpit of England as the venue for our first-ever romantic trip.

In truth, she's been a bit funny with me all week, a bit . . . reluctant, is the best word I can come up with. So much so that I'm beginning to regard her coolness the morning after we slept together as a high point. I could be imagining it – although I'm obviously hoping it's nothing to do with any, ahem, *performance issues* – and maybe it's simply that my 'treat her like we're in a relationship' idea has reared up and bitten me, in that blowing hot and cold, sometimes taking much longer to respond to my texts (or the lack of 'smiley faces' when she does) is what you *do* in a relationship. Even though it's not something I've seen before. In anyone I've ever gone out with.

Though I appreciate that's not the largest of samples for comparison, so I'm trying not to read too much into it. Besides, she has agreed to come away for the weekend – although given her reaction to where we're going, whether she'll even get on the train is something I wouldn't bet on right now.

'Margate,' she says again, and at once, I want to say 'ha, ha, just kidding, we're off to Paris!' or something like that, and she'll punch me on the shoulder in a 'you kidder' kind of way, and I'll try not to rub the spot where I know I'll have a bruise later because I do bruise easily (and I'm guessing that Angel's got quite a punch on her), then I'll hurry across to the Eurostar ticket counter and she'll be none the wiser.

In her defence, maybe I've made a mistake in us travelling to Margate from St. Pancras – because it's the Eurostar terminal, so of course Angel might have thought we were going somewhere exotic rather than the far reaches of Kent. But it's too late to do anything about that now, because for one thing, I've already paid for the train tickets (the best part of forty-two pounds each, because I've gone for the high-speed service rather than the clanky old train from Victoria), and the hotel reservation is non-refundable (although I've saved 22 per cent, thanks to booking.com, because I'm no mug) *and* because I run a gallery that's hardly Richmond's top-grossing arts venue (and which, thanks to Angel's repeated requests, is about to give Nick from her work a free exhibition), so I'm not made of money. Besides, she can't expect *every* date to be some adrenaline-fuelled, zip-wire, roller-coaster ride. If she does, I'm – *we're* – in trouble.

'That's right,' I say, batting that last thought away as best I can, though like an angry wasp at a picnic, I fear it's going to bother me for a while.

'Great,' says Angel, bless her, but it's in that same flat tone, so I force a smile and do my best not to make eye contact as I escort her towards our platform.

'Have you ever been?'

'Once,' she says, which leads me to infer that as far as Angel's concerned, once was enough.

'Oh,' I say, then add, as enthusiastically as I can: 'But this still counts as a new experience.'

'How do you work that out?'

'Well, because – apparently – it's changed a lot.'

Angel gives me an 'it'd have to have' look. 'Really?'

'It's almost trendy now. There's a new retro funfair, if that's not a contradiction in terms, and loads of vintage shops, and some great cafés and bars, and the hotel we're staying at looks right out over the sea, and . . .' I stop talking, conscious I might be over-egging it on the basis of the article I read in the *Independent* last week. Despite the paper's name, these things are never really independent, are they?

'You've been recently, have you?'

'Well, no – never, actually, but . . .' In truth, I'm a little deflated. Angel should be happy to be spending the weekend with me *wherever* we're going, shouldn't she? Instead, she's still wearing the expression of someone who wants her weekends to count, and who thinks going somewhere like Margate, especially with someone who thinks that a weekend in Margate is a fun thing to do, is a waste of a couple of days off, when she could be spending them trekking up Machu Picchu, or diving the Great Barrier Reef, or dancing in some muddy field to some band I've – and probably even she's – never heard of. But if it's music she wants . . .

'*Da-ahn to Margit*,' I sing, in a terrible mockney rendition of the Chas 'n' Dave eighties novelty hit, grabbing my imaginary braces at nipple height and doing a little 'cheeky chappie' dance for added effect, but Angel just stares at me as if I've started frothing at the mouth.

'Come on,' I say, handing over her train ticket, then nodding towards the barriers. 'It'll be *fun*.'

Angel looks at me, eyes the barriers as if they're the point of no return, then sighs loudly. 'Fine,' she says, making her way reluctantly through onto the platform, her body language suggesting she thinks having fun is the last thing we'll do.

And I can already tell that unless I can salvage the weekend, and take a significant step towards the 'thirteen dates' mark, it just might be.

I adore trains. And planes. Any form of travel, really: I love having the opportunity to look out of the window, appreciate the scenery, read, listen to music, eat an overpriced sandwich and then get off *somewhere completely different*, whereas Angel seems to see the just-over-an-hour-and-half journey as an opportunity to nap. Which is just as well, given that I think she's still mad at me for my choice of weekend destination.

Though I could be reading her wrong, of course. It's early days, and I've never dated someone so . . . unpredictable. Which is fun. And maddening. And exciting. And frustrating. And, by definition, something I shouldn't expect to be all plain sailing, I suppose. Plus, we hardly know each other – Angel's been pretty miserly in sharing details about her family, for example, and reluctant to ask me about mine, though in her defence, I suppose it's hard to find out about someone when you're hanging off a rock face, or galloping (well, plodding) on horseback through Richmond Park. Unless, of course – and it's something I try not to let bother me – that's her strategy.

Still, at least her being asleep means the ninety-three minutes of awkward silence I'd been dreading is actually ninety-three minutes of comfortable silence (though now I'm thinking I should have saved some money by taking the slower train, with the added benefit of being saved an additional eighteen minutes of awkwardness), during which time I can look out of the window and watch the Kent landscape whizz by. And while admittedly 'whizzing by' is the best thing for some bits of it, I have to stop myself from waking Angel up for the various highlights: the view of Canterbury Cathedral as we approach the city, Rochester's castle and Dickensian streets, the rusty old submarine floating in the Medway (though that's possibly more of a boys' thing), the buffet trolley arriving – though the noise that makes does make me wonder whether she is in fact pretending to be asleep. Still, by the time we pull into Margate and I nudge her awake, she seems to be in a better mood.

The train's been pretty full – there are a lot of people getting off here with us – and I take this as an encouraging sign, though as we exit the station and head towards the seafront, the huge grey tower block that's the first thing we see doesn't give the best impression. And nor do the derelict, boarded-up shops beneath it.

'Welcome to Margate,' says Angel sweetly, though it sounds like she's silently putting the word 'you're' at the front of that sentence. She nods down at the litter swirling around our feet in the brisk sea breeze. 'When you said we were coming away for a dirty weekend, I didn't think you meant it literally.'

But the beach itself is amazing – a long curve of golden sand stretched out before us, peppered with sunbathers despite the relatively early hour; a few hardy souls even braving the sea. In the distance, the harbour wall is topped by a strip of multicoloured buildings that the *Independent* has reliably informed me are a series of bars, cafés and art 'spaces' (though not in the inside-the-frame 'Hanksy' art space way, I hope) – a fact I relate excitedly to Angel – and dominated at one end by the town's new box-like art gallery.

'Interesting building,' she says, squinting at it.

'That's the Turner Contemporary.'

'Because when people see it they *turner* round and head back to the station?'

It's a terrible joke, but the fact that she's making jokes at least suggests her mood's lifted a little, so I pretend-glare at her. 'It's a gallery.'

'Right,' says Angel.

'Named after Turner.'

'Okay.'

'The artist.'

'He lived here, did he, Mister TripAdvisor?'

'Well, no. But he used to paint here.'

'He should come back,' says Angel, nodding towards the faded, peeling facade of the seafront shelter in front of us, where a number of pensioners are trying to escape from the wind.

'He'd be about two hundred and forty years old.'

'He'd fit right in, then.'

It's now I should perhaps say something. Ask Angel what's wrong. But I don't – or rather, don't dare – because I'm worried her answer might include the words 'you' and 'me'. So instead, we stroll in silence along the seafront, crossing the road by the entrance to the newly restored Dreamland funfair, walk on past the amusement arcades that bleep and buzz at us, then carry on beneath a clock tower that resembles Big Ben's younger (stunted) brother. After a few minutes, we reach our hotel, a large, smart-looking Victorian building opposite the harbour.

'Here we are!' I announce, worried that 'ta-da!' might be overdoing it a little.

'Right.' For the first time today, Angel's sounding . . . if not impressed, exactly, then not disgusted, so I pick up her wheelie bag, hold open the door and follow her into the plush-carpeted reception. As she helps herself to a piece of peppermint rock with 'MARGATE' written through it from a bowl on the table by the door, I stride up to the front desk and clear my throat.

'Can I help you?'

'Booking for Wilson?' I'm saying it like it's a question, I realise, so I pull out my phone and navigate to the booking.com app, and the receptionist – a young girl with an Eastern European accent – taps a few keys on the computer in front of her, though when I peer at the screen to try to spot my reservation, she's simply minimising Facebook. 'I've got a reference, if you need . . .'

'No,' says the girl, abruptly, scrolling down the screen. 'Twin room, sea view, one night.'

'Double.'

She consults the screen again. 'You booked through booking.com, right?'

The way she says it – inferring that I'm a cheapskate – makes my hackles rise a little. 'Yes, but I chose a double room.'

'That's more of an "if available" thing.'

'And are any available?'

The girl taps a few more keys, squints at the screen, then smiles up at me. 'Yes.'

'Great.'

'But they only have a partial sea view.'

'Ah. How partial?'

'Very.'

'Right. But I – I mean, *we*, really wanted a double room.' I glance meaningfully across at Angel, who's currently marvelling at the view of the sea through the doorway, in an attempt to infer that this is our first weekend away, and right now I need all the help I can get. 'And with a sea view. Can you double-check?'

The girl sighs, then goes through the same keyboard-tapping routine. 'Sorry,' she says, after a moment. 'No double with a sea view.'

'But . . .' I glance across at Angel again. 'Twin beds?'

'You can push the beds together?'

I sigh. It's all about making an impression, after all. And even though I suspect there's already a bit of a gap between us that won't be helped by a space between our mattresses, the sea view's why I booked it in the first place.

'I'll take it,' I say. Even though I don't seem to have a choice.

'This is *perfect*,' says Angel enthusiastically, once we've navigated the narrow flight of stairs to our room (and finally got the key card to work in the door).

I'm assuming she means the view, rather than the sleeping arrangements, though twin beds aside, the room *is* perfect – our double doors overlook the seafront, and have what's known as a Juliet balcony, which of course isn't a real balcony, just a set of waist-high railings that stop you falling out when you open the doors. As Angel dumps her bag by the wardrobe, rushes towards the doors and throws them open, I have to stop myself from chasing after her and grabbing her.

'Careful!'

'Noah, we're one floor up. Besides I'm hardly going to fall out.'

I give her a look, hoping that *we* won't. 'Even so. These Juliet balconies are dangerous. In fact, I never understood why Juliet kills herself with a dagger when she could have just as easily leant forward and—'

'I can look after myself, you know.'

'Sorry. Yes. You're right. Knock yourself out. Well, not *literally* . . .'

Angel grins at me as she walks around the room, peers inside the wardrobe, sticks her head into the en suite, then flops down on the armchair in the corner.

'Which side do you want?'

'What?'

'The bed. Where do you normally sleep? Left or right? Or are you one of those middle-hoggers? I don't remember from the other night. Although that's because we didn't do a lot of sleeping . . .'

'We can push them together . . .'

'You'll still need to pick a side.'

'Right.'

'Okay, I'll take the left, then.'

'No, I was saying "right" as in "right, I'll pick one, then" . . .'

'So you want the left side?'

'Um, no, actually. I'll take the, you know, right . . .'

'Right.'

'Right.'

'You already said that.'

'You don't mind?'

'Nope.'

'You're sure?'

'Positive.'

'Great.'

Angel hauls herself out of the armchair and jumps backwards onto the left-hand bed. 'We are talking "right" as in when you look at them, rather than "right" when you're on them?'

'Right,' I say, though I realise it's not the most helpful answer, but Angel just smiles.

'Sorry if I was a little grumpy earlier,' she says, propping herself up against the headboard. 'It's just . . . every day needs to count. You know?'

I nod, even though I don't. 'Come on,' I say, grabbing her hand, hauling her to her feet and leading her towards the door. 'Let's go and have that fun I promised you!'

'Look at that!'

I follow Angel's pointing finger towards an old-fashioned seafood stand on the harbour wall. So far, Margate's been full of trendy 'retro' stalls selling ironic kiss-me-quick hats (for somewhat un-ironic prices) and sticks of achingly sweet rock with the town's name (and type 2 diabetes) running all the way through them, and men in vintage ice cream vans selling 99s who gave me the answer 'one hundred and ninety-eight' when I asked for two of them, so I suppose I shouldn't be surprised at the Victorian-style sign for jellied eels swinging gently in the breeze.

'Have you ever had jellied eels?'

Angel shudders. 'That would be *no*.'

'Well, now's your chance,' I say. 'That's what weekends like this are all about. New experiences.'

'*Jellied eels?*'

'Yup.' I'm almost dragging her over towards the stand now. 'And they've got winkles.'

'Which they can keep as well.'

'Chicken!'

'Now, if they had *that* . . .'

I march confidently up to the window and rap lightly on the counter, and a bored-looking woman engrossed in something on her mobile phone looks up, a little startled, as if I'm her first customer all day. Judging by the huge, untouched tubs of assorted seafood in front of her, I wouldn't be surprised if I am.

'A jellied eel, please,' I say confidently, loud enough for Angel to hear from where she's waiting a few metres away, perched precariously on top of the light-blue-painted railings overlooking the harbour.

'We don't sell them by the eel.'

'Oh. Right. Well, how do you . . . ?'

'Small or large.'

'Eel?'

'Pot.'

'How many do you get in a pot?'

'Eels? Or bits?'

'Either.'

'Dunno. Never counted.'

'Okay, then. Well, how big is a small?'

The woman sighs, as if humouring an idiot, then holds up a couple of polystyrene containers, both of which look like they'd probably contain more eels than I'd like.

'Can I try one first?'

'See that sign that says "Free Tasters"?'

I quickly scan the front of the stall. 'Er, no.'

'Well, there's your answer.'

'Oh-kay.' I look round at Angel, rub my hands together, then smile at the woman. 'In that case, I'll have a small, please.'

The woman gives me a 'last of the big spenders' look, then pulls a metal lid off a tub in front of her, picks up a ladle and scoops a gelatinous mass of something unidentifiable into the smaller of the two cups.

'So, um, what's in this?' I ask as she hands it over.

The woman looks at me flatly. 'Eels.'

'No, I meant . . . I mean, I knew it was *eels*, obviously.' I let out a small laugh, though the woman seems about as amused as Angel was when I announced my Margate plans earlier. 'How is it made? Do you put the eels in the jelly before you cook them, or is it the other way round?'

'You really want to know?'

Something about her tone suggests I really don't, but I nod anyway.

'We catch the eels. We cut them up. Then we boil them. The jelly comes out.'

'From the *eels*?'

The woman nods, as if I've just asked the stupidest of questions. 'We leave it to cool. It sets. *Et voilà!*' She makes a little flourish with her hands that, when combined with the French, seems a bit over the top given the contents of the pot. 'Now don't you be going and telling everyone our trade secrets.'

I glance back across to Angel, who's watching me intently, an amused expression on her face.

'And how do you eat them?'

'With a fork.'

'No, I mean . . .' The woman looks at me with disdain, which, when I replay the question in my head, I suppose I deserve.

'You put them in your mouth. And chew. Then swallow.'

'*Cold?*'

'Otherwise the jelly would be all runny.'

'And that would be bad because . . . ?'

'Because then you couldn't pick it up with the fork,' she says, though she's struggling not to add the word 'obviously'.

'Right.' I stare into my cup. It looks as if I've sneezed onto the thing that bursts out of John Hurt's chest in *Alien*, and if there's a more unappetising-looking foodstuff, I can't think what it might be. But I can't back out now. Especially with Angel watching. 'Thanks.'

'Four ninety-nine.'

It seems a lot for a cup of something that looks like it's been scooped out of a fishmonger's drains, and I don't want to imagine what the larger portion might cost, but I find a fiver in my wallet and hand it over, then as the woman roots around in a small metal cash box, face that always-awkward period of deciding whether or not to wait for what's only a penny in change. I of course don't want the penny, but I take it anyway, as it seems churlish to wave it away seeing as she's gone to so much effort to find it, or to tell her to 'keep the change' (which would surely be more of an insult than a tip). Then I spot one of those plastic charity tins (are they *all* called tins, even though they're not made of metal anymore?) with 'Lifeboats' written on the side, so I put it in there instead, which the woman says 'thank you' for, even though I doubt a penny's going to help pay for any new tins, let alone any lifeboats.

'You'll be needing one of these.' The woman gives me a wooden two-pronged fork. 'Unless you want to eat them with your fingers.'

'Thanks,' I say, though the more I look at the contents of the cup, the more I realise I don't want to eat them *full stop*.

'Enjoy.'

I ignore what's more than a trace of sarcasm in her voice, and – carrying my prize – stroll nonchalantly back across to where Angel is waiting, staring at a flock of screeching seagulls fighting over what looks like a discarded version of exactly what I've just bought.

'Ta-da!'

Angel peers into the cup, scrunches up her nose, then grins at me. 'Go on, then.'

I root around in the cup with my fork, trying to find the smallest of the eel chunks, eventually locating one that should go down whole, then I spear it with my fork, tentatively lift the quivering mass to my nose and sniff it. It doesn't smell so bad – not exactly appetising, but not awful, either – so I pop it in my mouth and swallow it whole.

'Yum!' I say, with as much conviction as I can muster, then I spear a larger piece and hold it out. 'Your turn.'

'What did it taste like?'

'Not much, to be honest.'

'That's because you didn't chew it.'

'I did.'

'You didn't.' Angel gently grabs my wrist, and steers the fork back towards me. 'Go on. Properly, this time.'

'Um . . .'

She flutters her eyelashes. 'For me . . .'

'Fine,' I say, then I pop the piece of eel in my mouth, hoping my gag reflex can take it.

'Now chew!' says Angel.

Reluctantly, I steer the piece of eel between my back teeth with my tongue and gently bite down. The texture's somewhere between rubber and sick, and the flavour's not a lot better – I can see why they don't do free tasters – and as I try to stop myself from heaving, Angel raises both eyebrows.

'So?'

To be honest, I'm more interested in *not* thinking about what it tastes like than trying to describe it, so 'fishy snot' is the best description I can come up with, and it's not a description that does anything for my nausea.

With a last, defiant look at Angel, I hand her the cup of jellied eels, rush towards the metal railings and spit the contents of my mouth into the sea below.

'Ew,' says Angel. 'Are you okay?'

I stare out to sea, where the water's churning as much as my stomach, and take a few deep breaths. 'Yeah. Just thought I'd better return it to where it came from.'

'Here,' says Angel, upending the contents of the cup over the railings, where it's immediately set upon by the flock of seagulls. 'Let's cut out the middle man.'

'Good idea.'

'Are you sure you're okay?'

'Yeah. I just need something to get rid of the taste in my mouth.'

'How about this?' says Angel, standing up on tiptoe and kissing me tenderly on the lips.

'That works,' I say.

'Do you need to go and lie down for a while?'

'No, I think I'll be . . .'

'Because I do,' says Angel seductively.

It takes me a few moments to cotton on to what she's suggesting. But not quite as long to pick Angel up in a fireman's lift and run back to the hotel when I do.

'So . . .'

It's Sunday morning, and – having graciously let Angel use it first – I'm in the shower, giving myself an extra scrub *down there* with what's left of the minuscule bottle of Bliss (a name that pretty much sums up the weekend, as far as I'm concerned) shower gel the hotel's provided, just in case Angel feels amorous after breakfast. Though given how she already felt amorous after yesterday's jellied eels incident and twice last night, I'm probably kidding myself that I'd be able to respond in kind.

'So, what?'

I peer around the frosted shower screen, enjoying the sight of the little jiggle-dance Angel does when pulling her jeans on. We're already packed, seeing as check-out time is eleven o'clock, and while she's seemed a little quiet this morning, I put that down to her crushing disappointment at having to leave Margate.

'I've got something I need to tell you.'

'Sounds ominous.'

'I have . . .' I hesitate as I lather up again, unsure quite how to phrase it.

'A third nipple? Skeletons in your closet? A fantasy involving a horse and a—'

'No! Nothing like that.'

'Well?'

'Feelings for you, I was about to say. I like you.'

I know I've maybe put my cards on the table a little early on in our relationship, but after a weekend like the one we've just shared, I just can't help myself. And maybe it's the noise of the shower, or the soap bubbles covering my ears, because I think I hear Angel say 'Me too', although before my heart can leap, and in fact before it even gets a chance to begin its run-up, I realise I must have misheard her, because she follows whatever it was she said with: 'Which is a shame.'

'What?' I stick my head back around the shower screen and stare confusedly at her. 'Why is it a shame?'

'Because it means we can't see each other anymore.'

And before I can stop her, she's thrown on her coat, picked up her bag and headed out through the door.

I'm out of the shower and pulling on my jeans in record speed, but by the time I get down to reception, she's long gone. And although the puzzled looks I get from the receptionist are probably more to do with the fact that I'm dripping wet, barefoot and only half dressed, rather than Angel sprinting out through the door a few moments earlier, she's not the only one who's confused.

There's a couple checking in who are staring at me, but I don't care. My heart's pounding, I feel physically sick, and my head starts spinning as I try to understand what's just happened.

I take the stairs back to the room two at a time, find the nearest pair of shoes, jam them onto my feet, snatch up my phone from the bedside table and run desperately to the station. The London train's just leaving as I get there, probably with Angel on it, and while it occurs to me to do a James Bond/Jason Bourne and make a run and a leap for it, there's a part of me that wants to let her go – simply so I'll have time to work out what on earth's gone wrong.

I collapse dejectedly onto the nearest bench and call her mobile, but Angel doesn't answer, and short of hanging around at the station for the rest of the day, I don't know what to do. There's a pain in my chest that won't go away, and I have to swallow really hard to stop the tears from coming.

I can guess what I've done: I crossed the line. Right from day one, she told me that relationships and her didn't really go together, so what did I really think would happen – Angel would respond with 'you're so lovely, I know I said what I said but you're right, and I was wrong'? And besides, if it *really* takes thirteen dates, why oh why did I play my hand after – well, coffee plus the opening plus rock climbing plus horse riding plus this weekend (which at best was three, if you include yesterday's lunch and dinner, and breakfast this morning) – a grand total of seven?

And the trouble is, even though Angel might have said she has feelings for me, I can guess exactly what they are. Disappointment, for one. Disgust, maybe. Because I've ignored what she's been saying, and perhaps misinterpreted what she *hasn't* been saying. Hurt her feelings by declaring mine – and in the process, hurt myself as well. And maybe, been stupid in convincing myself that *this* was something I could do.

I hang around for the next train to London just in case she's taken the scenic route to the station, even waiting hopefully by the barriers when the next train *from* London pulls in, just in case Angel's gone as far as Ramsgate, changed her mind and hopped across the platforms, but when there's no sign of her, I head miserably back to the hotel to collect my bag.

'Checking out?' says the girl, fortunately a different receptionist from the one who witnessed the earlier drama, and when I nod, she smiles. 'Did you have a nice time?'

'We did,' I say, somewhat confused.

Because for some reason, that seems to have been the problem.

I call her mobile again from the train home, but Angel diverts me to voicemail – and, after the tenth or so attempt, switches her phone off (either that, or my repeated ringing has run her battery flat). But even after I'm probably entering restraining-order territory, I still haven't thought things through enough to be able to leave an appropriate message, so I don't.

Nor does she answer her front door, though to be fair, there aren't any lights on when I go round that evening, and even though it's blowing a gale and raining, I still hang around on her steps for a good hour longer than I'd originally planned, on the off chance I'll catch her.

I even call Nick at Angel's work the following morning, under the pretence of something about his forthcoming show, and when I ask him oh-so-casually to put me through to Angel, he sounds a little surprised and tells me she's phoned in sick. And though I tell him to ask Angel to call me, my phone doesn't ring the once, though that's possibly because I've run *my* battery down with all my attempts to get in touch with her – but even when I realise my stupid mistake, scramble around for my charger and desperately switch it back on, there's still no message. And when Marlon ever-so-helpfully points out to me when I eventually show my miserable face in the gallery that, sometimes, no message *is* a message, it's all I can do not to throw my phone at him.

'You obviously scared her off,' he says.

'How is "I have feelings for you" scary?'

Marlon looks at me as if I've just broken his favourite mug. 'Maybe she wasn't ready for that. Thirteen dates, remember? And you're at, what, six?'

'Seven,' I say, though 'sixes and sevens' is perhaps a more accurate description of where I'm actually at. 'But I shouldn't have to *persuade* her to fall in love with me. If she doesn't feel it, she obviously doesn't . . .'

'She obviously feels *something*.'

'How do you work that out?'

'Because of the way she reacted.'

'I'm sorry, Marlon. This is just . . .' I slump forward and put my head in my hands. 'How could I have got it so wrong?'

'You might not have got it wrong. You might just have played your cards too early.'

'And that's it? Game over. Just like that.'

Marlon holds both hands up. 'Hey. You're talking to the guy who does the leaving. But if I told someone I had feelings for them – as far-fetched as that might sound – and they hightailed it out of there so quickly they'd leave Usain Bolt eating their dust, I'd be pretty sure they didn't want to see me again. You've told me that on paper the two of you aren't compatible. And it looks like Angel's just done a pretty good job of confirming that.'

I lean back in my chair and stare hopelessly up at the ceiling. 'I just don't get it. She seems to want to be with me. But it just feels like there's something stopping her.'

'As long as that something isn't . . .'

'Isn't what?'

'You.' Marlon pats me on the shoulder sympathetically. 'I'm sorry, Noah.'

'Me too,' I say, then I sit bolt upright, nearly falling off my chair in the process. '*Me too!*'

'I heard you the first time.'

'No – that's what she said.'

'What?'

'*Me too*. After I told her I had feelings for her.'

'And *then* she did a runner? You're sure?'

'I'd assumed I'd misheard her. Because she did a runner. But yes. Now I think about it. Definitely. "Me too", she said.'

'And we're *back* in the game!' announces Marlon. He's holding his hand up, and though I think he wants to ask a question, it's actually for a high five.

'So what should I do?' I say, half-heartedly clapping my hand against his, then trying not to wince at my stinging palm.

'Get her back,' he says, as if things are as simple as that.

But in the end, of course, things turn out to be a *lot* more complicated.

13.

The next few days are some of the worst of my life. Getting out of bed, getting dressed and going to work take the greatest of efforts, as does resisting the temptation to change my regular running route to go past Angel's flat (or even stake-out her street 24/7 from the comfort of my car), and while Marlon tells me I should give her a bit of space – in truth, I'd give her the whole universe if it would help get her back.

On the Thursday morning I send her a text, just saying I'd love to talk when she's ready, and when she doesn't respond straight away, I spend the rest of the day analysing what I've written for flaws. That evening, when my mum and dad phone because they're worried that they haven't heard from me, I end up mumbling something about being busy and put the phone down on them. And by the Friday, I've decided if I ever meet the person who coined the phrase 'better to have loved and lost, than never to have loved at all', I'm going to punch them squarely in the face.

After almost a week of no communication whatsoever from Angel – which, to paraphrase Marlon, is about as clear a message as I can imagine – Saturday morning finds me back at the hospital. Mary's having her cast removed – and even though my mumbled reply of 'I should be so lucky' to her 'If you're sure you've got nothing better to do?' when I insist on going with her is hardly the most gracious of responses, it's all I can muster up the energy to say. Though as we're sat in the waiting room, hoping the screen will display Mary's number before we both lose the will to live, it turns out that 'lucky' is *exactly* what I am.

'Isn't that your young lady?'

'Pardon?'

Mary leans towards me, raises her purple-plastered arm and points towards the far end of the corridor. 'There. Walking towards us.'

I peer along Mary's cast, like you might a gun sight (albeit a purple one), and nearly fall off my chair: Heading in our direction, glued to her phone, is Angel. But instead of leaping out of my seat and going over to talk to her, my first instinct is to pick up the discarded magazine from the chair next to me and hide behind it.

'Aren't you going to talk to her?' says Mary, peering at me over the top of what I now realise is this month's *Mother & Baby*.

'Um . . . no.'

'Why not?'

'Because she made it perfectly clear to me she's not interested.'

'Whatever makes you think that?'

'Apart from the fact that she cold-heartedly abandoned me at the hotel, and has maintained a frosty silence ever since?'

'She doesn't look that happy.'

'That makes two of us. Besides, I wouldn't know what to say.'

'"Sorry" might be a good start?'

'Pardon?'

'That always seems to me to be the traditional thing to say after a falling-out. And that's what the two of you have had, isn't it? A falling-out?'

'You could say that.'

Mary sighs. 'So just go over there and apologise.'

'What for?'

'Whatever it was you did.'

I open my mouth to start to explain, but I'm not sure Mary will understand, though thinking about it, maybe I do owe Angel an apology. At least it would be a conversation-opener. But just to march across and say sorry . . .

'I'm not sure she'll want to hear it.'

'She's not that heartless, Noah, surely?'

'I don't know about that.' As Angel pauses by the door to type something into her phone, then heads quickly outside, I sigh. 'Too late now, anyway.'

'Not if you get a move on, it isn't. And all those runs you've been going on must be good for *something* . . .'

'But I'm here with you.'

It's a lame excuse, and I know it. And so does Mary, bless her. 'You go and talk to her. I'll be fine.'

'But . . .'

'Honestly. My appointment's not until . . .' She peers up at the clock on the wall. 'Half an hour ago. So I'm sure I'll still be here when you get back.'

I frown at her, but Mary's stern 'Noah!' reassures me, so I get up from my seat and head towards the exit, wondering what on earth to say. Though I'm on the back foot almost immediately, as Angel, still staring at her phone, suddenly walks back through the door and crashes straight into me. And in the end, it's me who apologises for this as well.

'Sorry!'

Startled, Angel looks up from her phone and beams at me, before she remembers we're not speaking. Then she suddenly looks concerned, and it seems as if we *are* speaking, as she tenderly puts a hand on my arm and says, 'Noah! What are you doing here? Are you okay?'

'What? Oh, yes. What are *you* doing here?'

'Just . . . a check-up.'

'You weren't answering your phone. I was worried.'

'I know.' Angel stares down at the floor. 'I didn't know what to say.'

'Why did you leave like that? Things were going so well. Weren't they?'

'That was the problem.'

'Huh? All I said was that I had feelings for you. It wasn't like I got down on one knee or anything. And you can't think that was out of the blue? I mean, we've been having a great time, and some really fun dates, and then there's the' – I lower my voice – 'physical side, where I think we really connect, you know? And then, the moment I say something emotional . . .' I stop talking, because I'm actually feeling pretty emotional myself, and besides, the more I talk, the less chance Angel has to actually say anything.

She looks at me for a moment, as if waiting to be sure I've finished, then she sits down in the nearest chair, grabs my hand and pulls me down onto the seat next to her. 'There's something wrong with me,' she says quietly.

'What?'

'Medically.'

I stare at her for a second or two, then say 'What?' again, and Angel takes my other hand, as if she's about to give me some bad news. And while it turns out that it *is* bad news for me (from a purely selfish point of view), it's *really* bad news for her.

'I've got something called . . . well, the actual technical name wouldn't really help you. But in layman's terms, I'm suffering from congenital heart disease. Well, not suffering, exactly. I've got it. But it's not like I can't get out of bed in the morning or anything like that.'

'Ri-ight,' I say, in that elongated way that means 'go on', not knowing how else to respond, and Angel takes a deep breath, then exhales slowly, as if she's had to explain this a thousand times.

'So . . . my heart . . . it has a fault.'

'A fault?'

'Think of it like a crack in a dam wall. Or a tyre with a thin bit that could go *pop* at any minute.' Angel puts her index finger into her mouth, then pulls it out against the inside of her cheek, making a popping noise like I used to as a kid, and although it strikes me as very childish, it's also more than a little scary. 'Not that it would actually make that noise.'

'But how does it – I mean, *what* does it . . . ?'

'Well, it means that any moment, if I'm really unlucky, my heart could just . . . stop.'

'Stop? As in . . .' I pause, mid-question. It's pretty self-explanatory, really. '*Stop* stop?'

Angel nods. ''Fraid so.'

'But that's . . .' I shake my head in disbelief. 'How long have you . . . ?'

Angel shrugs. 'I was born like this, so I've been living with it for as long as I can remember. And I mean *living*, Noah. When I first found out, of course I was a bit pissed off, but then I thought, what can I do about it? I mean, you play the hand you're dealt, don't you? The worst thing would be not to live my life, or to keep myself wrapped in cotton wool just in case. Which is what my parents wanted to do with me.'

'Past tense? You've never mentioned them.'

'Oh no, we get on fine, most of the time. They live here in Richmond. It's just . . .' Angel takes a deep breath. 'Every time I see them, it's only a matter of time before my mum gets that look on her face, or my dad says something, and it drives me *mad*.'

'What look?'

'The one you're doing right now.'

'I'm not doing any look.'

'Yes, you are. People can't help it.'

'Help what?'

'Feeling sorry for me. Wondering whether I'm about to drop dead. Staring at me to check I'm still breathing, just because I haven't spoken for a couple of minutes. Thinking there's something they should be doing to minimise my excitement levels, *just in case* . . .' She sighs. 'And that's exactly why I don't tell people. And can't commit to anything, long-term. And it's why I hardly date. And I certainly don't tell anyone who I *do* date.'

'But . . . that's not fair.'

'Not fair?' Angel snorts indignantly. 'What's not fair is being born with a condition that makes you feel like you're walking on a tightrope for your whole life. But that's what's happened to me, so I can either stand still, do nothing and try desperately not to fall off, or I can keep moving forward, knowing I might lose my balance, but at least I've gone somewhere.' She sits back as a small child who's been circling the waiting room on a scooter comes barrelling past us, closely followed by his exasperated mum. 'The only thing I can control is who else this affects. By not letting anyone get too close.'

'Oh,' I say, followed by a much longer 'Ohhh!'

'So Margate—'

'I get it,' I say, realising my second 'oh' wasn't quite as self-explanatory as I'd thought. 'Is there not a—'

'Cure?' Angel shakes her head. 'Not really, no. I manage the symptoms with drugs for the most part, but the only real cure, if you can call it that, is a heart transplant.' She makes the 'scary' face. 'In the meantime, as long as I come in here for my monthly check-ups, and make sure I don't overexert myself . . .' She looks at me, as if trying to decipher my expression, then obviously decides I need things simplified. 'Think of it like driving a car around that you know has a fault. You don't take it straight in and replace the engine, not when you suspect it might have a good many more miles left in it if you drive carefully. So you keep going, and then, if it breaks down, that's when you take it into the garage.'

'Assuming you get it there in time.'

Angel nods. 'There is that, yes.'

'But . . . we went rock climbing! And horse riding!'

'We did.' She squeezes my hand, then lets it go, and it's only now I remember she's been holding it the whole time. 'And it was *fun*. Exactly the kind of thing I don't want to miss out on. And admit it – you wouldn't have suggested either of those things if you knew.'

I lean back in my chair and stare up at the ceiling. 'Wow.'

'So there you have it.'

Out of the corner of my eye, I can see Angel looking at me as if she's expecting a response, but to be honest, I'm a little shell-shocked, and, 'It's a lot to take in,' is the best I can do.

'Take your time. I've had a lot longer than you to get used to this, and there are days I still don't believe it.'

'Wow. That's . . .' My head's spinning, so I puff air out of my cheeks, wishing the world would slow down a little. An announcement like this *is* something you need a while to process – but as I've just found out, time is the one thing Angel might not have. Besides, as announcements go, this one's pretty momentous: the woman I'm in love with – and I realised this is still the case within approximately half a second of seeing her – has just admitted that we may not possibly have a future, though that's because *she* might not have a future. And while everything about Angel suddenly makes sense, everything about the two of us – my desire to get married, start a family, plan for a life together – suddenly doesn't. Or at least, it wouldn't, if I wasn't absolutely crazy about her.

I can't think of the right thing to do, the right thing to say, so I stand up, pace anxiously around in front of her for the best part of ten seconds, then sit back down again. 'I'm so sorry . . .'

'I don't want your sympathy,' snaps Angel.

'Sorry.'

'And you've got nothing to apologise for.' Her expression softens. 'I just want – no, *need* you to understand.'

'Understand?'

'Why I'm like this.'

I smile to myself. I've a feeling understanding Angel is always going to be a work in progress. 'When you didn't answer my calls, I thought . . .'

'What would I have said?'

'What you've just told me would have been a start.' I shake my head. 'I thought you were . . .'

'Dead?'

'Ignoring me. Though, of course, now I know that was a possibility too.'

'Perhaps . . . Well, maybe it was wrong of me.'

'Which bit?'

'All of it. To behave like I did. To leave you in Margate. To not tell you in the first place. And I'm sorry.' Angel holds a hand out for me to shake. 'Friends?'

I blanch at the word, and stand up again. 'I don't want to be just your friend, Angel. That's the problem.' Though a bigger problem might be where else we can go from here.

She stares at me for a moment, then nods towards the vending machine in the corner. 'Can I at least buy you a coffee to apologise?'

'I can't. I'm with someone.'

Angel raises both eyebrows. 'Well, *you* didn't waste any time.'

'Not like *that*.' I point to where Mary is doing a bad job of not watching us. 'That's Mary. My landlady. She broke her arm. I'm just keeping her company while she gets the cast removed.'

As if reinforcing her part in our little play, Mary raises her bad arm, points at the bright purple cast and makes a sad face.

'Oh,' says Angel, then she glares at me. 'Noah!'

'What?'

'Every time I try to convince myself you're not right for me, you go and show me a side of you that . . .' She gives a little shudder and a grimace, as if someone's dropped an ice cube down the back of her shirt.

'Right,' I say, not quite sure whether what she's just said helps my overall cause or not. 'But if that's the case, then surely you owe it to yourself to spend more time with me? Just to see how it goes. *Where* it goes.'

'Noah, I can't promise—'

'I'm not asking you to promise anything. Especially now.'

Angel meets my gaze for the longest time, as if we're in a 'blink first' competition, and then, to my delight, she 'blinks' spectacularly. 'Well, how about dinner? This evening. On me. So I can apologise properly for not telling you. And so we can talk – properly. About this. About us.'

At the hint there might still be an 'us', I almost want to do a somersault in delight. And while the pre-Angel, boring, sensible, plan-for-the-future me wouldn't have dreamed of getting involved with someone who a) tries to convince themselves I'm not right for them and b) apparently might not even make it to dinner this evening, trouble is, I *am* involved, and I already know if Angel offered to punch me in the face to apologise, I'd still say yes. So 'Yes' is what I say. Followed by: 'But I want dessert.'

Angel leans across and kisses me in a way that makes me suspect that dessert might not be the only thing I'll be getting. Which, in turn, is something else I need to think about.

'Hold on,' I say. 'You could drop dead *at any moment?*'

'Well, I'd get a bit of notice.'

'How much notice?'

'Somewhere between none and . . .' She grins sheepishly. 'Well, I'm not sure, really.'

'Right. So is, you know, *it* . . . safe?'

'Is what safe?' says Angel innocently, though her expression suggests she knows exactly what I'm talking about.

'You know.' I lower my voice and lean in, in case scooter kid comes back, though when I check on his whereabouts, he's in the corner, flailing around in full tantrum-mode, like he's doing some weird interpretive dance. 'S-E-X.'

Angel nods. 'Weren't you listening earlier? It's *excitement* that could kill me . . .'

She fixes me with a blank stare for a second or two, then bursts out laughing as if she's just made the best joke in the history of comedy, and while I suppose it is quite amusing, and Angel has one of those infectious laughs (a few people sitting near us – including Exasperated Scooter Mum – start to snigger too, despite having no idea what Angel's just said), all I can do is smile weakly back.

Because the truth is, right now, I don't find any of this the slightest bit funny.

I don't say much on the drive home, partly due to the fact that Mary's insisted on having the roof down and the subsequent wind noise makes conversation almost impossible, but mainly because – for the second time today – I don't know what to say. On the one hand, it's great news that Angel is prepared to talk – but on the other, there's nothing great about her news at all. And while I'm really pleased she was able to tell me, I'm also really wishing there wasn't anything *to* tell in the first place.

'Are you all right?' says Mary, as we make our way up the garden path.

'I should be asking you that.'

She holds her hand up to show me her cast-free wrist, though I'm shocked to see just how thin her arm's become. 'All good. Though they've advised I give up the arm-wrestling for a while. Or at least, use my other hand.'

She reaches for the front door, wincing a little as she tries to turn her key in the lock, so I lean across and open it for her. 'Does it hurt?' I ask, steadying her as she makes her way inside, but Mary waves my hand away.

'Don't worry about me. How did *you* get on?'

'Well . . .' I follow her through to the kitchen. 'I'm not sure, really. I mean, she apologised and everything . . .'

'*She* said sorry to *you*?'

I nod, in a can't-quite-believe-it-myself kind of way. 'And we're going out for dinner tonight, but . . .'

'But?'

I pick the kettle up to gauge how full it is, then click it on. 'She's got this . . . thing . . .'

'Thing?'

'. . . wrong with her. With her heart, to be more specific.'

'So it's *not* made of ice, then?'

'Okay, okay. There's a possibility I overreacted a bit there.' I smile at her. 'No. Some medical problem she was born with.'

'Hence the reason she's always at the hospital.'

'I guess.'

'Is it serious? And curable?'

I find a couple of mugs in the cupboard and set them down on the kitchen table. 'Serious, yes, in that she might drop dead at any minute. Curable – not so much.'

'I'm sorry to hear that, Noah. But I suppose you should look on the bright side.'

'There's a bright side?'

'That she cares enough about you to tell you something like that. I'm sure it's not something she goes around broadcasting to everybody. Imagine how hard it must be to tell anyone, especially someone you care about, knowing that it might scare them off.'

'I know, I know.' I give her a look. 'You're not as decrepit as you think you are, you know.'

'Thank goodness!' Mary chuckles. 'And what will you do if she tells you she wants to give things another try?'

I think for a moment, grateful that having to locate the end of the little plastic pull-strip in order to open a new packet of PG Tips affords me a bit more time. 'Under normal circumstances, I'd bite her hand off.'

'Not literally, I hope?' Mary chuckles again. 'But it seems to me these aren't normal circumstances.'

'Ever since I first met Angel, there's been nothing normal about my circumstances at all.'

Mary absent-mindedly fingers her wedding ring. 'It wouldn't worry you that your girlfriend might – how did you put it – drop dead at any minute?'

'Of course it worries me!' I say, not really wanting to get into the complexities, let alone the likelihood, of Angel being my girlfriend. 'Everything about it worries me. But walking away worries me even more.' I deposit a couple of teabags in the mugs, wait until the kettle clicks off, then drown them in boiling water. 'But I guess there's two things to consider. I've only known her for a little more than a month, so it's probably worth getting to know each other better to see what's what. And if we do decide we want to be together, there's a chance she'll be okay. That nothing will happen. She might live for ages.'

'She told you that, did she?'

I take my phone out of my pocket and tap the screen. 'I checked with Doctor Google while you were in having your cast removed.'

'Oh, I do like those Indian doctors.'

'No, I mean . . . Never mind.'

'But there's a chance she won't?'

'I suppose. But better to have loved and lost, and all that? And let's face it – who really knows what's around the corner?'

'But, Noah, you're someone who always *likes* to think you do.'

'Yes, well, maybe this is different. Maybe I should be different.' I give our drinks a stir, fish the teabags out and splash some milk in each one. 'In any case, we're just dating. No strings. Nothing serious, and all that.'

Mary regards me suspiciously. 'So what you're saying is, the only time this is ever going to be a problem is if you decide you really like her.'

'Exactly,' I say, as I carefully hand Mary her tea. Though I don't want to tell her that ship's already sailed.

14.

I'm waiting for Angel outside a restaurant called 'Lentil/Burger' on George Street. It's the latest 'hot' chain to eat at, apparently – hence the queue snaking around the corner – catering for both meat-lovers *and* vegetarians (though not at the same table, I'd imagine), and new enough to count as one of Angel's 'new experiences'. I hope.

I made sure I got here early enough to nab a place that should get me to the door in time for her arrival: Angel's literal interpretation of her 'life's too short to wait in line' philosophy is still fresh in my mind, and the last thing I want is for her to try to push in front of all these people (even though, after this afternoon's revelation, I can see why she might want to. And that she'd probably have grounds).

By the time she arrives – at seven, as arranged – I've timed it almost perfectly, as I've reached the 'two minutes' wait' section, and surely even Angel can't complain about two minutes. She's dressed in a pair of dungarees, a fake-fur jacket and yet another pair of Converse, a combination that on anyone else might look like they were wearing it for a dare, but on Angel it just *works* – though I suspect she could turn up wearing a Lidl shopping bag with holes cut for her legs and I'd probably feel the same. As I wave her over, she casts her eye over the hundred or so people lined up behind me.

'Have you been waiting long?'

I know she means in the queue, rather than for her, given how she's precisely on time, so I just shrug as casually as I can, though that's partly to disguise the fact that I don't know whether to give her a kiss on the cheek, or a hug, or say something like 'you're worth waiting for', or just stand there like an idiot – but in the end, standing there like an idiot seems like the easiest option.

'"Lentil/Burger"?' she says, switching her quizzical look from the restaurant's sign to me.

'That's right. Though, strictly speaking, I suppose it should be called "Lentil *or* Burger", as apparently those are the only two items on the menu.' I take a step forwards as the couple in front of the couple in front of me is shown inside, and Angel obediently slots in beside me. 'Although apparently the lentil part of the name refers to a lentil burger, so maybe "Burger/Burger" would be more appropriate. Though it's perhaps more of a patty, so . . .' I'm conscious that I'm rambling a bit, but that's because I'm nervous, so I stop talking and grin at her, then a thought occurs to me. 'I take it you like, you know . . . ?'

'Burgers and lentils? Have I not mentioned I only eat fish?'

I laugh, then stop abruptly when it occurs to me that Angel might not be joking, and I'm playing a film of all our previous encounters in fast-forward in my head, trying to find evidence of her eating something and whether it was drownable, when she breaks into a grin. 'I'm kidding, Noah.'

'I knew that,' I tell her, unconvincingly.

The couple in front of us are being escorted in, which puts us at the front of the queue, where a black-clad woman clutching an iPad as if she thinks we're about to try to steal it is giving us the once-over.

'How many?' she asks, once she's evidently decided we're fit to spend our money in her restaurant.

'Two please,' I say, backing up the statement by holding two fingers up, just in case she doesn't understand me, even though it's probably obvious to her that we're not part of the Spanish family having an animated discussion behind us.

The woman peers at her iPad, then at us again, then says, 'Fine,' as if she's just lost an argument and she's not happy about it. 'Jemima will take you to Prudence, who'll take you to your server.'

As Angel says 'Thank you so much' so cheerfully it's verging on the sarcastic, the woman nods at a similarly dressed girl (I'm guessing the aforementioned Jemima) standing just behind her, who smiles humourlessly, then silently escorts us inside, where we're met by another member of staff (Prudence, I think, and I wonder if we'll be meeting the two of them again and whether remembering their names would be a good idea), who – like we're a couple of batons in a strange relay race, takes us over to where a waiter (sorry, *server*) is, well, *waiting* in the main room.

As Angel rolls her eyes at me, he leads us through the cavernous, industrial-themed dining room, past groups of people eating, perhaps not surprisingly, burgers. And while it's too dark to tell whether they're meat or lentil burgers, not being able to see much turns out not to be a bad thing, particularly given the prices on the – admittedly very short – menu waiting for us on our table.

I peer closely at it, wondering if I should switch on the torch app on my phone so we can read it, then notice the waiter's still, well, *waiting*.

'Can we help you?' says Angel.

The waiter glances down at the iPad mini he's just produced, magician-like, from his apron. 'Your order?'

'We've only just sat down,' she says. 'We haven't had a chance to look at the menu.'

The waiter points towards the window, where the restaurant's name is stencilled in huge gold letters on the outside. 'You do know what we're called?'

Angel narrows her eyes at the glass. 'Regrub Litnel?'

'What?' The waiter frowns at her, then realises she's reading it from the back. 'Yes, very good.'

'Lentil/Burger?' I suggest quickly, which gets a whispered 'teacher's pet' from Angel.

The waiter nods. 'Well, they're your choices. A meat burger, or a lentil one. And most people tend to make their mind up while they're waiting out there' – he points towards the window again – 'rather than in here.' *Wasting my time*, he's obviously implying.

'Right.' Angel consults her menu again, and makes a play of studying it closely. 'What to have, what to have . . .'

'Perhaps sir would like to order first?' says the waiter through nearly gritted teeth, when Angel still doesn't make a choice.

'Oh, I'll have what she's having.'

The waiter sighs, loudly enough for the people on the next-door table to look up from their meals. 'Would you like me to come back later?'

'That's what we wanted in the first place!' says Angel, though just as he turns to go, Angel slaps her menu down on the table. 'Burger,' she announces. Then, when he's tapped it into his screen: 'No, lentils.'

The waiter raises one eyebrow. 'You mean you want to change your burger for the lentils, or did you mean you wanted a burger without any lentils?'

'Do the burgers come with lentils?'

'No.'

'Then yes,' says Angel.

'Which?'

'The second one.'

'Right. And you, sir?' he says, although this time the 'sir' doesn't sound like a term of respect.

'Like I said.' I shut my menu, and hand it to him. 'I'll have what she's having.'

'Right.' The waiter jabs angrily at his screen, then, keeping his eyes fixed on it: 'Anything on the side?'

Angel raises one eyebrow. 'Oh, you mean like chips and stuff?'

'Yes,' he says flatly. 'Like chips. And stuff.'

'What would you recommend?'

'Chips.'

'Then that's what we'll have.'

The waiter looks at us both, as if he fears he's going to regret asking his next question. 'And to drink?'

'Drink?' Angel picks her menu up again, and consults the list on the back as if it's a GCSE paper and she hasn't revised. 'Um . . .' She turns to face me. 'Well, keeping with the theme of the restaurant, it seems to be beer or water.'

'I'll have a beer,' I say quickly, already convinced the waiter's going to be doing something to our burgers that might possibly poison us.

'Me too,' says Angel sweetly.

'Two beers,' says the waiter, tapping so hard on his iPad that I fear the screen might shatter, and as he walks – or rather, *stomps* – away, I sit back in my chair.

'That was cruel.'

'He started it.' She laughs. 'These places are just so . . .'

'They are a bit pretentious, I suppose.'

'I was going to say "up themselves", but your description is better.' She peers around the room. 'They make you queue for ages, expect you to feel grateful that they've let you in, and then they try to get you fed and out again as quickly as possible . . . I mean, we're the customers, right? We're paying for this.'

'The food's supposed to be good.'

'It's a burger, either made of meat or lentils, and chips. Two of the simplest things to prepare. If they can't get *them* right, as opposed to another restaurant that has to make twenty different things each night . . .'

'Hey,' I say, a little annoyed at her attitude, especially since I've queued for forty-five minutes outside, simply so she won't have to. 'How about we just try to enjoy ourselves, rather than pick apart—'

'Sorry. I'm just a bit . . .'

'Me too. So . . .'

'So?'

'So . . . We need to talk?'

Angel raises both eyebrows. 'Are you asking me, or telling me?'

'Both.'

'You look like you want to go first.'

'Okay. So . . .' I clear my throat, and look around for the waiter, suddenly desperate for my beer. 'How are you?'

She tuts loudly. 'Don't start.'

'Start what?'

She folds her arms, resting her elbows on the table as if she's about to interrogate me. 'Don't start treating me like I'm about to die. Because I'm not. I might. But then, we *all* might. Even you. You could fall under a bus.' She nods out through the window, where the number 65 is rumbling past. 'Tonight, if you're not careful.'

'Is that a threat?'

'Depends if you let me share your pudding or not. But I'm serious, Noah. The moment you start thinking of me like an invalid, it's over. It's one of the reasons I work where I work – when everyone's got problems, like they've lost a limb or are suffering from PTSD – things that make yours look pretty ordinary – you don't feel so . . .' Angel frowns. 'Whatever the opposite of special is.'

'Fine, fine.' I hold both hands up. 'But *you* can't think that every time I say "how are you?", or ask how you're feeling, I'm referring to, you know . . .' I point at her left breast, which is unfortunate, because the waiter's chosen that exact moment to deliver our beer, so I quickly change the movement into a finger-waving, as if I'm making an important point. Which, actually, I am. 'Especially if we *are* going to be . . .'

'Be?'

I hesitate, running through quite a long list of words in my mind before I think I've found the right one. 'Together.'

'Is that what you want?'

'If by "that" you mean "us as girlfriend and boyfriend", then yes.'

'Noah, I'm really not sure I'm girlfriend material.'

'I am. Sure, I mean. Not, you know . . .'

Angel picks up her glass, takes a sip of beer, then regards me from behind it for almost as long as she spent choosing from the menu. 'Okay,' she says eventually, but just as I'm mentally sliding towards the corner flag on my knees in delight, she follows it up with: 'But if this is going to work, we'd better set out some conditions.'

'Conditions?'

She nods. 'One. If we are going to be together, then you can't tell anyone.'

'Anyone?'

'Nope.'

'That seems a little weird.'

'Them's the rules!'

'What's wrong with people knowing you're my girlfriend?'

'No, dummy. I meant that you can't tell anyone that I've got something wrong with me.'

'Ah.'

Angel narrows her eyes at me. 'What does "ah" mean?'

'I may have . . .' I take a quick gulp of beer. 'Mentioned something. In passing. To Mary. The other day. I'd tell her to forget it, but she's worried she's got Alzheimer's, so she probably already has.'

Angel thinks for a moment, and for a second, I fear that I've already blown it, though it turns out she's deciding whether to laugh at my joke or not. 'Okay. But no one else. *Or* else.'

'Got it.'

'Two. No talk of transplants, and in fact, no mentioning my condition in relation to anything we do. *Ever.* Which includes you not trying to stop me if ever you feel we're going to be doing something' – she makes air quotes with her fingers – 'dangerous.'

'Okay.'

'Three. Don't expect any big declarations of love, anything slushy or sentimental. That's just not my style.'

'How will I know how you . . . ?'

'Feel about you?' Angel grins. 'Don't worry. You'll know. Remember, "action is character".'

'Right.'

'Four.'

'There's more?'

'Four,' repeats Angel. 'Whatever my parents say to you, you ignore. Especially if it's about the t-word.'

I nod, partly because I don't want to be tricked into breaking condition two so soon. Besides, from what I can tell, Angel hardly sees her mum and dad anyway, so that shouldn't be too hard.

'Five. If I *ever* catch you staring at me when I'm asleep just to check I'm still alive, I will kill you. Slowly, and painfully.'

I laugh.

'Don't doubt that I could. And would.'

'Okay, okay.'

'Six.'

'Don't tell me we're not allowed to do it?'

'*Six*, Noah. Not "sex".'

'Sorry.'

'Six,' she repeats. 'Never, ever tell me I can't do something.'

'What? Why?'

'Just don't.'

'But . . . that's silly.'

'Is it? All my life, people have been telling me I can't do stuff because of this.' She places both hands over her left breast, as if proclaiming her love for something. 'And all my life, I've hated it. So whenever someone says "you can't" to me, I just have to prove them wrong.'

'Okay.'

'And finally, seven – and this is the most important one – no making plans, no talking about the future, no regrets that we might not be able to do something, or go somewhere . . .' Angel reaches across the table and takes my hand. 'You're a planner. I'm not. For you, belt and braces is a way of life, for me it's a fashion statement. And trying to plan for the future with me is like trying to keep your eyes open when you sneeze: impossible, and potentially dangerous. Let's just live for the day, Noah. After all, no one knows how much time they've got left. So it's silly to try to look forward to a future you might not have.'

'Fine,' I say, after a moment, though I already suspect that'll be the hardest one to stick to (well, that and the 'checking she's breathing' one, though I can, of course, just say I'm staring at her chest for, ahem, *other* reasons). And while I've never dated anyone with 'conditions' before – or anyone with Angel's condition – I've never dated anyone like Angel before either, so I suppose I shouldn't be surprised. Besides, as I'm continually being reminded, these thirteen dates are as much for me to be sure about Angel as they are for Angel to fall in love with me. 'Did you want to write these things down, so I can sign them?'

'Would you mind?'

I pat my trouser pockets, then the front of my shirt (just as I remember my shirt doesn't have pockets), as if I'm looking for a piece of paper and a pen. 'Sorry. Nothing to write with. Unless you want me to ask the waiter if we can borrow his iPad . . .'

'Probably best not. Well, you know what they say about verbal contracts, and all that.'

'That they're not worth the paper they're written on?'

Angel frowns as she tries to digest that, then she gives a little shake of the head. 'So . . . do we have a deal?'

There's a smile playing on her lips, and she's holding her hand out, so I look at it for just long enough, as if I'm weighing up buying a second-hand car, then I shake it.

'Deal,' I say.

Angel gets up from her chair, and for a moment, I fear that she's leaving, but instead, she marches round the table, throws her arms around my neck and kisses me for a long, long time – so long, in fact, that when we eventually break breathlessly away from each other, our burgers have materialised on the table.

And just like that, and in what feels like the most formal of arrangements, Angel and I are back on.

15.

Angel and I aren't the only ones making arrangements. It's the following day, and as promised, I'm taking Mary to look at some homes, and even though that means I might have to look at some myself – just like with Angel, my needs aren't the most important ones.

I've already phoned a couple of stairlift companies, spoken to the council about whether there's any home help available and even called some private-care organisations, but I've decided to keep all that from Mary until today's over. Hopefully she'll see the homes, then see sense, but like I've learned from my dealings with Angel, sometimes people need a bit of persuading.

We've arranged to leave at ten, but like most old people, Mary's waiting with her coat on by the door a good half an hour before then, and though she says not to rush, I can tell she's eager to get today over with.

'Ready?'

'As I'll ever be.' Mary stands in the hallway and stares into space for a moment, then: 'Keys,' she says, collecting her bunch from the table by the front door.

'Are you doing that a lot?'

'Doing what?'

'Forgetting things.'

Mary frowns at me, before hurrying back into the kitchen to retrieve her handbag. 'I forget,' she says, then she raises both eyebrows and digs a bony elbow into my ribs. 'Come on.'

'So, where's first?'

'I thought we'd start with this place.' Mary reaches into her bag and passes me a leaflet.

'Parkview Rest Home?'

'It seems like the best.'

I flick through the leaflet, wondering whether Mary should have added '. . . of a bad bunch' to the end of that sentence. 'You like the look of it, do you?'

'On paper, yes,' says Mary, as I lock the front door behind us and help her to the car. 'It's hard to tell until you're actually there, I suppose. But "Parkview" sounds nice. I've always loved the park.'

'Well, let's just hope it lives up to expectations.'

'Yes,' says Mary, patting the back of my hand. 'Let's.'

Though given the way her voice seems to be wavering, I suspect her expectations really aren't that high at all.

We're on the back foot the moment we arrive at Parkview, because it's not actually anywhere *near* the park, and even peering out of one of the poky-looking rooms at the top of the slightly rundown two-storey building with a pair of powerful binoculars, I doubt you'd have a view of anywhere that has so much as a distant view of the park. The only park it does overlook is the next-door car park, a huge concrete monstrosity that blocks out the light, and while it occurs to me to mention that perhaps that's where the home got its name from, given the look of disappointment on Mary's face, that wouldn't be such a great idea.

She gives the doorbell a firm push, and after a moment, a stern-looking middle-aged woman dressed in a blue nurse's uniform cracks it open.

'Can I help you?' she says suspiciously.

'Mary Davidson. I phoned yesterday.'

The woman – Candice, according to the badge pinned to her chest – stares blankly back at her in an 'a lot of people phoned yesterday' kind of way.

'And?'

'I understand you have a vacancy?'

'To live here?'

'I think I'm a little old to apply for a job, dear.'

Candice narrows her eyes, as if trying to decide whether Mary might be trouble. 'Right. Well, you'd better come in, then.'

As she opens the door fully, Mary gives me a look, then I follow her inside, squeezing past Candice in the narrow hallway. She bolts the door carefully behind us, and Mary nudges me.

'Do you think that's to keep people out, or in?'

'I think we're about to find out.'

We're ushered into the reception area, a tiny space with a water cooler bubbling away like someone with a bad case of dysentery in the corner, and a small table at the far end, where Candice motions us towards what looks like a visitor's book.

'Did you want us to sign in?' I ask. 'Or is this for leaving a review?'

'Sign in,' says Candice flatly. 'We take security very seriously.'

I scan down the list of names. Given that the last few entries include a 'Pearl E. Gates' and a 'Jerry Atrics', it appears that's not a sentiment shared by the home's visitors.

'Okay. Do you have a pen?'

Candice pats her pockets, then sighs, as if the absence of a biro is the latest in a long line of things that have plagued her day. 'Don't worry,' she says, as if doing us the biggest favour possible. 'So, Mary, was it?'

'It still is, dear. I'm not dead yet.'

'When did you want to move in?'

Mary makes a face. 'I don't know if I do, yet. I thought I'd come for a tour first.'

'A tour?'

'Of the facilities. And perhaps meet some of the – what do you call them . . . ?'

'Residents,' says Candice, in the same way a prison governor might say 'inmates'.

'If that's all right?' says Mary sweetly.

'Fine,' says Candice, in a tone that suggests it isn't really, and as if we're already proving to be difficult customers.

Without another word, she marches us down the musty-carpeted corridor, Mary and I struggling to match her pace, then leads us into a large, overly central-heated lounge, where several residents are sitting, either watching the ridiculously loud TV in one corner, or sleeping, or staring listlessly at plates of unidentifiable foodstuffs that look like they've been sitting there for a day or so, and which make the other weekend's jellied eels seem almost appetising.

'This is the TV room,' Candice says, or rather shouts, trying to make herself heard above the volume of today's episode of *Bargain Hunt* and causing a couple of elderly women in the corner to start awake. 'The garden's out there,' she adds, pointing to a set of French doors at the far end of the room that lead to a tiny paved courtyard that'd surely challenge the definition of 'garden', where a couple of old men are hunched by the fence, smoking like chimneys and looking like they're plotting an escape.

Our arrival seems to have created a flutter of interest. In one corner, a lady halfway through completing a jigsaw puzzle waves me over, and though I think it's simply to see how well she's doing on her picture of what are either kittens or puppies – without the heads, it's difficult to tell – her whispered 'Take me with you', and the iron grip with which she latches on to my wrist make me step quickly away from the table.

'So,' says Mary, her voice not quite as strong as when we first arrived. 'Can we see the room?'

'It's still . . . occupied,' Candice says awkwardly.

'But I thought you said there wasn't anyone living in it?'

'There isn't,' says Candice flatly. 'Not living, at least.'

'Ah.'

Candice peers along the corridor, where an elderly man on a wheeled walking frame is inching his way towards us. 'But you can see a similar room,' she says. 'If you're quick.'

With another glance at the man, she leads us briskly to the other end of the corridor, and through a door with 'GEORGE' written in large letters on the small whiteboard fixed at eye height – and at once, the temporary nature of the sign makes me want to head for the exit.

Candice shows us inside, then stands guard in the doorway as we look around, which given the size of the room, doesn't take long at all. It's the size of what I imagine a prison cell to be – an impression not helped by the bars on the window, which she assures us are 'to stop anyone breaking in', rather than the other way round.

Mary casts an eye over the room, taking in the mismatched furniture, the small, uncomfortable-looking bed, the window with its train-track view, then jumps as the express to Waterloo rattles past. Though while that might make some people turn straight round and leave, she doesn't appear that concerned.

'Well, it's hardly The Ritz, but . . .'

'The trains don't bother you?'

'Pardon?'

'I asked if the trains bothered you,' I say, a little louder, and Mary shakes her head. 'One of the advantages of getting older. Hearing loss.

Saves you from a lot. Besides, it'll be handy being near the station. Especially if I ever need to get out,' she adds, in a whisper.

'For the day, you mean?'

Mary chuckles. 'That too.'

'So? What do you think?' asks Candice.

'It's . . .' Mary pauses as another train hurtles past, causing the few ornaments on top of the tiny television set in the corner to violently shake. 'And how much is this room?'

'It's not this room exactly,' says Candice, though by the lack of progress George has made down the corridor, she seems to be implying that it might soon be. 'Yours would have a better view.'

'Of?'

'The station.'

'But this has a view of the station.'

'Yes, but your view would be better.'

'Well, how much would *that* room be?'

'Six hundred and fifty pounds.'

Mary looks at me with a 'that's not so bad' expression on her face. 'And how much is that per week?'

'That *is* per week.'

As Mary reaches for the back of the nearest chair for support, I have to ask again. 'Six hundred and fifty pounds *a week?*'

Candice nods. 'That includes three meals a day.'

'Really,' says Mary, wrinkling her nose at the smells coming from the kitchen.

'Well?' says Candice, though it's not clear if it's a 'shall we go?' *well* or a 'do you want it?' *well*, because by the looks of Mary, the answer is very different for both of those things.

'Can I think about it?' she says, and Candice sighs.

'Fine. But don't take too long.'

'I don't *have* too long, dear.'

Suddenly, there's a commotion in the corridor, and as we make our way back out of the room, we almost get caught in a slow-motion stampede of elderly residents.

'Did the fire alarm go off?' asks Mary.

Candice shakes her head. 'It's music time. For an hour every morning, the TV goes off and we provide some live entertainment. Today, it's Dan the Music Man.'

'I thought the TV room was that way?' Mary points back towards the source of the commotion, where a couple of elderly men have tried to exit at the same time and have got their walking frames in a tangle, trapping the rest of the desperate residents behind them.

'It is,' says an old man, the wheel of the oxygen tank he's pulling behind him almost running over my toes. 'Run for your *life*.'

Candice hurries over and frees the Zimmer-jam in the doorway, and we walk back through the TV room, where an over-smiley man dressed in a wide-brimmed hat, head-to-toe matching denim and cowboy boots is randomly strumming a guitar as if he's just realised it makes a sound. There are two residents still in there, though they look like that's only because they can't get up under their own steam, and as Dan starts to sing, one of them reaches up and tugs out her hearing aid.

'Did you want to stay for the music?' asks Candice.

Mary cups a hand to her ear. 'What was that?'

'Did you want to stay?'

'Thank you, no. We should go,' says Mary. 'Noah? Shall we?'

I nod, take Mary's arm and lead her back along the corridor. Unlike her, I don't need to be asked twice.

My suggestion to 'make a day of it' turns out to be a very short day indeed, as the other two places we see are no better, and we're in and out of them both within an hour.

It's a miserable drive back home: I've got the roof down so Mary can feel the wind in her hair – 'While I've still got hair' – but even a detour through the (real, as opposed to car) park, where I regale her with my horse-riding date story, can't seem to get a smile out of her. As we sit in the traffic inching its way through Richmond town centre, she's unusually quiet. Until . . .

'I suppose that's that, then,' she says.

'Maybe they're not so awful. Or perhaps we just caught them at a bad time. You know, like sometimes you go to a hotel, and it's change-over day, so you don't quite see it working properly . . .'

'Maybe that *was* it working properly. Did you think of that?'

'I was just trying to cheer you up.'

Mary sighs. 'What's the name of that place that old people go to?'

'Eastbourne?'

'I was thinking of Dignitas.'

'Don't talk like that!'

'I'm sorry, Noah. It's just . . .' She looks back over her shoulder, then lowers her voice, as if worried someone from one of the care homes might be following us. 'That's hardly how I saw myself seeing out my days. When Stan died . . . well, it was all very sudden. He didn't go through any of this old-age malarkey. And he'd have hated to end up somewhere like *that* . . .' Her voice trails off, and she lets out a theatrical shudder. 'But if that's what they're like . . .'

'It's a shame there isn't some kind of TripAdvisor for rest homes.'

'*RIP*Advisor, they'd have to call it.'

I laugh. 'I'll do some research when we get home.'

'Please, don't mention the word "home".'

'Sorry.'

'Thank you for coming with me, though. When you don't have children, at my age . . . Well, it's nice to have someone else who looks out for you.'

'Why *didn't* you have kids?'

'Stan and I . . . Well, because we had each other, and all the time he was alive, that was enough. But now I can see we kind of painted ourselves into a corner . . .' She turns and smiles at me. 'If this Angel really is the one for you, even if you've just got the slightest feeling she might be . . . don't waste any time. Because you never know how much you've got left. And it's all about quality, rather than quantity.'

I do a funny little salute, then wonder why I have. 'Duly noted.'

We move the ten or so yards forward that the traffic lights allow, then Mary lets out an incredulous laugh. 'And they wanted six hundred and fifty pounds *a week*!'

'I know!'

We're stopped outside a travel agent's, and Mary points at a poster in the window. 'Look at that! I could go on a round-the-world cruise for the same amount of money.'

'Well, that's what you should do,' I tell her. And I'm only half joking.

16.

A ngel and I switch back into dating mode as if what went down in
Margate is a distant memory – and I decide it's probably best to
keep it that way, mainly by making sure I don't bring it up again –
and although I'm careful not to do anything that might overexert her,
I'm even more careful to make sure she doesn't think that's what I'm
doing.

So for date nine, the following Sunday, we hire a boat on the
Thames, and I insist on having the first 'go' at rowing, and then when
Angel insists it's her turn, I tell her we need to go back in because
I'm feeling seasick, even though (and she doesn't think to point this
out until afterwards) if you don't include the slight ripple caused by a
particularly speedy duck swimming past, there aren't any waves on the
Thames.

Afterwards, we go to the cinema, for the matinée performance of
the new Bond film, and while Angel points out this doesn't exactly
qualify under her 'new experiences' heading, as she's been to the cinema
before, I counter with the fact that she hasn't seen this particular film,
even though in the end neither of us see much of it due to a) the woman
with huge hair who sits right in front of us despite the cinema being
half empty, and b) the fact that we spend most of the film snogging.

On the way home, and in a rare public display of affection, Angel
and I are walking along George Street arm in arm – then, suddenly,

she lets go of me so quickly it's as if she's just realised she's mistakenly grabbed someone else.

'Hide!'

'What?'

'Quickly!'

'Are we playing some kind of game?'

'No. My mum!'

'What about her?'

'She's over there. Across the street.' I spin around, then rub the spot on my shoulder where Angel's just punched me. 'Don't look!'

'Why not?'

'She might see us,' says Angel, in a tone that sounds like the word 'dummy' belongs at the end of the sentence.

'And the problem with that is?'

'Because then she'll want to *talk* to us.'

'At the risk of repeating my earlier question . . .'

Angel glares at me, then grimaces as a loud 'Yoo-hoo!' comes from the middle-aged woman waving at us from the opposite pavement. 'You'll see,' she says, waving reluctantly back, a look I've never seen before on her face.

'Should we cross and . . . ?'

'No, let her come to us. A speeding car might do us a favour and—'

'Angel!'

As her mother crosses the road, I can't help notice that Angel has taken a step or two towards the kerb, and is now standing a respectable 'friend zone' distance away from me. Still, it's early days for the two of us, so I perhaps shouldn't be too concerned about this, especially if I want 'early days' to turn into not-so-early ones, so instead I fix my best meet-the-parents smile on my face, and brace myself for whatever the next few minutes might bring.

'Hi, Mum.'

'Darling,' says Angel's mum, though her eyes are on me as she speaks, and I think about making a joke – maybe saying 'sweetheart' back – but it's way too early for that kind of thing. She's a short, attractive woman, with slightly less-defined elements of Angel's features in hers, as if she's a prototype model of her daughter – to be honest, it's a bit spooky to see her, though if I were being selfish, I'd be looking forward to growing old with Angel if that's how she was going to turn out. Although I probably won't be growing old with Angel, I remember, and the thought stops me in my tracks. 'What are you doing here?' Angel says, in a 'this town ain't big enough for the both of us' tone, but the inference seems to be lost on her mum, who just nods towards the House of Fraser department store on the opposite side of the street.

'I need a new dress.'

'*Another* new dress?'

'For the golf club summer party.'

'Since when do you play golf?'

'I don't, silly. But your father . . .' Angel's mum rolls her eyes.

'He's not with you?'

'He's off at the rugby. Some corporate jolly. Besides, his surprise that none of – and I quote – the "walk-in wardrobe-full" I bought last year were good enough, means that I haven't told him what I'm doing. So here I am.'

As Angel's mum smiles in a 'what can you do?' kind of way, Angel makes a face. 'Well, don't let us keep you.'

'Angela, darling! You sound like you're trying to get rid of me. Not interrupting anything, am I?'

'No,' says Angel flatly.

The three of us stand there for an uncomfortable moment or two, until I can't stand it any longer.

'Hi,' I say, a little miffed Angel hasn't introduced me yet. 'I'm Noah.'

'Noah?' She peers closely at me, and narrows her eyes. 'And you are . . . ?'

I frown. Has her mum got Alzheimer's, too? 'Noah. I just told you . . .'

'No, I mean, and you *are* . . . ?' Her eyes are darting expectantly between me and her daughter, as if waiting for a secondary piece of information to be delivered, something that will clue her in to my role in this awkward little threesome, but Angel's remaining tight-lipped.

'Well, I suppose I'm Angel's—'

'Mum!' interrupts Angel, flashing me a look.

'What, darling?'

'Enough with the interrogation!'

'I'm simply trying to take an interest in your life, dear. And seeing as how you never tell your father and me anything . . .'

As Angel glares at her, and evidently deciding her daughter's not going to give anything else away, Angel's mum turns her attention back to me. 'So, Noah, how *do* you know Angel?' she asks, trying another tack. And I'm beginning to suspect if she could shine a light in my face, she'd do that too.

'Well . . .' For some reason, I'm stumped. *I met her in a coffee shop* is actually how I know her, though the question's not really meant to be taken literally, is it? It's an enquiry as to my status, my definition, my place within Angel's life. And I'd tell her, if something about Angel's expression wasn't giving me the strongest hint that I shouldn't.

'Um . . .'

'Okay,' says Angel suddenly. 'Caught red-handed. He's my fiancé.'

'What?' Angel's mum stares at me, then at Angel, then at me again, then she repeats herself. 'What?'

'Noah's my fiancé. We're getting married! We're just off to choose a ring.'

'But . . .' Angel's mum looks like she's about to burst, especially when she notices that, as luck would have it, we're standing outside a jeweller's.

'We were going to elope, but just my luck we had to bump into you . . .' Angel meets her mum's stunned gaze, then all of a sudden, she bursts out laughing. 'Your *face*!'

'What?' Angel's mum is staring at me in astonishment, though to be honest, I'm probably mirroring her expression.

'We're not really getting married. Noah's just a *friend*.'

'Just . . . a friend?' says Angel's mum, just before I can.

'That's right.'

'That wasn't very funny, darling.'

'Yes it was. And perhaps it'll teach you to stop grilling every man you see me with.'

'I was hardly grilling him.' Angel's mum smiles sweetly at me. 'I was hardly grilling you. Was I, Noah?'

I realise I'm on dangerous ground here. Side with her mother, and I might earn some brownie points for the next time we meet – although given how uncomfortable this little encounter has been, I'd bet money on there not being a next time. Plus I'm also busy wondering just how many 'every man you see me with' means.

'Trust me, Mum,' says Angel, before I can say anything. 'If I ever do decide to get married, you'll be the first to know.'

'Well, third,' I say, adding, 'you know, after Angel and whoever it is she's marrying,' when her mum looks murderously at me.

'Not that it's ever going to happen.'

Though I'm sure she tries to cover it up, her mum's flinch is easy to spot. 'Angela, don't talk like that!'

'I mean, weddings are just . . .' Angel shudders melodramatically. 'And placing so much emphasis on finding someone good enough for your children to end up spending every other weekend with? I tell you – marriage, settling down, having kids is so . . . over.'

'It worked out just fine for your father and me,' says Angel's mum. 'Mostly.'

Angel opens her mouth as if to say something, then evidently thinks better of it. 'Right,' she says, after another moment. 'Well, we have to go. Noah?'

'Um, yeah. Sorry. Nice to meet you, Mrs—'

But I don't get any further, as Angel's grabbed me by the bicep, put her other hand firmly on my lower back and is escorting me away along the pavement like I've been arrested.

I'm a little stunned about what's just happened: firstly, by not being introduced as her boyfriend, and secondly, by Angel's relationship with her mum. It's a side of her I've not seen before, and it's too early to tell whether it's a defence mechanism or they just genuinely don't get on. Given how her mum seemed genuinely hurt, I'd guess it's probably the former. Though a defence mechanism against what, exactly, I'm not quite sure.

But there's something else, too, and it's something a lot more worrying, and it's probably *my* fault: I've agreed to all of Angel's 'conditions' *just like that*, simply because I was desperate to get her back. But now, seeing what she feels about weddings, hearing her say out loud that marriage, settling down, having kids is 'over'. . . Given those three things are what I want, I'm not sure that's something I can *get* over.

So maybe, just maybe, I've been a little too hasty.

'What was all that about?' I say, once we're out of earshot and Angel's stopped peering over her shoulder to check we're not being followed.

'Noah, I—'

'Are you ashamed of me?'

'What? No! Not at all.' She smooths the indentations her fingers have made in my sleeve, then lets out an embarrassed laugh. 'I'm ashamed of *her*.'

'Why? She seemed perfectly nice . . .'

Angel makes a face. 'Oh, that's how it starts . . .'

'How what starts?'

'My mum, and her "when are you going to settle down, get married, make me a grandmother . . ." Actually, she's not so keen on the last thing, given how she's been telling everyone for years that she's ten years younger than she actually is. But you can imagine.'

'I'm sure she just wants you to be happy.'

'I'm sorry, Noah, but you've met her once. I've had this for almost thirty years, so I think I'm a little bit more qualified than you to . . .' She stops talking, aware she's getting a little loud, and her expression softens. 'Okay, okay. It's just . . . I've had boyfriends in the past . . .'

'Really? I thought I was your first!' I say in an attempt to lighten the mood, although it doesn't seem to work.

'And because of my *thing*, my mum's always been keen to get me married off to them sooner rather than later, just in case later is, well, *too* late – as if marriage is something I mustn't miss out on, even if it's just for five minutes, metaphorically speaking, or even to the wrong person.'

'Thanks very much!'

Angel gives me a look. 'All I'm trying to say is, she seems to be forcing me to hurry down this route as if it's something *she* needs to get done, rather than something that I might want.'

'Maybe. Though think about it from her point of view.'

'This better be good . . .'

'Well . . .' I hesitate as I run through the next few sentences in my mind, wary that they could cause offence. 'Perhaps when you have an ill child, you're always worried something's going to happen to them. Then, the longer they survive, perhaps you start to believe that actually, it's all going to work out, so you can't help projecting—'

Angel lets out the briefest of snorts, but it's enough to stop me mid-sentence. 'More likely, she's desperate to pass the responsibility of looking after me – and yes, I'm saying that ironically – onto someone else. Or maybe she's looking for a replacement – you know, once I've gone, the poor old widowed son-in-law, so she can play the bereaved mother, and the two of them can—'

'That's a bit harsh.'

'Sorry.' Angel sighs. 'I guess I'm just fed up of people trying to tell me what's best for me, that I should follow the path they've taken. Especially when, from where I'm sitting, what they have doesn't seem that great at all.'

'Is your dad the same?'

'Yes and no. On the one hand, of course he wants to get me married off. But on the other . . . Well, no one's ever going to be good enough for his little girl.'

'He should be happy you have a boyfriend. Someone to look aft – I mean, *out for* you.'

'I don't need looking out for, Noah.'

'Sorry. I didn't mean it like that,' I lie. 'What I meant was, that you had someone . . . Well, just had someone, I suppose.'

'You'd think, wouldn't you?' Angel shakes her head. 'But he generally ends up scaring them off. Which I suppose is fine. Saves me the job of dumping them . . .' Angel grins at me in a 'just kidding' kind of way.

'I'm sure your mum and dad just want what's best for you.'

'Best for *me*?' says Angel incredulously. 'How does anyone possibly know what's best for someone else? I tell you, if I had a pound for every time my mum and dad mentioned the word "transplant" . . .'

'They're probably just scared of losing you.'

'Oh, they're scared, all right, but not in the way you'd think. My mum once told me her greatest fear was that I died having sex!'

I burst out laughing, then rein my amusement back in given Angel's expression.

'I told her that would be the best way to go, but all she could say was, "Think about the embarrassment for your father and me." And that's how it's always been. Not about poor old me and how this stupid condition of mine affects my life, but how it affects her, how it might make *them* look.'

'She just cares about you.'

'There's only one person my mum cares about, Noah, and that's herself. All I'd get when I was growing up, whenever we'd have an argument, was her telling me I should feel sorry for *her*, because "no one should have to bury their own child". Honestly, she says it like she'd be the one expected to dig the grave!'

'Wow.'

'Yes, wow.' Angel shakes her head. 'It's almost as if from the moment I was born, I've ruined all the plans they had for me. Can you really blame me for not wanting to be around that? Not wanting to expose *you* to it, too?'

'Well, when you put it like that . . .'

'So yes, I'm sorry for not introducing you as my boyfriend, but knowing what they're like . . . Sometimes, it's easier to deal with your own negativity if you cut all external sources of it out of your life, and especially when the worst offenders are your own mum and dad.' Angel pauses for a moment, and briefly, I catch a glimpse of something vulnerable before her guard goes up again. 'Every time she looks at me, I can see the disappointment in her eyes, as if it's my fault I emerged kicking and screaming from her womb with this . . . defect. As if it's something I did on purpose. As if they resent me for not being perfect.'

Angel's gritting her teeth, though whether it's because she's so angry or is trying to stop herself from crying, I can't tell. And although I want to tell her she *is* perfect – that I think so, at least – I can't. Because if you're being precise – technically, at least, she isn't.

'Hey,' I say, putting an arm around her. 'Don't worry. I completely understand.'

But the weird thing is, given the prospect of losing her, the possibility that we won't ever get married and the probability that things won't work out the way I want them to, I completely understand her parents too.

17.

I t's the following Friday, and after a fabulous (tenth) date at the theatre, we're back at Angel's flat on the sofa (and each other, if you get what I mean), and even though, apart from at the cinema, we haven't been 'physical' since Margate, Angel's showing no sign of pulling away. (I only tell you this because of what happens next – don't think this is suddenly going to morph into some sort of *Fifty Shades*-type story.) But as I reach up and place a hand on her breast (my right hand, and her left breast, in case you liked *Fifty Shades* and you're trying to picture it), all of a sudden, there's a loud beeping sound, and I sit up in surprise.

'Have you got some sort of bra alarm?'

'What?'

'Hey – that's not a bad idea. A *bralarm* . . . Imagine how many we could sell to fathers of teenage girls! We'll be *rich* . . .'

It's a pretty good joke, I think, and I wait for Angel to jump on me – aren't women supposed to find a sense of humour attractive? – but instead, she wriggles out from my grasp, reaches into her handbag (which, I now realise, is where the beeping's coming from), pulls out a beeper and smiles at it.

'Anything urgent?'

Angel presses the 'Cancel' button and drops the beeper back into her bag. 'Nope,' she says, reassuming her earlier position.

'You're sure?'

'Yes!' she says, a little exasperatedly, then for added emphasis she grabs my hand and puts it back where it was, only for the beeper to go off again.

Angel keeps kissing me, and I do my best to ignore the sound, but eventually I have to pull away. 'You're sure you don't need to get that?'

'Yes, Noah, I'm sure.'

'Not someone desperate for a score?' I say, jokingly implying she's a drug dealer, though 'desperate for a score' kind of applies to me too right now. Especially when the beeping doesn't stop, and Angel jumps up from the sofa.

'Oh, for f— Hang on.'

She reaches back into her handbag, retrieves the beeper, hits 'mute' again, then walks across to the bed and hides it under her pillow. I'm a little miffed, as I'd hoped that was where we were going next, but just as I decide the sofa will do, the beeper sounds a third time. Frustrated, I haul myself back upright.

'Who *is* that?'

'Harefield,' says Angel matter-of-factly.

'The *hospital*?'

'No, my great uncle Harefield. He's paging me from the Dickens novel he lives in.'

It takes me a moment to realise Angel's being sarcastic. 'Um, if it's the hospital, then shouldn't you answer it?'

'Not really.'

'But it could be . . .' My eyes dart towards where my hand was, albeit briefly, a few moments ago.

'Yeah.'

I'm sitting bolt upright now, any thoughts of resuming our encounter long gone. 'So why . . . ?' I fold my arms, unfold them, then fold them again. 'I don't . . .'

Angel reaches over and takes my hand, though she doesn't put it back on her breast this time. 'It's complicated.'

'I've already got that part.'

She thinks for a moment, as if trying to formulate her thoughts into something I'll understand. 'Noah . . . I'm not really ill.'

'You've . . . been *lying*?'

She shakes her head vigorously. 'No. I mean, I do have this heart thing, so *technically* I'm ill. But normally, if people have something wrong with them, there would be lots of things they couldn't do. For me, it's different. There are lots of things I *shouldn't* do. And that's not really the same.'

'I don't follow.'

She jabs a thumb towards where she's hidden the beeper. 'That thing. A transplant. It's for people who are *really* ill.'

'*You're* really ill.'

'No, I mean bedridden. Can't walk more than a few steps unaided, or need to be on oxygen the whole time. Or who, whenever they wake up in the morning, punch the air in delight because they've made it through the night. Trust me, I've seen them: little kids who struggle with every breath. And what's worse is, I've seen their parents. A mum and dad who spend every waking hour wondering whether today will be their son's last. A family who dread every phone call, because it might be the one telling them their daughter's just died . . .' She swallows hard. 'Imagine watching your child gasping for life, unable to do the simplest things, things that other kids, other people, take for granted. How can I possibly put my needs in front of theirs?'

'Why do you have the beeper, then? If you're not intending to—'

'Every time a heart comes up, they look at the list and contact the most suitable candidate. If you're lucky, you're at the top of the list. And I got lucky. Twice. When I was younger. You've never seen a faster driver than my dad with me in the back of his Jag, taking me to hospital!' Angel smiles, though there's not a lot of humour in it. 'But for various reasons, it didn't work out, and they, *I*, couldn't go through with it. Which cost two other people the chance of . . .' She swallows even

177

harder. 'So now, if it ever goes off, I ignore it. Which means someone else, someone more deserving, gets . . .'

'. . . the heart that's meant for you.'

'Maybe I've *got* the heart that's meant for me, Noah. And this is my way to make amends for what happened.'

'That was hardly your fault.'

'Maybe not. But if you had the power to give someone's daughter, someone's loved one, a second chance by simply doing *nothing*, then why wouldn't you?'

'*You're* someone's daughter,' I remind her. 'Someone's . . .' I clear my throat awkwardly, '. . . *loved one.*'

'As my parents have reminded me a million times.' Angel sighs. 'But I'm not really, am I? At least, not in the same way as most of the people I'm talking about. Besides, how can I possibly deserve my place in the queue in front of them, when to all intents and purposes, I'm fine?'

'But you're not, are you?'

Angel shrugs. 'I'm more fine than most of them.'

I stare at her for a moment, wondering how on earth I can counter this – though it's not till later I realise that perhaps it's not my place to – and the best I can come up with is: 'But don't you want to *live*?'

'I *am* living, Noah. A lot better than most of those people. A lot better than most people *full stop*. And I'm more worried about being able to live with myself if my decision to take the heart that's been offered to me means someone else loses their baby, or their father, or mother.'

I open my mouth to argue, then shut it again. Angel's made a pretty strong case – but then again, she's had a while to think about it. And what would I say – that *I* want her to go through with it, that she should do it for *me*? Because that would be pretty selfish.

And besides, I realise as I sneak off early the following morning, careful not to disturb a sleeping Angel when I do, we're not at thirteen dates yet. So what would be the point?

18.

This morning's three laps around Old Deer Park turn out to be a nightmare. I haven't slept much given how much my head's been spinning after the events of yesterday evening, plus it's rained overnight, so the grassy course is more bog-jog than parkrun, and my trainers collect so much mud just walking to the start that it's going to be like running in heavy boots – and while I've been on a couple of training runs during the week, both times I've failed miserably to reach anything near the distance I'm expected to do today without stopping for a breather. At least there's no sign of Rocket (which means no sign of his obnoxious owner), so reluctantly I take my place at the start line, wait for the whistle, then set off round the course.

At first, it's not too bad – obviously my training's been paying off, as I manage the first lap without too many problems (or at least, without wanting to throw up, which I suppose is progress). Then, as I approach the finish line for the first of what'll (hopefully) be three times, I see Angel, stopwatch in hand.

This is a *disaster*. I'd assumed she'd still be at home in bed, but I obviously haven't reckoned with her impressive ability to be up and out of the house in five minutes. And while she knows I went that one time to try to find her, I haven't told her I'm *still* doing parkruns, mainly because I wanted to get (quite) a bit better before I did the big reveal

– plus I'm still a little embarrassed that whereas my main motivation used to be trying to track her down, at the moment, it's Rocket's owner I've got in my sights. But now, not only is she going to see me as an absolute sweaty mess, but she's also going to realise just how pathetically slowly I run.

I realise I'm faced with a dilemma – pace myself (i.e. walk most of it) just so I don't look an absolute wreck when I finish, or run as fast as I can, and run the risk of actually dying before I even get to her.

The fact that Angel's doing the timing at the end and not out on the course marshalling means I could, of course, miss out a lap. Pretend I'm faster than I am. But that would be cheating. And there's no way I'd dare cheat on Angel.

I could just stop. Sneak away. I'm still wearing my cap, hoodie and sunglasses (though now it's so Rocket's owner won't recognise me on the street and beat me up), but despite my outfit, Angel might have seen me turn up, and how is me buggering off without finishing the course going to look? Given my disguise, she might not recognise me, though I'm going to have to pass her three times, so that's unlikely. Alternatively, I could slow right down and try to lose myself in the crowd of pensioners/pregnant women/kids bringing up the rear, or I could keep going at what's my top speed, wave confidently at her each time I pass, and hope I don't look too bad by the time I've reached the finish – although given how my training's been going, and that I can't see a dog nearby I can borrow, that's probably unlikely. And while I could run by in the manner of those footballers who pull their shirts over their heads after they've scored a goal, given the fact that I'm hardly sporting a six-pack, that's more likely to be an own goal.

As I near the turn, I can see her calling out encouragingly to each runner that passes, enthusiastically clapping her hands, and I realise dejectedly there's no way she's not going to notice me. Then I have a brainwave: I can sprint up to her, then feign an injury. That way, I'll look impressive *and* won't have to run another two laps. I can 'pull' a hamstring, hobble to a stop right by where Angel is marshalling and . . . But that's dishonest, too. Plus, injuring myself on what's supposed to be a 'fun' run isn't the most impressive of feats.

Fortunately, the other runners aren't too spread out, so I can position myself in the middle of a group, and as I pass Angel for the first time, I seem to have got away with it. I decide to keep going – after all, if I'm here running, and Rocket and his owner aren't, then that's one extra training session I'm getting in that they're not. And one – albeit muddy – step I'm taking closer to beating them.

The next lap passes without incident – cardiac, or otherwise. I seem to have fallen into a bit of a rhythm, managing to keep up with the group, and while I'm hardly enjoying myself, by some miracle I'm hardly at death's door either. I still haven't decided when (or whether) I'm going to do the big reveal, and even though as I pass Angel a second time, she narrows her eyes then shakes her head, I'm starting to believe I might be able to get away with it.

But then something occurs to me, and it's something quite important. If Angel and I are going to have any sort of future together, however long that might last for, we need to be honest with each other. And from my point of view, that honesty needs to start – well, if not right now, in about another ten minutes.

The third lap's a slog, not helped by the ton-and-a-half of mud I've picked up on the way round, but eventually, I make it. And when I reach the finish, my panted 'Hi' nearly gives Angel a heart attack.

'*Noah?*'

I nod, fearing any more speech needs to wait for a moment or two.

'I didn't expect to see you here.'

'At the finish?' I say, doubled over, my hands on my knees.

'At another parkrun. I thought you were only doing them in an attempt to find me?'

'I was,' I pant. 'But I don't like to . . .' I take a couple of breaths. 'Give up on things.'

Angel gives me a look. 'So I'm beginning to understand. Are you still mad at me?'

'Mad?'

'I thought, when you left early this morning . . .'

'What would I be . . . ?' I hold up a hand, indicating Angel needs to wait before I can complete the sentence. 'Mad with you. About.'

'Yesterday.'

'Hey, your body, your decision.'

'But you wish it wasn't?'

'That's not for me to say, is it?'

Angel stares at me for a moment, then waves another of the volunteers over, hands her the stopwatch and leads me to one side. 'Noah . . .' She pauses, as if she wants to get what she's about to say just right. 'I know you'd probably like things to be different. Trust me, there's been many a day when I've felt that way too. But you soon realise that it is what it is, and that there's no point wishing for anything else, because you're only going to be wasting your time. And I don't have time to waste. Do you understand?'

It's heartfelt, and honest, and there's not really a lot I can say – not just because I'm still struggling to talk – so I say, 'Sure,' even though I'm *not* sure, and even though I'm not sure I can change her mind – or that I should even try. Because Angel's the one who has to have, if you excuse the phrase, a change of heart.

But something else occurs to me, and it gives me a glimmer of hope: Angel feels what she feels about her situation because that's how she's seen *her* world. She doesn't think she has a future, because everyone's told her she shouldn't expect to be having one. Doesn't believe in marriage, because she doesn't have the best of examples in her mum and dad. Won't go through with the transplant, because she doesn't feel she's worthy enough. Someone needs to tell her that she's wrong. Or at least, show her she might be mistaken. And that someone is going to be me.

And it doesn't have to happen today. Or tomorrow. After all, relationships are a marathon, not a sprint. Though unless something changes, I can't even be sure Angel and I are middle-distance.

19.

I don't see Angel later. Not for any negative reasons – she has a 'thing' with 'the girls from work' on the Saturday night, so I spend the evening keeping Mary company over a pizza and a *Downton Abbey* box set binge-watch. Not that it's much of a binge: Mary falls asleep after half an episode, so I turn it off and watch *Die Hard* instead, which leads to a bit of confusion when Mary wakes up again and expresses her surprise at how tall the Abbey's become, and that Alan Rickman's joined the *Downton* cast.

And while we meet briefly a couple of times during the week, neither of them are what you could technically call a 'date', which means we're still stuck on ten, though that has been over the course of eight weeks, so I suppose I shouldn't complain. At this rate, Angel should be in love with me some time in July. Which is a result, any way you look at it.

Date eleven finally comes on the following Saturday, post parkrun, and begins with a dressed-up-to-the-nines me knocking on her door. Though when Angel lets me in, her reaction isn't quite what I was expecting.

'A *suit?*'

She's looking me up and down with more than a hint of amusement on her face, so I adjust my cuffs as nonchalantly as I can manage, trying to ignore the chafing from my shirt collar. 'Why not? I don't get a chance to dress up that often . . .'

'And a tie? Who wears ties anymore?'

'Um . . . me?'

'So we're going somewhere posh?'

I nod. 'Fairly. So no jeans . . .'

'No jeans. Right.' Angel undoes her belt, unbuttons the faded, ripped-at-the-knees 501s she's wearing and steps out of them.

'You'll – you know, have to put something on in their place.'

'Oops. Silly me!' She sticks the tip of her little finger in her mouth and adopts a coquettish pose. 'Back in a mo . . .'

As she grabs a couple of things from the wardrobe, then disappears into her bathroom to do her make-up, I sit down on her sofa to wait. I'm a little nervous, I'll admit – while the surprise 'lunch date' I'm taking her to is technically still a date, it's not really lunch. But Martin (an artist we've exhibited a couple of times) and Annie's wedding reception is phase one (not that I'm sure what phase two is yet) of Operation Change of Heart, my grand plan to open Angel's eyes to a different future. And while I'm pretty sure Angel wouldn't have agreed to come if I'd told her what it was from the outset, given her anti-marriage rant in front of her mum– perhaps foolishly, I'm convinced if I can get her there, and she has a good time, I can convince her otherwise. Besides, Martin's really nice, and a friend of mine, and Angel's not really met any of my friends (I've been too busy making sure the thirteen dates consist of pretty much just me and her in order to maximise my chances of making her fall in love with me), so this will be her opportunity to. And my opportunity to show her off in public as my girlfriend.

I tap my feet nervously as I peer around her flat. It's in the same, cluttered state it was the first time I came here, though now I know Angel a bit better, I can perhaps understand why. While I wait, I take the opportunity to have a look around. Angel's not one for photos of friends or family, so instead, the shelves are crammed with mementos and souvenirs – stuff she's picked up on her travels, as if she wants some physical record of wherever she's been. Maybe to remind her she's had a fantastic life. Or because looking backwards is all she can do.

There's a book of arty photos titled *101 Places to See Before You Die* on the table – one of those coffee-table books, probably so-called because they're so big and heavy you could stick four legs on and use them for exactly that, and I'm just flicking through it, noticing the folded-over page corners and wondering whether Angel's taking the title literally, when a loud 'ta-da!' comes from the bathroom doorway, and when I look up, I have to remind myself to breathe. She's dressed in a short, floral summer dress, her hair tied up, her legs seemingly going on forever, and she's even swapped her beloved Converse for a pair of high heels – and it's all I can do not to start drooling down my tie.

'Well?' she says, once I manage to get my jaw off the floor.

'You look . . . That dress . . .' I'm shaking my head in admiration, but Angel misreads it.

'Not appropriate?'

I exaggerate my head-shaking. 'Exactly appropriate. You look . . . amazing!'

She walks over to me, and tousles my hair. 'Aw, shucks!'

'I'm serious. I had no idea you . . .'

'Scrubbed up so well?'

I stand up and walk round her, as if checking the bodywork of a rental car. 'Well, yes.'

'Thanks. I think.'

I'm still staring when Angel taps her watch. 'So?' she says.

'So what?'

'Shall we go?'

'Go?' I frown, and then: 'Oh, right. Sure.'

'Fantastic.'

'Which is the word that exactly sums up how you look.'

Angel nudges me. 'You're not so bad yourself.'

I make a face, hoping she'll still think that when she realises where we're going.

It's a short drive to the wedding venue, or rather, the 'hotel where we're eating', as I describe it to Angel, which is a shame, partly because I'm enjoying the view of her tanned knees (the right one of which I keep 'accidentally' brushing whenever I reach for the gear knob), but also because it doesn't give me a lot of time to formulate an *actual* reason for my sleight of hand. And while I could take a detour through Richmond Park, I don't want to be late and have Angel create a scene in front of everyone. Especially the bride and groom.

As I park the MG outside the hotel, Angel stares up at the building. 'This is posh,' she says, though I don't comment, mainly because I'm preoccupied with trying to get her inside without giving the game away. The invite's in my inside jacket pocket just in case, though Martin's hardly Damien Hirst, so I'm hoping I won't have to show it to security to get in, and I've a wedding present for the happy couple in the boot, although getting that out would surely look suspicious – either that, or Angel might think it's for her, and then I'd have to explain why I think she needs another toaster. Right now, the invite and the gift are both staying where they are. I've a feeling I'm going to have enough explaining to do without either of them making an appearance.

We stroll arm in arm through the door, where a spotty teenager in a slightly-too-big jacket-and-cap combination, who looks as if he knows exactly how ridiculous he looks, greets us with a sullen 'Help you?'

'Can you tell me where the . . .' I lower my voice as Angel heads over to the front desk and helps herself to a handful of mints from the bowl. '. . . *reception* is?'

'This is the reception,' says the teenager, pointing to a sign above Angel's head that, quite helpfully, says 'RECEPTION'.

'No, the *other* reception.'

The teenager stares at me as if I'm an idiot – though, quite frankly, he might have a point – then a wave of realization crosses his face. 'Oh, you mean the wed—'

'*Other* reception. That's right.'

'It's through there,' says the teenager, pointing towards a set of doors that lead out into the garden.

'Right. Great. Thanks. Angel?' I wave her over, and as she stuffs the mints into my jacket pocket, escort her through the doors.

'We're eating outside?'

'Apparently.'

She shrugs. 'Lead on,' she says.

As we stroll out into the garden, where around a hundred dressed-up people are standing around chatting, sipping champagne and generally doing the kind of things people do at weddings, I start to doubt the wisdom of my actions. My only hope is, given that Angel is so anti-marriage, she won't have been to many weddings, meaning she might not actually recognise that this is a wedding until it's too late. Though that hope lasts around five seconds, because Angel takes one look at the assembled crowd, and her face falls.

'Oh god!'

'What?'

'Looks like we've walked in on a wedding reception!'

She's said it with the same enthusiasm as if we've walked into a UKIP convention, and I freeze, not sure how to answer, suspecting that 'Surprise!' might make her turn round and walk straight back out again. Though my non-committal 'Uh-huh' probably doesn't do me any favours.

'*This* is where we're having lunch?'

'Supposed to be.' I stare at Angel, wondering how on earth I can get out of this, willing her not to see through my little ruse. But to my amazement, she doesn't.

'Incredible. You booked, and they didn't tell you this was going on?'

'No,' I say, though I'm really answering the 'you booked' part of her question.

'Nando's it is, then,' says Angel, taking me by the arm. 'Though we might be a little overdressed.'

Reluctantly, I start to follow her, disappointed that my plan has failed at the first hurdle, but at the same time, relieved I'm not going to be found out. But as we make for the exit, a waiter with a tray of drinks appears in front of us and offers us both a glass of champagne, and before I know what I'm doing, I've helped myself to a couple.

'What are you doing?' hisses Angel.

I glance nervously around. Martin's nowhere to be seen. If I can just get to him beforehand, perhaps convince him to pretend he doesn't know me, then convince Angel it'll be fun to 'crash' his wedding, even if it's only for a while, then maybe I can get away with this without having to admit to any underhand dealings on my part. *And* show Angel my 'wilder' side.

'Hey – if a couple of complete strangers want to buy us both a glass of champagne to celebrate their special day, who are we to refuse?'

'What?'

'Don't tell me you've never crashed a wedding before?'

'Actually, no,' she says, though it's with a mix of trepidation and admiration. 'What if people ask us who we are?'

'Just tell them . . . Tell them your boyfriend works with the groom. Or the bride,' I say, quickly.

'What if the bride or groom ask us?' says Angel.

'Well . . .' Inwardly, I'm still celebrating having got away with my 'boyfriend' reference. 'Same answer. Just, you know, the other way round.'

'Noah . . .'

'We'll be fine! Just watch out for the wedding police.' I smile, then hold a glass out to her. 'Here.'

Angel hesitates for a fraction of a second, then she beams at me and takes it. 'Don't mind if I do.'

'Now, you're sure? I know you don't like weddings, so . . .'

'One drink won't hurt.' Angel chinks her glass against mine. 'Especially since you've gone to all this trouble.'

I swallow so hard I hope she can't hear it. 'What do you mean?'

Angel reaches over and adjusts my tie. 'Putting *this* on.'

I breathe a sigh of relief, and wonder how long I can maintain this pretence without either getting found out or having to make a run for it, though the more I think about it, the more I'm convinced we might get through the whole event without me having to tell Angel what's going on. It *is* a buffet, after all, so there's no chance our names will be on any kind of seating plan, which means we can eat without the real reason for us being here coming out, and probably have a dance without Angel twigging. She might just treat this as one big free party, and even if someone or something does give the game away, by that time she'll have had a few champagnes, so she's bound to see the funny side.

I hope.

'Here.' Angel hands me her glass. 'Just off to powder my nose.'

'Right. I'll, you know, wait here.'

'Or you could see if there's any food . . .' says Angel mischievously.

'Will do.' I do a mental fist-pump and give her a little salute, nearly sloshing champagne down the front of my suit, then anxiously peer around the gathering until I spot Martin in the far corner, surrounded by well-wishers. Once I'm sure Angel's out of sight, I wade through the crowd and hover next to him, preparing to put my plan into action.

'Noah!' Martin's face lights up when he sees me. 'So pleased you could come! This' – he makes a show of presenting a meringue-clad

Annie to me, grabbing her by the shoulders and moving her forward as if she's a robot he's just invented – 'is Annie. My *wife!*'

He grins awkwardly, as if still getting used to the word, and Annie gives him a look as if she is too, and it's silly, I know, but I can't help feeling a little bit jealous.

'Noah,' I say. 'Lovely to meet you! And congratulations! And . . .' I pull Martin to one side. 'I need you to do me a favour.'

Martin laughs. 'This isn't that wedding from *The Godfather*, you know, where you can just turn up and ask—'

'Just pretend you don't know me.'

'What?'

'Pretend you've never met me before. And that you haven't invited me today.'

'Whatever for?'

'Long story. But it'll be a funny one. Maybe even at *my* wedding.'

Over his shoulder, Angel's approaching, a quizzical look on her face. Martin looks at where I'm nervously staring, then back at me, and fortunately does the math, as Hanksy might say.

'Gotcha,' he says with a wink.

As Martin heads off to greet some other guests, Angel joins me, so I take a risk and snake an arm around her waist. 'Angel, darling, this is Annie. She's the bride.'

For some reason I've gone all posh, and Angel gives me a look. 'Dressed like that, darling?' she says, slipping into her role with ease. 'I'd never have guessed.' She leans in and gives Annie a hug. 'Congratulations!'

'Nice to meet you,' says Annie, looking a little puzzled.

'And you,' says Angel brightly. 'Lovely wedding.'

'Thank you. And how do you know Martin?'

Angel looks at me, the briefest expression of panic flashing across her face. 'Noah . . . He and Martin . . .' she says hesitantly.

'We've worked together,' I say, quickly, pleased that I can finally admit to something that's actually true.

'Right.' Annie's still looking a little unsure about what's going on, although she quickly decides she doesn't want to waste any more of her wedding day with someone who's quite possibly mad. 'Well, I better go and circulate, so . . .'

We stand there a little awkwardly for a moment, then Angel grabs my hand. 'Us too! Darling, there's someone you simply *need* to meet . . .'

With a final beaming smile at the already departing Annie, she leads me away, only for Martin to come bearing down on us.

'Hi,' he announces loudly. 'Martin. The groom. And you are?'

He's grinning at me, obviously taking his role a little too seriously, though to her credit, Angel's doing the same.

'Angel and Noah,' she says, standing on tiptoe and kissing him on the cheek. 'Congratulations!'

'Angel and . . . ?'

'Noah,' I say formally, adding, 'Angel . . . works with Annie,' when Angel nudges me.

'Super!' says Martin, followed by a mischievous 'At . . . ?'

'The . . . office?' suggests Angel.

'Lovely! Well, Angel, lovely to meet you. Thanks for coming. And . . .'

'Noah,' I say, again.

Martin winks at me as he shakes my hand. 'Well, I'd love to stay and chat, but . . .'

'Sure. Totally understand.' For some reason I've gone all posh again, and Angel can't hide her smirk.

'I don't know about you, darling,' she says, mimicking my accent. 'But I could murder another glass of bubbly.'

'Me too,' I say, hoping Angel won't be murdering me by the end of the day. 'Congratulations again . . . Martin, was it?'

'That's right. And you were . . . ?'

'Noah.'

'Noah,' says Martin, then he nods in Angel's direction. 'Congratulations.'

'Thanks,' I say automatically. Though it's only when he's gone that I understand what he means.

We've attacked the buffet, and got through so much champagne that the car will be staying where it is until at least tomorrow morning, and the amazing thing is that *I seem to be getting away with it.*

The other amazing thing is that Angel appears to have had a good time: she's danced even when the cheesiest of music has been on, chatted to people she's never met before, and even led me behind the marquee for an impromptu snog after one particular slow dance got a little bit steamy. While I'm not about to suddenly admit what I've done, I'd guess any further wedding invitations might be greeted with a bit more enthusiasm, which can only be a good thing.

And later, as we're walking home, my arm round her shoulders, her shoes in my other hand (dancing in heels proving a step – or steps – too far for someone who spends their days in Converse), it's hard to put my finger on it, but something's changed: as Angel leans into me, there's a closeness that I've not felt before. A sense that she's holding me a little bit tighter. Almost like she doesn't want to let go.

Though I appreciate that could just be because she's cold, especially when her teeth start to chatter. We're already halfway down the hill when she remembers she's left her cardigan in the car. So rather than go back for it, thus delaying going back to *hers*, if you know what I mean, I give her my jacket.

'Aren't you the gentleman?'

'I do my best,' I say, though as I help her into it, her sudden 'Ow!', coupled with her hand moving quickly towards her chest, makes me panic for a moment.

'Are you okay?'

'Yeah. It's just . . .' She reaches a hand inside the jacket. 'There's something sharp in your pocket . . .'

I blame the champagne, because it takes me a second or two too long to realise what it is that's digging into Angel's chest. And before I can get rid of the evidence, she's waving the embossed, incriminatory and evidently sharp-cornered piece of card in front of my face.

'What's this?'

'That's, well, it's . . .'

'A wedding invitation?'

'Er . . .'

Wordlessly, Angel glares at me, then she studies the embossed card. '"Mr and Mrs Anderson request the presence of Noah Wilson *plus one* at their daughter Annie's wedding to Martin Smith, at the Richmond Hill Hotel, on . . ."' She stops reading. 'Either we were incredibly lucky and stumbled into a wedding where another Noah Wilson decided to not show up and you've decided to keep this for a souvenir, or . . .'

'It's, um, "or".'

'You took me to a *wedding*?'

'Well, technically I took you to the reception.'

'You said we were going for lunch!'

'It *was* lunch. A long lunch, admittedly. Buffet style. With dancing. Which just happened to be at a wedding.'

'The question, which I'm sure you can anticipate, is . . .'

'Why?'

Angel nods.

'Well, so you could see that . . .'

'That what?'

'That not everyone feels the same way about weddings, about *marriage*, that you do,' I suggest. Though judging by Angel's expression, I'm not getting out of this one any time soon. 'But you enjoyed yourself?'

'Maybe.' She scowls at me. 'That doesn't change the fact that you tricked me.'

'Tricked you into coming to an event where I thought you might have a good time. And you did have a good time. So what does that make me?'

Angel's smiling now, and I'm pretty pleased with myself, I must admit. I seem to be in the clear; in fact, more than in the clear – I might actually have had a result. But just then, I spot that it's one of those smiles that you see people make in films right before they do something really bad, and I realise it's not the result I was hoping for.

'Tell me something. If you knew I felt the same way about . . . tomatoes . . . would you trick me into eating them, just to see if you could change my mind?'

'Well, maybe.'

'Even though I might be allergic?'

'Yes, but you'd have told me, wouldn't you? If someone's got an allergy, that's what they do, isn't it? And you can't be allergic to *weddings*.'

Angel snorts, though in the same way a bull does, pre-charge. 'Okay, maybe it's my fault, because I didn't tell you *why* I feel that way.'

'Come on.' I nudge her playfully. 'No one *actually* feels that way. Look at you today: the champagne, the music . . .' I do a little shimmy, then worry it's more dad dancing than *Strictly*. 'That's like someone devouring a bacon sandwich, then claiming that they're vegetarian.' I reach into my pocket and remove a handful of mints, which throws me until I realise the slice of wedding cake I've taken for Mary is in the other one. 'On top of it all, you get *cake*! How can you not like *that*?'

'It's not *that* I don't like. It's . . . it's a lot more serious than you . . .'

'Come on. A wedding's just a big party, where everyone's out to have a good time. Why would anyone not want one?'

'It's not that I don't want one!' she says, on the verge of tears. 'It's . . . They represent something that I don't have. That I'll never have.'

'If you mean love, or commitment, that's not strictly—'

'A *future!*' shouts Angel. Then she shrugs off my jacket, hands it carefully over, gives me a don't-you-dare-follow-me look and stalks off into the night.

Just like when we first met, I hear Angel before I see her, though this time it's mainly because her sobs are so loud it's hard not to. She's hunched on a wooden bench overlooking the ornamental gardens that lead down to the river – in other circumstances, given that it's a clear night, the stars are out and the moonlight is twinkling off the water, it would be the perfect setting for romance, if I hadn't just possibly committed the biggest faux pas ever.

I've followed her, fully intending to say sorry, but when Angel sees me approaching, she beats me to it.

'I'm so sorry, Noah.'

'Hey. No need to—'

She sniffs loudly. 'There is, actually. I know going out with me probably isn't easy . . .' She pauses, just to sniff again, and while I'm wondering whether I should object to her last statement, the moment passes. 'And I know you've probably never gone out with someone like me before.'

'That's true.'

Angel's shivering, so I remove my jacket and drape it over her shoulders, and she pulls it around herself gratefully. 'It's just . . . this thing I've got. It's taken me a while, but I've finally learned to live with it – ironic phrase, huh? It even has its advantages sometimes.'

'*Advantages?*'

'Just that it makes you live for the day. And that's what everyone always tells you, yeah? That that's how we all should live. And it's good advice. Except it's not really "advice" in my case, because I've got no choice . . .' She sniffs again, then dabs at the mascara running from her eyes with her – or rather *my* – sleeve. 'But every now and then, something happens that catches me off guard, and makes me realise I don't quite have this as under control as I think I do, and that *only* living for the day can actually be a bit, well, *shitty*. When I met you, for example, and after we'd spent some time together, I realised you were different.'

'In a good way, I take it?'

Angel nods. 'Yeah. Which is why . . . Margate. I just had to get away.'

I sit down next to her. 'Margate's not *that* bad.'

'You know what I mean. This – you and me . . . I've never had it before.'

'Me neither.'

'In a good way too, I hope?' She forces a smile, then reaches over and takes my hand. 'I *like* how you plan, Noah. How you do stuff for us, for *me* – from rock climbing to horse riding, to standing in a queue outside the world's worst restaurant so I don't have to. That you take everything I throw at you, and you field it in the most delightful ways. Pick me up when other people put me down. You're the perfect boyfriend. Everything I could ever ask for. More than I deserve. Any girl would be so, so lucky to have you, so excited to be planning a life with you. But me? I'm not just any girl. I can't give you what you want, but only because I can't *be* what you want, and I know that probably hurts you, but it really, *really* hurts me to think that we can't have a future together. And events like today, with everyone so happy, the parents, grandparents, all looking forward to a lifetime of kids, and grandkids, and the happy couple knowing they'll be growing old together . . .' She takes a deep breath. 'Me? I don't even buy unripe avocados, just in case.'

'That's not funny,' I say. None of this is funny – and although Angel's the one with the heart defect, right now my heart feels like it's broken too. More than that, I'm angry. Angry I've misread her feelings about marriage so badly. Angry it's taken me until now to realise how vulnerable she actually is under the tough exterior she shows the world. And angry that I can't see a way to make any of it better for her.

'It's *true*, though,' says Angel. 'And the thing is, I'm not the jealous type. Sure, I sometimes think I've been dealt an unlucky hand, but you play the cards you're holding, don't you? And for the most part, I'm okay with that. But occasionally, I see something, and I realise it's silly, but I can't help feeling so . . . angry at the unfairness of it all, and I know that probably sounds selfish, but everyone's allowed to be selfish every once in a while, surely?'

'Of course.'

Angel's almost shouting now, but it's not angry shouting, it's that teary shouting that you have to do to stop yourself from crying, as if you're forcing out words where the sobs should be, and to be honest, I'm clueless as to what to do, what to say. It could be that she's just venting, or talking hypothetically, but it could also be that there's nothing I *can* say. As I'm beginning to understand, not everything has an answer.

'Look at me. I'm just about to turn thirty, with an approach to life summed up by the brand of trainers I wear, and a heart that might fail at any moment. I'm damaged goods. I've ruined my mum and dad's lives. You'll quite possibly end up hating me yourself for dragging you into this . . . mess of a world that I live in. And then I go to something like that, something magical, and witness the most amazing spectacle, a demonstration of love, of hope, of all that's best about us as human beings, where two people are making a commitment, a promise, to stay together *for ever*, and it's all I can do not to resent them because they've got something – or at least, have the courage to *go for* something – that I can't. Even with someone I've fallen in love with.'

I stare at her, open mouthed, for a moment. 'You mean me, right?'

'*Yes* you, you idiot.'

She's struggling to get the words out now, and all I can do is sit there and listen, convinced that this is it, that she's going to tell me that *we* have no future, that our relationship (unlike the wedding invitation that kicked this whole thing off) is pointless, so we might as well say our goodbyes now. And even though she's holding my hand as tightly as she ever has, I don't dare move, or try to put my arm around her, because I'm sure she's forgotten that she is, and I won't be able to deal with the rejection when she lets go for what's likely to be the last time. But when Angel eventually forces out her last sentence, I finally know exactly what to say, and it seems like the most natural response ever. Probably because it's how I've been feeling since day one.

'Be honest, Noah,' she sobs. 'Who wants to marry *me*?'

Hoping it won't be the last time I utter the words, I turn to face her and look deep into her eyes. 'I do,' I say, more confidently than I thought was possible.

'You . . . What?'

'I do. Want to. Marry you, that is. Because I love you too. So however long it might last . . . I mean, "till death do us part", right? That's what you say. And it's all anyone can ever promise, isn't it?'

Angel's jaw drops open – a sight that'd be funny if the moment wasn't so serious. 'Was that a *proposal*?' she says, after a moment.

'You started it!'

'Well, *that* escalated quickly,' she says, then she hugs me so hard I almost think *my* heart will burst.

And just like that, Angel and I are engaged.

20.

It's the following Monday, and Marlon and I are sitting at a pavement table outside The Spice Is Right, one eye on the gallery, having decided to try their 'express lunch'. Though we're still to find out what's 'express' about it, seeing as we ordered half an hour ago, and all we've seen so far is a poppadum each.

'Relax!' Marlon glares at where I'm nervously drumming my fingers on the table. 'The food's bound to arrive soon. And it's not as if we've got a crowd of people waiting to get in.'

'It's not that.'

'Angel?'

I nod, and Marlon sighs.

'Oh, Noah, I'm so sorry.'

'Nothing like that!' I snap. 'We're . . .' I pick up my beer and swallow down a large mouthful. 'Well, actually, we're *engaged.*'

'Christ!'

'I know!'

'Congratulations?'

'Are you asking me, or telling me?'

'That rather depends on how you feel about it.'

'I feel . . .' I hesitate. How *do* I feel? In truth, it's been a bit of a whirlwind, but if I think about it, that's exactly how my whole relationship with Angel's been so far, so I suppose I shouldn't complain. 'Great about it.'

'Well, in that case, I'm telling you.' Marlon clinks his pint glass against mine. 'When's the big day?'

'August eighth.'

'This August? As in . . .' He pulls his phone out of his pocket and consults the calendar. 'Five weeks' time?'

'Uh-huh.'

Marlon whistles.

'And it's not that big a day. Richmond registry office. She booked it this morning. In and out in half an hour.'

'That's what Angel wants, is it?'

'Apparently. And what Angel wants . . .'

'Excellent! But why the rush?'

I hesitate, aware that I promised Angel I wouldn't tell anyone else about her heart condition. 'Well, when you know, you know, and unless we wanted to jet off to Vegas for one of those drive-through weddings – and I didn't dare give Angel any ideas – the registry office was the quickest option. Plus they had a cancellation. So we're going in to give notice tomorrow.'

Marlon whistles again.

'So, if you're free on the day . . .'

'I'll ask my boss. See if I can get the time off work.'

'. . . and you'd do me the honour of being one of the witnesses?'

'Who's the other one? Is she single?'

'Yes. But she's also eighty-eight years old.'

Marlon beams across the table at me. 'It'll my pleasure. Especially since it was me who was responsible for the two of you meeting in the first place.'

'How do you . . . ?'

He breaks off a piece of poppadum, dips it in mango chutney, then curses under his breath when most of it snaps off in the pot. 'If I hadn't set you up on that disastrous blind date with Wei . . .'

'Well . . .' I pick my glass up and clink it against his. 'Cheers to that.'

'Cheers.' Marlon retrieves the shard of poppadum, pops it into his mouth, and licks his fingers. 'Though if you don't mind me saying . . .'

'Saying what?'

'A registry office?'

'What?'

'I always thought you were a bit more . . . traditional.'

'I was. But I'm beginning to think that maybe I shouldn't be. The big thing isn't how you get married. It's *that* you get married.' I jab a thumb back towards the gallery. 'If this Hanksy show has taught us anything, it's that it's what the frame *represents* that's important. Not the frame itself.'

Marlon raises both eyebrows. 'Wow.'

'Besides, it's what she wants. And she's what I want. So . . .'

'Good on you.' Marlon lets out a short laugh. 'Keep your eye on the prize, Noah.' He helps himself to another piece of poppadum. 'Only . . .'

'Only what?'

'When did the two of you meet?'

'About eight weeks ago. But that's not really—'

'Okay. Well, perhaps what I should have asked is: how many dates are you at?'

'Eleven.'

'Right.'

'What does "right" mean?'

'And you're getting married.'

'Right.'

'Not waiting for the full thirteen, then? Just to be sure?'

'Well, when you know, you know.'

'And you know, do you?'

I do the jab/thumb/gallery thing again. 'Look at where we work. Galleries depend on love at first sight. People don't come in thirteen times before they make a purchase. They buy it after seeing it the once.'

'Well, when you put it like that.' Marlon clinks glasses again. 'August eighth it is, then!'

'August eighth,' I say.

Five weeks away.

Plenty of time for another two dates.

21.

'Yes, Batman.'

Angel gives me a look I've come to know well over the past few weeks. 'I asked if you had your utility *bill*. Not belt.'

I wave my latest BT demand in the air. 'Proof of address, as required.'

'Right.' Angel roots around in one of those expandable file things. 'Passport – or birth certificate?' she says, holding up both of them in a 'pick one' kind of way.

'You'd better take both, just to prove you didn't just fly down from heaven.'

'You know you're not supposed to make jokes, don't you?'

'Huh?'

'It actually says. On the forums. Any attempts at humour will be frowned upon.'

'You frown at my jokes all the time anyway.'

'I'm serious. They're going to make us do this *Mr & Mrs* question-and-answer thing just to check this isn't one of those sham marriages, and unless we get it right, it might delay things. And . . .'

Angel stops talking and makes the 'enough said' face, and I grin at her. 'How hard can it be?'

'What's my middle name?'

'Um . . .'

Angel sighs. 'I don't *have* a middle name.'

'I knew that. Which, you know, is why I didn't know what it was. If you see what I mean?' Though judging by Angel's expression, she doesn't. She taps her watch, reminding me we've just got time for a quick run-through in Starbucks before our appointment, then turns her attention back to the list on the council's website.

'ID.'

'Check.'

'Fee.'

'Check. Well, debit card.'

Angel looks up to see me grinning again, then makes yet another face, this time as if today's going to be a long day. 'Noah . . .'

'I'm sorry, but "giving notice" . . . That sounds like you're evicting someone, or resigning from your job. It's hardly the most romantic description.'

'Still.'

'It's really what you want?'

Angel nods. 'No fuss. That's what we decided, right? Just you and me, and a couple of witnesses . . .'

'And "witnesses". Like at a murder.'

'There'll be a murder, in a minute, if you're not careful.'

'Sorry. As long as you're sure?'

'I am. A simple ceremony at the registry office. In, out, job done.'

'Are we talking about the wedding night now?'

Angel leans over and kisses me. 'We better not be!'

'Seriously, though. You don't want to do the "church" thing, or some tropical beach somewhere, standing under a palm tree, the waves lapping at our feet?'

'Is that an option?'

'Well, um . . .'

'I'm kidding, Noah. Simple is good. Just you and me. Making promises to each other. In front of each other. About the future. *Our* future.'

'Great.'

'Besides, the last thing I want is loads of people at some big wedding, because I know what they'll all be thinking.'

'Right.' I retrieve my car keys from the kitchen table. 'Although, what *will* they be thinking?'

'*Poor Noah.*'

'Because I'm marrying you?'

'No.' Angel punches me lightly on the shoulder. 'Well, yes, actually. Because who knows how long you'll have before you become a widower, and they'll—'

'Hey! We said we wouldn't mention that.'

'Sorry.' She takes my hand. 'No. No fuss is good.'

'No excitement, right?'

Angel gives me yet another look from her considerable repertoire. 'I'm marrying you. Excitement won't be a problem.'

It's called Richmond Register Office, but it's in Twickenham for some reason, so we drive rather than walk, until we spot York House (which, given all the different references, means I'm now suffering from some sort of location-based identity crisis) at the top of the road that leads down to the river. As usual, the council offices are the typical mix of beautiful old buildings and ugly 1950s concrete add-ons, and I'm hoping the wedding will be in one of the former, so when Angel spots a sign saying 'REGISTER OFFICE' on an imposing red-brick building to the left of the car park, I'm pleasantly reassured.

We follow the arrowed directions, though they lead us past the beautiful, carved-stone entrance, round the corner to a rickety uPVC side door and into a waiting room that looks more like the kind of place you'd go to order a late-night taxi than a wedding venue. There's a large reinforced glass window in the centre of the far wall, and when I walk across and press the bell, a woman sitting behind a computer looks up sharply, as if I've disturbed something really important. Or her nap.

'Can I help you?'

'I've – well, *we've* – got an appointment to give notice. At ten twenty.'

The woman consults her screen, taps away at her keyboard, then checks a piece of paper in her in tray. 'Noah and Angela?'

I nod.

'Take a seat. Someone will come for you in a moment.'

'Sounds ominous,' whispers Angel.

There's only one other person sitting there – a woman old enough to be my mum. I offer her a nervous smile, which she returns warmly as we take a seat next to her.

'Notice?'

The woman nods.

'Any tips?'

Angel is nudging me, but I ignore her.

The woman gives me a strange look, then points a finger in Angel's direction. 'Make sure you say what she says.'

'We've rehearsed. Just now. In Starbucks,' I say, with a confident smile. 'Where we first met,' I add, though I don't notice the large, sternly official-looking woman who's just appeared in the waiting room. Behind her, a small, much older man is giving the woman sitting next to me a covert thumbs-up.

As the registrar narrows her eyes at me, I feel myself start to sweat. 'I don't mean we met *just now*. Just that we've . . . well, we haven't rehearsed, exactly. We didn't need to. Because . . .' I'm suddenly aware that Angel's gripping my arm rather firmly, so I stop talking.

'Noah and Angela?' says the woman, consulting her clipboard.

'That's us,' I reply, putting an arm round Angel, just so the woman is in no doubt that I wasn't referring to the other lady. Even though she's probably already aware of that.

'Follow me, please.'

We do as we're told, heading in through one of those security doors where you have to press a button to let yourself back out, and ending up in a rather small office at the end of the corridor. There's a rather messy corkboard on the wall with about a thousand different notes pinned to it, a cluttered desk in the middle, and two uncomfortable-looking chairs, which we're guided into with a brusque 'Sit'.

'Right.' The woman consults her computer screen. 'What documents do you have with you today?'

Angel reaches into her bag, and hands over our utility bills and passports, which the woman studies closely, as if to check they're not forgeries. She types a couple of things into her computer, then turns and regards us over the top of her glasses.

'Okay. I have to ask you a few official questions. Firstly, are you both free to marry?'

'We are,' says Angel.

'And have you ever been married before?'

'To each other?'

The woman scowls at me. 'Of course not.'

'It could happen. Richard Burton and Elizabeth Taylor. And, um . . .'

'Well, have you?'

'No,' says Angel. 'Not to each other, and not to anyone else, either.'

'Thank you.' The woman taps a couple of keys on her keyboard. 'And you're not related?'

I look at Angel, and have to hide a smile. 'No,' she says.

'And have you got your ceremony date?'

I nod, glad that I can contribute something concrete. 'Eighth of August.'

'And where are you having that?'

'Here,' I say. 'Well, no, not *here*, exactly. But here at the registry office.'

The woman peers at her computer screen again, and frowns. 'Actually, it *is* here. In this office.' She turns to Angel. 'We have to warn people about this. Otherwise they can be a bit disappointed.'

'It's in *this* office?'

She angles her computer screen towards me, and indicates one of the boxes. 'You booked the statutory office. This is it.'

'Yes, but I didn't think . . .' I wave a hand around, attempting to indicate that getting married in this crummy office environment is surely no good for anyone.

'It's fine,' says Angel.

'I also have to inform you that you're only allowed two other people in here. As witnesses. If you bring anyone else, we can't make provision for them.'

I roll my eyes. 'You mean they wouldn't fit.'

'No,' says the woman.

'It's really in here?'

The woman sighs exasperatedly. 'We do have other venues.' She slides a leaflet across the table. 'There's the York Room. It holds a hundred and fifty people. But it's booked up until' – she tabs through to another screen – 'October seventeenth.' She looks at Angel, then back at me. 'And it's more expensive.'

I open my mouth to protest the implication that I'm cheap, but to be honest, if it is just going to be the two of us plus a couple of witnesses, even if we did ask my parents, and Angel's parents, and Marlon, and Mary – a venue that holds a hundred and fifty people would be a bit of an overkill.

'People actually get married in here?'

'They do,' says the woman, more pleasantly than perhaps I could expect, seeing as I'm slagging off the state of her office.

'It's hardly the most . . .' I struggle to find the word, but Angel rests a hand on my arm.

'It's fine,' she repeats levelly. 'We only want a small wedding.'

'It couldn't get any smaller.'

The woman turns her attention to Angel, obviously having decided I'm trouble. 'Okay,' she says. 'I now have to ask you a series of questions individually. So one of you will have to leave the room.'

I sit there for a moment, then realise she's referring to me. 'Oh. Right. Well, I'll just . . .'

So I do.

Back in the waiting room, I can't help wondering why the woman behind the glass screen is casting strange glances in my direction, until I catch sight of my reflection and realise I've been sitting here grinning like an idiot since I sat back down.

But I can't help it: I'm getting *married*. To *Angel.* And while it's perhaps not quite how I'd pictured it, what with everything happening so quickly, and the registry office, and Angel's illness – the fact that she's prepared to make a commitment to *me*, for however long that might last . . . it's all pretty amazing, to be honest.

There's nothing to read, apart from a couple of brochures about Richmond Council, which I manage to get through from cover to cover in about thirty seconds flat, and for some reason, there's a sign saying 'No Mobile Phones', perhaps to stop people from eavesdropping what's happening back in the office, so I'm faced with having to amuse myself for the ten-or-so minutes it takes Angel to undergo her grilling. By the time I'm so desperately bored that I'm counting the carpet tiles, the door opens, and Angel marches back into the waiting room, closely chaperoned by the registrar, as if to stop us comparing answers.

'Noah, would you follow me, please?' she says, so I briefly lock eyes with Angel, but she's giving me a look that could either be 'oh my god!' or 'get on with it!', so I ignore her and follow the woman back into the office. Once I'm sat in my original chair, the registrar turns to me.

'Noah.'

'Yes.'

'And what's the name of the person you're marrying?'

'Angel,' I say confidently. If this is going to be the level of the questioning, I'm going to ace it.

'*Full* name.'

'Angel Fallon.'

'A little bit fuller?'

'Um . . . Angel-a?'

'You sound like you're asking me.'

'No, it's definitely Angela. Angela Fallon.'

'And is she, or has she ever been known by another name?'

I think for a moment. 'Another name?'

'And I don't mean "Angel".'

'Oh. Well, in that case, no. I don't think so.'

'Right.'

'Unless . . .'

'Unless?'

'Well, all couples have got their pet names, haven't they? So sometimes I call her . . .'

'*Officially*, I mean. Has she ever changed her name?'

'I wouldn't know, would I? I mean, she was Angel when I met her. Though – funny story – the guy in Starbucks got *my* name wrong, and . . .' The registrar is glaring humourlessly at me across the desk, and I realise even if the story was peppered with jokes pinched from top comedians, it probably wouldn't be funny to her. 'I'll, um, save it for the wedding.'

The registrar looks as if she's not convinced there's going to be one. 'And your full name is?'

'Noah Wilson.'

'Right.' She narrows her eyes at me, as if she fears she's about to regret asking the next question. 'And have *you* ever been known by any other name? And I don't mean joke name, shortened name, pet name or name in the 'insult' way.'

'No,' I say, suitably chastised. 'That's "no" as in "no, I haven't", not "no" as in "short for Noah".'

'And what is it Angela does for a living.'

'Design.'

'So what's her profession?'

'Design . . . er?'

'I've got something different.'

'Design . . . person?'

'Consultant.'

'That's hardly *that* different, is it? I mean, we can all call ourselves a consultant. You could be a registry office wedding consultant, for example, and . . .' I stop talking, realising I'm not doing myself any favours. 'No, I'll go with what she said.'

'And what's her date of birth?'

I smile and reel it off, happy that this is one I know.

There are a few more questions – my father's full name and occupation, though when I say he 'was' a teacher, the registrar's face falls.

'When you say "was", is he not with us anymore?'

'Oh no. He's retired. Living the life of Riley in Stanmore. Well, as much as that's possible.'

'Fine.' She taps a few more keys on her keyboard, scans quickly through the form on the screen in front of her, then turns back to face me. 'Now, I need to take payment from you. It's seventy pounds.'

'That's it?'

'That's it.'

'No asking me what her favourite colour is?'

The registrar sighs. 'Do you *know* her favourite colour?'

'I do, actually! It's—'

'Seventy pounds,' she repeats.

Realising I better pay up and get out while the going's, well, if not exactly 'good', then in the right direction, I reach for my wallet, and the registrar produces a card machine, jabs a couple of the buttons, then passes it across the desk to me. And while this seems a little clinical – administrative, even – well, neither of us are religious, so really, it is just a formality. A tick in a box. A filling in of forms. Even though it means so much more.

'So, what happens now?' I ask as she hands me my receipt.

'Well, we display your notice to marry for twenty-eight days. If, during that time, we've received any legal objections, then the marriage authorities—'

'Will arrest us? What type of legal objections?' I ask, slightly panicky.

'Relax. The marriage authorities aren't *people*. They're the documents we need to issue so your wedding can go ahead. And by "legal objections", I mean whether it turns out you've given us, say, a false identity, or one of you is still married.'

'Phew. Right. Well, we haven't. And aren't. Not that either of us ever was . . .'

'Oh-kay. So, we're done here,' announces the registrar rather abruptly. 'And we'll see you back here on the . . .'

'Eighth.'

'That's right.'

'Great. And, um, will it be you who's doing the marrying? I mean, obviously we'll be doing the marrying, but will you be, you know, *doing* the . . .'

The registrar shrugs, in what looks like an 'I hope not' kind of way. 'Perhaps.'

'Right, well, thanks,' I say.

I head back to the waiting room, take Angel by the hand and lead her back outside into the sunshine, where she turns and smiles at me.

'Wow!' she says, glancing back towards the registry office. 'We're getting *married!*'

'I suppose.'

'Thanks very much!'

'I don't mean it like that. I just mean . . . That room. That *woman.* Talk about taking all the fun out of marriage.'

'Start as you mean to go on, I suppose,' says Angel, then she bursts out laughing so hard, so breathlessly, I worry something will happen to her.

And when she still hasn't stopped a good five minutes later, I'm worried something has.

22.

It's Thursday, two days after our 'notice giving', and my 'Happy birthday!' when Angel answers the door to her flat that evening isn't quite met with the reaction I'd been expecting.

'You sure about that, are you?'

'Oh. Have I got the wrong . . . ?'

'No, it is my birthday. It's just, you know, "happy", and turning thirty?' Angel makes a face as she kisses me hello, hopefully because of the 'ageing' thing. 'Though I suppose I should be glad to turn anything, given, you know . . .'

'You don't look so bad.'

'For a woman with a congenital heart condition?'

'For a woman of your age!'

Angel purses her lips at me. 'Thank you. I think.'

'I got you something.'

She takes the envelope I've been hiding behind my back, slits it open with a fingernail and peers inside.

'A card?'

'Not just a card.'

'Huh?'

'There's an envelope too.'

'Be still my beating heart!'

'I'm not sure that's something you of all people should say.'

'Sorry.'

'Besides, what do you get the woman who has everything?' I say, pointing at myself.

Angel gives me a look, and it's full of irony, though that's perhaps not aimed at me – as we both know, the one gift she really needs, she doesn't seem to want.

And even though I might not agree with that choice, I'm just going to have to accept it.

I offered to take her out to a restaurant of her choosing this evening to celebrate *à deux*, but it turns out (as she oh-so-casually informed me via text earlier, as if she were scheduling something as innocent as a coffee) we're going to her parents' for dinner. And while that should be something to celebrate too, given how last time I met her mum, Angel practically disowned me, her 'I suppose we'd better tell them we're getting married' has kind of cast the evening in a different light.

'Have you thought this through?' I say, staring at my reflection in the full-length mirror on Angel's wardrobe door, making a last, nervous check that I haven't got spinach in my teeth and that my flies are done up.

Angel walks over and undoes the top button on my shirt. 'Thinking things through where my parents are concerned is normally a waste of brain power.'

'So you're just going to rock up, and say, "Hi, remember Noah, the guy I told you was just a friend? The one I joked with you that I was going to marry? Well, we *are* getting married."'

'Pretty much.'

'Shouldn't we maybe make some sort of phased announcement? Maybe start tonight with the "boyfriend" bit, do that a couple of times and then drop the bombshell?'

'Noah, in case you've forgotten, we're getting married in a month. Even if we took your "phased" approach, there's no disguising that this is still going to be pretty quick. It's pointless dragging it out.'

'I suppose.'

'Relax. My mum will be thrilled at the news.'

'And your dad?'

'He'll be beside himself,' says Angel, as I follow her out through the door.

Though it's only when I'm pulling into Angel's parents' driveway that I realise that's not necessarily a good thing.

Angel's parents live in a big house on Queens Road. No, scratch that, the *biggest* house on Queens Road. And while most of the houses on Queens Road would probably fit the term 'mansion' more than simply 'house', her family home has a touch of Castle Dracula about it, given the gothic-style turrets and gargoyles staring menacingly down at us, which I hope aren't an omen for the evening.

And while Angel's a bit quiet on the drive here, I put that down to the fact that she's probably embarrassed about making me put the roof up when we last drove this way. Given what she's told me about her parents, I can understand her not wanting to be spotted with me back then. Although, now, things are somewhat different.

I steer the MG along the gravel driveway, squeeze it carefully in between the his-and-hers Range Rovers that make my car look like a toddler out with its parents, and climb apprehensively out. Up close, I can't help but marvel at the sheer size of the building: it's got three normal storeys, with what look like a couple of the type of bedrooms where your mad aunt would live in the pointy bits under the eaves, and one of those cellar/basement things that's exactly halfway under street level, though we have to climb up a set of stone steps to get to the rather imposing front door, so I'm not sure which one actually counts as the ground floor.

'Millions,' says Angel, in answer to the question that must be written across my face, as if she's admitting having a sixth toe, or a third nipple.

'Christ! What does your dad do?'

'Marry well, obviously – he does something high-powered in the City that I *still* don't understand, but this is all thanks to my mum's family. Some ancestor back in the day invented . . .' She mentions the name of an ointment that's about as household a name as you can get whenever you have a certain embarrassing affliction *down there*. 'Sold it to Johnson and Johnson. Made an absolute pile. From, you know . . .'

'Piles?'

Angel grins. 'Exactly.'

'But . . .'

'But what?'

'If your family's this rich, why do you live somewhere so . . .'

'Shit?'

'I was going to say *small*. But now you come to mention it . . .'

Angel digs me in the ribs. 'I work for a charity, remember? They're not the greatest of payers. And flats in Richmond aren't cheap.'

'Couldn't your mum and dad help?'

'They thought they were helping by having me live here so they could keep an eye on me, and no thank you to *that*. Plus, what's the point in getting used to this? I probably won't be around to inherit anything,' she adds, in a tone that makes me want to change the subject.

'Okay. Well . . . shall we?'

'Right. Now remember, it's Julia and Lawrence.'

'Julia and Lawrence. Right. With Julia being your mum, obviously?'

Angel leans over and pokes me in the stomach, then grabs me by the shoulders and looks at me earnestly. 'And good luck!'

'Why will I need—'

'Just ring the bell, will you? Quicker we're in . . .'

I do as instructed, then press it again when I don't hear it ring, then try a third time, suspecting it's broken, before I suddenly realise the reason I can't hear anything is simply because the house is so big, and in effect I've been ringing it repeatedly. After a few moments, a frantic barking comes from the other side of the door.

'Your parents have a dog?' I say, picturing a Dobermann, or some similar sharp-toothed attack hound about to leap out at me.

'Relax. That's just Rocket. His bark's a lot worse than his bite.'

'I sincerely hope . . . Hang on. What did you say his name was?'

'Rocket.'

I freeze, hoping against hope there are two dogs named Rocket in Richmond – either that, or Angel's dad loans him out to someone else for parkruns, but it's too late to do anything anyway (i.e. turn around and sprint for the car) as, following the sound of a rather sturdy lock being unfastened, Angel's mum – rather than the butler I'd almost been expecting – grinning from ear to ear, cracks the door open. Maybe I'm reading too much into it, but there's something about her that lights up when she sees Angel. Although it doesn't occur to me until later that that something is 'relief'.

'Hello, darling,' she says, throwing the door wide open and enveloping Angel in a one-armed hug that seems to squeeze the breath out of her. With her other hand, she's holding an over-exuberant Rocket by the collar, and when she lets him go he – perhaps not surprisingly – makes a beeline for me.

'Mum,' says Angel, smiling sheepishly.

'Happy birthday! And Noah,' she says, as Rocket leaps up at me, 'lovely to see you again.'

'Mrs . . .'

'Please. Call me Julia,' insists Angel's mum. 'Seeing as you *are* Angel's *boy*friend.'

'She told you?'

'A mother knows these things.' Julia winks at me. 'Come on through.'

With Rocket tailing me excitedly, Julia leads us through the house, down some stairs and back on ourselves, and it's so far that 'coming on through' takes a good thirty seconds until we eventually reach the semi-underground level. It's three times as big as Angel's whole flat, with one of those space-age kitchens that are all gadgets you'd need a degree in astrophysics to work and surfaces made from materials that sound like ancient Greek gods, supplied by companies whose names make you sound drunk when you try to pronounce them. At the far end, in front of a glass wall looking out over a garden that's probably half the size of Richmond Park, there's a dining area with the kind of table that would normally seat about twenty people. One end of it is currently set for four, though Angel's dad seems to be occupying around three of those places, and as we walk into the room, he hauls himself up out of his chair, blocking out most of the view of the garden. He's even more imposing than when he's in his running gear, dressed in that off-duty wealthy City uniform of chinos and a pink shirt, with a jumper draped around his shoulders in that way they must teach you at private school, and it takes all my effort not to turn around and run for the stairs. Though given our relative parkrun times, he'd probably catch me before I reached the door.

I brace myself for what I already know is going to be one of the firmest handshakes of my life, but even that can't prevent me from feeling I'm not going to be able to pick up my fork later with my broken fingers.

'Pleased to meet you, sir,' I say. Normally, this would be his cue to say 'Please, call me Lawrence', but Angel's dad is looking at me as if 'sir' is exactly the right way to address him. Though maybe, given the size of the house, 'lord' would be more appropriate.

'Noah,' says Lawrence, then he frowns at me. 'Have we met before?'

'I don't think so,' I say quickly, relieved he hasn't recognised me, despite the fact that Rocket won't leave me alone.

'Are you sure we haven't bumped into each other?' I freeze, but then Lawrence follows it up with: 'Perhaps at the golf club?'

'I'm sure we haven't met. At least, not in my official capacity.'

I mean it in an 'as Angel's boyfriend' kind of way, but given Lawrence's thunderous 'Official capacity . . . ?', I'm not sure it's the best introduction.

'Yes. You know, as Angel's, um . . .' The dark cloud that's just passed over his face isn't something I want to see again, particularly because he's looking at me as if I'm someone who's arrived to give him some bad news, which I'm already starting to worry is exactly how he's going to see this, so I stop talking and hand him the bottle of wine I've brought. It's the most expensive bottle I've ever purchased – thirty pounds, and recommended by the man in Majestic – but Lawrence looks at it as if he wouldn't even consider using it for cooking.

'Thanks,' he says, with about as much enthusiasm as I'm currently feeling for the rest of the evening, and as Angel and her dad exchange a perfunctory hug, I scuttle back into the kitchen with my bag.

'I brought this,' I say, removing the cupcake I bought that morning and did my best to conceal from Angel. 'I thought maybe we could stick a candle in it later and . . .' I hesitate, as Angel's mum takes my cake and places it on the kitchen worktop next to the kind of handmade, elaborately decorated birthday cake that would probably win *Bake Off* – *and* feed fifty people.

'Thank you, Noah. That's very thoughtful,' she says, removing the ornate '3' and '0' candles from the centre of her cake, peeling the wrapper from the one I've bought, placing the cupcake where the numbers had been and inserting them into it, and I immediately love her.

'Drink?' Lawrence's voice, only a few feet behind me, makes me jump.

'Yes. I do. I mean, not to excess, or anything, but I . . . Oh, you were asking if I *wanted* one?'

'Well spotted,' he says, narrowing his eyes at me, as if he's still trying to place me.

'Well, I'm driving, so . . .' Lawrence's expression darkens even further, though whether that's because I've turned down his olive-branch offer of a drink, or the fact that I look like I'm about to accept one and then still drive his daughter home, I'm not sure. 'I suppose just the one would be . . .'

'I wasn't offering to pour you two,' he snorts.

'Right. No. Of course.'

'So . . .'

'So?'

'What would you *like*?'

'Whatever you've got open,' I say, then realise that sounds pretty bad. I meant it to be as accommodating as possible, but it also suggests either that I don't have any preference about what I have as long as it contains alcohol, or that this is the kind of household that always has a bottle open. 'A glass of wine would be lovely.'

'Red or white? Or are you one of those *rosé* drinkers?'

It's a reasonable question – well, the first is, especially given the scornful way he's phrased the 'rosé' one – and I know the 'red with meat, white with fish' rule, and the last thing I want to do is make another faux pas. But from what I can tell, there's a bowl of olives and a bowl of almonds on the table, and I don't have a clue what colour wine goes with them.

'I'll have a glass of . . .' I mentally flip a coin. 'White, please.'

Lawrence strolls over to a huge, glass-fronted cabinet in the corner of the room, which, even though it's twice the size of the one in Mary's kitchen, appears to be a special fridge just for wine. 'Gewürztraminer do you?'

To tell the truth, I'm not sure. Whatever he said, it might even be a red, and for all I know, he could be testing me, so I settle for a 'Lovely . . .' and wait as he uncorks it.

'Here,' he says, handing me a glass the size of a goldfish bowl, and while it's the most delicious wine I've ever tasted, I decide I'd better drink it slowly. After all, I've been here for five minutes, and I can already tell it's going to be a very long night.

'That was delicious,' I say, putting my knife and fork together at approximately the four o'clock position on my plate and sliding it an inch or so away from me, not because dinner *was* delicious – Angel's mum's not the greatest of cooks, and moussaka's not exactly my favourite thing, given that it's a kind of lasagne with what appears to be black masking tape around the edge of extremely soggy pasta – but more to stop her piling a third slice of stodge onto my plate.

'Thank you, Noah.'

As Julia beams at me from across the table, I decide I've done enough buttering up on that front, and turn my focus onto her dad, though given his disdainful reaction to most of my previous attempts this evening – a fact that's not gone unnoticed by Angel – I'm still a long way away from getting a 'World's Best Son-in-Law' mug as a present this Christmas. 'By the way, you have a lovely house.'

It may be stating the blooming obvious, but it's what you say, isn't it? And while all Lawrence does is grunt at me, Julia seems pleased with the compliment.

'Thank you, Noah,' she says, waving away my attempt to help her collect up the plates. 'It's a bit big for just the two of us, I suppose, rattling around in here—'

'Especially since Angel decided to move out into that . . . place of hers,' interrupts Lawrence.

'Doesn't Angel have any brothers or sisters?'

I've asked it innocently enough, but the ensuing awkward silence and barely perceptible meetings-of-eyes that takes place across the table makes me wonder whether I've said something really bad.

'No,' says Angel, 'I don't.'

In truth, I'm happy to leave it there. I don't need an explanation. All I asked for were the facts, not a detailed presentation of the Fallon family tree. But Angel seems keen to tell me.

'Which is a surprise, if you think about it, because you'd have thought they might have wanted a back-up. A stand-in, just in case something happened to me.'

'Angel, that's enough!' snaps Lawrence.

'That's enough? What's *enough* is how rude you've been to Noah all evening.'

'Rude?'

'Yes, rude. Every time he tries to engage you in conversation.'

I've winced a little at the word 'engage', and I'm seriously having second thoughts about tonight's big announcement, especially since her dad is looking quite angry now, and as Angel smiles defiantly back at him, Julia touches me lightly on the arm.

'I hear you own a gallery, Noah?'

'I do. Well, not *own*, exactly. I mean, it's my gallery, insomuch as the *business* is mine, but I don't actually own the, you know, physical space . . .' My voice falters as I catch sight of Lawrence's 'who *is* this loser?' expression.

'That's just wonderful,' says Julia, giving me a smile of such kindly encouragement that I love her even more. 'Lawrence collects art. Don't you, darling?'

Angel's dad looks up from where he's been uncorking tonight's nth bottle of wine – most of which he's drunk himself. 'Sorry. I was miles away,' he says, which is funny, because I'm currently wishing *I* was. 'What was that?'

'I was telling Noah that you collect art.'

'Right. And?'

'And Noah owns a gallery . . .' says Angel, in a 'duh!' way.

'Oh.' Lawrence takes a large gulp of wine, then fills his glass up again, as if to give him some time to come up with a question. He's still looking as if he'd like to throw me manfully out through the French doors. And possibly without bothering to open them first. 'And what kind of art do you show?'

I shrug, which I then realise isn't the best demonstration of my encyclopaedic art knowledge. 'A variety, really.'

'None of that modern rubbish, I hope?' he sneers. 'All those pickled sharks that were selling for a fortune in the nineties passed me by, I'm afraid, and if I'd wanted to look at an unmade bed, I just had to go into Angel's room . . .'

'No, it's generally paintings, with the odd sculpture,' I say, once his roar of laughter at his own joke has subsided. 'Some conceptual pieces, but usually the kind of stuff someone like you would recognise.'

'What's that supposed to mean?'

'What? Oh, nothing. I just meant . . .' I glance around the room, and notice the traditional artwork that lines the walls. 'A lot of our stuff is a little . . . abstract.'

'It's very good,' says Angel, before her dad can make another rude comment. 'Noah has an excellent eye. And it's surprisingly affordable.'

At the mention of the financial side, though possibly more specifically the chance to make some money, Lawrence suddenly perks up. 'Good investment, is it? The stuff in the shows you – what's the technical term? Curate?'

'Um, "sell",' I say, realising that's not really a technical term at all. 'And that depends on the artist, really. Right now, for example, we're currently showing an artist called Hanksy, which is selling well, and his work is getting quite a reputation . . .'

'Never heard of him.'

'Well, he's quite famous, in certain circles . . .'

'Not *my* circles,' says Lawrence snootily.

Angel leans over and pokes him in his stomach. 'Don't be such a snob. I bet if you reeled off a list of the last few companies you dealt with, then Noah wouldn't have heard of them.'

Lawrence looks like that wouldn't surprise him at all. 'Would that say more about him or me, do you think?'

'Well, I think it's wonderful.' Julia stands up and looks at me. 'It really is nice to have you here, Noah. Angel's never brought any of her boyfriends home before.'

'Can you blame me?' says Angel, with a sideways glance in her dad's direction.

'I'm serious,' says Julia, fetching the cake, then extracting the kind of knife you might see a samurai wielding from a huge wooden block on the worktop. 'You're the only one of them we've met.'

'Out of them all? I'm flattered!'

I've meant it as a joke, but I obviously haven't learned my lesson yet, as Angel's dad looks like he can barely contain himself, and as we sit there in the latest of the round of awkward silences that have punctuated the evening so far, I'm eyeing the bottle of wine thirstily, wondering whether it's too late to change my mind and leave the car here. I might not be able to catch Lawrence at parkrun yet, but I can certainly have a good go at playing catch-up in the drinking stakes.

'Tell me,' says Angel's mum, eventually. 'How did you two meet?'

I look across to Angel, to give her the chance to tell the story, but with an almost-imperceptible nod, she swiftly heads the responsibility back to me. We've already decided it's her who'll be announcing the whole 'wedding' thing, so I prepare to tee it up for her. 'In Starbucks. Funny story . . .' I hesitate, then decide this one might actually qualify as funny. 'We accidentally took each other's coffee . . .'

'Or rather, Noah *stole* mine . . .'

I grimace, though it's more at the word than my actions: the last thing I want to do is give her dad more ammunition with which to hate me, and he's already looking like he's stockpiled enough for a good few years. 'Anyway, long story short . . .'

'Good idea,' says Lawrence, though when Angel's mum tuts, he looks up in surprise, as if not realising he'd said it out loud.

'Well, we ended up sharing a table. I wasn't sure if she was interested . . .'

'No?' says Lawrence, in a 'really?' kind of way.

'. . . and I couldn't ask her for her number because I was actually on my way to a— Well, that's not important. Anyway, I kept going back to Starbucks, hoping I'd bump into her again, but I didn't, and I didn't see her at any of the par—' I stop in horror at having nearly let the word 'parkrun' slip out. 'Parties I went to, then one day, I saw her at the hospital' – Angel's mum looks up sharply at this, so I soldier quickly on – 'but I was with someone else, and . . . well, it was my neighbour. And she's eighty-eight. So I wasn't actually *with* her . . .' Her dad is looking at me expectantly, both eyebrows raised, though I suspect it's to remind me about my earlier 'long story short' promise rather than because he's interested in the finer plot points of our meeting. 'So, I ended up following her to her office . . .' I pause for breath, worried that now I repeat this part of the story out loud, it's sounding more like stalking than romance. 'Anyway, I sent her an invite to our next gallery opening, and from there we went rock climbing. Not that the gallery's at the bottom of a cliff. Though admittedly, Church Road is pretty steep . . .'

'Rock climbing?' Julia's looking horrified, but she's directing the horror at Angel, who just meets her eyes defiantly.

'And the rest is history.'

Angel's dad mumbles something unintelligible (which sounds like 'I wish *he* was') as he tops his wine glass up again, but Julia reaches over and pats me on the back of the hand.

'Well, I think it's a lovely story,' she says. 'Faint heart never won fair lady, and all that.'

'Or a redhead one,' I say, then give a little cringe, as if to acknowledge the awfulness of my joke.

As Julia plunges the knife into the cake and begins carving off a slice that – if it's for me – I'll have to surreptitiously feed the majority of to Rocket, Angel takes a deep breath, gives me a look and then: 'So listen, Mum, Dad . . .' She reaches under the table for my hand and grips it firmly. 'Noah and I have an announcement to make.'

Julia stops, mid-cut, and looks up expectantly. 'Announcement?'

'We're . . . Noah and I . . . We're getting *married*!'

'Yes, very funny, darling.'

'I'm not joking. This time.'

For a moment, Julia just stares at Angel, then at me, then at Angel again, then she leaps out of her chair, rushes round the table and lunges for me. To be honest, I don't know whether she's pleased, not least because she's still got the cake knife in her hand. But as Angel gently disarms her, I allow myself to be enveloped in a huge hug that almost squeezes the breath out of me.

'That's just . . . I mean, it's . . . But the other day . . . ?'

'It's called a double-bluff, Mum. And anyway, we hadn't decided then.'

'Well that's . . . I mean . . .' Julia lets me go, gives the same hug to Angel, though a *lot* more gently, then turns to her husband. 'Lawrence?'

Angel's dad hasn't said a word. Or moved. Or, apparently, breathed, given how purple he seems to have turned. After a moment or two, 'This is all rather a surprise', is all he can manage.

'Isn't it?' says Angel, looking like she and her mum are in some kind of Cheshire cat grin-off. Her dad looks like he'd currently come last in that particular competition.

'And when did you decide on this?' he says, sounding like the words 'stupid' and 'idea' belong on the end of that sentence.

'Last Saturday,' says Angel. 'We'd just been at a wedding, and . . .'

'You'd been to a wedding?' Angel's mum is wide-eyed. 'I thought you didn't like weddings?'

'I don't. Not particularly.'

'Or the idea of marriage?'

'I changed my mind.'

'So we see,' says Lawrence tersely, as if mind-changing is something Angel tends to make a habit of.

'Or rather, Noah changed my mind.'

'Did he now?' Angel's dad narrows his eyes at me. 'You didn't even think it might be polite to ask me for her hand?' he says, in a tone that makes me worry the only 'hand' I'll be getting is the back of his.

'I'm sorry, Dad,' says Angel. 'I forgot you were still living in Victorian times.'

He glowers at her. 'And you said yes, did you? Just like that?'

Angel nods. 'Just like that.'

'With the same amount of consideration you've given to most of the major decisions in your life?'

'That's not fair, darling,' Julia pipes up. 'She's had a lot to deal with, as you well know.'

Lawrence turns to me, thunder in his eyes. 'You do understand how ill she is? That she could drop dead at any moment?'

'Dad!'

'He's got a right to know what he's getting himself into.'

'You mean by marrying an invalid? Or this family?' snaps Angel.

The two of them stare at each other for a moment, then I clear my throat.

'Of course I know,' I say evenly.

'And that doesn't matter to you?'

'If anything, it makes me want to marry her even more.'

'I bet it does,' says Angel's dad, though I don't quite get what he means.

229

'Well, I think it's wonderful news,' says Julia, adding, 'Just wonderful' in case we didn't hear her the first time. 'And it calls for champagne.'

Angel grins at me, and squeezes my hand even tighter beneath the table, which to be honest is beginning to hurt a little, but her dad shows no sign of moving.

'Lawrence?' says Julia.

'What?'

'*Champagne?*'

Unfortunately, Angel's dad looks like celebrating is the last thing on his mind, and as her mum retrieves a bottle of Bollinger from the wine fridge and places it pointedly in front of him on the table, he sighs loudly through his nostrils.

'This is for real, is it?'

'It is,' I say.

'And have you set a date yet?'

'August eighth,' says Angel.

'Well, at least that gives us just over a year.' Her dad seems to relax a little, perhaps because he thinks that's enough time to talk Angel out of what's clearly to him a ridiculous venture. 'Your mother will need to sort out caterers, and there's a chap I know at work who can get us into a decent hotel, so . . .'

'*This* August,' says Angel.

'What?'

'We thought we'd do it sooner rather than later.'

Angel's dad lets out a short, snorty laugh. He's still made no move to open the champagne, and by the looks of him, he's quite keen to put it back on ice. Or break the bottle over my head.

'You'll never get a church at such short notice.'

'Oh no. We just want to do it simply.' She smiles. 'Richmond registry office had a cancellation, which was why we booked . . .'

'*Registry office?*' he thunders.

'That's right,' says Angel.

'I'm not having a daughter of mine get married in a registry office!'

'Sorry, Dad. I didn't realise it was *your* wedding.'

'It *is* my wedding. At least in the sense that I'll be paying for it.'

'Noah's already paid for it, as a matter of—'

'Why is it impossible for you to do *one* thing the way we want?'

Angel finally lets go of my hand, though it's only so she can fold her arms. 'Not *this* again.'

'What's wrong with *this* again?' sputters Lawrence. 'I just don't understand your continued refusal to even consider an operation that could make you better.'

'Dad . . .'

'I've been reading up on it. Just the other day. There's all sorts of new techniques. Survival rates are much better than they were. And yes, I know there's a risk, but . . .' His eyes flick across to me. 'Risks are something you seem to be happy to take.'

'Dad!'

'Christ, Angela! Why is it so hard for you to behave like a normal girl?'

Angel's dad has turned a colour I've never known a human being to go, but I'm guessing Angel's seen this before, because she just shakes her head slowly.

'Because I'm not a normal girl. Am I?'

'Sweetheart, that's not what your father . . .' Her mum rests a hand on her shoulder, but she shakes it off and turns angrily to her dad.

'Why can't you just be happy for me?'

'I'm sorry, Angela, but you march in here after we haven't seen you for *weeks*, and announce that you're getting married *just like that.*' He clicks his fingers frighteningly loudly, then shoots me a disparaging glance, as if this is all my fault. 'We weren't even aware you had a boyfriend.'

'You're surprised, if this is the way you treat them?'

'I don't know the first thing about him . . .'

'I didn't realise you were the one marrying him.'

'. . . and I expect you probably don't either. Where did he go to school, for example? What are his parents like?'

'What's that got to do with anything?'

'It shows breeding.'

'Fat lot of good that did me! And besides, as long as he's nothing like you, I'm sure we won't have anything to worry about.'

'Look at him. He probably doesn't even own a tie! I don't doubt he's come here this evening, taken one look at this house and realised he's won the lottery. It's no wonder he can't wait to get you down that aisle – not that you're even going down an aisle – then you pop your clogs, and . . . bingo.'

'I'm not some sort of *prize*.'

I'm about to point out to Angel that her dad doesn't actually mean 'at bingo', but Lawrence doesn't give me the chance.

'I bet that's not how Noah sees it.'

'Dad, that's not fair.'

'Isn't it? Well, life's not fair, Angela. As you well know. And as your mother and I are reminded pretty much every day.'

'Lawrence . . .'

Angel's mum's been quiet for the last couple of minutes, and actually looks like she's on the verge of tears, but her dad's more than making up for his earlier silence. He stands up, reaches into his back pocket and retrieves what looks like a chequebook. 'What's it going to take, Noah? Five thousand? Ten? Fifty?'

'Pardon?'

'How much money,' he says, enunciating every word carefully, wanting to leave me in no doubt as to what he means, though I make myself ask. Just to hear him say it.

'For what?'

'For you to leave our daughter alone?'

Angel's dad's still on his feet, and if I were a betting man, I'd say it definitely looks like we're not getting that champagne – and I'm pretty sure we wouldn't even get decent odds on us getting a piece of birthday cake. The one thing I do get, finally, is his 'I bet it does' comment from earlier, and I realise that despite offers of birthday cake, or champagne, or even money, there's only one thing I want to leave this house with this evening. And that's the person I brought.

'I doubt even you have that much money,' I say flatly, then I remove my napkin from my lap, set it carefully on the table and stand up. 'Thanks, Julia, for a lovely evening. Lawrence.'

I think for a moment about offering him my hand to shake. Being the bigger man in all of this. Showing him there are no hard feelings. But in truth, there *are* hard feelings. How dare he think I'm just dating Angel for the money – and that I can be paid off. And to suggest I'm not good enough for his daughter – even though *I* might think that, he certainly can't.

But above all else, I may need to use my hand again to write, or at least sign my name on August eighth, and given the ferocity with which he shook it before he'd decided he hated me, I don't want to risk it a second time.

So in the end, I do the only thing I can do, which is to take Angel by the hand, lead her back up the stairs, past a bemused-looking Rocket, and out through the front door.

Angel and I drive in silence for a good minute or two, before her 'Well, *that* went well . . .' makes me let out an involuntary snigger.

'I'm sorry, Angel. I guess I'm just not what your dad was hoping you'd—'

'Stop right there, mister! Prince Harry wouldn't be good enough for me, in my dad's eyes. Prince William, mind you . . .' She grins. 'My mum seemed over the moon, though.'

'Even though she tried to decapitate me with the cake knife?'

'She'll get him to see sense. Don't worry.'

'I'm not worried,' I lie, convinced Angel's dad's probably already making calls to some dodgy business associates of his to arrange a contract on me. 'I just wish he'd been a bit more supportive of *you*.'

Angel rolls her eyes so exaggeratedly it almost makes a noise. 'Noah, he's never been supportive of me. This is just his way. Anyway, it's not like we need their blessing or anything, and let's face it, being cut out of the will is hardly my biggest problem.' She turns and stares out of the passenger window. 'I'm sure my dad will come round. Eventually.'

So I nod, and drive on, although the prospect of Angel's dad coming round – to my house, with a golf club or some other blunt instrument – is exactly what I'm worried about.

23.

Telling my parents is completely the opposite experience. In fact, my mum seems to sense something's up from the minute I call, and invites us round to theirs for Sunday lunch. Angel's offered to drive, given that it's raining and the roof of my car leaks so badly we might as well not bother to put it up, so we're in her bashed-up Ford Ka, and because her approach to driving mirrors her general approach to living life (in a 'breakneck speed' kind of way), we're ten minutes early, but even so, my mum is already waiting for us, clutching a large golf umbrella, in the porch.

'Hello, love,' she says, marching out to meet me as I climb out of the car.

'Hi, Mum. This is . . .' But that's as far as I get, as she goes rushing past me to where Angel's emerging from the driver's side.

'Angel,' says my mum reverently, like Angel's some sort of celebrity, holding the umbrella in one hand and almost manhandling her out of the car with the other. 'Of course it is.' She hands the umbrella to my dad, who's just materialised behind her, then envelops Angel in a huge hug, as if greeting a long-lost relative. 'You told us on the phone.'

'And let's face it, it'd be highly unlikely you'd get dumped, meet someone else, then decide to bring her instead, all in the space of four days,' says my dad, elbowing my mum out of the way to give Angel a squeeze. 'It took you long enough to meet *this* one.'

'Though the dumping could happen,' adds my mum. 'We've seen it before.'

'Unlike many of his previous girlfriends,' says my dad, nudging me in the side. 'He doesn't tend to bring them round.'

'So you're honoured,' says my mum.

'It's almost as if he's embarrassed of us,' adds my dad, escorting the two women towards the front door, where Albert, my parents' Labrador, is waiting out of the rain, wagging his tail like a windscreen wiper on full speed.

'Or his previous girlfriends,' says my mum, winking at Angel.

They're like this, my mum and dad. Like one of those old double acts, only they make the carefully choreographed routines of the likes of Morecambe and Wise seem amateurish. Not that they complete each other's sentences – it's more that they seem to bounce off each other with an effortlessness you'd think has taken years of rehearsal (though given that they've been together for nearly four decades, perhaps it has). And while it can be quite overwhelming, to be honest, like watching a fast-paced tennis match from a seat too close to the net, to her credit, Angel seems to be coping.

She reaches down and scratches Albert behind one ear, then takes a step backwards as he shoves his nose into her crotch. 'Well, it's lovely to meet you, Mr and Mrs—'

'Dave, please, and Lesley.'

'I'm Lesley. He's Dave,' says my mum, rather unnecessarily.

'You didn't need to say that, love,' scolds my dad.

'Lesley can be a boy's name too.'

'Dave can't be a girl's.'

'What about Davina? You could shorten that. Especially nowadays . . .' My mum makes a face, as if to convey 'anything goes', then she lets out a brief, high-pitched laugh.

I shake my head, and follow the three of them inside the house. 'Here,' I say, handing my dad the bottle of cava we've brought.

'Ooh,' says my dad, peering at the label. 'Are we celebrating something?'

My mum shushes him. 'Don't be silly, Dave,' she scolds, then she peers directly at me. 'Are we?'

We're still standing in the hallway, and unlike Angel's parents' place, it's not the kind of hallway that works for four people and a dog. Though theirs would possibly work for forty.

'Mum, traditionally we're supposed to have made it at least as far as the front room before the interrogation starts.'

'Oh, I'm sorry!' My mum makes a face, as if she's just been caught naked with one of the neighbours. 'Where are my manners? You go through and sit down. Lunch won't be long. Dave, get them a drink, will you? What would you like to drink, Angel? Shall we open yours? Is it cold enough? Do I need to put it in the freezer? You can do that trick with a wet paper towel, you know?'

My mum stares at the two of us, and I'm just replaying her last few sentences, wondering which of her questions to answer first, when Angel smiles. 'Actually, I'm driving, but why don't we open that. A small glass won't kill me. Or make me kill anyone else, hopefully . . .'

She nods at the cava, and my dad stares at her for a moment, then he hands her the bottle and nudges me again. 'She's offered to be designated driver, eh? I'd hang on to this one, son, if I were you.'

'I'm doing my best,' I say involuntarily, and Angel smiles at me.

'Right,' says my dad. 'Glass of cava for the lady coming up.' He takes a step towards the kitchen, then pauses, mid-stride. 'Anyone else?'

'*Everyone* else,' says my mum. 'Except for Albert.'

As Albert goes into another tail-wagging frenzy at the sound of his name, my mum escorts us into the front room. 'So, how did you two meet?' she says, directing us towards the sofa.

I look at Angel, and like at her parents' the other day, she nods in an 'after you' way. 'In Starbucks, actually. Funny story. I'd only gone in to use the toilet . . .'

Angel looks up from where she's peeling the foil from the top of the bottle. 'Actually, it's not that funny a story. Suffice to say, your son took my coffee by mistake – at least, he says it was a mistake – and we ended up having an argument about relationships being a leap of faith, and, well, I won. And that was that.'

'They must be, mustn't they?' says my dad, marching back into the room, with a tray with four champagne glasses and a bowl of vegetable crisps that have obviously been pre-debagged balanced on his fingertips, and at shoulder height, like waiters do. 'Otherwise she'd never have gone out with him, would she?'

As my mum shushes him, he makes the 'what?' face, then deposits the tray awkwardly on the coffee table. 'All I'm saying is, some people take a while to grow on you. And Noah's one of those people.'

'Exactly,' says Angel, levering the cork out of the bottle of cava with her thumbs. 'Although actually, he didn't take that long at all. Because we're getting married.'

There's a loud pop as the cork flies off towards the kitchen, Albert setting off in hot (well, lukewarm) pursuit, and my mum stares at me, then at Angel, then at my dad, lingering on each of us for a couple of seconds in a wooden-acted, soap-opera kind of way.

'What?' she says, in that way people do when they've actually heard what they think they've heard, but they just need a bit more time to digest it.

'We're getting married,' repeats Angel.

'You and Noah?' My dad this time, majestically leaping into first place in today's 'stupidest question' competition.

Angel nods. 'Me and Noah.'

My mum purses her lips as if she's trying hard to contain a burp, but it's no good, because all of a sudden she screams 'The smazzy!' – though a few seconds later, I realise she's *actually* screamed 'That's amazing!', but in such an incredibly high-pitched way that Albert probably got it before we did.

I beam guiltily at my mum and dad. I'd been a little worried we might get the same reaction as from Angel's dad, but instead, they're both looking like they've been marooned on a desert island for so long they'd given up hope of ever being rescued, and today, suddenly, there's a ship steaming towards them.

'That's fantastic news,' says my dad, eyeing the cava and then me as if to say, *so that's why you brought it.* 'Have you set a date?'

'The eighth of August.'

'Right,' says my dad. 'Well, that gives us just over a year, so . . .'

'This August,' says Angel, though the upward inflection at the end makes it sound like a question.

My mum and dad freeze, like they're playing a game of statues. Even Albert looks up from where he's chewing the cava cork into a thousand pieces.

'*This* August,' repeats my mum.

'That's right.'

'As in, next month?'

'Just over four weeks' time, to be pre—'

My mum screams even louder, then rushes round the coffee table to grab Angel, and I fear she's about to attack her – but as I rush to Angel's defence and try to intercept her, she grabs us both in a huge hug.

'Oh, *Angel* . . .' My mum frowns, then widens her eyes. '"I'm *driving*" . . . Good cover story!'

'What?'

My mum rests a hand on Angel's stomach. 'You're hardly showing, so does it really have to be so soon? Not that I'm complaining. Dave, we're going to be *grandparents!*'

Angel bursts out laughing. 'I'm sorry to disappoint you, Lesley, but that thing I'm "hardly showing" is a rather large breakfast.'

'What?'

'I'm not pregnant.'

'I don't understand.'

239

'Angel's not pregnant, Mum.'

My mum's face falls faster than a broken elevator. 'But . . . Why are you getting married so soon?'

'Well . . .' Angel and I exchange glances. We discussed this in the car on the way over, and decided it's easiest to just go with 'we're not getting any younger' for now, which is why Angel's answer confuses me a little.

'Because I've got this incurable disease, and we thought we'd better do it sooner rather than later. You know, *just in case* . . .' She's looking at my mum straight-faced as she says this, and there's a moment's silence, then my dad bursts out laughing.

'Ha ha, Angel. Good one. Just can't wait to be married to this one, eh?' He puts an arm around my shoulder. 'Can't blame you, really. Noah's mum was the same. Though it turned out, she *was* pregnant.'

'Dave!'

'Or at least, she was after our wedding night . . .'

'*Dave!*' shrieks my mum, but to be honest, she's still caught up in what thankfully seems to be – despite Angel's un-pregnant state, *and* her other revelation – the good news.

I stare at Angel, telepathically urging her to either explain fully or laugh it off as the joke my parents are convinced it is, but she just blanks me. Awkwardly. Until my dad exhales loudly, shaking his head in the manner of a good-natured schoolteacher who's just been pranked by his class.

'You kids today. Everything has to be *now*.'

'Well, when you know, you know,' says Angel. 'You know?'

I shrug, and nod, even though it's hard to tell who knows what. But I shake the hand my dad's thrusting towards me, then stand back as he squares up to Angel, although he doesn't seem to know whether to shake her hand or give her a hug, so she grabs him instead and puts him out of his misery, and that's, well, *it*.

And this is the great thing about my parents. There are no more questions, no 'are you sure you're doing the right thing?', no enquiries as to how long we've known each other, or what her parents do, or even what school she went to. They're just happy for me, for Angel, for *us* – and, I'm guessing, for *them*. Even Albert's tail-wagging seems to have upped its frequency. And isn't that how things should be?

Except – and this is a feeling that creeps up on me as the day progresses – things *aren't* as they should be, for me, at least. Because sitting there, looking at my mum and dad, seeing the bond they've built up over their forty years together, the home they've made for themselves, the life they've carved out, the family they've had, despite the fact it's just the three of us (although it's about to gain an additional member), it's hard not to feel emotional. The way things stand, unless she goes through with the transplant, Angel's only likely to be a temporary addition. Chances are, she and I aren't going to have *any* of this. And right now, while I'm sure Angel is *who* I want, I can't ignore the growing conviction that *this* is *what* I want.

But I swallow it down, along with a little too much to drink, because everyone's in a celebratory mood, and the roast is delicious, and the cava goes down nicely, and my dad even heads out into the shed to find that bottle of champagne he's been saving for a 'special occasion', and my mum does that trick with the freezer and the wet paper towel, and we all clap appropriately, and even though Angel probably suspects that my gene pool might not be as, well, *pure* as hers apparently is, she doesn't seem to mind.

Then later, just as we're leaving, my dad takes me to one side, and shakes my hand again. 'Congratulations, son,' he says, a slight quaver in his voice, but it looks like the smile will have to be surgically removed from his face. Whether that's because I'm getting married, or because I'm getting married to Angel, it's hard to tell, but I suspect it's a little of both.

And quite frankly, that only makes things worse.

'Your mum and dad are lovely.'

I look round at Angel from where I've been staring, more than a little preoccupied, out through the passenger-side window. 'Huh?'

'Your mum and dad.'

'What about them?'

'I said they're lovely. A bit mad, but lovely.'

'I think they felt the same about you. Apart from the mad part, obviously.'

Angel smiles as she switches the windscreen wipers onto full speed, floors the accelerator and wheelspins out into a barely-there gap in the traffic. 'They'll find that out soon enough.'

We drive on in silence for a while – then, as the huge blue-and-yellow bulk of the IKEA on the North Circular looms in the distance, I clear my throat.

'Do you really think just slipping it into the conversation was a good idea?'

'As opposed to making a big announcement? Look how well that went down with *my* parents. Besides, it doesn't really matter how they heard it, does it? The important thing is that they know we're getting married. And they seemed pretty happy about the news.'

'Not *that*. About your . . .' I'm staring at her chest, and I pat the area above my heart for added emphasis. I've only known about it for a month, so I still haven't worked out a good way to refer to Angel's condition. '. . . *thing*. Making a joke of it. If you were planning on telling them, you should have told them *properly*.'

'Noah, we've discussed this.' Angel pauses as she undertakes a slow-moving car that's hogging the middle lane, smiling at the elderly man behind the wheel, his nose about an inch away from his windscreen, as we pass. 'It's not the first thing I want people knowing about me. Plus, talk about how to burst someone's bubble . . . "Yay, we're getting married, but the bride might not make it down the aisle."'

'We're not going down an aisle.'

'Metaphorically.' She turns and looks earnestly at me. 'We'll tell them properly. When the time is right. I just thought I'd sow the seed.'

We drive on for a moment, then – and maybe it's the glass of brandy I consumed from the dusty bottle my dad produced after lunch from the back of their drinks cabinet, not to mention the cava and champagne, but I can't help myself – 'And when exactly will the time be right?'

'Noah, don't start.'

'Oh, and it's not strictly "incurable", is it?'

'What?'

'Your *thing*. It's not incurable. You could have a transplant. So perhaps you shouldn't describe it like that.'

Angel sighs loudly, pulls suddenly into a loading zone at the side of the road and switches the hazard lights on. 'Are we really going to do this again? And now? We've had a lovely, upbeat day. For once, I got to feel like a normal human being, with something to look forward to. We made your mum and dad really happy. Isn't that enough?'

'S'pose.'

'Good.' She flicks off the hazards and pulls out into the traffic again, zipping through the gears. 'Now, shall we listen to some music, or . . .'

'I just don't see why you don't want to *live*.'

Angel slams the brakes on in a driving-test 'sudden stop' kind of way, causing the same driver she smiled at earlier to beep his horn angrily as he swerves – or rather *steers*, given that he's only doing around twenty miles per hour – around us. 'I *am* living, Noah, in case you hadn't noticed. And doing a pretty good job of it, despite everything that's been thrown at me. And with all due respect, you've known me for five minutes, and you're trying to get me to change my mind on something that I've been thinking about for years. So please just respect my decision on this.'

'Yes, well. Maybe, but . . .'

'Are those four words connected? Or are you just coming out with random—'

'Angel . . .'

'What?'

She's shouted that last word, though that's possibly because she's incorrectly guessed what I'm about to say. 'Did you maybe want to start driving again? Because I'm pretty sure you're not allowed to park in the middle lane of the North Circular.'

'Oh. Right. Sorry.'

'No, I'm sorry.'

Angel gives me the briefest of smiles, then she puts the car in gear and we start moving again, which I'm relieved about, mainly because of the huge lorry bearing down on us. Though after a moment, and after I've surreptitiously checked there's nothing behind us within rear-ending distance, perhaps foolishly I decide I'll have another go, but this time, in what I understand might be a better, non-confrontational way.

'I just don't understand.'

'Oh, for . . .' Angel sighs loudly, glances sideways at me, then cuts violently across three lanes of traffic, jumps a red light and screeches to a halt in the McDonalds car park. 'What don't you understand, Noah?'

I wait a second or two for my breathing to return to normal, release my vice-like grip on the dashboard and swivel round in my seat to face her. 'Well . . . *why*, I suppose.'

'Why what?'

'Why you don't . . .'

'What?'

'. . . want to have a, you know . . .' I swallow hard, knowing I should probably leave it, but I can't. Spending time with my parents, realising what I might be missing out on, has hit home more than I thought. 'A transplant.'

'A transplant,' she says flatly.

'A heart transplant,' I add, somewhat unnecessarily. 'Because, well, your dad's, you know, *right*.'

'My *dad*?' she snaps.

'I've been reading up on it too,' I say, in a way that sounds like I'm taking an interest in one of Angel's hobbies, and expecting it to win me some brownie points. 'There *are* all sorts of new techniques. Survival rates *are* much better than they were. And yes, I know there's a risk, but I . . .' I stop talking. *Wouldn't mind* isn't perhaps the best end to that sentence, and *could help you through it* sounds more than a little patronising.

'You what?'

I frown back at her, not knowing if that's 'you what?' in a 'please finish your last sentence' kind of way, or 'you what?' in an 'I can't believe you said that' kind of way. And because I don't know, I don't answer. Which seems to provoke Angel even further.

'I'm scared, okay?' Angel's almost shouting now, and for a moment I worry I've overstepped the mark. But I'm more surprised than worried. Angel's not scared of anything. At least, she hasn't appeared to be.

'Of . . . ?'

'Have you ever seen a heart transplant operation?'

I shake my head – it's not the kind of thing I would have, surely? – so she reaches for her phone, quickly navigates to YouTube and locates a video, though I assume it's not something she's kept under 'Favourites'.

'There's lots on here, if you want to see the gory details.'

'It can't be *that* bad,' I say, nervously picturing the slightly rare roast beef I've just eaten, hoping I won't be seeing it again any time soon.

'No?' Angel jabs angrily at the 'Play' arrow on the screen, and thrusts the phone in my face. 'They cut you open, break through your breastbone, rip out your heart, pump you full of someone else's blood, all so they can stitch this alien thing inside you, then staple you up again in a way that makes the Frankenstein monster look like Kim Kardashian. It's not pretty, I can tell you. Then – and that's assuming you survive the operation – there's the weeks in intensive care, pumped full of drugs, all sorts of tubes hanging out of you, everyone hoping, praying you won't reject the donor heart . . . And don't forget a lifetime of medication, regular check-ups where people congratulate you for making it through another year, and every time you take a shower, or get dressed, or someone sees you naked there's this huge, vivid, jagged reminder running down your chest that your own body wasn't good enough, that you were broken, and that someone else had to *die* to give you a chance at a slightly better existence that, let's face it, might not be that much better at all . . .'

She's almost crying now, but I'm too scared to interrupt her, to try to comfort her, not because I don't think I'd be able to, but because I've realised I'm finally getting a glimpse of the real Angel. And something tells me it's something I need to see.

'Imagine, Noah, waking up every morning knowing you had a part of someone else inside you. That you couldn't make it through the day – no, scratch that, make it through the next two minutes, without them.'

'But that's exactly what I feel about you,' I say.

Angel silences me with a look. 'I'm sorry, but knowing that your very existence depends on this foreign body doing the job it's supposed to do, only somewhere it's not supposed to be . . . and even then, maybe not for that long.'

'But the statistics . . .'

'I've lived my life via statistics, Noah. Nine out of every thousand children are born with congenital heart disease. Just over half of them make it through to adulthood. A half again live until retirement. And only half of *them* actually get a heart transplant. Of those, while eighty-five per cent survive the operation, only sixty-two per cent actually survive for another ten years. If you work that out, then that's not painting a very positive picture statistically. And do you know what? At the moment, I might die, or I might not. That's fifty-fifty. And it might not be strictly accurate, but those are odds – if you excuse the phrase – I can live with.'

Angel turns and peers out into the downpour. There are people parked all around us, munching on Big Macs, tucking into fries, devouring Happy Meals, and since 'happy' is the last thing today's meal has turned out to be, all I can do is stare miserably at them through the rain-spattered windscreen. I've run out of things to say, and I certainly don't have any argument left – if I had any in the first place. After all, who am I to think I can know Angel for – and I quote – 'five minutes', and try to change her mind about something she's had her whole life to think about. And not only that, how can I do it without seeming selfish? I do want her to live for her, of course, but I'd quite like *us* to be a reason too.

'Noah . . .' Angel reaches across, grabs my hand and places it firmly on her left breast, causing the young couple who've just pulled their car into the space in front of us to hurriedly reverse out again. 'This broken heart of mine – I know it's not perfect, but it's what I am. It's a part of me. Just like some people have' – she peers at me – 'big ears, or a lopsided grin, or a nose that—'

'Okay, okay!' I glare at her, then see that she's smiling, but I suddenly don't feel like joking about this. 'Why are you marrying me, then?'

Angel lets out a short laugh. 'I was kidding about your ears.'

'Not *that*. I mean, if you've only, and I quote, "known me for five minutes"? Or is marriage just another one of those things you want to tick off on your bucket list, like rock climbing or eating jellied eels, so you made the first person who came along fall in love with you – and then, when they got down on one knee, you said, "Yeah, I'm not doing anything the second Tuesday in August, let's get hitched."'

Angel gives me a look I've never seen before. 'Is that really how you see it?' she says softly.

'Yes. Well, no. I don't know.' I throw my hands melodramatically up in the air. 'All I'm saying is, if you can change your mind about marriage, and make a decision like getting married after only five minutes, why can't you change your mind about the transplant? For me.'

'Yeah, sorry, I forgot this was all about you.'

'That's not what I mean,' I say, even though I suddenly realise that's how it sounds. 'It's just . . . All I'm trying to say is that, actually, life's pretty great. Having a future's pretty exciting.' I jerk a thumb back in the direction of my parents' house. 'Being able to think about what we might do in thirty years' time. Getting a dog. Buying a house. Having things to look forward to, things that give you a reason to get out of bed in the morning. While you still can. Because I'm worried that one day, you won't. And if that happens, well, then I won't want to either.'

Angel's crying now – not full-on shoulder-wracking sobs, but a steady leak from both eyes that shows no sign of stopping, and even in my limited experience, I'm pretty sure there's not a lot I can say that's going to help. Though in actual fact, I *don't* want to help. I want these shock tactics to hit home. To hurt. To *work*. Perhaps because my mum and dad have just reminded me what a future can look like, and I can't for the life of me understand why anyone wouldn't do all they can for some of that.

'I'm sorry, Angel,' I say, as I stare petulantly down at my feet. 'It just all seems so . . . unfair.'

'Yes, well, life's just not fair sometimes,' says Angel coldly. 'Especially when you're born with something that fucks up your life, fucks up your parents' lives, and in fact, does that to everyone you care about because you can't be what they want. Can't *do* what they want.'

'Yeah, well, it's tougher for the rest of us.'

'I'm sorry?' Angel's staring at me, open-mouthed. 'How is this tougher for *you*, exactly?'

I meet her gaze as I collect my thoughts, then realise I've got an answer for this one. 'Say you meet the most amazing girl in the world, fall head over heels in love with her, ask her to marry you, almost die of happiness when she says yes . . . but then reality hits home, and you realise that you're going to wake up next to her every day, and the *first thing* you're going to be doing is looking across at her to make sure she hasn't gone and died in the night.'

'We talked about this. At the restaurant. You promised me you wouldn't . . .'

'Yes, well, some promises turn out to be too much of an ask.' I shake my head. 'I know you're scared. I'm scared too. Scared that I'm already in over my head. Scared that your heart will fail, and that it'll rip *my* heart out in the process. And scared that I'll grow to resent you for not even investigating the possibility that you can get better. And that won't be fair on either of us.'

'That's not how—'

'Yes it is! Everyone who cares about you . . . you're just ignoring them. Being selfish. And while that's your right, to live how you want, what's not fair is to involve other people.'

'I never set out to—'

'That's not the point! "The only thing I can control is who else this affects," you said. "By not letting anyone get too close." Well, spoiler alert, you *can't* control it, because the reality is that me, your mum, your dad, we got too close. Despite your best efforts.'

'Noah . . .'

'I want to live with you, Angel. Really I do. So I'm sorry. Because I'm not sure I can live with that.'

'*Noah* . . .'

I reach for the door handle, pop the door open and make to get out of the car, though I've forgotten I've still got my seatbelt on, which ruins my dramatic exit somewhat, and while it's the sort of thing that normally Angel would laugh at, I don't need to look at her face to know that she's not laughing now. And in truth, I *can't* look at her face, because I know if I do, I don't want what's sure to be a look of complete and utter disappointment in me to be the last thing I remember about her.

So instead, I fumble for the button, fight my way out of the belt, climb out of the car, slam the door behind me and start walking in a random direction. And even though it's raining, and I don't have a coat *or* the faintest idea how to get home from here, being lost, wet, miserable and in the dark somehow feels kind of appropriate.

24.

I don't hear from Angel for the next couple of days, but then again, what was I expecting? Storming out of a car (at the second attempt) in the middle of a rainstorm while parked at a McDonalds is hardly the kind of mature behaviour you expect from a prospective life (however long that will be) partner.

And while I know I should probably call her and apologise, there's a bigger part of me that wants her to come running to me, to tell me she's finally seen sense, that what I said was, in fact, the right thing to do, and that she's booked in for her transplant next Tuesday, though as the week drags on, that starts to look more and more unlikely.

Besides, I've got some thinking to do, too. For the first time since we met, I've had to actually face up to the fact that I'm marrying someone who might *die*. And while I know that's true for everyone who gets married, when it's an actual, tangible chance it makes a difference. Perhaps it's something I won't be able to come to terms with. Or even worse, like I told her, Angel's refusal to do anything about it might be something I start to resent. And resentment is the last thing a relationship needs.

If she does die – at the risk of sounding callous (and without getting into some huge debate about the afterlife) – she won't know anything more about it. Won't have to deal with the aftermath. The consequences. Whereas I will. Every single day. And that's a pretty big deal.

'You win,' says Marlon when I tell him what happened. We're supposed to be going through Angel's colleague Nick's portfolio, and while he's really good – just the kind of young artist I love to exhibit – it's the exhibition I made of myself in front of Angel, or more importantly the reason for it, that's dominating the conversation.

'How do I *win*, exactly?'

He holds both hands up, like a fouling footballer protesting his innocence to the referee. 'I've been out with all sorts of women, but never one who might *die*.'

'Well, technically that's not—'

'You know what I mean.'

'So what should I do?'

Marlon folds his arms, and stares contemplatively out of the window. 'You should think about dating someone else,' he says, after a moment.

'What?'

'Whenever I'm seeing someone, and I'm not sure about them, I go out with someone else, just to see how I feel about the first one. Clarifies things.'

'You go out with different people all the time!'

'Proves my point. If I'd met the person I wanted to settle down with, then I wouldn't.'

I open my mouth to argue, then shut it again, because Marlon's already flicking through his phone contacts list. 'So,' he says, 'let's see how you get on with . . .' He stops scrolling, though I hope it's not randomly. 'April.'

'Who?'

'April. She's a friend of mine. You'll like her.' He jabs at the screen. 'I'm setting the two of you up on a date.'

'Um . . .'

'What?'

'Well, excuse the obvious question, but you do know I'm getting married in . . .' I look at the date on my watch. 'Four weeks?'

Marlon laughs. 'Doesn't look like that from where I'm sitting. Besides, you might need a—'

'Back-up? In case Angel suddenly drops dead?'

Marlon's grin fades. 'No. Although now you come to mention it . . .' He perches on the end of my desk. 'I just don't want you to be blinded by the situation.'

'The situation?'

'*Angel's* situation.'

'Are you suggesting this is some kind of . . . mercy relationship? I've met a pretty girl with the biggest sob story you can imagine, so I'm doing her a *favour*?'

'No. But you might think you can *save* her.' He shakes his head. 'I just think you should take a step back and think about what it is you really want. And one way to do that is to remind yourself what it's like to go out with someone normal.'

'Angel *is* normal. Ish. Besides, I suspect that's been my problem.'

'You know what I mean. You might just find it's a bit less . . . hassle, going out with someone who doesn't bring her kind of complications to the table.'

'I *like* her complications. Most of them.'

'Noah, relationships can be difficult at the best of times. A relationship with Angel, given her situation . . .' Marlon smiles. 'I just think you need to be sure that this is what you want.'

'And going out with someone else will help me decide?'

Marlon nods. 'I never said all thirteen dates had to be with the same person. So, I'll set it up?'

'No!'

He sighs. 'Okay. How about I arrange to meet her for a drink. You "happen" to bump into me, I'll invite you to join us and you see what you think?'

'I'm not sure—'

'Just talk to her. Spend a bit of time in the company of someone else.'

'That's all?'

'One drink. No pressure. Just think of it as window shopping. Or test-driving a car. Tasting the wine before you actually order a bottle. Or not even tasting it – sticking your nose in the glass and scenting the bouquet . . .'

'Okay, okay. One drink. But just to be clear, I'm not sleeping with her.'

Marlon looks at me for a moment, then bursts out laughing. And while I can perhaps see why, right now, I'm not finding *any* of this funny at all.

April's what most tabloid newspapers would call a 'stunna' – model-pretty, with long dark hair, and an amazing figure that the short, low-cut, so-tight-it's-amazing-she-can-breathe blue dress she's wearing gives me a comprehensive view of. She's so obviously out of my league – no, in a *different* league, and one where they play a completely different sport – that I'd have been in danger of not realising it was her at all, if not for the fact that, sitting next to her at the bar, is Marlon.

For a moment, I consider turning around and leaving. Not only to spare myself the embarrassment of April ignoring me all evening in favour of Mister Smooth, but also because there's a part of me that suspects Marlon's planning to give me a full rundown afterwards on my 'technique'. But I can't, because he's probably right – in the light of my situation with Angel, I could do with a yardstick – and also because his loud 'Noah! Come and join us!', coupled with some overenthusiastic waving, means I've already been spotted.

We've chosen a pub in Twickenham, on the river, and about as far away from Angel's normal stomping ground as possible (on my insistence, to reduce the chances of me being 'caught'), but even so, I check she's not here before giving them a quick wave back. I nod towards the toilet, tap my watch and do an anxious little dance to suggest I'm desperate – though the only thing I'm actually desperate for is to be anywhere but here. Then, after a quick freshen-up, I take a deep breath, head back out into the bar, do my best to walk over to where they're sitting without tripping over anything and climb a little awkwardly up onto the stool Marlon's leather jacket's been guarding.

'Noah!' says Marlon, leaping off his stool and enveloping me in a hug, as if I'm his long-lost bestie rather than someone he finished work with an hour ago. 'What a pleasant surprise.'

'Marlon.'

I'm in my newest, trendiest suit, my most expensive watch is on my wrist, and I've even polished my shoes as per his instructions – but though I'm in my Sunday best, I probably don't compare to even a Monday-morning April.

'April, this is my friend Noah,' he says. 'Noah, this is April.'

April extends a perfectly manicured hand towards me, and I'm not sure whether to shake it or kiss it. 'Hello, Noah,' she purrs, in a voice that's part public school, part forty-a-day. 'Marlon's been telling me all about you.'

'*All* about me?' I say, going for the safer 'shake' option while trying to hide my disappointment that I've been in the toilet for all of two minutes, and that's still long enough for him to divulge my life story.

'That's right.'

I raise both eyebrows at Marlon, wondering whether that included the 'Angel' part. 'I hope he's left us with something to talk about?'

'I'm sure we'll find something. Even if it's only me!' April lets out a honking laugh, and my nerves make me join in as if it's the best joke I've ever heard.

'Can I get anyone a drink?' I ask, just as I spot they've both got full glasses.

'I think we're fine,' says Marlon, then he slips his phone out of his pocket and frowns at it. 'Oh no!'

'What?'

'I've just remembered; I've got a thing.'

I do a double take, then realise he can't mean a 'thing' like Angel's. 'What?'

'You have to *go?*' says April.

'Really sorry, babe. Completely forgot.' Marlon gives me a look, then jumps down from his stool. 'Noah, you wouldn't mind keeping April company while she finishes her drink, would you?'

'What?' I say, in the split second before I realise what he's up to, and that there's not much I can say except for: 'Of course not.' Even though, by the looks of her, April wouldn't be on her own for very long.

'Thanks,' he says, sliding his untouched beer across to me.

'You can't even stay for five minutes?'

I must sound a little panicky, because for a moment, Marlon looks like he's considering it. 'No. Sorry. Much as I'd love to hang around and play gooseberry,' he says, his expression suggesting that actually, he would. 'I'll leave you two to get to know each other. Have fun!'

With a wink in my direction, followed by a hug and a kiss *on the lips* for April, he saunters off, and as she watches him go as if he's the last train home she's just missed, I shrug in a 'circumstances, eh?' kind of way.

'Well, this is awkward.'

'Isn't it?' April takes a sip of her cocktail – probably one of those 'slippery nipples' or 'screaming orgasms', though I don't dare ask. 'So, Noah . . .'

'So?'

'If I didn't know better, I'd say we've just been set up.'

'I'm not sure he—'

'Marlon tells me you're an art dealer?'

'That's' – I hesitate, although I suppose it's true. The Hanksys have been selling. Though as to whether they're actually *art* – 'right. And what else has he told you, exactly?'

'Not much. Art dealer . . .' She begins counting things off on her fingers. 'Sports car driver, horse rider, rock climber . . . Quite the gentleman. Or should that be *action man?*'

I narrow my eyes, only now realising how exactly Marlon's managed to convince April to hang around this evening – on the basis of that description, *I'd* probably be interested in meeting me too. 'Well . . .' Marlon's beer is looking increasingly tempting, so I gulp a third of it down, then think *what the hell?* 'Guilty as charged.'

'And how do you know Marlon?'

I'm tempted to say *he's a soon-to-be ex-employee who's set us up because I'm having doubts about my fiancée,* and put an end to this little charade right now. 'We work together. You?'

'Oh, we don't work together.' April laughs. 'Though I suppose you'd know that. Seeing as you and he do. We dated. For a while.'

'Right. And . . . ?'

'It's complicated.' April honk-laughs again, though the sound's beginning to get a little annoying. 'And are *you* seeing anyone right now?'

'Like you said. It's complicated.'

'How so?'

'Pardon?'

'How is it complicated?'

I down the next third of Marlon's beer, mainly to give me a bit of thinking time. Normally, 'it's complicated' is something you say, and it's accepted, and you move on. You certainly don't expect to be called on it, or have to explain yourself.

'I suppose . . . well . . . that's a good question.'

'And the answer is . . . ?' says April, when I don't say anything further.

'She . . . I'm just not sure if there's any future in it.'

'And a future's important to you, is it?'

'Yes, actually. It is.'

April pulls the cocktail stick out of her glass and – making eye contact the whole time – slowly pulls the cherry off with her teeth. 'Not into one-night stands, then?'

I almost drop my glass in shock. 'Well, um . . .'

'Relax, Noah. I'm teasing you.'

And this is how the evening goes. We have another drink, I do my best to maintain the action-man, art-dealing, fake Noah that Marlon's created, while April flirts with me (or rather, him) and quizzes me patiently about the girl I'd rather be here with. And the problem with this is, the more I talk about Angel – though I'm careful not to mention her by name – the more I know this evening's a mistake.

Eventually, April downs the last of her cocktail, reaches across the table and pulls my sleeve up.

'Is that a new watch?'

'I'm sorry?'

'Only you keep looking at it. So either it's new, and you're admiring it, or you're bored. I'm choosing to believe it's the first one.'

'I'm sorry, Angel. I—'

'What did you call me?'

'Um . . . April?'

'No you didn't. You called me Angel. So either that's a pet name you've come up with for me this evening – and trust me, it couldn't be more inappropriate – or it's the name of your "complication".'

'I don't think I—'

'Noah, *please*.'

'No, you must have misheard. Or perhaps it was a slip of the tongue. I mean, they're so similar. Listen . . .' I repeat 'Angel' and 'April' several times in succession, like a child trying to confuse themselves with 'red lorry, yellow lorry'. 'See? Easy mistake to—'

April sighs loudly. 'Sure,' she says, then she slips, snake-like, down from her stool and gathers up her coat.

'Where are you going?'

'*Home*, Noah.'

'Why?' I say, hoping I don't sound too relieved.

'Because of the way you've talked about *her* all evening.'

'What? I'm sorry. I—'

April rubs my upper arm as if trying to console me. 'It's okay, Noah. You're obviously still in love with her.'

'That's not . . . Do you think so?'

April smiles. 'A girl can tell.'

She stands on tiptoe, kisses me briefly on the cheek, then turns and walks – no, glides – out of the bar, and as I watch her go, I realise something important. April is funny, and smart, and beautiful, and sexy, and interesting, and fit, and probably not about to die any time soon – all the things I, or anyone, would normally look for in a woman. But there's one thing she isn't – she even said so herself – and it's the most important aspect.

She's no Angel.

25.

I ring Angel's work first thing, but there's no answer on her extension, and when the receptionist tells me she's called in sick, I initially start to panic, before realising that if she was *that* sick, she'd hardly be calling in.

When I eventually drag my miserable self downstairs, a preoccupied-looking Mary is waiting for me in the front room, though I don't get a chance to check what the matter is, because her 'Is everything all right?', said in the tone of someone who can see that, quite clearly, it isn't, quite unbelievably sets me off crying.

'It's Angel,' I manage, after a moment or two.

'She's okay?' says Mary quickly.

'Oh, it's nothing like that. Though that would almost be easier to deal with.'

'Don't be so sure.'

I blow my nose on the tissue Mary's produced from the constant supply up her sleeve, and flop down onto the sofa. 'We had an argument.'

'Is that all?'

'It was a pretty bad one. I said some things . . .'

'Can you take them back?'

'I don't know. Even if I could, I still meant them. And she knows that.'

'Was there any justification in what you said?'

I nod. 'I think so.'

'And did she have a valid response?'

'I suppose.'

'So it was a difference of opinion. Not an argument. Which means you can just talk about it. Put it behind you. Move on.'

'I'm not so sure.'

Mary hauls herself out of her chair, walks slowly across to where I'm sitting and lowers herself carefully down onto the sofa. 'Well, in that case, just apologise. Tell her you were out of order. Sometimes "sorry" is the most useful word.'

'Even though I'm not?'

'Oftentimes, we just have to accept people, Noah. Faults and all.' Mary smiles. 'I'm sure Angel knows that too.'

'But why does it hurt so much?'

She reaches over and pats the back of my hand. 'Because you're in love.'

'I'm beginning to wish I wasn't.'

'You don't mean that.'

'No, but . . . To have this feeling, and then face the prospect of it being taken away from you, and there's nothing you can do about it . . .'

'You don't know what's around the corner. No one does. And if there's one thing life has taught me, you've got to take your chance at happiness the moment it comes. Even if it *does* only last a moment. So find her. Talk to her. Apologise. Do whatever it takes.'

'Okay, okay.' I sigh. 'That's assuming she ever speaks to me again.'

'I'm sure she will. Remember, the course of true love never runs smoothly.'

'Is that another Shakespeare quote?'

'Actually, I think I heard it on *Downton Abbey*.' Mary lets out a short chuckle. 'You two were meant to be together. Something happened when you met. And you'd be silly not to give it another chance.'

'Even with everything stacked against us?'

'Why not?'

'Well, for one thing, she might hate me. I'm already pretty sure her dad hates me. Mine will probably hate me when they find out I haven't told them she might die at any moment. And the worst thing is, she might.'

Mary smiles, then waves all my arguments away. 'Just ask yourself one thing,' she says. 'Do you love her?'

I nod.

'Well, in that case,' says Mary, 'you know what you have to do.'

Doing it is harder than I'd thought, mainly because when I get outside, my car won't start. And while I hope that's not a metaphor for me and Angel given how it was working perfectly yesterday – at least in this case, the solution is a phone call away.

After half an hour or so, the familiar yellow AA van pulls up outside, and a smiley, grey-haired man my father's age jumps out.

'It's the MGB,' I say, 'parked outside the church hall on the corner,' and as I lead him across to it, the man's grin widens.

'I used to have one of these. Nineteen sixty-eight. Wire wheels, the lot.' He pats my car affectionately on the roof, then jumps into the driver's seat and lets out a happy sigh, as if trying on a comfortable pair of shoes. 'What seems to be the problem?'

I fold my arms and tilt my head to one side in the universal man-comments-to-another-man-on-a-mechanical-issue way. 'It, um, won't start.'

'Right.' The mechanic turns the key in the ignition, then cocks an ear. 'Has it been running okay up until now?'

'Yeah. I mean, occasionally it takes a couple of goes to fire, but generally . . .' I glance up at the sky, which is still a threatening grey colour. 'And it doesn't seem to like the rain much.'

'Who does?' The AA man pops the bonnet, climbs stiffly out of the front seat, then marches around to the front of the car. 'Try it again for me?'

I reach in and do as instructed, and he smiles knowingly. 'Sounds like your distributor cap.'

'How can you tell?'

'Like I said – used to have one of these. Lovely car, but always breaking down, it was. After a while, you learn to read the signs.'

'Can you fix it?'

He nods. 'I can get you going again. Might be worth you investing in a new one soon, though.'

'A new *car*?'

He grins. 'Distributor cap. They're only a few quid. In the meantime, I just need to employ a bit of specialist technology . . .'

I stand back and watch as he pops a couple of clips off a small, black plastic – well – *thing*, that looks like some robotic octopus, and pulls it from the engine bay. 'Here,' he says, showing me the octopus's innards. 'See that build-up of corrosion there? You just need to . . .' He reaches in with the end of a screwdriver, scrapes away at a couple of the metal bits, gives it a squirt of WD-40, then puts it back where it came from. 'Try it again,' he says.

I cross my fingers, and turn the key again, widening my eyes as the car starts first time. 'That's amazing!'

The man shrugs. 'Lovely thing like this wasn't really built to last. It's going to break down now and then. Trick is to know how to get it going again.'

As he hops back into his van and drives off, I catch sight of a poster on the noticeboard outside the church hall, and whether it's fate, or an omen, or finally something going my way, the timing just couldn't be better.

Mary's right, of course – which is why I find myself waiting outside Angel's office that evening. And while I perhaps wasn't expecting to be welcomed back with open arms, her brusque 'What do you want, Noah?' when she eventually emerges is a little frostier than I was hoping for.

'Um, to apologise?'

'Are you asking me, or telling me?'

'Telling you.' I hand Angel one of the flat whites I've carried all the way from Starbucks, which are probably a bit *too* flat now, given that I miscalculated what time she'd be finishing. When she takes the coffee, I see that as a good sign, although it could simply be that she's preparing to throw it back in my face, like it looks she's planning to do with my apology.

As she peels the lid off the cup and peers inside, I glance nervously at my watch, conscious I'm in danger of missing the CPR class I've booked onto in the light of the AA man's advice, though of course, if Angel *doesn't* accept my apology, there'll be no point me going.

'So . . . Sorry.'

'Is that it?'

'What more do you want me to say?'

'Quite a lot more, actually. I need to know that you're not going to throw a fit every time you don't get your own way. That you won't keep bringing this up every chance you get. That I won't have to constantly feel on edge that you're suddenly going to go out and buy one of those awful eighties 'Choose Life' T-shirts and parade around the house in it. That I'm not going to be made to feel guilty for not wanting to undergo something that you seem to think is as straightforward as going to the dentist for a filling . . .'

'I don't.'

'No?'

'No. Not anymore, at least. I, um, watched the video again. And did a bit of research. And realised that it, you know, wasn't, ahem, *fair* of me to try to enforce my ill-informed views on you. It showed a lack of respect for what you're going through. Of course you know better. And I should understand that, rather than attempt to change your mind.'

Angel stares at me for a moment, then her expression softens. 'Did you rehearse that?'

'Once or twice. With Marlon.'

'It was pretty good.' She puts the coffee cup to her lips, takes a long drag, then grimaces. 'It's a bit lukewarm.'

'You mean the coffee, right? And not my apology?'

'Right.'

'It's just . . .' I surreptitiously check the time again, then stare down at my shoes, wondering how long the sweet wrapper stuck to the sole of the left one has been there. 'Being at my parents, seeing how happy they are, knowing they've been together for so long . . . Can you blame me for wanting some of that?'

'You'll have some of that.'

'Yes, but *how much* some?' I say, then frown at my bad English. 'You could' – I swallow hard – 'go at any moment.'

'So could anyone. Hit by a bus. Car crash. Terrorist attack.' Angel's counting them off on her fingers. 'This is just another way. It could get me tomorrow; it might get me in twenty years' time. As could any of those other things.'

'Yes, but . . . you can't avoid most of that lot.'

She drops her coffee into a nearby bin. 'You seem to think I'm just standing in the bus lane, waiting for the number 49 to come along and run me over, and there's a simple way I could step back onto the pavement, and yet I won't do that, because the bus doesn't look like it's coming just yet, and I might trip on the kerb and kill myself that way.'

I replay what she's just said a couple of times, then grin guiltily. 'Yup.'

Angel grabs my hand and squeezes my fingers tightly. 'I'm fine as I am, Noah. It's a strategy you – and my parents – might not approve of, but it's gotten me to thirty. Who's to say it won't get me to sixty? Or even further?' She smiles grimly at me. 'Can't you just accept this?'

'Do I have a choice?'

'Of course you do.'

I know what she means. That I can walk away from her right now, out of her life, and get on with mine. But I already know there's no way that's going to happen. 'Actually, I don't,' I say. 'Because I love you.'

Angel stares at me for a second, then she takes a quick step forward and kisses me, but I don't know whether it's an 'apology accepted' kiss, or a 'goodbye' one, because she follows it with: 'That might not be enough.'

I look at my watch a third time, and Angel sighs exasperatedly. 'Is there somewhere you need to be?'

By your side, I want to tell her, but instead, I say, 'Actually, yes,' and Angel's eyes flash.

'Where?'

'I'd rather not—'

'Noah, what could possibly be more important than this?'

'I'm, um, doing a CPR course. I've just signed up. It's tonight. In the church hall at the end of my—'

'What?'

'CPR. It stands for Cardio—'

'I know what it stands for,' says Angel, looking at me in disbelief. 'What on earth are you doing that for?'

'Because I respect your decision. And I realise it's your decision. And . . .'

'And what?'

'And I don't want to lose you.'

And if I wasn't sure before, as she grabs me ever-so-tightly and pulls me close, even though she's burst into tears, I suddenly know a hundred per cent that Angel and I are back on.

26.

The church hall is somewhere I've never even stuck my head inside in the five or so years I've lived here, despite the hundreds of badly designed posters that have appeared on the noticeboard by the door, advertising everything from Keep Fit to Karate, Ballet to Badminton, and Jumble Sales to Judo, and as soon as I walk through the door, I can see I haven't been missing anything: it's draughty, and dusty, and the 'Toddlers Tae Kwon Do' class that's preceded us has left a strange smell of cheesy feet and wee in the air. But I'm here for an important reason, I remind myself: to turn myself into Angel's 'AA man'. And this is the quickest – and cheapest, given the added bonus that it's free – way to do that.

There's a dozen of us sitting in a semicircle on uncomfortable stackable chairs, their seats worn smooth by a decade or more's succession of bottoms, and at the front, a bouncy, middle-aged woman – the type you see in sitcoms as the overly-helpful-but-ultimately-annoying next-door neighbour – is standing over one of those rubber CPR dummies, waiting for the murmuring from the other attendees to die down.

I'm the youngest in the group by about thirty years – the rest are pensioners, obviously hoping they'll learn enough to keep their other halves going in case of an incident, which, let's face it, is exactly why I'm here.

The woman standing in front of us – Mandy, so her name tag tells us – glances up at the large clock on the wall, double-checks the time on her watch, then claps her hands together, causing the old man next to me to start awake.

'Is everybody here?'

There's a muted grumble from the assembled pensioners, along with the sound of creaking – furniture, and joints – as a few of them haul themselves upright in their chairs, and Mandy beams at us. Then an old man sitting two seats to my left raises his hand, and Mandy nods in acknowledgement.

'It's our first week. So unless that's addressed to the people who aren't, and therefore who can't answer because they're *not* here, how would we know?'

Mandy eyes him as a shopkeeper might an awkward customer. 'Well . . . you might have friends who are supposed to be coming, and aren't here yet. Or you might have come with someone who's still parking the car.'

She smiles, pleased with her answer, until an old lady at the back pipes up with: 'It's residents' parking around here. So chances are, people walked.'

'Or came on the bus,' says someone else.

'Besides, there was only twelve chairs put out,' says the gruff old man next to me.

Mandy's looking a little put-out herself. 'Well, in any case, shall we begin?' she says, not quite as cheerfully. Then, when there's no dissent: 'So, thank you for coming. For those of you who don't know me, or with poor eyesight' – she lets out a loud, slightly maniacal laugh as she taps her name badge – 'my name's Mandy.' She pauses to allow a muted chorus of 'Evening, Mandy' to die down. 'Now, a question. What's the most valuable skill anyone can have?'

There's silence around the room, then a croaky voice says, 'Knowing how to make crystal meth?'

'Pardon?'

The old man next to me has got his hand up. 'I seen it on that *Breaking Bad* on TV. And it seemed like a pretty valuable skill to me.'

Mandy frowns at him. 'Oh-kay,' she says, evidently not a *Breaking Bad* fan. 'Something else?'

I peer around the group. People are looking at their shoes, the floor, the hall's stained-glass windows. Anything to avoid answering the question.

'Anyone?' says Mandy, her cheerful veneer looking like it's about to crack. 'Anyone at all?'

With a sigh, I put my hand up, and she flashes a smile in my direction. 'Yes?'

'CPR?'

Mandy beams at me. 'CPR. Well done. What's your name?'

'Noah.'

'Thank you, Noah. Now, everyone, what does CPR stand for?'

The old man next to me leans across and lowers his voice. 'If she doesn't know, what's she doing teaching the class?'

'Anyone?' says Mandy. She's looking hopefully in my direction, and while I don't want to hog the limelight, if someone doesn't answer, I fear we might be here all night.

'Cardiopulmonary resuscitation.'

As Mandy looks at me like I've saved *her* life, there's a mumbled 'Teacher's pet' from behind me.

'Well done, Noah! And "cardio" is to do with . . . ?'

I'm willing someone else to answer. Anyone. But by the looks of them, the course is interrupting what would normally be nap-in-front-of-the-telly time.

'The heart,' I say. 'And, um, pulmonary is to do with breathing.'

I've anticipated her next question, mainly because I'm trying to hurry things along, but Mandy looks a little miffed, as if I've deviated off-script.

'So, that's the heart, and breathing. Now, what might be the signs of an episode?' she says, though I take it she doesn't mean of *Breaking Bad*.

'Well, there aren't any, are there?' says the man who answered the first question, and Mandy frowns.

'Pardon?'

'If someone's had an "episode". There won't *be* any signs. That's what we're here for. To learn how to get them going again.'

'Oh-kay,' says Mandy, again. 'Well, what signs *won't* there be?'

There's a polite cough behind me, from a grey-haired old lady with her hand up. 'Can *I* ask a question?' she says.

'Of course.' Mandy beams encouragingly at her. 'What do you want to know?'

'It's just that you seem to be asking all the questions. All the time. And they're questions we don't know the answers to. Otherwise we wouldn't be here. Obviously.'

Mandy's still looking at her, as if she's waiting for an actual question.

'So, could you perhaps just *tell* us about CPR? Rather than asking us about it? Otherwise we're never going to get anywhere, are we?'

'Including home,' says the man next to me.

Mandy's smile is beginning to falter, but to her credit, she manages to hold it together. 'Yes. Of course. I didn't realise you were all complete beginners.'

'Is there any other kind?' says the man two seats to my left. 'I mean, you're either a beginner or you've done it before. So to suggest there's such a thing as a *complete* beginner . . .'

'Exactly.' The old man next to the woman who's just taken Mandy to task – her husband, possibly, given how she's picking a bit of fluff from his jumper – pipes up. 'Plus the course is called "Beginners CPR".'

'I know that,' says Mandy, with a hint of exasperation. 'Seeing as I'm the tutor.'

'So who did you expect to turn up?' the old man behind me continues. 'A hall full of retired doctors who just wanted a bit of a refresher?'

Mandy surveys the class in an 'I've got your number' kind of way. 'Right,' she says, through gritted teeth. 'So, you walk into your front room, and you see that your partner has had an episode.'

Another hand goes up – the same man two seats away. 'I don't have a partner.'

'Really,' says Mandy, sounding not-at-all-surprised. 'Well, imagine you walk into a room – any room – and you see someone – anyone – having an episode, which you'll be able to tell, because they'll be non-responsive . . .'

'That sounds like my ex-wife,' says a man at the back, to a round of tittering.

'So, first of all, you need to check their breathing. See if their chest is rising and falling; put your ear to their nose and mouth and see whether you can hear anything . . .' She looks around the class, remind-ing herself of the average age. 'Actually, forget that. Look to see if they've got blue lips. Or you might want to check their pulse, either at the neck . . .' Mandy strides across to the man who made the *Breaking Bad* comment, and jabs a couple of fingers into the side of his neck. 'Or at the wrist,' she says, grabbing his arm and roughly twisting it upwards.

As the man rubs his shoulder, Mandy peers threateningly down at him. 'Then, the first thing you need to do is get them onto the floor,' she says, strolling back over to the dummy, much to the relief of the man she's just assaulted.

'What if they're already on the floor?'

This comes from a woman in the corner, and to tell the truth, I'm feeling a bit sorry for Mandy now, especially when a few of the other attendees start to murmur in agreement.

'Pardon?'

'If they've had an episode, like you say,' suggests someone else, 'they're probably going to be on the floor, aren't they?'

'They may have had it in a chair. Or a bed.'

'But they could have fallen out,' adds a man from the opposite side of the room.

As a debate starts amongst the attendees as to the most likely scenario, Mandy glances towards the fire exit, and I can't blame her – it's like it's open season. 'Okay,' she almost shouts. 'Let's assume they're on the floor. The first thing you do is check for a response.' She kneels down, grabs the dummy by the shoulders and shakes it violently, accompanied by a loud 'Can you hear me?', which the wag to my left points out is 'a waste of time as it hasn't got any ears'.

'So, we've established they're non-responsive, and breathing erratically, or not at all. And perhaps you can't feel a pulse . . .' She glances up to make sure no one is about to interrupt. 'Now, are there any circumstances when you *don't* want to begin CPR?'

'If you don't like them?'

'If they've left you a lot of money in their will?'

'If they've just eaten garlic?'

As a ripple of laughter runs around the room, Mandy sighs. 'Nooo,' she says, drawing the word out like a schoolteacher in front of a class of five-year-olds might. 'If there's any danger to *you*. If they've been electrocuted, for example, or are lying in the middle of a busy road.' She looks around the room and fixes a couple of the troublemakers with a murderous glance. 'If not, and it's safe to proceed, the first thing you do is . . . ?'

When no one answers, Mandy slips her phone out of her pocket. 'Call for help. And who are you going to call?' She glares at the class, daring them to say 'Ghostbusters'.

I put my hand up, and she smiles in relief at a sympathetic face. 'Emergency services?'

'That's right, Noah.' Mandy nods, then mimes punching three buttons on her phone. '999. Tell them where you are, and what's happened. But remember, they might take a while to arrive, so the next bit's the most important – and why we're all here, yes?'

There's a grumbling round the room, and Mandy takes a deep breath. 'So . . . let's CPR!'

She's announced it in a 'let's get ready to rumble' kind of way, but the assembled wannabe first-aiders are still busy writing down 'Call 999' in their notebooks. Or at least, the ones who remembered to bring one are.

'Okay. First of all, you have to check the airway.'

Mandy pulls open the dummy's mouth, and makes a show of peering carefully inside. 'If there's an obstruction – food, false teeth – it's imperative you remove it before you start. *Their* false teeth,' she adds, as the old man next to me starts to extract his.

'Then, you locate the bottom of their sternum, link your fingers like this . . .'

'Aren't you supposed to give them a thump first?' says the man whose pulse she took.

'What?'

'I saw it on *Casualty*. You give them a thump.'

Mandy looks at him as if, where he's concerned, she's considering doing exactly that. 'No. Not anymore. As I was saying, you link your fingers, rest one hand on top of the other, find a spot approximately two inches up from the bottom of the sternum, and then . . .' She leans over the dummy and begins to push down hard on its chest. 'Begin compressions. Thirty of them. At a rate of about a hundred per minute.'

The man to my left is showing a sudden interest in Mandy's technique, though that's probably because of the view down her top as she leans over the dummy and jigs up and down.

'Then,' continues Mandy, 'once you've done your thirty compressions, you give two rescue breaths . . .' She places one hand on the dummy's chin and the other on its forehead, and tilts the head back. 'So . . . Pinch the nose shut, make a seal over the mouth with *your* mouth, and then blow, twice, keeping an eye on the chest to ensure it inflates.'

The man to my left looks like he's about to pass out, given how closely he's keeping an eye on Mandy's chest.

'Right. Now it's your turn.'

The assembled oldies look at each other in consternation, as if they're expected to practise on each other, but after a moment, Mandy simply says the word 'dummies', which perhaps understandably, seems to give her a lot of satisfaction.

She nods to the back of the hall, where a series of dummies have been set up on trestle tables next to the wall, so dutifully we head over and practise, Mandy patrolling up and down in front of us until she's sure we've got the technique correct. In truth, it's harder than it looks: the breathing part takes a lot of effort, and if five minutes of compressions are raising a sweat in me, they're also making a few of the group look like they're in danger of having an episode themselves.

Eventually, once Mandy's happy, she directs us all back to our seats. 'Does anyone have any questions?' she says, with the look of someone who really hopes they don't.

Everyone's fidgeting, obviously keen to get home, but I tentatively raise my arm. 'I've got one.'

Mandy smiles. 'Yes, Noah?'

'How effective is this?'

She frowns. 'Well, it's hard to really say, but generally, around ten per cent of people who have CPR performed on them in this way will survive.'

'Ten per cent?!' the man next to me sputters, as if he's just given up two hours of his valuable napping-in-front-of-the-television-time for *this*. 'It's hardly worth it.'

He's right, of course. All things considered, a ten per cent chance is closer to no chance. But when you think about it – and I think about it a *lot* – it's certainly better than nothing.

27.

A funny thing happens at this morning's parkrun. Angel's not here – she's still boycotting her occasional volunteering role given her dad's behaviour at dinner the previous week – but I've dragged myself out of bed anyway. It's a hot day, and alongside my normal cap, hoodie and sunglasses combination, I'm wearing even more clothes than usual in the hope that Lawrence won't recognise me, so I'm a sweaty mess even before I get there; but it's just as well, as he's the first person I see when I arrive.

Making sure I keep as far away from him as I can at the start, partly because I don't want Rocket to pick up my scent, I let the two of them sprint away from me (though 'let' isn't quite correct, given that Rocket is pulling Lawrence through the first hundred metres at a speed I can only dream of), then settle into a steady rhythm. Pushing on, I manage to maintain the gap during the middle part of the race, and by the time I start the closing lap, I seem to be gradually beginning to reel them in.

Admittedly, it's not muddy, so I'm not carrying half the field round with me in the tread of my trainers this morning, and I've done more practice runs this week in an attempt to direct my frustration at Angel's intransigence into more positive things, plus I'm fuelled by adrenaline given the way Lawrence treated me over dinner – but even so, I'm more than a little surprised. And while there's still a fair bit of ground to cover, the sight of them up ahead is all the motivation I need.

I pick up my pace, though I'm already breathing hard, and get to within a hundred metres or so, but there's less than the same distance again to go to the finish line, so reluctantly I slow down when I realise I'm not going to catch them (and that I'm possibly going to collapse). Then Rocket suddenly plants all four legs into the ground, and like a speedboat that's just thrown out a (dog-shaped) anchor, the two of them come to an abrupt stop.

As Rocket squats down and *starts to do a poo*, and Lawrence's loud 'Gah!' echoes round the park, I can't believe my luck. 'Come *on*, Rocket,' says Lawrence, who looks like he's considering picking the dog up and carrying his still-defecating body over the line. But by the looks of Rocket, he's not going anywhere, and nor, as a result, is Lawrence. Which means the momentum has just seriously swung in my direction.

As Lawrence extracts a plastic bag from the little bone-shaped container dangling off Rocket's lead and attempts to hold it underneath the dog's bottom while simultaneously encouraging him to get going again, I dig deep and hit top speed. With a sarcastic '*meep meep!*' I go shooting past, just as Rocket is pawing the ground with his back legs in a 'finished' kind of way, though it's too late for Lawrence, who's frantically trying to tie a knot in the plastic bag and lob it into the nearest bin.

Nervously, I glance back over my shoulder. There's less than fifty metres to go, and by my estimations, even with the now considerably lighter Rocket, there's no way they'll possibly catch me. All I have to do is keep putting one foot in front of the other . . .

With a grin on my face, I sail across the line, then collapse against a nearby tree, just in time to see them sprinting desperately in behind me. Lawrence has a face like thunder, and I wouldn't bet on Rocket getting his dinner any time soon, and for a moment I consider doing the big reveal and showing him exactly who it is who's rubbed his face – proverbially, at least – in the (dog) dirt. But then I realise something, and it's something that doesn't just apply to parkrun.

I don't want to win by default. I want to win because I deserve it.

Saturday afternoon, however, isn't funny at all. Mary's decided to spend a 'trial' month at Parkview, and though we both suspect it's going to be a trial in all senses of the word, she's determined to go through with it.

Angel's offered to drive, because it's raining, and while we could just as easily take a taxi, I've gladly accepted, particularly because, with Mary and Marlon as our witnesses at the registry office next month, it'll be good for them to spend some time getting to know each other. Though after a pub lunch where the two of them get on so well I hardly get a word in edgeways, Angel almost seems more upset about dropping her at Parkview than I do.

'Now, it's only for a few weeks. Are you sure you'll be all right?'

'I should be saying the same thing to you,' I say. 'You don't have to do this, you know. You could stay at home, we could sort something out in terms of care . . .'

Mary sits down on the bed, and rocks back and forth to check the condition of the mattress. 'Yes, I do,' she says. 'Besides, the last thing you need is some old person getting in the way . . .'

'That's no way to talk about my husband-to-be,' says Angel, plonking herself down next to Mary. 'You're sure you've got everything?'

'I think so,' she says as she surveys the room. It's on the upper floor of the building, and not quite as 'palatial' as the one we saw a few weeks previously, with a few scuff-marks on the walls (that Angel whispers to me are probably from an attempted cat-swinging). But at least she's spared the train noise.

'It certainly seems like it,' I say, having struggled to lift her suitcase out of the car a few minutes earlier.

'Well, just call if there's anything else you need.' Angel gives her a hug. 'Clothes, food . . . We could smuggle in a mobile phone. Or some drugs . . .'

'Or arrange a jailbreak,' I suggest, trying to swallow the lump in my throat.

'Now now, Noah. This is the only way to find out whether I'm going to get on with this place.' She pauses as the sound of a guitar being tuned wafts up from downstairs. 'And I'm sure the time's going to absolutely fly by.'

'Right, well, we'll leave you to get settled in,' I say, giving her a hug myself. 'And I'll be back to visit.'

'Lovely.'

'Bye then.'

'Oh, I hate goodbyes,' says Mary. 'Let's just say "see you", and be done with it.'

'Okay. Well, see you,' I say.

'See you,' echoes Angel.

'Wouldn't want to be you!' says Mary, giggling like a five-year-old.

It's meant to be funny, but from the way Mary's smile falters as we leave, and even though she knows Angel's secret, I suspect she actually would.

We've hardly left the car park when Angel sighs loudly, and makes the kind of face you'd tell a child off for.

'Christ,' she says, accelerating into a gap in the traffic that's barely there.

'What?'

'Parkview. Talk about God's waiting room.'

'It's not that bad.'

'*Not that bad?* I was in there for five minutes, and I'm already thinking I'll have to burn these clothes to get rid of the smell of wee-soaked carpets and boiled cabbage and – hold on . . .' She lifts her sleeve to her face and sniffs it, as if she's sampling an expensive wine. 'Dettol.'

'You weren't impressed, I take it?'

'Being forced to end your days surrounded by a bunch of incontinent, slobbering old loons you've never met before; having to endure Tone Deaf Tony—'

'That wasn't his name.'

'—strumming away on an out-of-tune guitar; eating food that quite frankly makes school dinners look like Michelin-starred cuisine . . .' She shudders. 'No thank you. *And* you have to pay some exorbitant sum for the privilege.' Angel's taken both hands from the steering wheel and used her fingers to put air quotes round the last word, though her voice had already done a perfectly adequate job. 'Then there's your family, hanging around, willing you to pop off so they can get their hands on the house you spent a lifetime paying for – and that's if the government don't make you sell it to pay for your care home . . . Though by the looks of the staff in there, it's more of a *don't care* home.' In the space of about half a second, Angel puts one hand back on the steering wheel, grabs the gear knob with the other, shifts the car down a gear, and we speed through the lights just as they change to red. 'I tell you, there's not that many times I'm grateful for this condition of mine, but to know I'm probably going to be spared that . . .'

As she jabs a thumb back in the direction of where we've just driven from, I look at her incredulously. 'You can't possibly mean that.'

Angel glances across at me as if I'm mad. 'That appeals to you, does it?'

'Well, no, but that's not how everyone ends up. And even if you do, it's only a small part of it, isn't it?'

'Of what?'

'Life. What about all the getting there. It's better to travel, and all that?'

'It's certainly better to travel if you're going to end up somewhere like Parkview. I tell you, there's only one place I want to go if that's what I'm facing, and it's off the edge of a very high cliff.'

'So all old people should just kill themselves?'

'If that's the alternative, then yes.'

'That's . . .' I stare at her, open-mouthed. 'I mean, I think a few of them might tell you it's worth it.'

'For what?'

'For everything else. The life they've lived. The places they've been. The things they've seen. The memories. Friends. Work. Children.'

Angel lets out a short laugh. 'Yeah right.'

'*Yeah right*, actually.'

'So you could be a Nobel Prize winner, or a master criminal, or the Queen, and that would suddenly make an existence like that worthwhile?'

'Well . . .'

'You don't get it, do you, Noah? Living with something like mine frees you up from all of this. All of these worries. I don't have to think about saving for my future, making some provision for my retirement, because I probably won't have one. And that's . . . liberating. Knowing that, actually, you're going to go at your peak, rather than when you're a drooling mess who can't even remember their own name . . .'

'But if you're taken at your peak, then you're going to be missing out on . . .'

'What?'

'Well, a bit more peak. Or a descent from the peak, where the view's still pretty good, and it's a different view to the one you had on the way up, because you're going in the other direction.'

'Downhill, you mean?'

'Even so. Don't you care about that?'

Angel reaches over and grabs my hand – a slightly worrying manoeuvre, because it means she has to take her other one off the wheel to change gear. 'I won't know any different, will I?'

'How can you be so sure?'

She sighs. 'I'm sorry to be the one to break it to you, Noah, but there's no afterlife. No such thing as reincarnation. We're here for a good time, not a long time, and if I'm going to be on this earth for less than most, then I want to make sure my time is *better* than most. And that means no worrying about the future. No getting hung up on my career, or putting every penny into working my way up the property ladder, or worrying about what other people think of me.' She grabs the top of the steering wheel with both hands, much to my relief. 'Look at most people. They spend their whole working lives doing a job they don't enjoy, simply so they can retire and hopefully live long enough – and be well enough – to do the kind of things that they always wished they'd had the time to do while they were working, except now they can't, because they're too old, or infirm, or broke. All that time saving for a rainy day, except when the heavens actually open, it's too late. It should be the other way around – people should be able to do exactly what they want when they're young enough to be able to actually do it. To enjoy it. To . . . I don't know . . . play tennis without worrying whether their knees are going to give out, or join the local drama society before their memory gets so bad they can't remember their lines. That back there – that's not me. I want to live.'

'Life doesn't end just because you get old. Old age can be fun. Exciting. Exhilarating.'

'I think you're getting Eastbourne confused with Jason Bourne,' says Angel. 'Old age *isn't* fun. Apart from the ageing, there's the memory loss, and the incontinence, and the falling over, and the brittle bones, and the going grey, and the wrinkles . . .' She's counting them off on her fingers as she goes, her hands still on the wheel, as if giving some sort of special signal to any oncoming drivers, and I worry she's soon going to have to use her toes as well. 'And the loss of a partner, and the struggle to live on a pension, and the failing eyesight, and losing your hearing, and not being able to do any of the things you liked doing that made your life worthwhile. Look at Mary. She's seriously contemplating moving from that lovely house of hers to that . . . *place*, simply because she's seeing herself get worse on a daily basis, with no one to look after her, or look out for her, except for you, and she knows that's likely to change once we're married and in a place of our own. There's nothing she can do about it. Nothing. No medical treatment, no magic pill. All she's got to look forward to is a slow decline, until hopefully her mind's gone enough that she doesn't realise how miserable she is.' Angel shakes her head. 'And so tell me why exactly I would want to stay around for any of that?'

Because of me, I want to say. *Because I'll be with you. I'll look after you.* But looking at her expression, I can already tell there's no point. Despite the wedding, despite all the fun we're having, despite the fact that we're starting a new life together, it seems like none of my plan to show her that life is beautiful, and worth hanging on to, is working.

And while I'd begun to think I'd made some progress – the other day, I saw Angel hunt in the supermarket for the milk carton with the longest 'Best By' date – I fear that after what she's just witnessed, I'm right back to square one.

28.

The following Tuesday starts innocently enough. I open up the gallery, then nip out and fetch myself a bacon sandwich from the café round the corner (with a series of empty picture frames on the walls, it's not like there's anything to steal), then Marlon arrives and makes the coffee, and while I don't really want one because I've already had a cup this morning, plus it's only nine thirty, which is midway between breakfast and elevenses, and therefore seems like a funny time for a coffee, he's brought in some Krispy Kreme doughnuts, and it seems inappropriate to eat one *without* a coffee, so he makes me one, and I drink the minimum amount to wash the doughnut down (about a third of a cup, if you want to know), and he asks me if there's something wrong with the way he makes the coffee, and I tell him that after five years working together, surely that's the kind of thing I'd have told him already, and he tells me that in most relationships it's the not-telling that kind of stuff that leads to divorce, and I tell him we're not in a relationship, then almost fall off my chair laughing at the way he rolls his eyes.

I've already been for a run this morning, but it's a nice day, so when it's time for lunch I consider taking Marlon's bike around the park for a bit of exercise, but *because* I've already been for a run this morning (and despite the doughnut), I'm too hungry, so instead I just stroll down the hill and into town and buy myself something to eat from the Boots 'Meal Deal', which includes a Twix, and even though I tell myself I'll save it for tomorrow (because I've already had a doughnut), that idea lasts about halfway back to the gallery.

Then, the moment I walk in through the door, Marlon high-fives me, and answers my puzzled expression by showing me a receipt from a telephone order of the final Hanksy 'painting' to a Mr L. Fallon, to be delivered to a Queens Road address, which it takes me about a minute to realise is Angel's parents'. And even though I suppose I could deliver that one personally, I decide to give it a miss.

And because it's the 'final' Hanksy, it means we've sold the whole show, which is something we never do, so I give Marlon the rest of the day off, and sit there until closing time with a big grin on my face, wishing I could be a fly on the wall when Lawrence sees what he's bought. Though that grin only lasts until I'm just about to lock up and I hear someone at the door.

'I'm sorry, we're closed,' I call out, but Angel's voice surprises me.

'Got time for a drink?'

'Of course.' I buzz her in. 'Everything okay?'

Angel nods. 'Yeah. I just . . .'

'Hey. What's the matter?'

Angel swallows so loudly it makes a sound. 'It's Nick,' she sniffs.

'Yes, I've been meaning to ask you about him. I've left him a couple of messages, because we've sold all the Hanksy stuff, which means it might be a good time for him to get some of *his* stuff on the—'

'He *died*.'

'What?'

'Nick died.'

'When?'

'On Saturday.'

'You're kidding,' I say, though it's painfully obvious to me Angel isn't. 'How come?'

'How come he died, or how come I just found out?'

'Both.'

She looks at me, her face crinkles up and she starts to weep quietly, so I take her in my arms. 'He hasn't been in work this week, and I bumped into his mum.' Angel jerks a thumb back over her shoulder. 'On the high street just now. She saw me and started bawling her eyes out. He was in a motorbike accident, and . . .' She blows her nose on the tissue I've just handed her.

'Christ. It's such a . . . I mean, I hardly knew him, but . . .' My voice trails off. The mention of death has suddenly brought Angel's fragility front and centre.

'The funeral's on Friday,' she sobs. 'I wondered if you'd come with me?'

'It's a date,' I say, holding her tightly and rocking her gently, side to side. And though I don't exactly mean it like that, it turns out to be a rather significant one.

29.

Angel takes one look at me as she cracks the door open.

'Which one are you?'

'What?'

'Mr . . . ?'

'Huh?'

'You look like someone from a Quentin Tarantino film.'

'Ha ha.' I brush my lapels down. The suit's new, bought yesterday afternoon in the Primark sale for only twenty-eight pounds, and even if I do say so myself, it looks surprisingly good on. 'Well, I guess I'd say Mr Blue. Seeing as we're going to a funeral. And you're supposed to feel blue at—'

'I get it, Noah. Did you buy that specially?'

'Yup.'

Angel opens her door wide, revealing the same summer dress she wore to the wedding three weeks previously.

'Um . . .'

'What?'

'Do you really think that's . . . ?'

'What?'

'Appropriate?'

Angel sighs. 'Noah, funerals are a celebration of life. All this "wearing black" business . . .' She shakes her head, then nods at how I'm dressed. 'As long as you weren't planning to wear that at mine.'

'Of course not,' I say. Though mainly because I'm hoping it'll have long gone out of fashion by then.

We're a little early – Angel insists on driving my car, so the normal ten-minute trip to Mortlake Crematorium only takes us a white-knuckle five – and the crematorium's next to the municipal dump, which is making for some interesting smells (which I assume are coming from the dump, and not the red-brick chimney towering above us). At least it's a beautiful, sunny day – appropriate weather for Angel's dress, if perhaps not an appropriate occasion, as the glances and whispers coming from the other, soberly clad mourners waiting outside seem to be confirming.

By five past three, there's still no sign of the deceased, prompting a 'We always said Nick would be late for his own funeral' from someone, which sends a nervous ripple of laughter around the group, although the appearance of the hearse through the imposing wrought-iron gates puts a sudden stop to that. As the car makes its way along the driveway, Angel nudges me.

'So, what happens now?' she whispers.

'You sound like you've never been to a funeral before.'

'I haven't. They've been kind of up there with weddings, as far as I'm concerned.'

'Right. Well, essentially, we all file in behind the hearse, and someone fighting back tears gives a eulogy where they say something nice about the deceased, everyone else cries, then we all go for a drink.'

Angel frowns. 'Doesn't sound much like a celebration. Except for the drink part, obviously.'

The hearse stops just in front of us, followed by a convoy of black Bentleys that pull up behind it, from which a dozen or so sombre-looking people step out. I've no idea who the bereaved's mother (or wife – or any of the relatives) is, though if I had to guess, I'd imagine she's the devastated-looking, red-eyed woman in the black dress who's having her hand shaken/shoulder patted/being hugged by the succession of mourners.

Angel's gone quiet, and as the woman she tells me is Nick's mother walks into the chapel, she seems to almost be hiding behind my shoulder. Then the coffin is slid out from the back of the hearse, the pallbearers heft it up onto their shoulders and we follow it inside.

'Remember,' whispers Angel as we take a seat at the back, 'we're here to celebrate his life.' Though she's not sounding quite as confident as earlier, and I've a suspicion she's telling herself as much as me.

I look around at the assembled mourners. They don't look like they're in the mood to celebrate anything. Most of the women are crying, perhaps set off by Nick's mother, in the same way as when you see someone yawn it makes you want to yawn as well. Some of the men, too, are barely holding it together, and even I'm feeling a little teary, despite the fact that I only met Nick the once. Although I do have to keep reminding myself not to think too far ahead.

'I don't get it,' says Angel.

'Don't get what?'

'It's not as if they didn't know it was coming. Maybe not in a motorbike accident, but *still*.'

'That's like saying – I don't know – if you suspect you're about to get punched in the face, it's going to hurt less than if you don't. A punch in the face is a punch in the face, however much you might think it's coming.'

'Well, I don't want this at mine, FYI. I want—'

'A celebration. So you keep saying.'

'I mean, when someone's born with a condition like mine, you *should* be celebrating. You're not even expecting them to make it out of childhood, so for them to get to my age, Nick's age . . . it's quite an achievement.'

'Angel, you really don't understand, do you?' I say, perhaps a little too loudly, as an old lady in the pew in front of me turns round to shush me. 'A funeral isn't about what you want. It's not actually *for* you. Well, it is, but that's not what I mean. It's for everyone else. So they can grieve. Mourn. Say goodbye. And I'm sorry, but you don't get to dictate how they do that.'

Angel's staring at me, but before she can answer, a young woman climbs up behind a lectern at the front of the room. She looks pointedly to her right, where Nick's coffin is resting on a kind of trestle table, then smiles out at the assembled mourners.

'Hi,' she says. 'My name's Kate. And I'm a celebrant.'

At the word 'celebrant', Angel nudges me, as if to say *See?*, then the woman smiles again.

'Nick's family have asked me to say a few words today on their behalf . . .'

And it's at this point I kind of zone out, because at the mention of Nick's family, I've turned my attention to the group sitting in the front pew, just in front of where Kate is standing. And while I can't see their faces, I don't need to in order to know just how devastated they all are. How shattered they all seem. Though I hardly knew him, the loss of such a good person, such a talented person, at such a young age . . . Even I'm feeling what a tragedy it is.

And whether I'm just picking up on the atmosphere, or I'm feeling emotional, or, more likely, I'm thinking about how I'd feel if I had the rest of my life with Angel wrenched away from me, I don't know. But from deep inside me, I can feel something bubbling up, until it meets a tightness in my throat, and all of a sudden, I'm struggling to stop my chest from heaving, and trying to swallow it down only makes it worse, and eventually it all comes out of me in a silent wail, until eventually my shoulders are shaking, there's water streaming from my eyes, and it's all I can do to stop the snot from dripping out of my nose.

'Noah?'

I turn to face her, and the sight of what I might be losing is almost too much to bear.

'Are you okay?' she whispers.

It's a bit of a silly question. Of course I'm not okay. Especially since I can't help but picture *our* families sitting here, her mum in floods of tears, my mum probably exactly the same, our dads doing their best to maintain a stiff upper lip, with everyone waiting to line up outside to tell me how sorry they are for my loss, and me thinking how sorry I am I never managed to convince her to go through with the transplant.

And then something amazing happens. Angel looks at me, then her expression goes through a series of subtle changes, and all of a sudden, despite what she said earlier, I can tell that she finally gets it.

'Come on,' she says, her voice wavering a little.

So she takes me gently by the arm, whispers our excuses to the people sitting next to us, and – ignoring the fact that all heads in the crematorium have swivelled round in our direction, leads me back outside.

We stand there for a moment, blinking in the sunshine, Angel looking a bit shell-shocked. And while that might simply be the effect of seeing my meltdown rather than the overall 'death' thing, I can tell that something's changed.

'I didn't realise . . .' she says, staring off into the distance. 'I just didn't realise . . .'

So I do the only thing I can do, and take her in my arms, and hold her, and I keep holding her for as long as I can, because I don't know how long I'm going to be able to do this for, and I only let her go when I realise there's a crowd gathering, and though they're not there to watch us, but more likely there for the next service, the last thing I want right now is an audience.

'Shall we?' I say, and Angel nods, and we stroll, hand in hand, to where she's parked the car with one wheel on the kerb, then I take the keys from her and let her in.

'Did you want me to drive?' she says, but I shake my head.

'I've had enough of death for one day.'

As Angel gives me a playful shove, I throw my jacket in the back, loosen my tie and drive us back to her flat – past the entrance to the dump, past the retail park, along by Kew Gardens, up the hill and through the park.

I'm taking the scenic route, I'll admit, and why not? It's much, much better than the alternative.

30.

Hanksy comes in the following afternoon, carrying an empty wooden picture frame under his arm.

'Your latest?' I ask, nodding at the frame. 'You've been hard at work.'

'Not really,' he says, setting it down on the desk. 'I've got loads of these sitting around at the studio.'

'Well, I hate to break it to you, but the show's over.'

'Actually, it's not.' Hanksy flashes me a grin. 'I've sold loads of these since then. Can't produce them fast enough. Except, of course, I can. So this one's for you. A wedding present.'

I pick up the frame, and peer through it. 'That's the title? Or is it actually a wedding present?'

'Actually a wedding present. And a thank you gift.'

'An empty frame? For single-handedly saving your reputation, and making you about ten grand in the process?'

'Well, yeah.' He grins again. 'Loads of great artists have a collaborator, a muse. And this was certainly a-*muse*-ing . . .' He raises and lowers both eyebrows like a ventriloquist's dummy, and I smile sarcastically at his joke, then he turns his attention to the work on the walls. 'Hey! What's with all the new stuff?'

'This is . . . was, a friend of Angel's.'

'Was?'

'He died.'

Hanksy puffs air out of his cheeks. 'Bummer. Still, good marketing strategy. Most artists sell better after they're dead.'

'I'll bear that in mind for your next show,' I tell him, grabbing him by the arm and escorting him to the door.

'Right. Well, I can see you're busy, so—'

But I don't hear the end of the sentence, because I've thrown him out onto the pavement. Closely followed by a certain wedding present.

The funny thing is, Hanksy's right – I am busy. For an event that simply consists of turning up, saying a few words and signing a bit of paper, all within a half-hour slot on a weekday morning, there seems to be an awful lot for Angel and me to do, so much so that the next couple of weeks pass by in a blur. There's a reception to book, and rings to choose, and vows to write, and a honeymoon to organise – and thanks to the Hanksy show selling out (and I mean that in both senses of the phrase), we can afford the Maldives rather than a trip back to Margate. And even though Angel tells me she wouldn't *mind* Margate, the dreamy look on her face when she's flicking through the brochure suggests we'll end up going to a place where jellied eels definitely aren't on the menu.

In the meantime, the posthumous show of Nick's work at the gallery has sold well – because it's good, not because he's dead – and after the Hanksy debacle, it's exactly what I needed to reaffirm my belief in what I do. Plus the fact that we decide not to take any commission and give all the proceeds to Nick's wife makes Angel burst into tears when she finds out, and when, as a result, she tells me she couldn't love me more, that has the same effect on me.

My parents have been behaving like excited teenagers – crossing off the days until the wedding on a calendar they bought specially and hung on the back of the kitchen door. My mum's even taken Angel shopping for some shoes for the big day, though according to my dad, Angel's choice of a limited-edition pair of Converse apparently took my mum 'a little bit of getting used to'. Meanwhile, Angel's mum's been popping into the gallery on almost a daily basis, just to check how 'things' are going – though I suspect it's more to check that Angel's heart still is. Surprisingly, Angel's dad has even offered to pay for the rings, which Angel suggested was a 'gesture', though I haven't accepted, as I think it's a two-fingered one.

Since I told her about the wedding, Mary seems to have perked up quite considerably. She's said she's happier (on my regular Parkview visits), because for the first time in a while, and I quote, she's 'got something to look forward to', and it's nice to see a change in her. As it is in Marlon: he's asked me if he can 'bring someone' to the reception. And while he's still a long way from 'thirteen dates' territory, compared to his normal MO, it's definite progress.

And while all of this is quite exhausting – on top of running every day, and running the gallery every day – I'm glad there's so much going on. Because I'm doing it all for Angel. With Angel. Because of Angel. And I'm savouring every moment.

While I still can.

31.

Today is my final parkrun before Angel and I get married. I probably don't have to come anymore, seeing as I only started them in an attempt to track Angel down, but to my surprise I've started to enjoy these sessions, and while I'd prefer to spend every Saturday morning curled up in bed with her – after Tuesday, I'll get the chance to do that every day. Plus, the fact that Angel's here marshalling kind of puts paid to that idea.

Besides, my training's been getting easier – I'm in a notch on my belt – and fewer people seem to be finishing ahead of me each week, and while my aim has never been to beat every man and his dog, there's certainly *one* man (and dog) I've got in my sights.

This morning, it's Angel who's the starter, and because she and her dad still aren't speaking, the two of them are playing a funny 'trying to avoid each other' game, as if they both think the other one's 'it' at Tag. I, on the other hand, have marched right up to him and ditched my disguise in a *Mission: Impossible* facemask-peeling-off kind of way, and when Lawrence catches sight of me, to say he does a double take would be to severely underestimate the number of takes.

'You . . .' is the best he can come out with, as I reach down and pat Rocket on the head.

'Lawrence,' I say, trying to sound a lot more confident than I'm actually feeling.

'You know you only beat me the other week because of this one,' he says, giving Rocket's lead a sharp tug.

'If you say so.'

'I *know* so. As you're about to find out.'

'Is that so?'

'Yes, that's so,' says Lawrence, then his eyes flick across to where Angel is standing, marshalling everyone towards the start line. 'How would you like to make this . . . interesting?'

'It's already interesting. Interesting how much you're worried I'm going to beat you.'

'I mean *really* interesting. As in, a *bet*.'

'What kind of bet?'

'You win, I show up all smiles on Tuesday. You lose . . .'

'And?'

'*You* don't show up on Tuesday. Which means I'll *also* be all smiles.'

I stare at him in disbelief. 'You want me to think about calling off the wedding based on the result of a *run*?'

'Not just a run. *This* run. And not just the wedding . . .'

'What?'

'It's never going to work, Noah. Angel's always followed her own path. You need to let go of this stupid idea of some happy-ever-after.'

'That's . . . You can't be . . .' I'm a little stunned at this – firstly because Angel's dad has remembered my name, and secondly, that he'd really expect me to bet on something so monumentally important.

'Unless you're too *scared* . . . of a little competition, that is.'

I realise there and then that Lawrence isn't 'a little competition'. He's a bully. And while it no doubt used to work for him at whatever toffee-nosed, self-important public school he went to, and probably makes him fit right in at whichever bank he works at in the City, I can so see why Angel and he don't get on.

I know it's only a parkrun, but Lawrence seems determined to employ the kind of mind games you see at the start of the Olympic 100-metre final, and right now, I'm determined to give as good as I get.

'I've been training,' I say. 'Doing a lot of cardiovascular exercise, actually.' I glance over to where Angel's standing, making sure Lawrence knows who I'm looking at. 'With Angel. I guess you'd call it "cross training". Except she didn't seem that cross . . .'

'Wha . . . ?' he splutters, looking the exact opposite to how I've just described Angel's mood, and as he turns an almost comic-book shade of red, I pat Rocket a final time, then smile up at him. 'Good luck,' I say.

Lawrence scowls down at me. 'Luck is for losers.'

'Which is why I wished you it,' I say. Then I shuffle to the far end of the line and wait for Angel's whistle.

I've learned my lesson this time. I know I don't have much of a sprint finish – or much of a sprint start, or middle, to be honest – but I also know that, in running, as in life, as in relationships, if you put in the mileage, you're going to see the benefits. Plus I'm relying on Angel's dad being so angry at me that he's going to go out too quickly in his attempt to 'break' me. So all I have to do is hang on to him – not literally, of course – and (and the irony's not lost on me) wait for him to 'die'.

As Angel starts us off, I don't rush headlong off towards the first turn, but instead fall into a steady, manageable pace fifty or so metres behind Lawrence. I've checked online – his personal best's less than a minute faster than mine, and my times have been improving by just under that every week, so I'm convinced it's doable . . .

At least, I am until the end of the second lap. Lawrence is showing no sign of slowing down, and the pace is beginning to hurt. Although he's breathing hard, in comparison I'm doing a pretty good impression of Thomas the Tank Engine on his way up Everest, plus Rocket is straining at the lead like he's been left in no doubt there'll be consequences if he stops. I'm already knackered, but by my calculations, there are only about eight minutes of running left until the finish. And if Angel can survive thirty years of feeling her heart might burst, the least I can do is four hundred and eighty seconds' worth.

Somehow, though my legs and my lungs are on fire, I dig deep and manage to maintain the distance between us. In fact, I'm maybe even closing it a little, if Lawrence's increasingly frequent glances back over his shoulder are anything to go by. Eight minutes become seven, seven become six, then five, then four, and all of a sudden, all that's left is one more turn before the last, long uphill towards the finish line.

I pray for a second wind, even though I'm not sure I've had a first, and I take it as tight to the flag as I can, not wanting to run even an inch more than I have to, then gradually increase my pace. The theme from *Chariots of Fire* suddenly pops into my head, so I try to keep my technique as smooth as possible, imagining that I'm an athlete, in top condition, sprinting along the beach with my fellow competitors in 1924 – and given the age of some of the other parkrunners, that doesn't take too much imagination.

In the distance, I can see Angel, jumping up and down excitedly, and she's all the motivation I need, the reason I've put myself through hell every time I've laced up my running shoes, and why I've been dragging myself round a muddy park every Saturday morning for the last few months. And winning today, with her here, is doubly important – not because I'm expecting to run into her arms (though that would be nice), and not – actually – because I want to make her dad look small, but because I want him at her wedding, and I want him to be happy about it (or at least look like he is), and I don't want him to think I'm a loser. Even though I know I'm not, because I've managed to win (over) Angel.

There are a handful of runners in between us, and I manage to pick them off one by one until – by some miracle – I've caught Lawrence up, and though there's only a few hundred metres left, what's clear to me is that he's exhausted. Even Rocket's looking a bit wild-eyed, though that could simply be as a result of him needing – and not daring to go to – the toilet.

'Come. *On*. Rocket!' pants Lawrence, as I begin to draw level with the two of them. Desperately, he nudges Rocket to one side of the path, creating a barrier with his lead that prevents me going past, then when I try to overtake him on the other side, he switches Rocket's lead to the other hand and does the same.

'It's never going to happen, Sonny Jim,' says Lawrence, in between breaths. 'Just let it go . . .'

As I struggle to pass him, I realise Angel's dad is right. It isn't going to happen. Not as long as he's got this unfair advantage over me. By which, I mean how he's been Rocket-propelled.

'It's Noah!' I remind him. 'Not Jim!' Though I stop short of telling him it's not Sonny either. 'And you're the one who needs to let go.' Then, with a desperate lunge, I reach down and unclip Rocket's lead from his collar.

Like a water-skier who's let go of the rope, Lawrence slows down so suddenly, so dramatically, that I almost think he's been lassoed from behind, and as the newly liberated Rocket lives up to his name and sprints off to where Angel's waiting at the finish line, I happily run in too.

'That'll ruin his day.' Angel nods at her dad, who's jogging miserably towards the finish, and although I try to appear as nonchalant as I can, inside I'm cheering like I've just won the gold medal, and in world-record time.

Because hopefully now, he won't ruin ours.

Mary's not in her room when we visit her at Parkview that afternoon. And while at first I assume she's out in the garden, or maybe barricaded herself in the toilet to avoid Dan the Music Man, when Angel points out that her belongings are missing too, I start to get worried.

'She's gone,' says the nurse, when she eventually turns up, after we've been frantically pushing the 'Call' button for what seems like the last ten minutes.

'Gone?' My legs go weak, and I collapse down onto the bed. 'When?'

'Yesterday,' says the nurse.

'How . . . ? What . . . ?'

'Sometimes our residents just . . . leave us,' she says dismissively.

'I can't believe it.' I look up at Angel, my eyes brimming with tears. 'She seemed so . . . vital.'

'She was.' Angel rests a hand on my shoulder. 'But looks can be deceiving, remember.'

'How did it happen?'

'One minute she was here, the next minute . . .' The nurse shrugs. 'Gone.'

'At least it was sudden,' says Angel.

'You're telling me,' says the nurse. 'And we still don't know how she got past security.'

'Huh?'

'Mary's not *gone* gone,' interrupts Candice from the doorway. 'She went. Left. Yesterday. Best guess is sometime between eleven and twelve. Dan the Music Man was playing. Sometimes it's hard to keep track of everyone in the stampede from the lounge.'

'Where did she go?'

'She's not at home?'

I shake my head. 'Not unless she's hiding somewhere. Although maybe she's forgotten where she lives. Perhaps she's out, wandering the streets, scared, confused . . .'

'She didn't seem that confused to us.' Candice hands me an envelope that's been sitting on the bedside table. 'Oh, and she left you this.'

300

'What is it?'

'One way to find out,' says Angel.

As the two staff members head outside to deal with a disturbance in the TV room – an argument over which daytime antiques show to watch, by the sounds of it – I stare at my name on the front, written in Mary's elegant, unmistakeable, old-lady handwriting. 'I can't open it.'

'Why not?'

'It might be . . . a suicide note.'

'Let me.' Angel slits the envelope open with a fingernail, then scans through the letter. 'Actually,' she says, after a moment, 'it's the opposite.'

'Huh?'

Angel sits down next to me on the bed. 'Dear Noah,' she reads. 'Please forgive me for leaving like this, but like I told you, I've never liked goodbyes, perhaps because I never had the chance to say a proper one to Stan. You're the grandson I never had – though I suppose that's my fault for not having a son or daughter first, so I'm sorry I'll miss your wedding. But I know you and Angel will be very happy.

'And so will I. In fact, it's you I have to thank for this. Remember we saw that sign in the travel agent's window, and realised it'd be cheaper to go on a round-the-world cruise? "That's what you should do," you said. So that's what I'm doing. By the time you read this, I'll be on my way to Miami, and then round the Caribbean, across to the Indian Ocean, and then Asia – all the places I always wanted to see. Economy class, mind you – I don't want to go overboard. Ha ha, see what I did there? And who knows – I might find somewhere I want to stay, where the weather's warm, where I can afford to be properly looked after. Perhaps even with an actual view of an actual park.

'The other thing I'm leaving is the house, to you. Think of it as a wedding present. If you and Angel can be half as happy as Stan and I were there, then I'll consider it a worthy gift. All the legal documents are in the bottom drawer in the kitchen, and it'll be yours when I'm gone. Think of it as yours *while* I'm gone, too.

301

'In the meantime, I'll send you a postcard from every place I visit. And when I stop writing, well, that's when you'll know my journey's over. Take care, Noah. And take care of Angel. Though I suspect it might be the other way round. P.S. Tell Angel she can redecorate how she likes.'

It takes me a moment to realise Angel's stopped reading, and as she slots the letter back into the envelope, she lets out a short laugh.

'What's so funny?'

'I've got a confession to make.'

'Which is?'

'I made up the part about redecorating. And you didn't even notice!'

'Very funny.' I slump forward, and put my head in my hands. 'I can't believe it!'

'Which part?'

'All of it!'

'People can surprise you.'

'I can't believe I'll never see her again.'

'She's gone to a better place.' Angel slides an arm around my shoulders. 'Several better places, by the sound of it. Mind you, given *this* place, that wouldn't be hard.'

'It's not funny!'

'I don't think it's funny.' Angel kneels down on the floor in front of me, and takes my face gently in her hands. 'I think it's amazing. And wonderful. And brave. And . . . inspirational.'

'Inspirational?'

Angel nods, then raises herself up on her knees and kisses me softly on the lips.

'Definitely,' she says, with a smile.

32.

I'm sitting in the gallery on Monday morning, still a little shell-shocked by the whole Mary-leaving/beating-Lawrence-at-parkrun/getting-married-tomorrow situation, when there's a loud bang from outside, so I look up from the hundredth game of solitaire I'm playing on my laptop, expecting to see the stunned pigeon I assume has just flown into the window flapping around on the pavement outside, only to see my mum and dad grinning inanely at me through the glass. I wave them towards the door and buzz them in, and my mum hurries over to kiss me on the top of my head.

'Surprise!'

'What are you doing here?'

'Lovely to see you too!' She ruffles my hair, something I didn't enjoy when I was a toddler, and the feeling's the same some thirty-plus years later.

'We thought we'd take you out for a pre-wedding lunch,' says my dad. 'Condemned man, last meal, that sort of thing.'

'I'm hardly condemned.'

'Call it a stag lunch, then.'

'I'm busy.'

My mum peers at the gallery's bare walls – all of Nick's paintings have been parcelled up, and the next show's yet to be hung. 'Looks like it.'

My dad picks up the last remaining Hanksy from my desk – the one I haven't yet shipped off to Angel's dad, not wishing to give him another reason to hate me before tomorrow. 'What's this? *You've Been Framed?*' He grins at his joke. 'No Angel?'

'What did you expect – to find her sitting on my lap?'

'Well, no, but . . .' My mum looks at me imploringly. 'Unless she's out shopping? At Mothercare? Or Baby Gap?'

'Mum, for the millionth time, I don't even know if we're going to have kids. In fact, we probably won't . . .' I catch sight of my mother's crestfallen expression, and quickly add: '. . . rush into it.'

'Well, why the rush to get married then?'

'We . . . well . . .'

My dad leans in close to me and lowers his voice, as if the gallery might be bugged. 'This isn't one of those staged marriages, is it? She needs a British passport, so she's paying you to marry her?' He nods at the empty walls. 'We knew things were bad, but if you needed money, you could have come to us. Not gone down the—'

'Dad, Mum, it's nothing like that. Angel and I just don't want to waste any time, that's all.'

My parents exchange glances. 'Why not?' says my mum.

'Just because.'

'I know you're not getting any younger. But you kids nowadays, it's all about instant gratification. And I don't just mean sexually.'

'Mum!'

'Your dad and me, we went out for two years before he popped the question.'

'Couldn't afford the ring,' says my dad.

'And even then, it took a while before we'd saved up enough to get married,' says my mum. 'There was none of this running off to Las Vegas to do one of those drive-by weddings.'

'Drive-through, Mum. A drive-by is a shooting.'

'Which I've thought about many a time since then,' says my dad with a wink.

'And we're not running off to Vegas. We just wanted a simple ceremony here in Richmond, with no fuss, and it just so happened they had a cancellation . . .'

My mum folds her arms. 'And what do Angel's parents think? She does have parents, I take it? Because we haven't even been introduced to them. Our future in-laws. They might be nutters. Or UKIP supporters.'

'Same thing,' says my dad, picking up a copy of the *Informer* from the desk and flicking through to the classifieds.

'They're perfectly . . .' I think for a moment. I've still not worked out the right adjective for Angel's dad. 'Besides, you might not be seeing them tomorrow.'

'Why ever not?' says my mum.

'Because her dad doesn't approve of Angel getting married.'

'To you? Bloody cheek. I mean, I know you probably don't seem like the greatest of catches . . .'

'Thanks very much!'

My mum rests a hand on my cheek. 'Not like that, Noah. I mean with the business and all that. And not owning your own house. And that old car of yours.'

'You might actually have a point. They're quite rich, and—'

'Rich?' My dad looks up from the paper. 'How rich?'

'Big-house-on-Queens-Road rich.'

'*Richmond* rich, eh?' He nudges me. 'Good on you, son.'

'I didn't know that when I met her.'

'Even so.'

'So that's it, is it?' says my mum. 'They think you're marrying her for her money?'

'She, um, doesn't have any.'

'Yes, but she'll be in line for—'

'Not necessarily.' My mum and dad are looking at each other, then me, then each other, in what's almost a comedy-confused kind of way, and I know I shouldn't tell them – mainly because I promised Angel I wouldn't. But these are my parents. And they've got a right to know. 'Angel's . . . not well.'

My mum makes a sympathetic face. 'Oh, well, please tell her we hope she gets better in time for tomorrow. Nothing worse than having a cold on your wedding day.'

'Especially if it's in your feet,' says my dad.

'She, um, won't be getting better any time soon.'

'Why not? Is it some sort of allergy?'

'Not an allergy, no.'

My mum frowns, then she looks at my dad, though perhaps not surprisingly, he's looking equally as confused. 'I don't understand.'

I take a deep breath. 'You remember that joke she made? When we came to yours for lunch?'

'She made lots of jokes,' says my dad. 'The biggest one was something about marrying you!' He bursts out laughing, then stops abruptly when he sees my face.

'Well, the one I'm talking about wasn't strictly a joke. Angel suffers from . . . Well, she doesn't actually suffer from it. She's got this . . . *thing* wrong with her. With her heart, to be specific.'

'Her heart?' says my mum.

'Is it serious?' says my dad, suddenly serious himself, and I nod.

'Could she die?'

I nod again, and have to swallow hard twice, then wonder if this will ever be something I can talk about without feeling like this. 'Apparently,' I say, my voice trembling a little.

'When?' he asks.

'Any time.'

'*Any* time?' says my mum.

I nod again as I haul myself out of my chair, conscious that this is a conversation best had standing up.

'But . . .' She frowns in my dad's direction, evidently half a step behind the two of us. 'But . . .'

'Which is kind of why we're going for this soon-as-possible wedding.'

My dad clears his throat. 'How long have you known?'

'A little while. Though I didn't find out until after.'

'After what?' says my mum.

'After he fell in love with her,' says my dad, unusually perceptively.

My mum is shaking her head. 'No. No!' she says, retrieving a tissue from her bag and dabbing at her eyes. 'You can't marry her. You just can't. Not like this.'

'I have to.'

'Why do you have to?'

'For the same reason I married you, love, I'd imagine,' says my dad softly, and we stand there in silence for a moment – at least, as much silence as there can be with my mum snuffling and blowing her nose.

'It's just so sad!' she says, eventually. 'Boy meets girl, boy and girl decide to get married, then *this* . . . You couldn't make it up, could you?'

'I don't know,' says my dad. 'If you can make up a story about scientists cloning dinosaurs and them running amok in a theme park, then Noah falling in love with a girl with a heart condition isn't that hard to imagine.'

My mum gives him a look. 'The poor thing,' she says, giving me a squeeze.

'I'll be okay.'

'Not *you*!' snaps my mum. '*Angel.* Imagine having to live with something so miserable.'

'You mean her condition, right, and not, you know, *me*?'

My dad lets out a short whistle, then he gently elbows my mum aside and, uncharacteristically, places an arm around my shoulders. 'You're sure this is what you want?'

'It is. Though I could obviously do without the "death" part.'

'Well, in that case, you've got our full support.' He gives me a quick 'manly' hug, then lets go of me and taps his watch. 'Now, how about that lunch?'

'Marlon's not in till later. And I can hardly leave the gallery unattended.'

My dad picks up the Hanksy again, then sticks his head through the space in the middle of the frame and gives me a look. So with a sigh, I pick up my keys, turn out the lights and follow the two of them out through the door.

'Where shall we go?' says my mum.

'How about The Spice Is . . .' I'm just about to say 'Right' when my phone bleeps with a text, so I fish it out of my pocket.

'That'll be Angel,' says my dad. 'Calling it off!' He roars with laughter, then cuts it suddenly short. Because while it *is* Angel, I only have to see the word 'hospital' and I'm already on the move.

33.

I'm running at top speed up Church Road before I register the 'at the' in front of the h-word, and while I debate taking the car, to be honest, I'm not sure I'd be able to drive with the tears streaming down my face. And if three months of parkrun has done anything for me, now's the time to find out.

I check my phone again, curse the fact that I've not noticed Angel's earlier missed call, and try to ring her back, but there's no answer, so I realise there's nothing for it. I cover the two or so miles to the hospital in a time that would wow them on a Saturday morning, rush headlong into reception and lean heavily against the desk. 'Is there an . . .' I gasp, '. . . Angel here?'

I'm sweating profusely, and the woman behind the glass panel glances across at the security guard in the corner. 'Have you tried the church next door?'

'What?'

'There are no angels here. This is a hospital.'

'No . . .' I wave a hand in front of me, as if the last thing I said is on a whiteboard in front of me and I'm trying to erase it. 'Fallon. Angel Fallon.'

'I told you. We don't have any angels. Fallen, or otherwise.'

'Her *name*'s Angel,' I say desperately. 'Angel Fallon. She just texted me. She's here . . .'

The receptionist peers at the computer screen in front of her. 'Fallon, Fallon, Fallon,' she says, scanning infuriatingly slowly through her list. 'There's a Fallon, but it's not "Angel".'

'Is it "Angela"?'

The receptionist looks at me sternly. 'I'm sorry, I can't give out that kind of information.'

But then I hear my name being called from the other end of the corridor – Angel's mum – so I sprint down to meet her. She's crying, which I can't possibly take as a good sign.

'What's happened? Has she . . . ? I mean, is she . . . ?'

Julia grips my arm tightly and nods frantically, which alarms me even further, until I remember I haven't actually asked her anything specific enough that a nod might answer – then Lawrence marches across to us from the coffee machine and I brace myself for an onslaught, and he gives me a strange look, as if he's considering where exactly to punch me, but instead, to my surprise, he envelops me in a huge, Old Spice-scented hug. I'm so sure it's bad news, I find myself hugging him back, then I break away, trying to ignore the fact my sweatiness has left an ugly stain on his crisp pink shirt.

'When . . . ?'

'An hour ago. She said you weren't answering your phone, so she rang us instead. We went straight round to pick her up and brought her here.'

'Why didn't she call an ambulance? Why didn't *you* call an ambulance?'

'Why would she need an ambulance?'

Now I'm *completely* lost. Her dad seems rather calm if, as I've been fearing, the worst has happened. But what other reason would they have – would Angel have – for being here?

'I'm sorry, I don't understand,' I say, and Lawrence suddenly puts two and two together.

'She's not dead, Noah. Her beeper went off. They've found a donor. She's having a transplant.'

'A . . . transplant?'

'That's right,' says her mum, and it's only now I see there's a smile behind her tears.

My knees suddenly go weak, and I flail around for some support, so Lawrence steers me to a chair and I collapse into it. 'I don't know what you did or how you did it, Noah, but she's agreed to go through with it,' he announces, pumping my hand like he's operating one of those old-fashioned wells. 'Well done, son! *Well done!*'

'She's . . . not dead?'

'Quite the opposite,' says Lawrence.

The room's still spinning, so I lean forward and put my head between my knees, taking deep breaths until the dizziness passes, then I haul myself back to my feet. 'Can I see her?'

'She's been waiting for you,' says Julia, then she takes my other hand and holds it very, very tight. 'As, it seems, we all have.'

Angel's sitting up in her hospital bed when I go in, looking all kinds of bored and scared, though her face lights up when she sees me. I've got us both a coffee, but then I notice there's a 'Nil by Mouth' sign above her bed, so I just put them on the table next to her.

'You took your time.'

'Sorry. People to see. Places to go. Things to do.'

'You're soaked.' Angel wrinkles her nose as I lean down to kiss her. 'Is it raining out?'

'That's, um, sweat.'

She makes a face, but takes my hand anyway. 'I'm supposed to be the one who's nervous about this operation. Not you.'

'It's not that.' I sit down on the edge of the bed and fix a smile on my face, trying to appear relaxed, even though I'm feeling anything but. 'I ran here. From the gallery. When I got your text.'

'Impressive.' Angel puffs air out of her cheeks, and glances anxiously up at the clock on the wall. 'So . . .'

'So?'

She smiles, matter-of-factly. 'So, I'm sorry, but we'll probably have to postpone tomorrow.'

'You mean the wedding – right. And not *actually* tomorrow.'

'Right.'

'Right. So . . .' I blink a couple of times, still unable to believe we've ended up here and trying desperately to wipe the images from those YouTube videos of the operation from my mind. 'Why the change of heart?'

Angel rolls her eyes. 'You've been saving that one, haven't you?'

'Might have been. Seriously, though.'

'Isn't "woman's prerogative" enough?' She lets out a short, nervous laugh. 'Though to actually answer your question, lots of things: Nick, and the funeral, and how he might not have been able to avoid the car that knocked him off his bike, but I realised I've got a chance to avoid the one that's coming for me. And Mary, and the cruise, which made me think that it's never too late to change, except for me it might be. And, of course, you.'

'Me?'

She nods. 'Yeah. You changed. For me. No one's ever done that before. And I'd been thinking about this "live for the day" philosophy of mine, and I realised that, thanks to you, that day might be some time in the future, and how else am I going to give myself a chance of making that? Then, would you believe it . . .'

'What?'

'My beeper beeped.'

'Right.' I sit there for a moment, my mind racing, not knowing what to say, as Angel rubs the back of my hand with her thumb. 'Angel, this is a pretty big deal, and—'

'Hey!' She reaches over and places a finger on my lips. 'It'll be fine. I've been reading up on it. There's all sorts of new techniques. Survival rates are much better than they were. And yes, I know there's a risk, but . . .'

'. . . risks are something you're prepared to take.'

Angel leans forward so she can make eye contact. 'Exactly.'

I squeeze her hand, *my* heart feeling like it's about to burst. 'So. When are you . . . ?'

'Any moment now, apparently. They've given me this mild sedative, which seems to be making me a little *too* honest, to be honest. Then they wheel me in for some final tests, and then . . .' She draws her index finger up the middle of her chest, in the way potential killers do across their throats.

'What kind of tests?'

'Blood tests. For compatibility. Just to limit the chance of rejection.'

'I'm glad you didn't put *me* through those when we met.' I grin sheepishly at her, and Angel laughs. 'Do you know who . . . ? No. Forget I asked.'

'The donor?' Angel sighs. 'Some serial killer, apparently. Died in a police shoot-out. The doctors say you better watch out, just in case I start looking at you funny . . .' She stares at me with narrowed eyes, then throws her head back and roars with laughter. 'Your *face*!'

'That wasn't funny!'

'Sorry. And no, I didn't ask.'

'Probably wise.' I pull her hand to my lips and kiss the back of it, savouring her warmth, the smell of her skin. 'You know I'd be happy, even if you don't . . .'

'I think we both might be happier if I do.'

'You're sure?'

'As I can be. Or at least, as I need to be. I've had a lot of decisions to make recently. And when it came down to it, surprisingly, this one didn't seem that hard.'

'Well . . .' I pick up my coffee, still doing my best to keep it together, 'cheers' it against hers for luck, and Angel smiles.

'This is just like our first date.'

'Hey,' I say, realising something. 'It's our thirteenth!'

'Thirteenth date?' Angel looks puzzled. 'And that's significant because . . . ?'

I feel myself start to colour. 'Oh, just some stupid theory Marlon told me about a while back. About how it takes thirteen dates to fall in love.'

'Right.' Angel narrows her eyes at me, then breaks into a huge grin. 'Now I see what you've been doing.'

'What?'

She tries – and fails – to hold in a yawn. 'Tricking me into going out with you thirteen times, so I'd fall in love with you!'

'As if I'd do such a thing!' I say.

Angel's looking drowsy, so I sit on the bed next to her, stroking her hair as her breathing slows, wishing I could sit here forever – but forever doesn't even last the best part of a minute, as a white-coated doctor appears at the door.

'It's time,' he says simply, and Angel reaches for my other hand, and holds them both tightly.

'Thanks, Noah,' she says, and I don't reply, because, to be honest, I'm suddenly having difficulty talking, and I'm considering asking the doctor if there's a chance of having the lump in my throat surgically removed, when Angel pulls me in for a kiss goodbye.

'No tongues,' she says, pointing towards the 'Nil by Mouth' sign.

So I kiss her, and tell her I love her, and that I'll see her afterwards, and then her mum and dad come in, so I get up and start to walk away, but Angel beckons me back towards the bed.

'What?'

'It's been fun, hasn't it?'

'Hasn't what?'

'Doing new things. Living life as if each day can surprise you.'

She's looking at me in an 'I told you so' kind of way, so I nod. 'Surprisingly, yes.'

'So, you're a fan now?'

'Of?'

Angel looks like she's struggling to find the word. 'Spontaneity.'

I nod again. 'It's this particular spontaneous act that's my favourite so far,' I say. Though I only hope I feel the same way tomorrow.

'Oh, and that "thirteen dates" thing,' she says, her voice slurring a little from the meds.

'What about it?'

She reaches up, gently places a hand on the back of my neck, then pulls me down so she can whisper in my ear.

'It worked,' she says, as her eyes begin to droop.

And right there, right then, I know that if the worst scenario possible happens, then this'll be the thing, the moment, the *time*, that I remember the most.

34.

It's funny, sitting here, looking at Angel's empty hospital bed, her few belongings neatly packed in a small retro Adidas sports bag by my feet. Her mum and dad have gone – it's been a long and stressful day for them, and I suppose there was nothing more they could have done here, and besides, I told them I'd sort everything out. Whatever *that* means.

I knew the risks. We all did. I'd read up on them, like any responsible person with a vested interest would do. Because you've got to be in possession of all the facts, haven't you? That way, there aren't likely to be any surprises. Although none of us would probably say we were expecting this.

In truth, I'm still reeling from the news, but it's been a real roller coaster of a day. Angel – *we* – came *so close*. And now what? Wait for someone else . . .

A noise from the bathroom disturbs my thoughts, and I look up sharply.

'Ready to go?'

'Not any time soon,' says Angel, walking over to kiss me.

I pick her bag up, glad to be leaving this place – although I know we'll be spending a lot more time here soon. 'We still on for tomorrow?'

'That's the most romantic thing I've ever heard!'

'You know what I mean.'

'You still want to get married?'

'Even more so now.' I beam down at her, then gently put my arm around her shoulders, and Angel shakes her head.

'Something wrong?'

'What did I tell you about treating me like an invalid?'

'Sorry,' I say as I escort her from the room. 'Of all the reasons you couldn't go through with it . . .'

'Hey!' Angel nudges me in the ribs. 'Whose fault is that?'

'Are you suggesting it's *my* fault?' I say, falling into step with her along the hospital corridor, though I have to resist the temptation to skip down it, high-fiving the nurses as I go.

'Of course it's your fault.' Angel fixes me with a grin, and rests a hand on her stomach as she walks. 'Because *you're* the one who got me pregnant.'

35.

Ow!' says Angel, grimacing up at me.

'Sorry.'

'Try shifting a bit to the right.'

'It's not wide enough.'

'Yes it is. You just need to approach it from a different angle.'

'I'm never going to get in this way.'

'Maybe if you take a run-up.'

'A *run-up?*' I look down at her. 'I'm supposed to be carrying you over the threshold. Not competing in this year's World's Strongest Man competition.'

It's Tuesday afternoon, and I'm a little tipsy after our post-wedding celebrations in the pub, where – given my joy about Angel's current 'eating for two' status – I've been doing something similar on the drinking front.

'Do you want me to carry *you?*'

'In your condition? And before you say anything, I'm referring to the pregnancy, and not . . .'

Angel makes a face. 'Don't remind me,' she says, as I turn her side-on and steer us both carefully through Mary's – sorry, *our* – front door. 'Of either of those things.'

'Okay. But I'm going to have to put you down now. You're too heavy.'

'I might get a *lot* heavier.'

'I think the technical term is "fat",' I say, lowering her gratefully to the floor.

'At least I'll have an excuse!' She pokes me in my stomach, then peers around the cavernous hallway. 'This place is amazing.'

'Not compared to your mum and dad's.'

'Would you rather we moved in with them?'

'No wife of mine is going to slum it! And besides, I'm not sure your dad would be so keen on the idea.'

'You'd be surprised. He seems to be . . .' She thinks for a moment or two. 'I'm going to go with "warming to you". Though I'd avoid parkrun for a while, if I were you. Besides, it's my mum you should worry about now.'

'What for?'

'You saw her smile waver when I told her she was going to be a grandmother?' Angel laughs, and turns her attention back to the house. 'Well, at least now we don't have to worry where the baby's going to sleep.'

'You're having it, then?'

'*We're* having it, I think you mean.'

'Sorry. Yes, of course. *We're* having it.'

'Thank you.'

When Angel doesn't say anything further, I clear my throat. 'Aren't we?'

'I'm thinking about it,' she says nervously. 'I mean, a *baby*. There's a lot to consider. And what if it . . . ?' Angel pales, and her hand goes automatically to her left breast.

'It's not hereditary.'

'How do you know?'

'Like I said the other day, I've been reading up. Nine out of every thousand, remember? And if you think about it, the odds of one of those nine out of every thousand having one of those nine out of every thousand . . .' I pull my phone out, open the calculator app, stare at the screen for a moment, then put it away again without pressing a button. 'Well, to be honest, the maths is a bit beyond me.'

'But I don't know the first thing about being a mum. And there's just so much to—'

'Hey.' I put my arm around her shoulders. 'Or we could just take it one day at a time. Make it up as we go along. See what happens . . .'

Angel looks at me, mock-horrified, then pulls *her* phone out of her pocket and jabs at the screen.

'What are you doing?'

'Calling the police. Someone's stolen your personality and replaced it with Captain Unsensible.' She slips her phone away as she leads me through into the lounge. 'You really want to have a baby with me?'

'Angel – us, together, starting a family, it's all I *ever* wanted.'

'Less of the "starting", mister! "Starting" suggests more to come. This might be our only one.'

'Fine by me,' I say. And it *is* fine by me. If I've learned anything over the past three months, it's that if you're always looking off into the distance, you can't really focus on what's right in front of you.

Angel collapses onto the sofa, just as I do the same. It's been an exhausting couple of days for us both. 'Even though, to use your delightful term, I'll get "fat"?'

'More of you to love, as far as I'm concerned.'

'That's so *sweet*.' She mimes sticking her fingers down her throat. 'But seriously, Noah. You're sure?'

'I'm sure. New experiences, and all that,' I add, surprised to hear myself speaking in the same upbeat tone as when Angel ordered that first flat white in Starbucks.

'As new experiences go, it's going to be pretty full on.'

'"Full on" is my new middle name,' I say, for some reason in an American accent. 'Unlike "Fallon". Which is your old surname.'

Angel widens her eyes. 'I know! Married!' She holds her left hand up and proudly inspects her wedding ring, almost as if it's a prize she never thought she'd win. 'Was it what you expected?'

I shrug, and look at my watch. 'I don't know. It's only been five hours.'

'The *ceremony*.'

'Not really. But then again, nothing's been as I expected, since I met you.'

'In a good way, I hope?'

'In a good way.'

Angel swings her legs up and rests them across my lap. 'Pleased to hear it.'

'I'll say this, though. For a half-hour slot in a windowless office with a couple of witnesses and a fair bit of form-filling, it felt much more . . . momentous than I thought it would be. And a *lot* more emotional.'

'Was that why you blubbed like a girl?'

'I did not!' I fold my arms defiantly, though Angel's right. I did cry. And I wasn't the only one, despite a red-eyed Marlon's denials afterwards. But in my defence, I'd suggest that pledging your eternal devotion to the love of your life the day after you've found out not only that she's prepared to go through with a transplant operation, but also that she's *pregnant*, would make even the hardest-hearted person well up. 'I . . . had something in my eye.'

'Funny how that happened right when the registrar said "in sickness and in health" . . .'

I try – and fail – to appear indignant. 'About that. Those promises. I meant them, you know?'

'Noah . . . the transplant . . .' Angel sits up straight again and looks suddenly serious. '*I* can't promise—'

'I don't need you to.'

'Especially now.'

'I understand.'

'But I'm thinking about it.'

'Your body, your decision. "In sickness and in health", remember?'

'You didn't have your fingers crossed during that part?'

'Angel, I've had my fingers crossed since the day I met you.'

She glances down at her stomach, then across at me, and makes a 'terrified' face. 'Well, you'd better keep them like that for another nine months,' she says.

So I smile back at her, cross *all* my fingers, then hold both hands up so Angel can see. Although, somehow, I have a feeling that everything's going to work out just fine.

ACKNOWLEDGMENTS

Thanks: To Emilie Marneur, Sana Chebaro, Sammia Hamer, Bekah Graham and the rest of the amazing Amazon Publishing team.

To Sophie 'don't kill your darlings, make them stronger' Wilson.

To the usual suspects (Tina Patel, Tony Heywood, Lawrence Davison, John Lennard) for their ongoing friendship and support. Keep it coming. Along with the material.

To the Board. We've still got it.

And lastly, as ever, to you, my fantastic, enthusiastic, appreciative readers. You're* the reason I sit down at my desk and write.

*along with my mortgage.

ABOUT THE AUTHOR

Photo: © 2014 Cassandra Nelson

British writer Matt Dunn is the author of eleven (and counting) romantic comedy novels, including *A Day at the Office* (a Kindle bestseller) and *The Ex-Boyfriend's Handbook* (shortlisted for both the Romantic Novel of the Year Award and the Melissa Nathan Award for Comedy Romance). He's also written about life, love and relationships for various publications including *The Times*, the *Guardian*, *Glamour*, *Cosmopolitan*, *Company*, *Elle* and the *Sun*. Before becoming a full-time writer, Matt worked as a lifeguard, a fitness-equipment salesman and an IT headhunter.